Roma, Underground

By Gabriel Valjan

Winter Goose Publishing

2701 Del Paso Road, 130-92

Sacramento, CA 95835

www.wintergoosepublishing.com

Contact Information: info@wintergoosepublishing.com

Roma, Underground

COPYRIGHT © 2012 by Gabriel Valjan

ISBN: 978-0-9836764-8-5

First Edition, February 2012

Cover Art by Winter Goose Publishing
Typeset by Victoriakumar Yallamelli

Published in the United States of America

For Andrea Camilleri & Warren Larivee

1

The cell phone was ringing again.

The light crept white and warm through the high balcony doors, across the gray marble flooring, up the sides of the walls, and almost intentionally focused on the recumbent form alone in the bed big enough for two. She twisted in a shroud of sheets as the telephone chirped again.

"Leave me alone."

But she was pulled into that familiar haze of half-waking, still tired from the overnight trip, the July heat. Back home she could sleep through most sounds, but in a different country she never would've imagined that a phone would sound so different.

It stopped and she sighed. "Thank God."

The laziness called her back to sleep, enveloped her after she relaxed into a long stretch. She smiled to herself with thoughts of how she might spend the day. It felt like a day for curling up with a good book or a film. Or better, pampering herself with a self-made spa treatment, remaining half-naked in her nightshirt if—

The phone interrupted again.

She snapped up the micro-thin mobile from the nightstand. *"Pronto!"*
"Buon—"

"What is it, Dante?" She brushed her hair back with her hand as she watched the drapes billow in a small breeze, the gauzy material providing a barrier from the punishing sunlight.

"Thought I'd call to ask if you had plans for today."

She tried not to sound annoyed, but she couldn't help it. "You've been persistent with your calling."

"What do you mean? I just called . . . this instant."

Even half-awake, she could hear him translating in his head when his Italian brain meant *adesso* or 'now'. She could also hear either hurt or confusion in his voice.

"Sorry, woke up on the wrong side of the bed."

"Well, the little hand is on eleven and the big hand is walking towards twelve, Bianca."

She laughed. Dante, unlike some Italians she had met, didn't brood over minor matters or perceived insults. He just went on as if nothing had happened.

"You want a date, don't you?" she said.

"Only if Lady Bianca would be so gracious to grant me one."

She felt his smile through the phone. "I don't know. I'm quite tired. I returned from Milan late last night after a shopping binge. The train ride with no air conditioning left me drained."

"Ah, yes, *soldi* season. You're a determined huntress to go by train. Four hours is a long ride when you could've shopped here in Rome. What did you capture that was not local to our woods?"

"Shoes, Via della Spiga, and Corso Buenos Aires, of course."

"I would've been flattered if you said you visited the shops on Via Dante and thought of me, but I'll stay modest, as always. So how about I take you on a special adventure and treat you to a late lunch?"

She hesitated for a moment. But what the hell, she was up anyway. She had no book in mind, and she always wasted far too much time in deciding on a movie. Besides, she was intrigued by what Dante might consider an adventure. "Uh, what do you have planned? I'm concerned about the heat and what to wear. I want to be comfortable today."

"Uh, don't worry about the heat so much."

So, it will be someplace cool. "Ah, a romantic date. Perhaps Bagnaia?" She was sure that he was thinking of taking Via Cassia to Viterbo to spend the day in that small town. Dante had mentioned the town's medieval center, the *città di dentro*, the last time they had lunch together. A tour of dark, old Romanesque churches would be pleasantly cool.

"No. I'm thinking something far older than medieval. You decide: clean or dirty?"

"Excuse me?"

"Where we go is your choice: clean or dirty? Pick one," he said with a dry tone.

This was . . . unexpected. They had been seeing one another for a month-and-a-half or so, but the relationship hadn't yet gotten terribly physical. She had not felt quite ready for intimacy, and Dante, flying in the face of the Italian stereotype, had not pushed. "Okay, naughty boy, I will disappoint you and say 'clean.' Where do we meet?"

"Near the Domus Aurea in an hour? This sounds good to you?" He knew she lived in an apartment not far from Hotel Diocleziano, and it was within walking distance, or by fast taxi with time to spare if she didn't fuss.

"Sounds like a plan. Ciao."

She snapped the phone closed and dropped back in the bed for a moment. Dante had said that he had called her only once that morning. So where did the earlier plague of calls come from? Bianca took all the necessary measures to make sure that her cell was unlisted—only Dante had the number, and giving it to him had been a monumental decision. Even though he knew whereabouts she lived, she had never had him over to the apartment.

She opened the phone and toggled through the Italian version of CALLER ID HISTORY; she saw numerous calls identified as UN-KNOWN or BLOCKED. She verified Dante's call: ten-thirty am.

How had this happened? Bianca refrained from giving out her residential details to retailers and acquaintances. Bianca had no phone in the apartment. She received no postal mail except for the quarterly utility bills that she paid in cash at various kiosks throughout the city.

It was time to get rid of the SIM card. Someone had found her. Someone who knew that Bianca was not Bianca.

2

The irony of divesting herself of her history and then moving to Rome, where all kinds of history surrounded, was not lost on her. Everywhere in Rome, history is stacked up on itself, from the incidental and dross to haunting echoes of the parochial, warring tribes of Latium to the ascendant dynastic sweep of the *Imperium*, the emperors and their monuments in various states of disrepair.

And yet nothing changes. The newspaper, the *Corriere della Sera*, was running a series of exposé articles about a bishop who not only shielded pedophile priests from prosecution for decades, but upon further investigation amassed a respectable bank account and maintained a luxurious Tuscan villa with servants and an extensive art collection.

The calls unnerved her and they should have. It wasn't as if she were in the US Federal Witness Relocation Program because she had turned state's evidence and provided damning testimony. No. The very people that she was hiding from were the emblematic WE THE PEOPLE—the United States Government, the all-encompassing monolith at home and abroad. She should know. She used to work for them.

Once upon a time, before she became Bianca (or the various other characters she'd been in the last two years), she had moved from General Accounting in the Congressional Budget Office to Reconciliations. She remained a GA5 (General Accounting level 5 clerk) even though what she was now doing was more accurately *forensic accounting*. Her new position in Reconciliations—itself an early name for forensic accounting—started around the time Congress was reviewing numerous legal iterations in the definition of *victim* in recent white-collar crimes like the S&L scandals.

Then she was approached discreetly to join Rendition.

This department had been little more than a vague rumor around the office bordering on urban legend, until the white business card with nothing but a red R on it showed up on her kitchen table with a time written on the back. She had just come out of the shower and was drying her hair when she saw the card. It had not been there when she had come home. She felt naked and looked around. No sign of forced entry. After reading the time on the card, she looked at the clock. It was less than a minute away.

When the second hand clicked to the minute on the card, the phone rang. Without thinking, she picked it up.

"I represent Rendition," a factual voice said without preamble. "We are very interested in having you work with us. We apologize for leaving the card on your table. We respect your privacy and you have our word that it will never happen again. One of our representatives is at the coffee shop down the street from your apartment. If you are interested, please go to the shop and sit on one of the stools facing the street. If you are not interested, then have a good night."

The line went dead.

Wet hair, no make-up, she jumped into a pair of jeans and threw on her oversized college sweatshirt, grabbed her coat and keys, opened the door, looked around—no one in sight—then closed it behind her.

She walked fast down the sidewalk, looking around without knowing what to look for, towards the corner coffee shop. It was cold. Car horns blared in the traffic that night and she heard the occasional cursing between taxi drivers and jaywalkers weaving around them. The steam rose up through the manhole covers. She arrived at the diner, ordered coffee, turned around, surveyed the place, and picked a stool that faced the street. It was uninspired coffee, as this was not one of those places where a specialty caffeine dose was the price of a decent lunch.

She sat down.

"Thank you for coming."

A man's voice. She looked at him but only saw half of his face before turning to look out the glass window.

"You've heard of Rendition?" he asked.

"Yes, but it was always in very vague terms. I didn't think it existed."

"It does. We don't have time to correct your misconceptions about it. What you need to know is this: none of us know each other, which means you always work alone, without backup or support. Assignments come to you through this e-mail account."

He placed a typewritten slip of paper in front of her. She saw that the domain name was a government host name.

"As you have already noticed," he continued in a calm, thorough voice, "the e-mail address is official, so make no mistake that you are on the right side."

She took a sip of her coffee. "Why the secrecy then?"

"Our legal system is not up to date, and there are individuals who have become greedy beyond tolerable levels, to the point where they threaten the general welfare. Your assignments are to do forensic investigations on these individuals and provide detailed reports of your findings. Should you have corroborating evidence to supplement your reports, then those items, whatever they may be, are to be dropped off at a secure location to be determined at a later time. If your assignment requires more information, we will get it to you when you make the requests by e-mail. Our response is fast and we'll do everything we can to assure your success."

"Then what happens after the report?"

"That is not your concern. You will be paid quite well in a separate account: tax-free, the income recognized by the IRS as compensation for your service to your country." The man held his cup up, speaking through the small swirl of steam above his coffee. It bothered her that she couldn't see much of the man's face. He seemed to be an ordinary-looking man from the half of him that she saw.

"What makes you think I'm qualified for this line of work? There are analysts who—"

"You are more than qualified. Do not doubt yourself. We picked you for a reason."

"You . . . know me?"

"You were born Alabaster Black. Only child. Parents deceased but otherwise a loving family of grandparents and distant relatives, now also deceased. We know that you were the tallest girl in the sixth grade. We know that your best friend in ninth grade was Sarah-Jane Martin. We know that you lost your virginity at fourteen to Louie Patrone and that it hurt and the experience was less than satisfying. We know that you didn't write your second-semester psychology paper. We also know that you always read the second flap of the dust jacket before you buy your books at Borders. We know the sins you confessed to the last time that you went to Confession, which was ten years ago. We wouldn't exactly call you a practicing Catholic, but we list the denomination as your religious preference. We know that you wash your clothes in cold water, because you believe it's easier on the environment. We know that you're wary of relationships. You experimented with pot, tried one homosexual—"

"I get the point!"

She became aware that the other patrons were looking at her. The man was still looking straight ahead, out the window.

"I'm sorry, Ms. Black. We're not judging you. I simply pointed out those things that are outside of public files, medical records, and banking history."

He said this in a calm, even tone, but she was less than reassured. Yet, at the same time, she felt strangely . . . flattered. Whoever and whatever Rendition was, they had cared enough to really dig into her past (and where had they gotten Louie Patrone from?). Also . . . she found herself intrigued by the possibilities. She'd come to love Reconciliation, found she had a real gift for looking at numbers and seeing the story behind them. Particularly the story that the numbers' creators wanted to keep hidden. So perhaps Rendition was just the next level for her. If she could trust them. Secretive organizations did not have a good reputation.

"And what if I get in over my head on an assignment?" she asked.

"You're on your own."

"And if I don't want an assignment?"

"Reply in the e-mail, and type 'No' in the message."

"And if I want out completely?" she asked the man, still facing the street.

"Reply to the e-mail, place UNSUBSCRIBE in caps in the subject line." He sipped his coffee. "If you accept an assignment, however, you have to complete it to the best of your ability. You can't back out in the middle."

She turned herself sideways on the stool to face the man's profile. "And you're not afraid that I'll talk to someone about Rendition?"

"You won't."

"Because . . ."

"There's nothing to tell. Nobody in Rendition knows what anyone else looks like, where we live, where we work, and the pay comes out of numerous government agencies with no signature for disbursement. The operation is completely decentralized and compartmentalized, with each member contributing his or her own expertise."

She had a sudden vision of every bad conspiracy-theory movie she'd ever seen. "Expertise doing what? Providing for the public welfare, but how exactly?"

"Rendition exists to protect our country's internal financial system until laws come into existence sufficiently sophisticated to prosecute offenders. Or, to put it another way, Rendition was created to stop unmitigated, dangerous greed. Profit is one thing. A CEO salary hundreds of times that of the lowest employee is tolerable. Outright willful action to maximize profit in a way that would leave publically necessary industries bankrupt, leaving the taxpayer in the lurch, is considered unacceptable. Unfortunately, the laws to punish this type of greed are not on the books yet. Think of Rendition as interim, gap analysis."

"And you believe in loyalty to something that you can't see? Something so 'decentralized'? You have complete faith that I might not jeopardize that?"

"It wouldn't be wise." He said it simply, without so much as a second's hesitation.

"And why me?" Her final question.

"Very simple, Ms. Black. We picked you for your forensic-accounting skills, but we also picked you for another reason. Please don't be insecure about your aptitude when I tell you this. We picked you because the majority of those who run these rogue companies are men. The one thing that they never expect . . ." He paused for a final sip of coffee. ". . . is a woman."

That clinched it for her. "I'm in."

Alabaster created her 3-D avatar with minimal skills, using a graphic software kit. She took a photograph of her mouth, her white teeth clenching the open manacle of a pair of stainless-steel handcuffs, her lips done in black lip-gloss, her hair combed while it was wet, and she wore a small leather band around her neck with small pointed studs. That picture was the sexiest she had ever felt.

Alabaster did her first assignment and was stunned when she checked and saw $100,000 deposited into her account. She soon found there was no fixed fee. Some of the cases paid $200,000 and others $250,000; and every year on her birthday she received an e-mail informing her that she had received a ten-percent payment based on her account balance as a bonus. She enjoyed her money but never did anything outrageous or ostentatious. Her one indulgence was her loft.

Over the next couple of years, Alabaster Black became the mastermind to the Reconciliation department. All the final reports, when they appeared in court, had the names of other, non-Rendition analysts to whom she had been told to delegate the task of writing up her findings. Her analytical skills and research had taken down Pegasus Enterprises' CEO for embezzlement. She had almost single-handedly dismantled Alliance Industries, whose CEO had established fictitious companies and an elaborate Ponzi-like investment scheme. She dismantled Manor Enterprises and exposed its CFO who was defrauding investors with falsified earnings statements.

Alabaster wasn't bothered by what happened to her "assignments" after she submitted her reports. Not all of Rendition's assignments were

tied to criminal activity. In many cases Rendition simply wanted assurance that there were no improprieties, and occasionally there weren't. And when she did uncover serious malfeasance . . .

Well, she did see in the news that Ray Hoskins of Pegasus died of a heart attack shortly after his indictment. Edward Wilburs of Alliance had an aneurysm and died at home. Milton Horowitz of Manor Enterprises had a massive cerebral hemorrhage. Randall Wilcox of Fox Engineering, who had cut costs on military deliverables and defrauded the government of billions of dollars, had the misfortune of driving an SUV that was later recalled for safety flaws in the rain.

Alabaster had no problems at all with outcomes until five years after she joined Rendition, when she took the Strand assignment.

3

After she'd dressed and replaced the SIM card with one she had purchased at the pharmacy, Bianca set out to meet Dante with her laptop slung over her shoulder and wearing casual clothes. She tossed the old SIM card into one of the green domed receptacles near the curb for the side-loading garbage trucks that would come the next day. Unlike the rear loaders back home, the Italian garbage truck was an engineering marvel. A respectable-sized truck that was easily mistaken for a city bus would pull up to the curb. A small bar, shaped like a stunted candy cane of red and white stripes minus the shepherd's crook, unfolds to prevent last-minute access to the green carrier or to size up its location on the curb, before a mechanical arm descends and lifts up the green tote overhead, where, mysteriously another mechanism slides the cover off, unloads the trash, and returns it back gently to the curb. Not one person will emerge from the truck or handle the trash. Clean, elegant, efficient.

Dante had said to meet him at the Domus Aurea, Nero's monstrosity of a palace between the Esquiline and Palatine Hills. After the fire of 64 AD Nero had the architects Severus and Celer start construction on a series of rooms, halls, and galleries to glorify his divinity, crowning his arrogance with the largest bronze statue of the day, a 36-meter likeness of him to rival the Colossus of Rhodes, out in front like a lawn gnome. Hadrian would later have it removed. Bianca felt all matters related to Nero had a grotesque overcompensation to them, but she suppressed her opinion when Dante had suggested it as their meeting place. She found some consolation that Nero had been forced into committing suicide less than a decade after building the Domus, and that his fellow Romans, as they had done with so many of their emperors, including Constantine, had made his likeness *damnatio memoriae*. History had yet to rehabilitate him.

She spotted Dante in the distance, more to the southern part of the Esquiline from the Domus, on the grass near a tree. He waved and she reflexively waved back.

Unlike most Italians, Dante Allegretti knew the value of time, which meant that if he said he would be somewhere in an hour, you could bank on his being there. The majority of Italians had a more fluid sense of time, and Bianca saw this during the high tide of tourism. Throngs of foreigners waiting for a guide would pace; the individual waiting on an acquaintance for dinner would starve; the shopper eyeing merchandise would languish for the return of the shopkeeper. And when the expected parties did arrive, it was always with a flourish and fanfare as if nothing was ever wrong, because that was the way things were done, had been done, and would always be done.

In addition to betraying his countrymen with his punctuality, Dante respected her presence when he spent time with her, looking at her and not the moving mass of well-dressed or half-dressed women, domestic or foreign, that flooded the narrow streets. Italian men were notorious for their easily distracted eyes for breasts, bottoms, and legs. Dante was also not a grabber: he kept his hands to himself. But the quality that she respected most, which also seemed to set him apart from the others, was that he was not what Italian women called a *mammone*, or mama's boy, the kind who, despite a good job and pay, would run home to Mama's table during the lunch hour or have Mama do his laundry. Bianca had concluded long ago that Italian men will attempt to bed every single woman, strut around and think secretly (or not so secretly) that they are the greatest of all lovers before they age and break down, then marry a clone of their mother because she is a divine, nurturing goddess. Dante was his own man, independent and self-sufficient. And like his last name, he was a friendly good-tempered man.

"Welcome to Colle Oppio," he said as his hands worked . . . a set of ropes for a harness.

"You said Domus Aurea," she said.

He shook his head, looking down at a particular loop of rope. "Nope. I said near the Domus. But anybody can see that any day."

"Okay, then. I've heard of the Oppian gardens, and parks are nice enough for walking and a picnic—"

"*Fini!* The rope and harness is as I like it." He pointed to the strap across her shoulder. "What is this you carry? One of those men purses?"

"No. It's my laptop."

He sighed. "Sundays are days for friends and family, to enjoy life, for tomorrow we work." He pulled a jumpsuit out of his messenger bag. "I suppose you have a mobile with you."

"No cell phone. This jumpsuit for me?"

"Good, no mosquito," which was his word in English for cell phones because he found them annoying and pervasive. "Jumpsuit is for you to slide on and then step into harness, please."

Apparently, this romantic adventure was going to be a costume drama. She took off her laptop and suited up, finding the jumpsuit not quite heavy but not exactly light. The material breathed but could keep out fluid. She put one foot into one leg of the harness and then the other, balancing one hand on his shoulder as Dante leaned over to slide the harness up to her hips, giving them a firm lift up. The straps were rather . . . intimate, but Dante seemed so engrossed in verifying the buckles and placement that he hardly noticed.

"Trying to give me a wedgie?" she said, her hand still on his shoulder. Dante pulled the next set of straps up in front of her breasts, pushing them into the center of her chest and doing some kind of mental calculation with the connecting hoist that would somehow keep it in front of her chin, according to his secret estimates.

Bianca had a wry smile, as he handled her body in the most nonsexual way. She had gotten enough hints from their time together to know he wasn't gay. He was just incredibly focused on her safety. He turned away and repeated the whole exercise with his own jumpsuit and harness, attaching his messenger bag to one of his straps.

"What about my laptop?" She pointed to the black square body on the grass.

He toddled over like a cowboy and attached it to her harness.

"It won't fall, I promise," he said. "Oh." He fetched from his bag two white helmets with headlamps. People walking by looked at the two of them askance, but went about their business as if the sight of two people suited up for a biohazard disaster was just another odd scene in Rome.

"Okay, Dante, I've been patient enough. What are we doing in these outfits?"

"We go to the tree there. A few years ago there was rain, and a big hole appeared near the tree, and like in one of your science fictions in your cinema, the hole opened up to another time and place. We go there now."

"Wait. You mean to tell me we're going into another dimension, a worm hole?"

"No worms, I hope, but yes, another dimension. This is Rome. The living, the dead, the past and the present—it's all the same here in Rome." Dante pointed out and named all Seven Hills of Rome. "This one, Colle Oppio, like any section of Rome, is built upon and built upon, over 3,000 years. I show you now."

Dante took Bianca over to the tree, behind which there was a platform. She saw a sign in Italian that said the equivalent of "Authorized Personnel Only." The sign had a color scheme that matched the logo on the vest that Dante was wearing. She said nothing as he connected her to the line, attached himself to the line, and then clipped himself to one of her lines so they were bound together for the descent.

"Afraid of heights?" he said.

"I don't think so."

"Then look at my face. Bend your knees like you are sitting as we move. I control us moving down. Stay still and trust me, understand?"

"Okay, but how far are we going down?"

"Ah . . . conversion . . . let me think. About forty feet."

"That's not far to the bottom."

"Bottom? That is longer way down. Forty feet is to see what I want to show you. No need to be scared. I take care of you. You are safe with me."

"I'm not scared." Actually, she was grinding her teeth, but he hadn't noticed because he was working the ropes with gloved hands now. This was a side of him she had never imagined.

Dante lowered them with a slow, knowledgeable handling of the belay ropes into the darkness. As indescribable mustiness came up from someplace below, Bianca felt as she had when she was a kid on a rollercoaster that went into a dark tunnel and then did a free fall into the blackness. The sudden weightlessness and the liberation of that lightness was dizzying, except here they were moving in fits and starts, which was admittedly a little scarier. Dante knew how to work the ropes and descend without using his headlamp. He was talking, but she was ignoring him, because the hair on the back of her neck prickled when she felt an errant breeze from nowhere waft over her.

"Ready?" Dante said.

"Ready for what?"

"Ready for the surprise."

"Ah, sure."

"Stay very still a moment."

She held still as she felt his arm move through the blackness. Her light went on with a click, and she saw his proud, smiling face. He turned his headlamp on. "Now close your eyes for a second, Bianca. I will turn us around, so no need to panic."

Both of them twirled ever so slightly and she felt his hand on her shoulder. She couldn't recall him ever having touched her before, and she wondered whether he had planned on that moment occurring or whether it had merely been a move to steady the two of them so that they would not unwind on the rope in the opposite direction.

"Open your eyes, please."

She opened her eyes, and there in front of her was a mosaic of grape harvesters, all male and nude, directly in front of them as they hung in mid-air. It was about ten feet long, and six or eight feet high, done in polished red marble and other stones. Three men looked almost satyr-like as they danced in an elevated press in a frenzy to crush grapes, while another man to the left of them was shown dragging more grapes in another basket up an incline from the vineyard and about to pass a reveler who seemed to be blowing a triumphant song through two reeds. It was full of movement, of excitement, of sheer joy.

•

"Oh my God . . . it's beautiful," she said.

"A colleague of mine, Marco, discovered this a few years ago, and you are one of but a handful of people in the modern world to be looking at this splendid piece of history." He ended with a proud smile and a squeeze of her shoulder.

"What is it? I mean—what is it called?" She tried to drink the art in, from left to right and then right to left and then up and down.

"It is 'The Grape Harvest' or in Italian, '*Vendemmia*,' which as you may know occurs from July to October in my country. Our experts believe this was created between the time Nero built his Domus, about 65 AD, and The Baths of Trajan, about 109 AD, give or take."

"This is amazing, so beautiful," Bianca said. "How do you have access to this? You told me that you're an auditor."

"I'll explain it to you over lunch. I cook for you this afternoon." He started to move the ropes for them to ascend up to the hole near the tree. "But first we must return to the world of the living."

The air above ground was both refreshing and alien; and in some ways, despite the greenery of the park and the less oppressive presence of cars and tourists in this part of Rome on a Sunday, the modern world seemed vulgar.

"Where do we take lunch?" she asked.

"My place. Let me have the jumpsuit so I can stow all this away and lock it up." He unhooked her laptop and handed it to her. Bianca felt nervous since she had never been to Dante's place and she wasn't sure whether she was ready for anything after lunch, if that was his intention. She watched him fold up the jumpsuits, coil up the ropes professionally, and place all of it in a duffle bag with a logo like the one she had seen on his vest. He put the bag into a lockbox near the platform by the tree and dusted his hands off. "Ready?"

She nodded and let him lead the way.

As they walked, Bianca thought more about the qualities she liked in Dante. He was a decent, friendly guy. They'd known and seen each other for three months, which is a reasonable amount of time, but she really wasn't ready to have a lover. Then again, he was not giving any indication that he wanted that from her. Perhaps she was making assumptions.

Dante was handsome, about her height, 5'7", trim and lean. He dressed well, spoke well, and he had that Italian face that, depending on the lighting or shade, could reveal all the different corners of the Mediterranean that had visited the peninsula over the millennia. His face had all the virtuous features one might expect of Rome during the Punic Wars, fierce and determined to oppose Carthage, or of a loyal foot soldier to Caesar in Gaul with blood-stained gladius in hand. But Bianca occasionally caught glimpses of a face holding the duplicity of the elitist Senators of later Rome, or partaking in the machinations of the Borghese or Medici families.

"Where do you live?" she asked, surprised that after all this time she had never asked him.

"Il Pigneto. Just a short ride on my Vespa."

In other words, she wouldn't have to hold on for dear life because all distances to a Roman are short, with pedestrians on the point system and traffic lights merely advisories. No doubt the ancient Romans thought that meeting Hannibal in the Alps was just a day trip.

Pigneto was one of those gritty, up-and-coming working-class neighborhoods, once covered with graffiti, but now trying to gentrify itself after the massive bombardments of the Second World War. Slowly, through an unspoken collaboration between young and old, it was turning into an area that offered a little bit of something for everyone—a vibrant art scene, bars for everything from watching soccer with your mates to a romantic tryst to dinner with your boss, and a reputation for incredible restaurants, specializing in *casareccia*, or home-style cooking. The latest trend was *aperitivo*, where, for a reasonable fee, a diner can enjoy a decent glass of wine and a spread of good food. Bianca knew about this neighborhood east of Porta Maggiore; about the immigrants; about Pasolini filming *Accattone* there, and she also knew that there were no hotels there and public transportation to this northwest part of the city was nonexistent. If the evening went late, she would have to stay the night.

"Dante, we can always grab a bite nearby. There's no need for you to cook in this heat."

But he had just unlocked and, with a flick of his foot, swept the Vespa's kickstand up. "Don't worry. The meal is quick and I can drive you home afterward, or wherever you wish."

She took the helmet and gave in to the ineluctable: sitting behind him and wrapping her arms around his midsection for the ride.

4

Bianca did have to hold on for dear life, feeling Dante's heart beat against the palms of her hands. It was her first time on a Vespa.

Freedom of the road is an American concept. In Rome, it is bare-knuckle survival that borders on the Darwinian, with a cosmopolitan twist. In terms of pecking order, one need only look at traffic at stand-still or as it zoomed around the roundabout: the Fiats are at the top of the list for the indigenous species. Then there is the occasional Citroën or Peugeot for the fun-to-ridicule French, and the Mercedes or BMWs make their proxy statement for German engineering. The rare-as-a-unicorn Ferrari or Lamborghini will always part the traffic out of respect. But it is the Vespa that is the mercenary of the herd because nothing instills more terror or a thrill for all concerned than a scooter zooming between moving automobiles. The Italian driver respects the Vespa; pedestrians rank with pigeons.

He parked his Vespa and Bianca handed him her helmet without saying a word. He said nothing as he led her into a nondescript exterior from the cobbled street. There was a marble foyer after he opened the main door with his key, some steps to an elevator not far from the metal lockboxes. His apartment, on the top floor, was really a loft and a very cozy one at that. The floors were white resin and parquet. The walls, also white, at first appeared austere, having no decorations. But they did have nice archways for windows, and she could soon see the elegance of proportion and balance that decorations would undermine. The place was immaculately kept, which surprised her since until then she hadn't thought of men as being particularly neat. The sofa was a modular model in three pieces: also white, also pristine. The personality of the room was modern. The color of life inside Dante's abode came from the bindings of the books he kept on easel book-cases; from the light streaming through the arches, and from the dark walnut stairs that led upstairs to his bed and bath. Near those books he had two nice chairs: a vintage Milo Baughman and another one that looked lovingly used—a wide and deep dark leather chair decorated with nail heads around some of its edges. The stairs went up a few feet to a small landing and then turned sharply at a right angle before they continued upward. Bianca realized that soft lighting emanated from a light fixture in the wall at the landing and that the mysterious second floor also had a ledge, so that when upstairs she imagined that you look downstairs.

Dante put his keys into a small, cut-crystal bowl near the door. He asked her to follow him into the kitchen, which you entered by walking through one of the arches. The kitchen, though small, was long, with counter-space all in marble, which reminded her of the Verde marble she once had in her loft back home. He had a gas stove, and like any self-respecting Italian, a DeLonghi for his morning espresso. In that small space he also had a dishwasher, while a hidden closet housed an earth-friendly dual-function washer and dryer that she could see only because he had the door slightly ajar. Impressive, although she wondered where he took his meals.

Dante said something that she didn't catch. He slid open the small door to the terrace, where he had a small table and some potted herbs. This must be where he ate when the weather was good, then inside with the same table when the weather was bad. She hadn't seen a television or plasma screen yet. She sat down in a chair on the balcony, placing her laptop bag near her chair. A gentle breeze swept in from her left and she closed her eyes to enjoy the solitude.

"Tired?" he said.

"Oh, no, just relaxing. You have a very nice place, Dante."

"I'd give you a tour but I figure you're hungry. Lunch will be ready shortly. I'm serving *bistecca tagliata,* and I'm taking the liberty of pairing it with a rosé."

"Sounds wonderful." She put her hand up to block some of the sunlight. "I wasn't aware you cooked."

"I wouldn't call this 'cooking.' This is a quick dish: grill the steak to rare, rest it before slicing against the grain, bed it on arugula and lemon wedges, save the juices, drizzle with olive oil and sea salt, and done." He sounded almost apologetic for its simplicity.

"Sounds delicious. Can I help you in the kitchen?"

"No, please stay. I will be out with some fried squash blossoms for *primi*, but stay here because it's a secret recipe, and I like to pair it with a nice white wine. We'll eat here *sulla terrazza*."

"That sounds perfect, thank you." She didn't mind eating on the terrace; it was the chef's prerogative.

Behind her she heard plates yawning out of the cupboard and a clink of wine glasses and a refrigerator door open and close. If there was a sound of the cork it was altogether too silent and skillfully pulled.

He came out and poured the white wine and returned to the kitchen where she heard the sound of sizzling and the occasional muttered curse word. More culinary noises came later and she yelled out to him, offering again to help him, but he declined, telling her it would be only a few more minutes and to have patience.

Bianca gave into the temptation and picked up her laptop. He must have Wi-Fi because the connection was relatively instant. She reflexively suppressed cookies, caching, and search histories, but everything digital was moving to full traceability. The world was becoming a paranoiac's paradise, with data endlessly collected, but the question was whether there was ever enough staffing to analyze it. The NSA had only so many people at its disposal. She punched in a search on Fabi shoes since she had seen a pair in Milan that were gorgeous but sold-out in her size. A nice pair of hand-made shoes was a treat. She wanted to see whether someone out there had her size and the color she liked in their inventory. She copied the name of a retailer she had found and closed Firefox.

As she was about to put her long fingers down to paste the name of the retailer into her command line to start hacking into their inventory, an IM dialog box popped up.

"Did you work for Rendition?"

Oh, shit.

Dante appeared with two plates of fried blossoms. She closed the lid of the laptop quickly. He eyed it with disapproval.

"Sorry, I'll put it away." She placed the laptop down onto the ground next to her chair.

He arranged his napkin on his lap. "You seem inseparable from that thing."

Bianca set her own napkin down. "I didn't mean to be rude. The blossoms look very elegant. Thank you for cooking for me and for that surprise trip underground. I still can't get over the mosaic."

He lifted up his glass and she followed suit, tipping her glass when he had called for a toast. *"Salute!"*

Dante closed his eyes and munched on a blossom. "I hope you like them. As for the computer, I see them as aids, not accessories. It bothers me sometimes to see people so mesmerized with technology. I worry that the day will come when we stop writing letters or making a phone call. I much prefer to read, as you can see from my books in the other room."

"Well, there's e-mail and chatting for personal contact, and there are many books online, especially literature before 1924. Public domain."

"Oh, I know that, but something has to be said about a handwritten letter, unfolding it and seeing the writing, wondering about the choice of paper, the pen, or for that matter, hearing the voice. There are times I miss that. There are times when I feel that the web offers nothing more than ephemera. But that is my humble opinion." He took a delicate sip of his wine. "The world shouldn't be reduced to bytes on a screen that live on a swirling disk inside a computer or uploaded, downloaded, retrieved or stored in some server half a continent away."

"You're a romantic." She smiled and then added, "And a bit . . . mysterious."

"Me, mysterious?" he said with a shrug. "I'm not mysterious."

"C'mon, you told me you were an auditor with the *Guardia di Finanza*, which I know is the Italian Financial Police, yet you deny saying that you're a cop. No, you say you're an auditor who focuses on corporations. Not mysterious? And this afternoon we go exploring a two-thousand-year-old mosaic. You were wearing some logo but I—"

Dante's face turned pink. "Logo? Oh, that—that's a group of financial types that are part of the Roma Underground."

She put her glass up to her lips. "The Roma what?"

Dante leaned forward. "Have another blossom as I explain." She did. "The Roma Underground is a group of speleologists. We have specialized training in the basics of archaeology, climbing, and SCUBA, and our objective is to explore and map the underground city of Rome. We're all amateurs and we formed groups. You can say that some of us have become competitive and, you might think, territorial in a playful way."

"Competitive?" Sometimes his English required a little clarification.

He folded his hands over his dish. "Not really territorial, since we communicate with each other openly. I meant 'competitive' in the sense, we formed groups. We have the doctors, the lawyers, the policemen, and us, the financial types. It is like teams. We compete over how much of the underground we can map. It is healthy."

Another crunchy blossom later, she said, "Healthy in what way?"

He mused for a second. "Every profession has their unique way of looking at things. What I mean is that a surgeon will look at something differently than the way a detective would."

Bianca tilted her dish to show she had finished her blossoms. "Of course they'll look at data differently, Dante, because their objectives are different. A surgeon wants to remove something and a detective wants to catch someone and—"

He took her dish and placed it on top of his. "Hold that thought. I need to slice the *bistecca*."

Dante moved back to the kitchen and Bianca retrieved the laptop and pried back the screen. Over another symphonic clashing of dishes and self-talk directing the food preparation, she studied the IM dialog box. Whoever was on the other end had a few more additional lines, with the second entry in screaming caps. "I NEED YOUR HELP, PLEASE." But the one that sent a chill down her spine was the final, almost-casual line, "THEY know where you are."

She powered down the laptop and closed the cover and set the computer down onto the floor before Dante returned. She took a bigger gulp of wine.

Dante returned with the sweating bottle of rosé and two fresh glasses, set everything down, and poured the wine before returning with the *bistecca tagliata*, a Tuscan dish. He said something about the beef being grass-fed. The lean pink meat lay like thin planks on a bed of arugula and she could see the juices still bubbling. Dante had placed some bright wedges of lemon on the rim of the dish.

He had a vegetable peeler in hand with a fragrant wedge of Parmigiano-Reggiano cheese. "I usually don't use cheese, but I know some cooks use it with this dish. Like some?"

"No, thank you, Dante. Please sit down and enjoy this dish with me."

As he found his chair and pulled himself in she asked, "So you and your fellow auditors go exploring subterranean Rome on the weekends?"

He cut a small piece of meat. "When we can. As a rule we always go in pairs for safety reasons, so sometimes scheduling is difficult. But I have gone down alone along established routes and ventured occasionally into some unknown areas. You'd be surprised how much of the underground is not documented. One can imagine the treasures left to be discovered."

"Must beat auditing any day. Tell me a little about your work. By the way, this *bistecca* is marvelous. Thank you."

He took in some arugula, chewed, and made a point using his fork by jabbing the air close to his dish. "I like auditing, and it isn't always boring. I work for the Guardia di Finanza. You know that."

"You mentioned it. You're a special type of police, right."

"You can say that. We still have a paramilitary function, like the American Coast Guard, but I'm afraid my duties are much more mundane. I analyze financial reports and check them for compliance."

"So no exciting James Bond type of work?" She wanted to taunt his ego and see what came of it.

"Exciting for me yes, but it's cerebral. I leave the breaking down doors and waving pistols in the air to others. Sorry. No license to kill. The criminals that I'm after are very clever and often conduct their crimes where laws are poorly defined. In fact, I'm working on a case right now. Not sure that it'll lead anywhere but it's very interesting nonetheless."

"How's it interesting?" Bianca found the meat perfectly seasoned and the acidity in the arugula just right. It was almost enough to make her forget her troubles.

He finished chewing. "The file I'm working is an *Importazione-Esportazione* scam, or at least it looks and feels like a scam. I have not yet found evidence or even worked out the details of the mechanism. It's all inconclusive." He made a rolling motion with knife and fork as he turned over some arugula.

She took a small sip of the chilled rosé. Perfect. "What makes you think it's a scam?"

"The government has asked us to investigate the unusual, if not suspicious, flood of Roman antiquities onto the world market. The thought at the moment is this one company or possibly a ring of them is handpicking items from the Roman underground and selling them on the international black market to connoisseurs in the private sector. The problem is, we go around in circles with nothing conclusive. There have been some arrests, mostly small-time operators, but they clam up tight. The company at the center of it all calls itself *Amici di Roma*. There are hundreds of cultural associations throughout the world that call themselves 'the friends of Rome,' but this one is definitely an import and export business with a list of subsidiaries longer than the Appian Way."

"What about museums? They have to show documentation on acquisitions, and I thought excavations are supposed to be documented."

"No museum in their right mind would get mixed up in this sort of trafficking—at least not in an obvious way. The ones we thought might be involved have ironclad documentation from here to Hell. Museums aren't stupid. They learned something after watching the Greek government fight with the British over the Elgin Marbles. We figure—the team that I work with, that is—either a speleologist is siphoning artifacts before the Beni Culturali catalogues them or there is an inside man within the Culturali. In either case all of this is conjecture because there is no hard proof."

She reflected on what he had just said, wanting to offer a suggestion. But she refrained. She didn't want to get caught up in her old life, not when her old life seemed to be catching up with her.

Dante was too caught up in explaining to notice her hesitation. "See, Rome has a bureaucracy for everything. So one day somebody goes to tear down their wall to make some addition to their house and they uncover a pipe or a jar or a mosaic, and everything comes to a standstill—and I mean everything stops. *Basta!* You can't move so much as a shovel before an assessment is made. Whatever is found is carted off if it *can* be carted off, or it sits at the scene and the scene is photographed and subjected to technical tests."

"Like a crime scene."

"Much like a crime scene. But . . . ," his index finger went in the air, "we Italians are known for moving things along, either with a little monetary lubrication or a little forceful persuasion. Everyone knows of this, but again, you have to catch them in the act."

"Bribery and Mafiosi: the two seem to go hand-in-hand."

He nodded his head as he chewed. "But, of course, the problem is tracing the shell companies, and also Customs being a virtual Hydra with bribery. It's almost impossible to keep on top of it all. Tons of artifacts are piling up, God knows where, so that the paperwork can be checked; if it even gets documented. So you see, who is to know if a relic goes missing from a warehouse somewhere?"

"Might I make a suggestion?" Bianca said, giving in to the urge.

As he worked on some arugula, his hand motioned to come forward with the suggestion.

"Maybe you're thinking too locally about this and you need to start thinking global. What I would do is look at the top museums with respectable, growing antiquities collections, and—" She put her hand up, anticipating his repeating the earlier point about museums staying away from illicit acquisitions. "Wait—hear me out, Dante. You look at their contributors, the private collectors, and you see if they've made purchases. Look for auction houses, trades between collectors—that sort of thing."

"And you think one of these rich types is going around having his picture taken in a newsletter or he wrote in his diary that he had lunch and—wait, let me see—*Today I purchased a three-thousand-year-old stolen statue?*"

Bianca didn't take it as sarcasm. "No, but the tax records, especially if any of them owns or has partners in *Importazione-Esportazione* firms, might prove interesting. Don't forget that sometimes these rich types, as you put it, don't buy things but rather they trade one item for another to complete their collection."

"So they make an illicit purchase, donate it to the museum, and in return the museum acquires something with a more reliable provenance?"

"Something that might fit their collection better. Of course there is another way to uncover the method." Her eyes narrowed after she put the wineglass down. "You could set a trap."

"A trap?"

"Create a rumor that some artifact of inestimable value was recovered—something one of a kind; you'd need to shroud this new find in mystery—and see what happens. I think you'll find people coming out of the walls. Of course, you'd need the cooperation of a very small group of people you can trust to maintain the secrecy of the hoax. Start the rumor and see what interesting things unfold is what I would do. Let them come to you."

Dante looked stunned, a small piece of green hung from his lips. He wagged his finger at her, "You make it sound so easy. 'Let them come to you.' I suppose you suggest one creates the web and sits on the outer edge with . . . *la pazienza del ragno*, the patience of a spider?"

"Why not? Let greed do the work for you." She was feeling strangely excited. She'd forgotten how much she enjoyed this sort of thing. "Never underestimate human avarice. Collectors are obsessive creatures; their psychology is all about obtaining, owning, and completing their collections. Besides, spiders are quite successful, using nothing but their webs. All you have to do is wait for the vibrations when something lands. In this case it's likely to be a go-between who does the buying so someone else far more important doesn't get their hands dirty. But money always leaves a trail."

Dante picked up the bottle and split the remainder between the glasses. "You can always count on a woman."

"Only if you want the job done right. Oh my, the time! I really should be going. Will you drive me home?"

He put down his napkin. "Sure. I'm sorry that I didn't have a chance to fetch dessert. Sweets are not my forte."

"Forget it, Dante. I'm full. We'll get gelato one night. There's a nice shop, run by Sicilians, on Via della Fontinella, unless you prefer the Gelateria Duse."

"I've always been partial to San Crispino on Via della Panetteria, but I'm open to persuasion." She could swear that he had winked at her as he pointed to the door where he had his keys.

She collected her laptop, slung the shoulder strap, and as she walked out of his nice furnished apartment she looked upwards to the second floor and smiled. *Get a man to talk about his work and you stand a chance of avoiding his bed without impoliteness.*

Both were unaware that across the street, in a green Fiat with plates from Palermo, a man with a zoom-lens camera was snapping photographs. Helmet on, and on the back of the Vespa holding on for her life, she had Dante drive her and drop her off in front of the Hotel Diocleziano.

The Fiat had chosen not to follow them.

5

She arrived home and set down the laptop and started to pace. Her feet found it soothing to touch the cold marble floor. She looked at the walls and pushed back her hair with both hands.

THEY know where you are. To her surprise, she found it made her angry.

She liked Rome. She liked Dante, and she liked having some semblance of a normal life: enjoying museums, the cinema, and everything the city had to offer her. She liked being Bianca. Rome was better than Lucerne, which was dry and grey and far too full of the Swiss. Yet as much she liked her life, it now seemed logical to run. She had money. She didn't have to work. She reasoned that it was okay to start over since she had no ties, not really. Dante would forget her and she could and would forget him. It would be easy enough for her to find another city, assume another identity and start over. Life, experience had proven, was easy enough to revise. She'd only started out as Alabaster Black. Since then, she had been numerous other women, and she would be someone else again.

But she was excited about this trap for smugglers. It stirred something deep in her that had been sleeping since she'd run.

The laptop sat there. She opened it, powered it up. She looked at the three IM prompts:

Did you work for Rendition?
I NEED YOUR HELP, PLEASE.
THEY know where you are.

The avatar was a female head, faceless. How creative. She stared at the prompts. The first one was casual, the second one was urgent and insistent with its caps, and the third one was muddled. Had her petitioner started the third request to underscore Rendition with the *THEY*?

Bianca found herself immersed in Alabaster's old habits. Was this Rendition's trap to draw her out? She didn't concern herself with the plea for help. The third one was meant to induce paranoia. She hesitated, thinking that if she did a diagnostic on the origin of the prompts then she might spring their trap, whoever *THEY* might be.

She chose to delete the prompts and close the laptop.

The wine made her feel sleepy, relaxed, but certainly not careless. She lay down on the bed, propped up the pillow and thought about the Strand job, which was what had started all this. It was relatively close in time but so far away from her present life that she felt as if she was watching herself in the third person.

It was old advice for doing well at an interview: break out your best dress, your breath mints, best blouse and nylons. Don't forget your best answers and updated résumé. No perfume and follow up with a hand-written thank-you note for the opportunity, sounding eager, but not desperate, remembering some small detail and closing it with why you belong. And most important of all, don't forget to do your research.

Ms. Alabaster Black had done her research on the Strand Corporation. Then she sat on the other side of the desk in her navy pant suit, white blouse, wearing light, barely noticeable makeup; her dark hair brushed back, long, cut even and lightly curling inward to her exposed throat. She allowed herself one luxury though as she waited for the Human Resources person on the opposite side of the desk to look up at her; she had casually crossed her leg.

In a way, she was still doing her research. She watched the young Resources person, all of twenty-two, ten years younger than she was, make her serious-reading face as she perused the résumé Alabaster had printed on porcelain bond paper in Garamond font—twelve point for company, title, and year, and ten point for description and accomplishments. For Ms. Alabaster Black was having the fourth interview that morning after a gauntlet of meetings: first with another Human Resources team member, who had given her a tour of the office, then with a project manager, then a team lead, and finally, this last interview with the Human Resources person who probably had received milestone status reports by phone during each phase of her ascent through the hierarchy.

Alabaster watched the eyes opposite her move from left to right, doing carriage-returns to the left margins as they read her extensive accomplishments. She watched the woman's right hand rotate a pen round and round while the rock of an engagement ring sparkled and glimmered. Alabaster looked at the store-bought cup of coffee to the woman's left; above the ubiquitous orange and hot-pink logo she saw the lower-lip lipstick smudge imprinted on the beltway rim of white Styrofoam. That lipstick bothered Alabaster.

The desk itself presented a confused mess of collected papers, white pages bound together with new paper clips that shone in the sunlight slanting through the blinds. And then there were the many multi-colored manila file folders organizing yet more documents, haphazardly placed into a wire rack next to a phone console with multiple communication lines pulsing, or lighting up, then disappearing. That was not how Alabaster would keep her own desk.

Alabaster continued to observe the other woman's lips as they slowed down, pausing, getting ready to state their part in this final scene of the game. It was a deliberate ploy to build tension. It was all part of the interview process, part of seeing how hungry the candidate was for the job.

"I see that you've had only one employer." The statement, inflected as a question, was meant to provoke insecurity and self-justification. For Alabaster Black, it had not. She jingled the ankle bracelet that she had trapped under her nylons and enjoyed the sensations up and along her inner thigh.

"Yes. I began in General Accounting and then moved into my specialty: Reconciliations." She did not elaborate beyond what she had explicitly outlined in her work history.

"Hmm, I can see that and . . ." and her cell phone buzzed on the desk. "Excuse me, but I need to take this call. Sorry."

The young Resources woman turned her large leather chair around and spoke in a soft voice on the other side. It was the fourth interruption by cell phone alone. A few poor souls had each come to the door but each had gone away after looking through the glass and seeing that an interview was in progress. Alabaster read the walls a fourth time: achievement award there, excellence award below it, a quality management award to the left, and a few smaller handshake-and-smile photographs and plaques with Robert Strand, the CEO, in the center. Then the one non-corporate item: a framed photograph taken in Rome, looking down the ancient processional street between the Temple of the Vestal Virgins and the Roman Coliseum. It was a nice photograph and the photographer showed a talent for composition.

Alabaster turned to the back of the chair in front of her upon hearing the cell phone click shut. She put her company smile back on.

"Very sorry about that," the young woman said, apparently shaken by the call.

"Are you all right?" Alabaster asked her with her head tilted in faux concern, the eyes observing her young guide.

"Yes, of course, thank you. It seems that your interviews this morning have gone very well. I've heard nothing but very good things. We would need to check on your references, of course, but I've been asked to present you with this as our offer." The young woman scribbled numbers on a slip of company letterhead and slid it towards Alabaster, who looked down at the paper and smiled. Then she stood up.

"Thank you, but no thank you, Ms. Hutchins. I should be going now," Alabaster said clearly, sliding the slip of paper back to the young Strand employee.

The young lady behind the desk had not been expecting this, her hand still resting on the letterhead. "Ms. Black, I would strongly advise you to reconsider. This isn't the way to go at it if more money is what you want. This offer is quite generous, especially for someone with such a limited employment history, and the Strand Corporation has had many more qualified candidates with extensive experience that qualify for the position."

Alabaster leaned over the desk and took back her one-page résumé. "Excellent, then hire one of them."

Ms. Hutchins' eyes widened. "Are you saying that you're not interested in working for the Strand Corporation?"

"That's correct."

"But, I don't understand." She almost sounded as if she were about to sputter. "Nobody has ever turned down a job offer from the Strand Corporation."

"I'm honored to be the first," Alabaster said. "Have a nice rest of the day."

Alabaster was already moving, out of the woman's office and down the cubicle alleyway toward the square light of the front entrance. She had seen what she needed to see. She had been inside the main Strand office and had done what she needed to do.

The Strand interview process was, in her mind, a reminder that an employee was nothing more than a whore. Call the kink a skill, name your price, shake hands, and then go somewhere private. That was the way Alabaster felt. She had seen it again and again, especially in the upper echelons of corporate America, despite the warm, nauseating false intimacy of the buzzwords: 'family', 'commitment', 'caring'. She would hear HR types shorten her name into what they thought were affectionate diminutives, like 'Al,' 'Allie' and the inexplicable, 'Ala Bee.' But at heart, it was mutual use for profit.

She rationalized that experienced workers knew the psychological subtext and went along with it as they had a commodity to sell and were going with the highest bidder, despite the marketing of 'a meaningful relationship' in brochures, by-words, and posters for any given company. She had seen that some companies revolved around some guru deity who gave mesmerizing annual or (if they were particularly egotistical) quarterly speeches to galvanize workers to work twice as hard for less pay than the previous year, while he and his inner circle would give themselves sickening bonuses and vote unanimously on lowering their option prices before dumping their shares on the Stock Market.

Ms. Hutchins' day had just grown worse because now she had to tell Mr. Robert Strand by phone that Ms. Alabaster Black had turned down his offer. Alabaster's play was afoot. She was counting on Strand's ego to interpret her rejection as a challenge.

When her résumé had been keyed into the Strand HR database and Mr. Strand's weekly spider program had crawled through the résumés, the word 'Reconciliation' combined with 'General Accounting 5' triggered an e-mail. Strand's little spider had alerted him that a prize morsel had wandered into his web.

Alabaster's own spider, much smaller and more secretive, had alerted her by e-mail that her résumé had been opened and forwarded to Strand's e-mail account.

Strand called down to HR to have them invite Alabaster Black in for an interview. The HR types had doubtless assumed that she would be another burnt-out government clerk who had become an information mercenary. Her selling point, they had thought, would be her accounting skills. But she knew that, for Robert Strand, the interest lay in her experience and working knowledge of government investigative methodology. Strand might've assumed Ms. Alabaster Black could become his private bitch on a leash that he could use to disembowel his enemies and feed their entrails to underpaid government lawyers who worked all day and all night in spite of all the resources of the federal government behind them. His idea had been to steal one of the government's own. Alabaster had applied to the Strand Corporation knowing that Robert Strand might think this way. He would not expect a GA5 to decline a job offer that included a six-figure salary.

Then it became a matter of wait and see, a game Alabaster knew how to play like a professional.

As CEO, Robert Strand had amassed hundreds of millions of dollars in assets and built his flagship hexagonal buildings in every European country; and he had just started building them in Asia, too. He had achieved little success in the Middle Eastern countries, like Israel, where the highest rate of entrepreneurial enterprises in the world could be found, and he had had an even more difficult time dealing with the older Israeli businessmen, who held a tight fist on everything. Strand had experienced no problem with Russia and the Eastern European countries, where he was practically a national hero for creating jobs.

Everything that Strand did, however, was slippery. He would sub-contract construction to the point that it could take years for auditors to figure out who had installed the plumbing and wiring on a particular site. He fought unions to a standstill. Strand would use minority firms and local businesses as front companies to get low-interest government loans. Given the way all his licenses were expedited and none of his legal paperwork second-guessed, it was hard not to suspect bribery. Strand's business had become so multinational, so diversified that, like an octopus, he had to have his tentacles in everything and everywhere and thus be able to propel himself forward mysteriously and gracefully.

Then the Strand Corporation had started failing, for no apparent reason. There had been no lay-offs, no executives leaving with sever-ance packages, but financial reporting had indicated that there were revenue issues.

Mr. Robert Strand, summa cum laude of Wharton and guest lec-turer at the London School of Economics, titan of technology, medi-cal visionary, engineering whiz kid, darling of Wall Street, man of the people, hero of distressed neighborhoods and patron saint of the urban poor, master manipulator of media—the man who walked on water—was starting to sink. When his businesses had started to slide inex-plicably downward on the quarterly reports, the GA swarmed down to identify irregularities but found none. Creating confusion for the financial review was that thousands of Strand employees had started to return portions of their paychecks, adding up in the millions, to show their loyalty for their captain.

The employees seemed determined that they would not let his ship sink, even though somehow he was, as the CEO, making the decisions that were blowing holes in the hull. The news media had shown crying employees, even interviewing a single mother who had written out a hundred-dollar check personally to Mr. Strand because "he's a good man that has fallen on hard times, like the rest of us."

The GA had found that the Strand Corporation had set aside all the employee money into a reserve account and had properly reported the income. The GA had been trying to wrap up its analysis before the EU and the Asian countries could start offering rescue money to shore up the Strand Corporation.

To Rendition, Robert Strand was suspicious. They just needed the evidence.

Alabaster had no problem with the assignment. In fact, she had suspected that his dossier would show up one day. She had gone to the train station and pulled out two eight-inch-by-ten-inch plain brown envelopes from lockbox 411. The pickup spot was never the same twice. One time it had been a certain shelf in the library. Another time it had been inside one of those hanging phone books at a public pay-phone. There had even been the pickup at the magazine stand where the documents had been placed next to some peculiar hentai porn. Her assignments would come at odd intervals: sometimes they would show up once a month; other times, four months would go by without any-thing. She would do one assignment at a time. There had never been any sense of urgency until she received the Strand assignment.

She went home after the interview and waited. Her keys made a light, metallic sound on the Vermont Verde Antique green-marble countertop that she had installed in her kitchen. She opened up one of the doors to her Viking refrigerator, pulled out a cut of loin steak that she had been marinating, and some green beans to steam.

She was debating whether she wanted wine or not when the phone rang.

From that first day when Rendition had left its calling card, it had honored its word and never stepped foot into her personal space or contacted her directly. Alabaster had never given her home number out. Only trusted social contacts and the rare date had her cell number. She had never brought a date home to her loft. She had listed her home phone on only one document recently.

She picked up the phone, and in the most casual, nonchalant tone, said, "Hello, Mr. Strand."

"How did you know?" The man was clearly caught off guard.

Alabaster decided on wine—a Malbec for the bold mouth feel and soft to medium tannins that would pair well with the meat. She silently eased the cork out of the bottle as she cradled the phone between her cheek and shoulder.

"I understand that you declined my offer this morning," Strand then said, composed in such a manner over the phone as to sound inquisitive, but concerned, with a small touch of hurt pride. He was back in control.

"I did." She poured her wine into one of her Riedel glasses. "I indicated to Ms. Hutchins that I was not interested. I would've told her earlier but she had to keep answering her cell while I was with her." After the first sip, she set the glass aside so she could focus on her conversation with Strand.

"I can understand that she might've appeared rude to have answered her cell phone, but what if I told you that it was me who was calling her? I'm very interested in you. It's rare that I have such talent walk through my doors."

"And you don't use the office phones, like everyone else? Or are you so close to all your employees that you have their cell phone numbers?" Alabaster was enjoying the game of one-upmanship.

"In fact, Ms. Black, I do have all my employees' cell numbers."

"Well, Mr. Strand, you don't have my cell and I don't think you're likely to have it in the future."

"Really?"

"Yes, really," she said as her cell buzzed with an incoming call, number not listed.

She rested the other phone on her shoulder, flipped it open and was about to say hello when he said, "As I was saying, Ms. Black, I do have all my employee cell phone numbers, and I can get the ones I don't have. Why don't you allow me to persuade you to come work for me? In person, say over dinner? I'm sure a government G5 accounting clerk can enjoy a nice dinner without any conflict of interest. How about eight this evening? I'll send my car over."

Alabaster hung up her other phone.

"Just dinner?"

"You know that I won't be able to resist trying to charm you to come work for me. You do have to allow me one opportunity before dessert. How 'bout it?"

"I've heard that you can be an insistent man, Mr. Strand, so it would seem that I would have no choice but to say yes."

"Call me Robert, please. As to the matter of free will, if you're genuinely not interested in working for me and having dinner with me, I'll let the matter rest. We all have the right to say 'yes' or 'no' to opportunities. If you say 'no,' you have my word that you won't hear from me again."

The turn in the conversation genuinely surprised her. "Really?" she said, trying to be slightly coy, which was something she had never been very good at.

"Yes, really, Ms. Black. I respect your time as you should respect mine. I won't waste yours and I hope you wouldn't waste mine. Dinner at eight, or not?"

Alabaster pushed aside the wine. "Fair enough; pick me up at eight then."

After returning the marinated meat to the fridge, she took her wine with her and got ready for the evening. The limousine pulled up in front of her building at eight pm sharp. The chauffeur tipped his hat and opened the door for her. Alabaster had chosen to wear a vintage black dress with pink embroidered roses, a posh little number that had been meant to show that she had a playful sense of humor with every intention of dispelling any dowdy misconception Strand might have about accountants. The cat-eye glasses had been meant to complete the half-serious and all-sexy look. She entered the back seat and adjusted her skirt before realizing that Robert Strand was sitting there admiring her with an appreciative smile.

"'Evening, Ms. Black," he said.

Alabaster had not expected him but recovered quickly. She offered her hand. "'Evening."

He shook it, his eyes meeting hers. "I'm taking you to a special place where we can enjoy a nice dinner and have privacy. And then we can see if we wish to work together."

"I thought you were trying to *persuade* me to work for you."

"We'll see. We might just decide to remain friends in the end." He knocked on the glass divider and the car drove off.

Strand had reserved the top floor of one of the city's premiere restaurants. The floor of the restaurant would make one slow-moving revolution per hour, offering, during its circular journey, a three-hundred-sixty-degree panoramic view of the city. The meal was staged with courses; it paired wine or sake selections, depending on the course. Alabaster started her meal with a steamed scallop with ginger and scallion. Strand himself opted for the pumpkin ravioli with sage brown butter. He persuaded Alabaster to have what he was having: Kobe beef paired with a robust Australian Shiraz.

The Kobe beef was a near-mystical experience. Zen-like in its paradox to move her to tears both for pleasure, because it was so soft that it required neither knife nor teeth, and for pity, because the animal had been raised to move so little, fed Kirin beer until it had become arthritic, then slaughtered. For dessert, he chose wasabi tiramisu while she had indulged her sweet tooth with the double chocolate mousse.

"Are you enjoying yourself?" he asked over his Grand Marnier Cent-Cinquantenaire.

She raised her Penfolds Great Grandfather's Old Tawny Port, which was simply majestic.

"As I promised, I want to persuade you to come work for me," he announced after a sip.

"Do you lavish this much attention on all your candidates?"

"Quite honestly, no, I don't, Ms. Black. I reserve such attention for people who are either my allies or my enemies."

Feeling the seductive draw of the port, with its slight mandarin note, she smiled and deadpanned, "I see. Deciding if I am a combatant, are we?"

He toyed with his snifter using both hands, enjoying seeing the citrus liqueur move against the side of the glass. "I know enough to know that you are investigating me, or shall I say the government is investigating me. I would go so far as to say that you are just the person Rendition would send after me and—"

Alabaster tried to look surprised. "Rendition? Not sure I understand what you're alluding to, Mr. Strand. I'm an accounting clerk with, grant you, unique skills that have a specific legal application, but Rendition is not something I know anything about."

"No offense, but you don't make a very compelling liar, which might of course explain why you never appeared in court to give testimony. More port?"

"Thank you. I worked as part of a team on those cases, and other analysts wrote up the final reports." She stopped when she caught him admiring her.

"Partial truth, Ms. Black. What would you say if I proposed the following: that you did indeed work as part of a team, but that you were the analytical mind behind all the findings, the one who put it all together? Your so-called team simply transcribed the results."

"I'm not that bright, Mr. Strand. And besides, what would make you jump to that conclusion?"

He enjoyed another sip of the Cent-Cinquantenaire. "Humility is the inverse of pride: that is the lesson of medieval theology. Let me be direct, Alabaster. You know that most high-powered corporations, the ones that really move things on this planet, film applicants during their interviews, paying particular attention to body language and their use of language to see if they are telling the truth, hiding something, and so forth. The films are often analyzed by behavioral specialists and occupational psychologists. It is very scientific and military-like and—"

"And will lead to a point, Mr. Strand?"

"I combined the vocal patterns in your answers and had the logic analyzed by my people when you did the routine 'how would you solve this problem?' question with the project manager. A very interesting thing emerged. It would seem, improbable or not, that whole phrases or parts of phrases in your speech matched the most damning sections of reports on the Pegasus, Alliance, and Manor reports. But most interesting to me was the high rate of perfect matches that came when I matched your phrasing to the Fox report."

"So what?" Alabaster said, not having much more interest in the indulgent port.

"Well, I could be completely wrong and it could all be a fantastic coincidence, but I would wager that the Fox fiasco was of personal interest to you, which could explain your fingerprints, so to speak, all over it. I could be completely wrong about you and Rendition, but let me put this observation out there to you. Rendition, like most covert government groups, picks the most innocuous, discreet people it can find. You—and I don't mean to offend you—are a very plain girl. What I mean by that is you are not flashy and draw next to no attention to yourself; you don't have any discernible vices or indulgences and have no attachments. In other words, you could and can vanish without anyone ever knowing."

Alabaster felt her cheeks flushed, and not from the port. The angle at which he sat in the chair across from her, which earlier had denoted cool comfort, now suggested cruelty and calculated sadism.

She touched her lips with the napkin. "I think you should take me home, or have your driver do it while you go to hell."

Strand put his hand on the table as some attempt at peace but she wouldn't look at his face. "I'm sorry if I struck a nerve, but give me a chance to prove myself. I'm not the bad guy that you think I am, Ms. Black. I'm merely suggesting that you think about whom you work for and their motivations."

"Fine," she said before she could help herself. "Riddle me this, Mr. Strand: Why are your enterprises suddenly failing? It does seem rather curious."

Strand pulled out a piece of paper. Alabaster looked perplexed. He held it up and momentarily refrained from handing it to her. "I ask one thing from you."

"What?"

He took another sip. "I know you are *that* good and I have no doubt you will figure it out, but I ask that if you do find anything you think is incriminating you notify me so I can prepare my defense. That is perfectly within my legal right as an American citizen."

"How do I know you aren't showing me only what you want me to see? And what if I'm not bright enough to find where you've hidden the improprieties?"

"If you don't find anything, then you file your findings with the GA folks or whomever you work for. Deal or no deal?"

She looked him over, looked at the piece of paper that he was still holding.

"You seem so determined to prove your innocence, Mr. Strand. If you have nothing to hide then you should have nothing to worry about." She took the last sip of her port, her eyes never leaving him.

"It's Robert, and we all have something to hide. The only people innocent in this world are those who are born this very minute. After that, we develop secrets that we'll carry with us until the day someone throws dirt over us."

He handed the paper to her. It held the access codes to the Strand Corporation's server.

Back at her loft later that evening, Alabaster sat with her laptop and a bottle of water, reviewing the voluminous amounts of data in the Strand computer systems. Financial data is a fluid entity, but everything that she was looking at in intervals for the necessary legal documentation was looking kosher. Not squeaky clean—there were some issues subject to interpretation—but nothing that could be remotely considered illegal. She plumbed the electronic depths hoping for something murky, but found nothing. Including any sign of the source of Strand's monetary losses.

As she was working, a window console popped up, an IM chat prompt, one of the very few real-time intrusions Rendition had foisted on her work. Alabaster figured that the Rendition analysts had likely been reviewing the same files as she was and drawing their own conclusions. She stared at the blinking cursor next to the Rendition avatar—a simple but static red 'R' on the screen.

The Rendition cursor moved left to right, leaving a trail of letters behind it. "WHAT DO YOU MAKE OF THESE FILES?"

Alabaster always despised screaming in caps. She typed in, "Same as you. Nothing conclusive yet."

The cursor pulsed in the gray windowpane. She waited. Alabaster never liked interruptions and overt displays of Rendition monitoring her work, but she rationalized it as their enthusiasm to nail Strand.

The cursor moved again, informing her that she ought to navigate to a certain drive. She copied the address onto her notepad, and there the cursor instructed her to analyze a folder named *Terra*. The cursor stopped, pulsed, and Rendition signed off. She opened up her diagnostic console and pinged the remote host to locate the Rendition chatter, and about a hundred IP addresses rolled down her screen. She imported the IP addresses into an address-locator program and found a hundred different locations around the globe.

Alabaster was annoyed, and not a little suspicious, that she was being led to a specific file pathway. If Rendition knew where the answer was then why did they need her? Then she thought that maybe they needed another set of eyes on the data. She typed in the pathway, and her cell phone started ringing.

"Hello?"

"It's me, Robert. I see that you found Terra. Suggestion: use disposable cell phones for communication."

The line then went dead.

"Great, everyone knows something but me. Thanks, guys." She closed the cell phone, powered down the device, and turned her eyes to the Terra folder. After three hours of devoted scrutiny, Alabaster was able to see that the Terra folder was the electronic repository for the Strand Corporation's secret project in geo-engineering 'dark soil.' She came across the concept in passing in a survey course she had once taken on geology. Scientists claimed that global warming could slowly be mitigated with the creation of biochar, or smoldering biomass, to generate a charcoal-like substance, which in turn could be added to the soil and retain, or as the geologists termed it, 'sequester,' carbon. The beauty of the process was that no carbon dioxide was released into the environment during the slow burning, and once added to the soil, the terra preta, or 'dark soil,' was found to be renewable and sustainable, adding nutrients to the soil, which had the potential to improve farming around the globe. Alabaster was impressed, but she was looking for the money trail.

And there it was. The Strand Corporation had been making significant investments for constructing preta plants in the Amazon Basin, Australia, the African Congo, and the remotest areas of Scotland. Alabaster inferred quickly the implications, from biochar to creating bio-oil, but Strand's documentation seemed centered on farming. He seemed focused on creating an inexpensive fertilizer that would also sequester carbon. After a bit more refinement, she found the money losses had been coming from their having sunk money into "charging carbon." She went back to one of the five technical assessment documents to understand what "charging" meant, but by then, she needed a break.

Alabaster jumped into the shower. The hot water soothed her tight shoulders and lower back from all that slouching at the computer. She couldn't stop thinking about Rendition's intrusion: it wasn't like them to do that. Only once had they done that to her. In the Fox case, her research and the IM chats had melded together into a furious search for facts. She hadn't thought of it so much as an intrusion but as a collaborative analysis. This time it perturbed her. She brushed her teeth again because it always refreshed her, put on some new panties and sweatpants, a light t-shirt, no bra, and threw on a hoodie. It was a sloppy look but she wasn't out to impress anyone. She decided that Robert's idea of getting a disposable cell phone was a good one. The bodega a block from the infamous coffee shop sold some.

After buying a couple of disposable phones, she tore the annoying plastic off one of them and called Robert. He then called her back on his own disposable cell phone.

"Look," she said, "I've been at this for the last several hours, so if you can save me some brain cells, I'd appreciate it. What can you tell me about *charging carbon*?"

"In simple layman's terms, charcoal is very limited, but it has the potential to provide nutrients over a very long period of time, like thousands of years. The problem is ordinary charcoal is a poor biotope and it requires a kick start and—"

"These are layman's terms, are they? You must know some extraordinarily well-educated laymen."

She could tell that Strand enjoyed explaining because he paused to lick his lips. "Okay, biotope simply means life-giving. Think of it this way: charcoal has to be soaked like a sponge before it can be squeezed, but when it's squeezed, and I mean metaphorically in terms of providing a yield and not geological compression, which is what you would need for oil and diamonds, but that is another process altogether and—"

"I think I understand. What is it that you need to soak the stuff in? I assume that is the problem."

"Exactly. You're right, Alabaster. The charcoal has to be soaked in another nutrient."

She was trying to connect what she was hearing with the financial picture. "So, this nutrient, or whatever it is, is the cause of your money pit, right? It's something very expensive?"

"Not exactly. The nutrient is actually very inexpensive, and very easy to come by. There are two parts to the problem. The first is that you have to soak the charcoal for two to four weeks and that should do the job. That soaking charges the charcoal with phosphorous and nitrogen, but you also need calcium, magnesium, and potassium already in the soil before you add the charged charcoal. Partial combustion and the biomass from plant life can get me everything, except the phosphorous and nitrogen that I need."

"Roundabout way of saying that the problem goes back to charging the charcoal, right?"

"Correct."

She was able to hear that his exasperation had been with his findings and not with her. "But you just told me that it's cheap and plentiful, so what's the problem?" She was approaching the entrance of her building. She knew that she would have to wrap up the conversation before getting into the elevator, as she would lose reception. "I have to go soon before this phone cuts out. Tell me what it is that you're up against. If it's cheap and plentiful then I can't see how the technology could be so expensive."

"Political lobbyists for other companies and human short-sightedness have made it costly. I'm up against massive corruption."

Alabaster was nearing her elevator door. "So what is it that charges the charcoal?"

She heard a pause. The elevator bell chimed and she heard his answer, "Human excrement." And then the call dropped.

She turned the key, walked into the loft and pulled back her hood, running her one hand through her wet hair and keying in his number with the other. He picked up.

"You're telling me all you need is shit?" she said.

"Plenty of it. Feces and urine, particularly from humans, are rich in phosphorous and nitrogen and—"

Something was wrong. She silenced Strand with a "Ssssh" that shot into the phone as quietly as possible.

"Why are you shushing me?"

"Shut up."

Alabaster walked in and walked over to her curtains. She eyed the chair near her closet. The curtains were swaying to the right on the rod and the chair was sideways to the wall instead of back against it. Alabaster looked at her laptop. The IM chat cursor indicated that contact had been aborted. She looked at the two avatars on the screen with the repeated "ARE YOU THERE?" and her empty responses next to her avatar. She wasn't feeling too sexy anymore.

Rendition had visited her apartment.

Bianca realized that she had been dozing in and out in her haze of recollection.

She felt tired and ran her hands over her face. Something had to be done if *THEY* knew where she was now. She felt restless so she decided to visit one of the all-night cyber cafés rather than work on her laptop in the apartment. If she paid in cash, the Internet usage would be harder to trace until she had a better idea who and what she was dealing with. Her mind settled: she would do some research and help Dante with his project.

Dante was a nice guy and could use the help—assuming, that is, that she found anything worthwhile to give him. But chances were, she would. She had the impression that Dante was of the paper-and-pencil variety of auditor and possibly a bit of a technophobe, or at least didn't make full use of the web and databases. She didn't give any thought to how she would explain her skills. It was the challenge of his special project at work that intrigued her.

Before she left, she disengaged the hard drive from her laptop. She verified that she had her jump key. She was leaving the apartment clean.

6

Dante was sitting at his desk with piles of paperwork neatly arranged in stacks all around him. At the rate it was accumulating, it would be about a month before he saw his blotter again.

"Psst! Gennaro incoming," said Alessandro, his office mate.

Dante looked over his shoulder and saw his superior stampeding toward his office, papers in hand.

Gennaro was a shorter version of Robert Mitchum from the early '70s, around the time of *Friends of Eddie Coyle*. A barrel chest, an unruly lock of hair that still clung to the original black color, and between them a pair of deadly-charming blue eyes. Gennaro hailed from Naples; he had only recently been transferred to the Rome branch office. He had earned this transfer after exposing a money-laundering scheme that had included all the major agricultural cities in the south of Italy, with kickbacks and bribes running north all the way into the major finance houses in Milan. While not condoning what the southern cities had done, Gennaro had been able to show that the farmers had been trying to control prices for their products so that they wouldn't be screwed into subsistence.

As the case had slowly passed through the courts—like a peach pit through a dog's digestive system, as he had been wont to allude to the subsequent trials—it exposed all the discriminatory business practices the North would use on the South. The newspapers and discussion panels on RAI television had had a field day grilling the local politicians. In a backward sort of way, Gennaro had helped his fellow countrymen even while exposing their corruption, and he had become something of a celebrity in Naples, despite the serious damage his exposé had done to local economies. He had peeled back the skin on animosities that went back to Garibaldi. And was punished for it with a transfer to Rome, putting him in the middle of the Northern wolves' den.

Although everyone in the firm knew that Gennaro was all heart and lived for the good fight, diplomacy had never been his strong suit. He was less than eloquent with his metaphors, and this made him a bit difficult to deal with.

"What the fuck is this?" Gennaro said, several papers and Dante's sealed envelope now torn open and rustling in his hand.

Dante said, "Sandro, please close the door and the blinds."

Gennaro watched Alessandro close the door and shutter the blinds to shut out the spectators who were hoping to see a bloodbath. Gennaro waved the papers again. "Did I make it in time for the matinee? Did the top of your head not close up when you were a child, Dante?"

"I think my proposal speaks for itself, Chief. You read it, right?"

"Of course I read it," Gennaro flicked the first page. "Here you say you want to create an archaeological hoax. And here—" jabbing a paragraph—"you want to run the details in the newspapers and on the news. Are you out of your mind? You're thinking of fraud and—"

"Not fraud, Chief. Bait."

"Oh, so let me see whether I understand. It's not fraud, merely entrapment." Gennaro had reached the point where a vein in his forehead was broadcasting his pulse. "You think I have the budget for this?"

Alessandro cautiously sat down, holding a pencil, enjoying the exchange.

"Chief, my proposal is cheaper than if we do it this way." Dante pointed to the lawn of files on his desk.

"Convince me."

"I can sit here and you can have how many lazy bums out there shuffle this paperwork for months. That's time and salary and at the end of the day your boss will ask you for a status. You won't have one and they'll tsk tsk in your ear and maybe they'll send you to Milan for your next assignment. You'd love that, wouldn't you?"

Gennaro relaxed some. The forehead vein went away. "I'm listening."

Dante shrugged. "It's simple, Chief. We set the mousetrap and let the rat come out to us. With all this paperwork, we focus only on a few mice, but with this trap we might get the big, ugly rat. We make a case and let the lawyers have all this shit paperwork so they can build their case and add names to the indictments."

Gennaro, reeled in part way, pulled up a chair and sat down before he asked, "This hoax . . . what did you have in mind? And how do we pull it off?"

Dante leaned forward. Alessandro also leaned forward. Gennaro glared at Alessandro a moment and then ignored him.

"One-of-a-kind and irresistible beyond belief," Dante said. "We say that we've found the last of the three standards of Augustus Caesar's lost legions from the Battle of Teutoburg."

Alessandro's chair creaked. "The last eagle. Holy shit! That would be huge."

Gennaro's eyes were blinking. "Help me. I'm not following."

"Sandro," Dante said, "explain it to the man."

Sandro hunched forward, "Chief, it goes like this. Augustus Caesar wanted to teach the Germans a lesson up north. He sends three legions. They get their butts handed to them—twenty thousand men slaughtered and left on the field. Then the Germans humiliate Rome by not only decimating three legions but also by stealing their standard bearer's eagles. It's like stealing the flag."

Gennaro's forehead wrinkled. "Damn Tedeschi."

"Augustus would agree. The defeat sends him into the grave. Up next comes Tiberius. He's all about power, as expected, but he has a young general named Germanicus who happened to be his nephew, which means his rival. When you don't want a rival at home, what do you do with him? You send him off on a military campaign and hope he gets killed. Off goes Germanicus, who marches north right up the Rhine River and attacks left and right. And instead of getting killed like he was supposed to, he recovers two of the three lost eagles. So Tiberius calls him back home."

Gennaro, taken with the story, said, "Why the fuck did he do that?"

"Because Tiberius was afraid of Germanicus' growing popularity," Dante said. "The people of Rome knew he was bringing two emotional treasures home, and that might have been enough to get him put on Tiberius' throne. It seems obvious Tiberius was worried about the politics, although historians have argued that he was critical of Germanicus' strategy and worried about the boundary at the Rhine River between Rome and Germania."

"Idiots," said Gennaro.

Dante saw that he had Gennaro sold. He wasn't surprised. The man was unpleasant, but not stupid. "See, Chief, if we can convince our rat that we have the third eagle, then our rat won't be able to resist. We can get some academic type to say he saw it and have him spin some reason why the third eagle was in Rome all this time—like Germanicus did actually recover all three but Tiberius tried to discredit him and revised history texts, or something like that. We can sell this with no problems. But . . ."

"But what?" Gennaro asked.

"We have to keep this absolutely secret. We don't know who is sharing cheese with the rat."

Gennaro tore up the papers. "Let's do it. You and Sandro know; and you, Dante, you decide who is in this circle. But like you said, keep it small."

Just like that, swift and decisive. *Damn, that felt good.* "Right, Chief. And what about all this paperwork in the meanwhile?"

Gennaro looked at the stacks. "Shuffle them around. Put a stack on the ledge over there so the circus outside the window thinks you're making progress. And Sandro—"

"Yes, Boss."

"Whatever happened to Germanicus?"

Alessandro made a sad face. "It is said that a heel named Piso murdered him by order of Tiberius, but nobody knows for sure because Piso was murdered before he could be tried."

"Same old shit. The good guy gets fucked. And what happened to dear uncle Tiberius?"

"The usual, as expected," Sandro said. "Germanicus' son Caligula, when he was old enough to kill people, had Tiberius smothered."

Gennaro smiled. "Good."

"That's not the part I think you would enjoy most, Chief," Dante said.

His manager's eyebrows rose.

"Tiberius was so unpopular after the murder of Germanicus that he had to flee Rome. This part you'll enjoy, Chief. You know where? Tiberius had to flee south to Misenum for his own safety. And that's where he was smothered."

Gennaro smiled broadly. "Ah, he died in Campania. My Napoli is her capital. Served the bastard right." He turned for the door. "Make it happen."

After the door closed Alessandro said to Dante, "Hey, he called me Sandro. I think the guy might like me. You know they say the blood of San Gennaro liquefies three times a year."

"Don't get ahead of yourself, Sandro," Dante said. "We don't pull this off and we might be sharing an office in Milan with him. And one of us will be close to the window."

Dante began thinking of the circle of those who needed to know. He made the proposal, of course. Alessandro knew, Gennaro knew. They would have to tell an academic of some kind, and maybe a member of the press. Or maybe not, if the academic had press connections he could trust.

And, of course, Bianca knew. But Dante felt deeply that he could trust her.

7

Bianca placed the printouts for Dante on her bed, then began a sweep of her place.

Screwdriver in hand, she disassembled all the switch plates. Nothing. She unhinged the thermostat. Nothing. Under the bed, along hidden corners and odd edges, moldings, she eyed and fingered all of them for anything suspicious, anything miniature and unobtrusive. Nothing. Not having satisfied her paranoia, she examined all her clothes, from hem to lining, for any tracking devices. Nothing. She scrutinized the little jewelry she had, then barrettes, her watch, her cell phone, the laptop and printer, their peripherals, and anything she considered an accessory, from scarves to her shoes. Nothing. Last but not least, she took apart her bed: sheets first, the padding, examining the mattress and then the frame, and the headboard last. Nothing. There were no signs of surveillance.

Yet.

THEY know where you are.

She sat on the floor of her apartment, pulled a strand of hair back and curled it around her left ear. Bad as it was that the IM prompts had spooked her, thinking that someone might have been in her apartment resurrected that monumental day when the tide in trust had receded, permanently.

She knew that Rendition's search of her apartment in the middle of the Strand investigation had ignited the theme of violation that she tried to forget, like the one with Louie Patrone when she was fourteen. It had started slowly. It had even been pleasurable; that is, until it had turned unpleasant. And then unstoppable.

Alabaster had tried to remain clinical about Rendition's violation. Patrone was the past. Both Rendition and Strand were the present. And it may not have been Rendition who searched her apartment. They seemed anxious about Strand; they knew about the Terra folder. Had Rendition understood the Terra folder's technology or was it that they simply were validating its conclusions with her? Had Strand induced her paranoia to make her think that it was Rendition, or had Rendition been trying to make her think it was Strand?

But no matter how rational she fought to be, having Rendition in her apartment frightened her. It was time to leave, to find some genuine privacy. Alabaster walked over to her laptop, picked up her original cell phone and turned it on. She decided against taking the laptop, though she placed financial files and the Terra folder on her jump key along with some personal files. She figured that the cell phone's GPS would make it look as if she was still in the loft and that the laptop would be too much to carry, even if it didn't act as another transponder. She threw some clothes into a small sports duffle and extricated a considerable amount of money from a secret hiding place. Rendition and Strand would be contacting her soon. She had to be gone before they did. She left her credit and debit cards behind because they were traceable: everything would have to be paid for in cash.

Alabaster left the building with her hair pulled back and tied, her hood pulled up, wearing sunglasses, looking like a female D.B. Cooper. She went to the Public Library and sat down at a public computer in a remote corner. It was in the Stacks, as the graduate students called it—where they did their research, gossiped, occasionally had sex, and hung out to all odd hours. The City Public Library had upgraded all its computers from the bulbous monitors and old hard drives collecting dust to sleek flat-screen monitors, elegant keyboards, and nicely wired external and main hard drives. She plugged in her flash key and started looking at the Terra financials.

Strand had been telling the truth. The money he was losing was not from Strand business endeavors. He was paying it out to the two main political parties and myriad lobbyist groups in the US. The common denominator to all the groups was that they were tied to environmental efforts: clean water; better waste management; lowering greenhouse emissions; alternative fuels; saving this or that animal or ecosystem; growing more trees; improving and establishing better organic-farming standards, and the list went on. Strand had, like most corporations, seeded his money everywhere so as to give the impression that there was no partiality. But Alabaster could see that of all the groups, most of Strand's money went to the greenhouse/alternative-fuel groups as donations. No surprises there.

There was no documentation indicating that any of the particular groups or specific individuals was blackmailing Strand, although they were technically bleeding his company dry. Strand reported all the donations, so there was nothing improper there for the IRS. A US Attorney might make a case for bribery, but that would be a stretch as there was no clear quid pro quo. If Strand were to roll on the groups, then his biochar efforts would either get disclosed or tied up and die on the vine, so to speak. She clicked open another financial folder.

That folder proved interesting, if not disturbing. Two sister corporations Strand had set up—Strand International in Europe, and particularly Strand Asia, were also making donations to political groups. Alabaster bit her lower lip. Strand might be clean under domestic law, but international law was a different matter, especially with all the EU strictures around environmental and industry practices. She scrutinized the money flow—the issue manifested itself very clearly. The Europeans might not be so kindly disposed to the issue of bribery but an environmental project that sequesters carbon cheaply and efficiently—that might earn Strand some clemency.

China, for the most part, was not regulated, and with China building cities the size of Los Angeles every six months since 1990, consuming concrete, oil, and steel, and driving world market prices for those items, somebody had to be scrambling for the contracts to do all the sanitation for those cities. That somebody, Alabaster knew, had to be organized crime, same as it was here. That was whom Strand was fighting to get access to the necessities for charging his carbon. The irony was that there were so many people determined to retain their hold on the excrement business.

secuting Strand for bribery, the difference between the US legal systems is that the Chinese seem to have a disturb- ̄ ̄ ̄ ̄ ̄ ̄ ̄ ̄ ̄ ̄ ̄tion with their high-ranking executives and public officials on the verge of discovery and disgrace: suicide or public parade into a stadium for a bullet through the back of the head. Russia was Russia. Bribery was an implicit business practice. From the looks of it, pillory-ing Strand would make him an international pariah.

Alabaster had heard enough. She disengaged the jump key from the USB port and sat there to think about her next move. The Feds wouldn't have a strong-enough case to prove bribery without short-circuiting the political wires. That simply wouldn't do and would prove too volatile. Going after Strand in an international court system was too risky, especially if foreign counsel and savvy politicians started air-ing dirty US laundry. Also, Strand was essentially no guiltier than any other businessman, and there was nothing in the files that suggested that he was planning to stick the taxpayer with the bill or give all the candy away to his friends or keep it for himself. Rendition hired her to evaluate the files and that she did. There was really nothing there.

She zipped up her hood and put on her glasses. She left the library and walked over to the pretzel stand and bought herself one of the huge salty ones and asked for mustard. The hot, doughy softness and spiciness felt like a nice indulgence. She went into the park, enjoying the sights. She picked up one of the disposable cell phones and called Strand on *his* disposable one.

It rang twice before he picked up.

"Mr. Strand, it's me."

"Who else would it be?"

"I reviewed the files. My report is simply that there is the appearance of domestic and international bribes disguised as donations to various environmental lobbyist groups. Personally, I don't think there's much water to the case but that's not to say the legal types won't enjoy drag-ging your name through the mud since the appearance of impropriety is damning, and sprinkling a few distortions here and there throughout the media to inflict a dent or two in your armor. My suggestion to you is to hire an army of corporate lawyers, specifically ones with expertise in international law and intellectual property. And retaining a PR firm wouldn't hurt. You and I both know that the big legal drama is to freeze your assets and put a lockdown on Terra. I doubt the Feds would want the public to know about Terra or let it go to the jury, since it would take a fair amount of explaining to twelve people the implications of what you are doing for the future of the planet."

Strand paused, clearly impressed, then said, "I'm not sure whether to thank you or not, but I appreciate your honesty, Alabaster. I do have one question."

"Fair enough. I have two." She looked around. Nothing peculiar; no one appeared to be listening. "Shoot."

"Do you work for Rendition?"

She paused. "I don't think it matters, Mr. Strand."

She could hear him a-hem over the phone. "I guess that's true, Ms. Black. It doesn't matter. I didn't ask out of personal satisfaction. It's quite possible that your life will change for working on this case. Governments, like businesses, are motivated to adapt and survive, sometimes by any means necessary, even if it also means destroying something that can affect the greater good. Darwin versus John Stuart Mill."

"I was just doing my job. Facts do the rest." She then modulated her tone, infusing it with a drop of venom. "Now, I have a question. Were you or one of your people in my apartment when I went to get the disposable cell phones?"

"No to both."

Alabaster was silent.

"You said a moment ago that you had two questions. What's the second?"

Alabaster hesitated for a second. "The night we had dinner together. Did you mean what you said when you told me I was a plain girl?"

She could hear him smile. "Far from plain, but it would've been inappropriate for me to take an interest in a potential employee. You're a remarkable woman, Alabaster, and nobody can deny that you have integrity. As much as I would like to be like any other man, I think we know that is highly unlikely, especially now. My advice to you is to think about your relationship to Rendition—if it were in your life, hypothetically speaking, of course—and decide if you want that relationship; otherwise, contemplate disappearing for a while. You are valuable but at what point are you merely expendable."

Alabaster felt conflicting emotions. There was more that she wanted to say but all she could manage was, "Thank you, Robert."

But that was then and this was now. "They" had found her. Someone had been in her apartment and she should probably pack up and run again.

But there was this project of Dante's, and she hated leaving projects unfinished.

She hunted around and found an envelope for the research she'd done for him. She peeled the adhesive on the back flap of the office-sized envelope. She looked at the strip and made a mental note: looks like flypaper but nice way of keeping matters sanitary with not having to lick it. It also meant no DNA. She printed a label out with Dante's name on it, peeled off the adhesive butterfly flaps and affixed it to the front. Envelope in her bag, she picked up her cell phone to give Dante a call and see whether she could visit him at work.

8

The door of the stuffy elevator opened up onto the fifth floor of the building to which Dante had given her directions. Like most places in Rome, there was no connection between façade and interior. The outside can look good while the inside has gone to seed, or vice versa. Dante's office building's exterior was calm and cold with no ornamentation—form following function in government office building tradition. The lobby and the elevators there, in stark contrast, an ostentatious display of baroque marbles that looked as if they had come from a bad flea market and had been buffed to a glare. The elevators themselves were burnished brass with strange magical-creature motifs narrating some confused mythological tale. The inside of the elevator was hot and humid as if it were a ventilation shaft to Hell.

The bell chimed at Dante's floor. Bianca looked both ways, as Dante had not specified which way to go out of the elevator. Then she saw Dante leaning out an office door, waving to her with a phone pressed to his ear. She raised her hand to indicate that she had seen him. Bianca made way for a young man, barely out of his teens, in a white shirt, no tie, too much cologne, rolled-up sleeves, pushing mail on a double-decker wire-mesh cart. He flashed her a smile, and with his attention diverted for that second or two, crashed into someone.

She made her way to Dante's office, ignoring the stream of curse words from behind her.

"Please close the door behind you, Bianca," Dante said, as he stood up. He pointed to another occupant: a tall, lanky but trim man, and without removing the phone from his ear, said, "Alessandro Monotti. Alessandro, Bianca . . ."

Bianca smiled and extended her hand to Alessandro. "Just Bianca, thank you."

Alessandro took it. "Charmed. Would you like something to drink? Coffee? Tea?"

"Thank you, no." Bianca opened her purse and was about to pull out the envelope when Alessandro turned to face Dante and said in a loud-enough whisper, "Incoming," and seeing that Bianca was about to turn her head, said to her, "Gennaro, the boss. Don't look."

The door opened and shut hard enough to rattle the blinds. Bianca casually turned to find a red-faced man with papers in hand. "Dante, you are—who are you?"

"Bianca. I'm Dante's friend," she said without getting up.

Gennaro clutched the papers to his chest and looked the question at Alessandro. Alessandro twiddled a sharpened pencil. "She's Dante's friend."

"So I heard." Gennaro turned to Bianca and extended his hand. "Gennaro DiBello, manager."

She shook it. "Bianca, a friend."

Dante slammed the phone down. "Sorry, I hate dealing with incompetence. I made a request on some financial reports, and supposedly they're not electronic so the request process for a paper copy is like dealing with the Vatican. I see you've met my boss, Bianca."

She nodded and crossed her legs.

There was a buzzing sound and all three looked at Gennaro.

He held up an index finger. "Oh shit. Excuse me, my ass is vibrating," and with that he extricated a bulky cell phone from his back pocket and stepped into the hallway.

"He doesn't use a belt clip?" Bianca said softly.

"He doesn't think he'd feel it," Dante said.

"But doesn't he sit on his phone?"

"When he's at his desk," Sandro said, "he takes it out and places it on the desk."

"Doesn't he leave it behind?"

"Yes," Dante said.

"Usually it vibrates until it walks off the edge of the desk and falls into his trash," Sandro said. "He misses a lot of calls."

Gennaro returned to the room and set his mobile on the desk. "Stupid assholes."

Dante raised his eyebrows. "Higher-ups?"

Gennaro nodded. "They're riding me like a newlywed." Then he realized Bianca was there and actually blushed. It was charming. "Pardon my language," he said, and suddenly seemed to regain his composure. "Dante, I almost forgot why I came here. We need to talk about that project but I'll come back, since you have company."

"Why not now, Chief?" Dante said. "She knows."

"She knows?" Gennaro said and Alessandro looked at Dante, his face asking the same question.

"It was her idea; planting the hoax, that is. I hadn't had the chance to give her the specifics of how I planned to go about it."

Gennaro let go of the unturned doorknob. "We agreed to keep this in a small circle, right? And here you're bringing your girlfriend into the mix. I don't care if it was her idea or not."

Dante looked at Bianca and she looked at him.

Gennaro's face resumed its earlier pepper red and his eyes scoured them both, with his heat more directed at Dante. "She isn't one of us and I can't afford seeing someone getting hurt, Dante. What the hell were you thinking?"

Dante sank into his chair.

Bianca cleared her throat. "No, I'm not one of you; that you got right. But I'm the one who had the idea that apparently the three of you couldn't think up. I won't ask for a thank-you-very-much."

Gennaro straightened his shirt around his waistline. "Thank you. Thank you very much for thinking for us. You might've done the thinking, but the infantry here has to make it happen. I doubt that you got that far ahead, with your long legs and ingenious brain. I forgot us men don't think higher up than our legs."

Bianca stood up. "It's usually the case." The office suddenly got smaller.

"Please," Dante said, "settle down you two."

Gennaro pointed at her. "We don't need liabilities. We're heading into deep shit and none of us can afford distractions, the emotions and—"

Suddenly, Bianca was tired of Italian men. "You chauvinistic little—no wonder you don't wear a wedding band. What woman would put up with you?"

Alessandro made a sound as if someone had punched him in the stomach. The fingers of Gennaro's hand felt his wedding finger. He shut up and found a chair. He remained quiet.

Dante let the air settle. "Please. We can do this. I drafted some notes that we can give journalists, and I know someone over at the television studio who can float this upstream for a newscast. But before we do this we need to line up someone academic who can give all this credibility."

Bianca sat there still as a stone. She had evidently triggered something, but she wasn't sure what. Gennaro looked strangely placid.

Alessandro finally spoke up. "Look, I had a professor at the University of Salerno who made me passionate about classical history. The guy has charm and he's well respected in the field. He'd play beautifully in front of a television camera. We've kept in touch on and off again so I know I can contact him. I can feel him out and see whether he buys into it. If there were anyone who wouldn't want to see our history flying out of the country into the hands of unscrupulous thieves, it would be him. Let me pitch the idea to him."

"He's a professor," Gennaro said softly. "Probably has a pension. This could be career suicide for him."

Alessandro played with that pencil again. "Last I heard, Boss, the University was cutting back on hiring and other expenses and gave his department the once-over. There was a lot of blood on the walls. They've cut his hours and moved him to a closet for an office. I've also heard that they've been reducing retirement benefits drastically. Who knows? There's a good chance my professor has a personal motivation to help us, aside from not wanting to see our national past being stolen. He's got the rocks on his back and he may want to see a few people drown with him."

Gennaro nodded slowly and then stood up. "You look into it, Sandro, and let me know as soon as you can." He left, closing the door.

"He seemed to calm down rather quickly," Bianca said.

Dante and Alessandro looked at each other. It was not a happy look. Alessandro was the one to say it. "Well, that comment of yours about no woman wanting to put up with his shit was what shut him up."

"Well, who would? He's a blustery and crotchety old man. Just because he's your boss doesn't mean that I—"

"He lost his wife a few years ago. It was not pretty."

Oh. Oh, damn, she thought to herself.

Bianca stood up. "I think I should go. Walk me out, Dante?"

As they approached the elevator, she handed him the envelope. "Here, take this."

Dante looked down at the brown manila office envelope she had pressed to his chest. "What is it?"

"Some research I did for you. I didn't give this to you in there because I don't know whom to trust."

Dante curled the envelope in his hand. "Alessandro is a good nut. The boss I have to have in the loop because he's my boss. I trust them."

"Don't trust anyone, Dante. Always hold back a little of what you discover. Keep them guessing, because it's when they stop talking that you have to start worrying."

He smiled. "I never knew you were a paranoid."

"Experienced. Where is Gennaro's office?"

Dante pointed to it and she started walking there while he pressed the elevator button.

His door was open but she knocked on the wooden doorframe. He looked up while he was reviewing paperwork.

"About my remark earlier," she said. "I didn't know, and it was insensitive of me. I'm sorry."

"Ah, don't worry about it. I just don't want to see you get hurt. My guess is that the people involved in this are not very nice."

He looked down to continue with his paperwork, apparently assuming she was finished. She stayed there until he looked up again, his forehead wrinkled.

"Word of advice about your superiors who are busting your balls?"

He watched her, but kept silent.

"Drag them through the weeds, nice and slow. When they fuck with you make sure that you fuck them back."

She winked and smiled. Gennaro had a look that said his day had just improved.

Bianca walked back and the Elevator of the Apocalypse announced its arrival with a chime. Dante held the door open.

"Call me," she told him. He nodded.

Dante returned to his desk, ignored Alessandro's questions about Bianca and why he had never told him that he had a girlfriend. Alessandro kept jabbering away as Dante opened the oversized envelope and paged through twenty-five pages of dense revelation.

He returned to the beginning of the documentation, paged slowly to repeat what his eyes had seen the first time, and then thumbed his way through the pages quickly, lifted his eyes up in the direction of the elevator. "Holy shit!"

On the street below, Bianca hailed a taxi. She leaned down into the car to instruct the driver of her destination.

Amidst all the commotion and noise around her—people, cars, Vespas, and buses—a green Fiat turned over its engine and pulled out into traffic behind her.

9

Dante didn't call until the next day.

She had hoped that he would call sooner. She admitted that she wanted to hear his gratitude for her research and also to answer his inevitable questions. He must have been wondering how she had uncovered all this information on a certain Lorenzo Bevilacqua, when there are thousands of *Amici di Roma* organizations worldwide, decentralized and without oversight, run by individuals or committees.

She knew the questions were inescapable and she had prepared her script that would answer his questions without compromising herself and revealing her former identity. Bianca didn't like the idea of lying to anyone, but there was too much at stake not to stretch the fabric of truth just a little, if it meant securing her personal safety.

Dante was a good guy. They had met three months before at a café. She had gone in and queued up for her morning cappuccino and whatever was available for a pastry. Just as any Roman, she lined up quietly behind the person in front of her, ready to give out her order, step aside and slurp her drink standing up, munch on breakfast, and move on. This particular morning, however, the oversized espresso machine— one of those copper ones from the last century, with the eagle on top and a steam system from the time of Robert Fulton—decided to be temperamental. Moreover, one of the two brothers who ran the establishment was out ill, leaving the remaining brother frantic and frayed. At first the poor man simply resigned himself to the stress, figuring his customers would get their morning jolt when they got it. But as the steam-pulled machine progressed from unpredictable to unreliable, he became more agitated and the chaos reached critical mass, even by Roman standards.

In walked Dante. As soon as he saw the problem, he jumped behind the counter to man the machine while the other one took the orders. It was obvious from the way Dante handled the machine that these two men knew each other well, because they worked together seamlessly. Dante quickly fixed the problem and had the machine hissing in no time. He began slamming spent espresso grounds down into the collection trough and rinsing the portafilter body and clicking fresh espresso into the basket from the Lavazza grinder, tamping and extracting the precious jet fluid into the thimble cups.

Bianca was engrossed in her observation of Dante. He was attractive, but it was another quality, his precision focus, that drew her deeper into watching him. That, and the fact that it had been implicit loyalty to his friends that had compelled him to work the counter. She took her breakfast standing up near the window, where she remained until the morning crowd left. After hearing the sole brother yell at Dante and refuse to take any money for his espresso and pastry, she saw him go sit outside on the small ledge under the window.

He tilted back his demitasse and picked up the round dish of pastry. A small child, a Turkish girl, was eyeing him with curiosity and hunger. Dante must have sensed her hunger because he broke his pastry into two pieces and gave her half. She sat closer to him and Bianca saw from behind the glass the moving lips of spoken Italian and the girl's brown face break into a smile of beautiful teeth and powdered sugar at the corners of her lips and the tip of her nose.

Over the ensuing week, she learned from the oblique stalking called daily observation that Dante frequented the *Due Fratelli Café*. She began to arrive twenty minutes later than her usual time, as she had that disastrous day, so she could see him. Finally she met him standing up at one of the makeshift tables, initiating the conversation with a remark at how crowded the place had become that particular morning. He saw her the next morning and the morning after, and one conversation led to another, and the casual progressed to the informal, which progressed to small disclosures about each other that were the beginning of the intimate.

He disclosed a little bit about himself after the seventh or eighth time they had met. Dante was a corporate auditor who covered Provincia di Roma, which is a third of Regione Lazio, although he had on occasion, he explained, gone out on loan to work on projects in the other four provinces surrounding the city: Frosinone, Latina, Rieti and Viterbo. Bianca, for her part, kept her information to a minimum, explaining that she was on sabbatical and visiting Rome to take in the art. She did nothing to correct his assumption that she was simply an academic who was unleashed abroad after toiling in the tower for seven years. Her facility for the language was more than serviceable, and Dante, like any educated Italian, appreciated the effort, knowing from the first instant that she was an American. He had asked her to speak English since he had very few opportunities to practice.

That morning she wasn't too annoyed that he hadn't called. It was just a day. She opened her laptop and let it boot up.

Setting herself up with a computer in Italy was no small accomplishment. First, the keyboard was different. The Italian keyboard uses the QZERTY layout, which is not far afield from the antiquated typewriter. There is no tilde character. Brackets are only available if both AltGr and Shift are pressed. And since Bianca had next to no need to correspond in Italian, she ignored that the keyboard lacked the È key. Her main concern was connectivity and protecting her data, so she backed up constantly and used a surge protector.

She typed in her password and waited. The phone rang.

"Bianca, it's Dante. Please turn on the Free Channel."

She did so just as some talking head in a nice suit, starched shirt, luminous teeth and perfectly coiffed spray-on hair announced that there was late-breaking news. A small banner ran across the bottom of the newsman's desk with some dramatic music playing in the background. He adopted a very serious speaking tone. Bianca thumbed the volume button. The camera cut to a woman in an office with a distinguished man fumbling with a small device on his lapel that looked more like a large fly than an inconspicuous microphone.

"Professor Moretti, please explain to our audience this miraculous find from under our very feet here in Rome," she said.

The man with graying hair lit up in a smile. "A most remarkable and significant archaeological discovery has been unearthed. As you know, Rome boasts of some industrious amateur speleologists who donate their off-hours and personal time to exploring and mapping the ancient underground of your magnificent city."

Bianca wondered why he had said 'your city' and her answer came promptly with a small box that appeared under the man's moving lips. It said: Professor Renato Moretti, Emeritus Professor of Classical Studies from the University of Salerno.

The man spoke pleasantly and with animation. "Under Via Cavour, which is poorly explored, there was released from captivity, so to speak, the last eagle of one of three legions sent into Germania during the time of Augustus Caesar."

"You are referring, of course, to the three legions the barbarians to the north had decimated. Augustus Caesar had sent these legions to their destruction."

The man winced, briefly. "I wouldn't want to suggest that our German neighbors to the north are barbarians, but for the sake of historical accuracy: anyone not a citizen of Rome or speaking the language was considered a barbarian. Our ancient forebears had adopted this perspective from the ancient Greeks whom they admired. And yes, Augustus Caesar had sent three legions to their destruction. But the point must be made that, in that day, nobody expected barbarians to annihilate a legion, and to lose three was astounding. And annihilation is an accurate description for what had happened to these three legions."

"In relative terms, what would be the modern equivalent?"

This time the man squirmed. She was doing her best to add color to her coverage, but apparently at the cost of historical integrity and international relations. "I hesitate at drawing modern parallels since technology was so different, life spans were shorter, warfare was radically different, and a host of other contributing factors make it difficult to make comparisons."

"A rough estimate."

"It would be like the most powerful nation in the world today sending their elite forces into battle against a nonentity and having their forces slaughtered and desecrated on the field. The difference, however, is that in today's terms the defeat has to be so psychologically debilitating that both leader and citizen agree tacitly that persisting further would be foolhardy."

"I see, Professor. But we, as children, were told that the eagles had been lost. Now you are saying one of these eagles has been found here in Rome and not in the wooded forests where the battle occurred. How do you explain that unexpected turn?"

The man seemed to be more in his element now. "My academic career has focused on Tiberius and the Five Good Emperors. As to your question about why here and not there, I believe that Germanicus, nephew of Tiberius, did indeed return to Rome with the last eagle. But his uncle, for political survival, suppressed the fantastic recovery. Bear in mind that Germanicus was building himself quite the popular reputation at all levels of society, which was a dangerous development from Tiberius' perspective."

"Professor, I'd like to know, as would our viewers, whether there is any other evidence to support the idea that the eagles had returned to Rome, because this seems to be an unprecedented find."

The man winked and folded his hands. "What we know of the original defeat comes from four accounts that are at odds with each other. We have Velleius Paterculus' account, which frankly is somewhat biased because he was a friend of Tiberius. Then we have Tacitus who, as we all know, is highly esteemed as historian and stylist. He presents a very dichotomous portrait: the very noble Germanicus at odds with the very evil Tiberius. But unfortunately, his details about the battle are too exaggerated to be trusted. A third account comes from Publius Annius Florus, but in many ways this paraphrases Tacitus. That account, however, is important because we can date the recovery of two of the eagles, mainly because our fourth account, from Cassius Dio, spoke of two eagles recovered in the year 41 AD. I have contended through my own publications that Dio, like Tacitus, had consulted Pliny the Elder's account of the Germanic wars and interviewed former legionaries. We also need to remember that Pliny himself, as a veteran, had relieved the men captured in the Teutoburg Forest. I believe Dio continued writing about the Germanic episode, speaking to Germanicus' recovery of the eagle, but the evidence is scanty."

"Very interesting. Do you believe that his literary efforts were quashed?"

"That's a separate discussion, but I think a sound argument can be made for the case. Historians know that Dio had run afoul of the Praetorian Guards, who had become quite powerful under Tiberius and Sejanus, his prefect. And we know that Emperors themselves fell in and out of favor through the practice of *damnatio memoriae*. I would like to emphasize that of eighty books attributed to Dio, only thirty-six remain and do so in fragments. We are left to conjecture to fill in the gaps. I've always maintained that Tiberius would have done anything to suppress Germanicus' rising reputation, and had his nephew returned to Rome with the last eagle then Tiberius would have seized it. The Roman people of his day would have known that the eagle had come home. Who is to say that Tiberius didn't have the eagle tossed down the Cloaca Maxima?"

"So what happens now to the eagle? Have you seen it?"

The man's fingers danced against each other and through his smile. "It is quite well preserved and one of the most beautiful things I have ever seen with my own eyes. To have held this precious artifact with my own hands is the crowning achievement of my career."

This guy was good. He had just made antiquities collectors around the world salivate and contemplate pulling out their eyeteeth just to get a peek.

The woman's voice was winding down, because the small banner about some politician caught with his mistress danced across the bottom of the screen.

"It remains guarded, where it will be examined, cleaned, and documented until it is presented to the world and to other scholars, like myself."

The woman turned to face the camera and said in bland, stripped-down Italian, "Back to you."

"Think we sold it?"

It was Dante's voice. Bianca had forgotten she was holding her cell phone. "No pictures were released, right?"

"None. We don't have the budget to conjure up something convincing. But I don't know how long we can hold off on that. The buzz is moving like wildfire."

"You mean spreading like wildfire."

He imitated a teenager, "Uh, whatever. Think it'll work?"

She laughed. "I think so, but tell me more about the buzz this is generating?"

"First, Sandro's choice was brilliant: intentional or not. Renato Moretti teaches at the University of Salerno, so there's this contingent of viewers screaming, 'Why isn't there some professor from Sapienza, Tor Vegata, or Tre on the eagle?' I hadn't thought about the political ramifications that would come of a *Professore* from the south handling this for us. It reminds me of the right-wing Northern League, who clack their dentures and threaten secession."

"Don't worry about that. The goal is to draw out other people. Keep focused on the prize, Dante."

"So what do you think?"

"I think you're off to a good start. As we say in America: keep your eyes peeled."

"I hear you. You know I keep hearing Gennaro in the back of my head."

"Really? What is he saying?"

"He is turning a quote from Sciascia inside out. He said, 'We may jump into the well for Truth, but best we not forget about the sun or the moon and hope to not get caught bare-assed.'"

10

The phone rang and rang and rang.

IM prompts appeared with their incessant pleas for help that never deviated from the monotonous mantra in screaming caps, 'I NEED YOUR HELP, PLEASE.' There was no name, other information, or ominous observations or updates about 'THEM.'

Bianca ignored them, avoiding her phone and computer and focusing on the TV.

Soon after Professor Moretti's announcement, the Free Channel ran a two-day piece on speleologists and their work on the Roman underground. The coverage instigated discussion panels with intense-looking professionals from several fields who debated the ethics around archaeological finds, the methods used, and the disposition of the finds. There were the usual desiccated academic types propped up in chairs, dusted off, and pinned like butterflies with microphones. Sure enough one of these mannequins informed the lay audience that Mussolini had burned down sections of Rome, thinking himself the next Augustus Caesar, when he was actually a bald-headed incarnation of Nero. For historical context one of the academic cadavers, who could have been a Black Shirt himself, mentioned that the Germans in his day had regressed into the mists of an idealized time with Wagner's *Ring Cycle* playing in the background, while the crazy half-mustache was national conductor. So having Il Duce orchestrating his new Pax Romana from a gaudy villa in Lake Como while parts of Rome burned would not seem so surreal.

Of course, Mussolini's inglorious end came up. Bianca knew that she had walked past the very spot, an Esso station then but a bank now, at the Piazzale Loreto, near the Corso Buenos Aires, where the deposed dictator and his lover, Clara Petacci, were hung upside down along with five others. All this and more bantered back and forth between the suits in studio chairs in the spirit of *Sic transit gloria mundi*.

Bianca ignored the academics and paid attention to the speleologists. Dante had mentioned that different professional groups formed into cliques. Aside from names and occupations in the little box on the screen, the viewer would have no idea that these amateur, although well-trained spelunkers, were competitive and territorial. She detected a strain of anger in one speleologist who spoke passionately of the Cloaca Maxima. The anger he had lay coiled in his statement that speleologists were a close-knit group that blogged about their progress, and this recent find under Via Cavour had shocked many in their community. He let slip with a tinge of possessiveness that it was surgeons who were trying to map the unexplored paths from the Cloaca to the Baths of Diocletian.

Today, a television crew followed the man down into the dark passage at the Forum of Nerva. It didn't take much imagination to know that the tunnel down was rank and disgusting. The camera provided but a small glimpse of static sludge and gradations of swirled brown, black, and tan fluids with the occasional floating signs of modern life mired with the ancient—dead rats and diaphanous spent condoms. Sight suggested the odor. The featured speleologist, a surgeon by day, wore a body suit and a mask, and had every joint of his clothing sealed off with duct tape.

It was a day of relentless summer heat. The air over the entire city felt as if it would not move. Everyone felt as if they were forced to breathe through a wet washcloth. Wearing the lightest of clothing like linen offered no respite because clothes stuck to the skin by the time you reached the bottom stair on the way out to work. Worse yet, air conditioners failed and the mid-day news recounted tales of the elderly whisked away to the regional hospitals for respiratory distress or heat stroke. It seemed all of Rome was on edge, ready to bribe whomever they had to in order to get a breeze.

The phone rang and rang and rang.

Bianca decided to turn the damn thing off, but not before looking at the caller ID screen.

It was Dante.

"Hello," she said for variety.

"You answered the phone finally. I've been trying for hours."

The voice wasn't Dante's. It was familiar, though. "Alessandro?"

"Yes, it's Alessandro. I tried to call you on my phone, but there was no answer, so finally out of desperation I borrowed Dante's home mobile and called you."

That explained why her caller ID had said UNKNOWN CALLER. Maybe she was being a little too paranoid.

"I'm so sorry, Alessandro. I have a habit of not answering calls if I don't know who's calling me. Dante's number is programmed in, so I answer when I see his name."

"Look, I didn't ring you to make a social call. I just left the hospital. Something has happened and we're worried, Gennaro and I."

"What? What happened to you?"

"Not me. Dante. He was attacked."

Bianca pressed the cell phone harder into her ear. She didn't hear the usual sounds of the hospital behind him: overhead paging, code calls, and other urgencies. "Where are you now?"

There was no answer.

"Alessandro, where are you now?" she said, raising her voice, although it had nothing to compete against.

"At Dante's place with Dante."

"How is he?" *He must be okay if the hospital discharged him.*

"He's banged up good, but he'll manage with a night's rest. The thing is he won't explain what the hell happened. He refused to help the *carabinieri*. All he did was talk nonsense and in circles. I guess the police gave up on a quick report. They'll try later."

Either Dante was that traumatized and his mind scattered from having his marbles shaken up, or he was deliberately minimizing what the news people would do with this development, if anyone connected his office with Professor Moretti. An assault on a state employee would be bound to make the news.

"Bianca, he keeps asking for you. Can you come over? He refuses to talk to me."

She looked around the room for her purse. "Yeah . . . I mean, yes. I will get there soon as I can."

"Good. Oh, and another thing. I gave your number to Gennaro, so he might be calling."

Bianca frowned. Now there were three people who had her phone number. A little act of socializing, and her number had gone viral.

"Fine. Do you need anything?"

"No. Wait. If Gennaro calls, please ask him to bring some food. I haven't looked in Dante's refrigerator, and I want to keep an eye on him. The doctors say with knocks to the head that he has to be observed for the first few hours. I don't get doctors. They tell the man to get rest but they tell me to make sure that he doesn't fall asleep. What kind of advice is that?"

While he talked she removed her hard drive and rummaged through her purse. "Typical for doctors, but you know it's in their oath: 'first do no harm, then make no sense.' I'll see you in a few." She ended the call.

As she was walking down the stairs, the phone rang again, but this time she answered instinctively, assuming it was Alessandro again. But as soon as she flipped the phone open, she realized she was letting her security slip far too much.

"*Pronto*," she said.

"It's me, Gennaro. You hear from Alessandro?"

Thank God, she had gotten away with it. She had to be more careful, had to be.

"I did," she said. "I'm going over there now."

Gennaro's voice seemed timid, as if he were nervous talking to her. "How is he?"

Walking outside and looking for a taxi she answered, "Don't know. He won't talk to anyone. It seems he got banged up good, but the hospital let him go. Sandro—" she shortened the name because she was tired of all the syllables, "said that he keeps asking for me."

"I was told the same thing. I will see you there then."

"Oh, Gennaro, are you still there?"

"Yes. What is it?"

She flagged a taxi; the automobile moved towards her. "Alessandro said bring food. Maybe we should do takeout."

"This is strange English."

The taxi stood still, the driver was waiting for the destination. Bianca was scrambling for an alternate phrase. "I don't know the Italian, Gennaro. Food. Food you buy at a restaurant and bring home."

"Ah, take-away. That's a sin. I don't do take-away," he said with all the solemnity of a cardinal.

"Whatever." She clicked the cover down, ending their conversation. She threw the cell phone into the purse, gave the driver the address and did the one thing that Romans do only with extreme caution: she told the taxi driver, "I'm in a hurry."

11

Alessandro answered the door. He looked worn. She could see that stress didn't wear well on him.

He was a thin, tall man, the opposite of many assumptions: born in Tuscany but educated in the south (his father had been relocated when Alessandro was a teen). He lived in Salerno but never assimilated the standard Italian accent—not that there is such a thing as standard Italian, despite the efforts of Manzoni and Mussolini (were there ever two opposites on a topic) and despite the arguments for and against the Florentine and Venetian ways with the language. In addition to being blonde with green eyes, the antihero of the Mediterranean stereotype, Alessandro enjoyed throwing confusion over those who annoyed him by dropping the *re* in his infinitives, using *te* when *tu* was expected, and if he felt particularly sadistic he would unleash a string of skillful sentences with double accusatives and double datives that left his quarry bewildered.

"Dante is in the bedroom and Gennaro is on his way with food," he said.

Bianca stood there as Alessandro walked away, presumably to the kitchen. This saved her the embarrassment of showing she didn't know where the bedroom was. She set down her purse, looked at the stairs and figured it was as good a time as any to map out the path.

There was another sitting area—she could see that this was where Dante did most of his writing, or personal work. Books were strewn respectfully on a table, parted and stacked on top of each other with a computer in the background. There were numerous notebooks with different-color spines and covers. The mélange of pens, pencils, and Post-its scattered everywhere on the table contradicted the order of the books and notebooks. A small hallway speared to the right from where she stood and appeared to lead to two rooms. One must be to a bathroom (confirmed as she passed it) and the other, by default, his bedroom.

Dante was propped up on some pillows, his hair uncharacteristically chaotic, and his face was bruised and darkening into a shade of eggplant under the right eye and on the cheek. He saw her but said nothing, just patted the bed next to him.

She sat down, gently so as not to bounce him. "I'm afraid to ask you how much it hurts."

He shrugged. "The eye will recover. I feel like someone rearranged my brains. The doctor said one of my ribs is broken but it'll heal on its own. I didn't know these days they don't bind you up around the midsection like you see in the movies. Scary, isn't it? Of course, they checked to see that it didn't poke a hole in my lung."

She grimaced, wanting to touch him but refraining. "Any idea who might've done this? A rival speleologist? Somebody connected with Lorenzo Bevilacqua? We never had a chance to review the research I gave you on his *Amici di Roma*."

He shifted himself upwards on the pillows. "I know it's not them, but I do think you might know who did this to me." Bianca felt both disconcerted and perplexed.

"I just gave you my complete list. Who else could it be?"

For a moment he simply stared at her. It was a tired, ragged look. "I think you have an idea. I'm trying hard not to be angry with you, Bianca."

Now she felt off-center. "Angry with me? Whatever for? Why would you be angry with me?"

"Because while one goon held me and the other one decided to use my ribs for a xylophone, the one restraining me kept saying over and over, 'Tell us what you know about alabaster.' And me, like a moron, I told them 'I have no idea what you're talking about and I don't know a thing about marble.' It wasn't until I was halfway unconscious and stopped feeling anything that I realized these two imbeciles were talking about a name."

Bianca was quiet and avoided looking at him.

"Have anything to tell me?" he asked.

She searched for words.

His hand came forward on the bed sheet to touch hers but she pulled away.

Dante crossed his arms. "Fine. I get attacked for no reason. My gut—the one that got kicked in—tells me these two diplomats are looking for you, for whatever reason. But, hey, you don't want to tell me. Fantastic. And you have the balls to tell me *I'm* mysterious."

"Stop it, already. I'm thinking."

"Yes, I tried thinking," he breathed in a short spasm, "while I was taking measurements of the man's foot," an exhalation followed, "with my face. It seemed they got frustrated and left me on the stairwell. Thank God. They went through my wallet, stomped my work cell phone into pieces. Cheap shit Chinese plastic. I wonder if Pinolo will reimburse me for a replacement?"

"Did they look through the pieces?" she asked.

"Of my work cell phone? How the hell do I know; I was on the ground finding religion. You're unbelievable, Bianca. I don't know you."

Then, to her great relief, both of them noticed a wonderful smell permeating the room that wafted up to the second floor. Either Alessandro or Gennaro was cooking.

She finally had enough of the secrecy. It was costing too much. "My name is not Bianca. It's Alabaster Black. I used to work in intelligence. American."

Dante took it in. "These two men, they are looking for you because of something you did?"

She nodded just as they heard Gennaro summon them downstairs.

Her hand reached out to his and rested on top of it. "I promise I'll explain it all to you. After we eat."

Alabaster reached the kitchen first. Dante insisted she go ahead of him and let him come down the stairs at his own pace. Alessandro had pulled the terrace table inside and had set it with placemats and cutlery. Gennaro was in the kitchen wearing an apron and plating his creations.

"Get him to talk?"

She nodded yes, to which he replied as a way of congratulating her, *"Auguri!"*

Fortune teller. She wished. "He talked a little but he tires easily. Maybe we just eat and let him get his strength back?"

Gennaro said nothing but she knew that he agreed. The man was focused on the geography of the dishes in front of him.

Alessandro clapped his hands to announce his presence in the kitchen. "Boss, what can I do to help here?"

"Want to help? Do like you do at the office: nothing. Get out of my kitchen! Instead of twirling your pencil, go pour the wine and sit down. Take Bianca with you and make sure Dante finds his chair. Think you can do that?"

They sat down and out came Gennaro with the starter: a stroke of mascarpone topped with grilled white asparagus and sautéed morel mushrooms.

"Unbelievable, Boss," Alessandro said. "I didn't know that you were a chef."

Gennaro stared at him. "Put your tongue to use and eat. Dante? You feel better?"

"But Chief, we need to toast."

Gennaro, seeing that they were sitting in a circle and had their glasses lifted, said, *"Cent'anni!"* They clinked their glasses and wet their mouths with the wine.

"Getting there," Dante said. "Thank you for this."

"We talk when you're rested. And you, Bianca, how you like my first course?"

"Magnificent," she answered, truthfully.

Gennaro looked down at his wine and took a moment to relish its nose. He had paired the asparagus with a Sicilian white wine, a blend of catarratto and chardonnay grapes: 2004 Leone d'Almerita that sang clean citrus notes and concluded the song with an outstanding finish.

Gennaro collected the dishes and came out with his second dish. "My apologies for this. I figured that since it's disgustingly hot out, I would keep it simple but refreshing. This is nothing fancy, just a quick recipe the women in my family used to make: Neapolitan calamari and shrimp salad."

He placed a large bowl of the colorful mix of seafood, arugula, fragrant basil, grilled eggplant and zucchini with a small amount of orzo thrown in. He left the table and returned to the kitchen to fetch their bowls. As they ate, Gennaro started small talk, for which Bianca was grateful. She was still working on what Dante had told her. It made no sense. Someone had found her, someone who knew her as Alabaster. But two thugs, beating a man and cracking his cell phone for the SIM card—that didn't sound like Rendition. They were more subtle than that. But if not them, then who? Strand's people? One of her other subjects?

And what should she do? Pack up and move on again? But she was starting to feel something here in Rome, something she had only rarely felt earlier in her life—at home before Patrone and before the Strand investigation. Feel safe? Trust going back to the States, back to Rendition's backyard? She loved the pace of Rome, the nonchalant attitude of the populace toward authority, including the authority of the clock, the history that literally lay underfoot, as Dante had shown her.

And there was Dante.

He had introduced her to Gennaro as "a friend," and that was accurate. But . . . she wasn't sure "friend" was the right word. They weren't lovers and were both comfortable with that, which went against both the stereotype of Italian men and her own, rather promiscuous, history. Men were easy. This time, with him, she was enjoying herself getting to know another person. She felt close to him in a way she'd never felt to a man. To see him beaten, because of her, was hard. And his trust, his willingness to listen, left her feeling . . . she didn't know what.

While she tried to feel her way through all this, Gennaro nattered on about the local news. There was a rumor on all three news stations and in every paper, including the free *Metro*, that another *sciopero,* a massive strike, was expected. All the whispers across Rome were saying that the annual public transportation strike, which occurs often in mid-August, would come earlier this year.

"Chief, how about I run and get some pastries?" Alessandro said after everyone had finished the meal. The heat was oppressive, so they nixed the idea of dessert, but agreed about indulging in a round of after-dinner drinks—except Dante, who thought it was a bad idea for his condition. He excused himself.

After the three of them had washed the dishes up, Gennaro rummaged through the cabinet and fished out three short glasses and a bottle of Sambuca. He found the coffee beans, placed three of them into each of the glasses, and introduced Bianca to *Sambuca con la mosca*. As Gennaro poured, Alessandro explained that the three beans, or flies, represented happiness, health, and prosperity.

After Alessandro had drunk his Sambuca, he checked on Dante who, he reported upon his return, should sleep, since enough time had passed between his injuries and discharge. Dante had tolerated food and hadn't complained of a headache or shown any symptoms of losing consciousness.

Alessandro was the first to depart. "I need to go. Thank you again for the wonderful meal, Boss. I'll see you tomorrow. Bianca, I see you when I see you."

Without asking, Gennaro poured himself and Bianca another round. She rotated the small glass in a circle on the tablecloth and watched the clear liquid coat the walls.

"So . . . Dante is attacked," Gennaro said slowly.

She stared right at him. "Are you blaming me?"

"Ssh!" he said, finger to lips, pointing upstairs and then twirling his finger in a circle. Which meant, what, exactly? Gennaro walked over to the kitchen wall and motioned for her to come over. She followed. He pointed to the switch plate screws to indicate that he had removed them earlier. Then the man took the edge of a knife and wedged the blade into the seam of the switch plate against the wall and gently pulled the metal away until it unhinged in his hands.

On the inside she saw a small black surveillance device.

He pushed the plate flush with the wall and tilted his head to the terrace.

She nodded and followed.

He slid open the door for her. They walked out together and went over to the ledge, away from the potted herbs and plants to where Dante had some open earthenware awaiting more plantings. Her opinion of Gennaro rose to a new level: the man might not like cell phones but he was no fool.

"I'm not blaming you for what happened," he said. "While it might have been your idea, nobody twisted Dante's arm. I liked the idea too, still think it's a good one, but we have to realize now that someone is sending us a message. I might seem to be an old man to you, a little bureaucrat a few years shy of a pension, but I earned my few gray hairs the hard way."

Bianca went to say something but he held his hand up. "There is serious money in the art world, and allow me to paraphrase Balzac: 'Behind every great fortune there is a crime.' I know as an auditor the lengths to which people will go to protect what they have or plan to get. People may look at me and think I'm some *campagnolo*, what you call a country bumpkin, but I've seen my share of things. Our Dante is an idealist. We have a term in Italy; it's called a 'witness for justice.' You've heard of it?"

"Yes, when I read about Rita Atria and the Falcone and Borsellino assassinations."

He wet his lips. "Funny you mention them, because I was one of the auditors examining files on suspected Mafia activities back then. It's neither here or there now because it's all history, but you develop a sense in the bones when you're walking into something bigger than you. The little fly in there—he nodded toward the switch plate bug—"tells me the opponent is at both ends. It tells me one should be careful of whom we trust and what we say, when we say it, and where we say it."

"I understand," she said.

"My intuition told me you would. At my age you recognize human 'types' and you act accordingly."

"Types? You think people are types?"

He leaned on the square edge of the empty pots. "Oh, most definitely. Call me old-fashioned or blame it on the Catholicism in the air in this country, but I do believe in it. You have the simple-hearted, who stumbles his or her way through life trusting everyone and everything without a care in the world. You have the self-centered, who trample everything because it's always about them. Every simple little thing has to reflect their image like a mirror. You have the good who get victimized, the good who somehow survive. And then there are the evil ones."

She turned and looked at him, not even trying to conceal her surprise. "You mean to tell me that you believe there is good and evil. Straight and simple down the line, black and white."

He pursed his lips and nodded. "I do. Much of this life is gray but there are those among us who are evil, those of us who are dangerous."

"And you're suggesting, I imagine, that you, Dante, and Alessandro—that we've all stumbled into something sinister and evil."

He waved his hand. "We've stumbled into something all right. But you miss my point, Bianca. Evil is very easy to recognize for the most part; finding it is difficult. The issue is Dante, the issue is you."

"What, I'm evil? Dante is evil?"

He squared off and looked her in the face. "Dante is passionate and you are analytical; and therein is the problem. The two of you help each other, because alone, individually, you are both dangerous."

"You know what I think? I think you've gotten too philosophical in your old age. You aren't looking at facts and thinking objectively." She wasn't sure it worked in Italian, but she thought the pitch of her voice suggested he was full of shit.

"Ah, you look at things objectively. You came up with the idea and he," pointing to the second floor, "ran with it. Your analysis and his passion and look at what has happened."

She hit the ledge of the container for the unplanted herbs. "Fine, in your roundabout way you're saying this is all my fault."

"You know there are two types of stories: the hero's journey and stranger-comes-to-town. Every story is either *The Illiad* or *The Odyssey*. All I'm saying is Dante is the hero on a journey and you are the stranger who came to town. Maybe your lesson is to help him by thinking through all the strategy in this big game of chess, knowing which piece to move into place and which ones to sacrifice."

She had crossed her arms and said over her shoulder to Gennaro. "You're suggesting I play the part of the chess master?"

Gennaro put his hands into his pockets. "Dante doesn't know how to play chess. Alessandro doesn't either, nor do I." He leaned over, close to her ear. "But I suspect that the stranger knows how to play."

12

Bianca stayed the night, sitting in a chair watching Dante until she fell asleep. After Dante had awoken and they had eaten breakfast together, and taken their separate showers, she sat Dante down out on the terrace and told him the story of Alabaster Black. She explained Rendition, her past projects, and the defining project, Robert Strand. She told him of the mysterious phone calls and the IM messages. She held absolutely nothing back. The time for that was past.

She watched him as she explained to see whether she could detect any signs of judgment in his face or in his body language. He sat quietly and listened like a schoolboy, saving his questions to the end.

"And he told you to 'disappear for a while,' so that explains why you're here. But how long has been 'a while'?"

"Over a year, going on two. I'd been elsewhere before I came to Rome."

"Different identities?"

She nodded.

The next question was the obvious one. She was expecting it, but it still hurt. "What happened to Robert Strand?"

"His last words to me were: 'You know it's time for me to go, Alabaster. Please be safe for me.'"

Dante waited for more.

"It was a scary time for me. I said nothing and ended the call, pressing a button on my cell. I didn't bother to check my bank account because I knew that would trigger a software program with Rendition, but I did send them my report from a cyber café with the time card purchased with cash. Rendition acknowledged the report without any questions, but I knew that they knew. A separate e-mail arrived after the report on Strand. This new e-mail detailed another assignment about some businessman setting up retirement homes across the US. I looked at it, read the teaser details, hit the Reply button, and typed in the Subject line, UNSUBSCRIBE."

"What was it exactly that changed your mind about Rendition?"

"Strand disappeared. I started to doubt myself, started to doubt Rendition, doubt what I was doing with them, with my life. In all my cases I was certain that I was right. Facts were facts. I was convinced that Strand was a criminal and up to no good. I was convinced that it was up to me to discover what it was that he was hiding."

Dante moved the pillow. "It seems that what you found were minor things, which are technically illegal but everyone knows they happen daily in business. I'm not sure I understand the geo-engineering project you described."

"That was the problem. Strand's project threatened the waste disposal companies and would've forced environmental groups to rethink their policies. If you can sequester carbon, there's no motive to conserve. You know how people are resistant to change. What made Strand dangerous to Rendition was that it was possible that his preta project could've created chaos in American politics. I was told from the start that one of Rendition's objectives was to protect the American economy. Strand comes along and upsets energy treaties and fuel economics on a grand scale. It came back Rendition wanting to maintain American economic hegemony. Strand was about to change all that."

"What did you do?"

"In the middle of the night, I left my dinky hotel room and went to a different café, where I uploaded the Terra folder's technological reports and all the details on Strand's findings on how to create terrapreta soil to all the major scientific-institute servers around the world, from MIT to CERN and everyone else in between, north and south of the Equator."

"That must've made someone stand on a cactus."

"Nice phrase. I created a small program that specifically targeted geo-engineers at these institutes with an e-mail and an extracting file for them to find the Strand documents on their server. I made sure that I did this at an odd hour because I knew that file servers were often reset for maintenance routines in the middle of the night for the next day. That was then and I don't see anyone implementing the technology, so I assume governments have made some tacit agreement to suppress the information. That's neither here or there because Rendition would know that I was the one that put the data out there."

Dante refreshed their coffee. He had decided that since he was deviating from the espresso shot, he would try coffee the long way. He set up the filter basket, heaped in the coffee, boiled some water and when it had come to a boil, poured it in and let the filter do its job. He made their second round and freshened up their mugs.

"I assume that you took it as your cue to leave the US?" he asked as he poured her the coffee.

She sipped. "For two days I was in a remote part of the world. I sat in a chair overlooking the ocean from a balcony, enjoying the orange hues of a sunset with a new laptop. I had assumed another identity. Then I got an unexpected ping of an IM chat. It made me nervous but I figured I couldn't hide forever."

"Rendition?" he said.

"Sort of . . . a red 'R' appeared which made me nervous as hell, but then an animation drew in an 'S' next to the 'R' and a cursor appeared, typing across my gray console screen. 'If you are receiving this, Alabaster, it's likely that I'm dead. No surprise there. Please grab pen and paper. Click on the image that appears in ten seconds.'"

Dante held the steaming cup of coffee near his lips. "Impressive and scary. What were the image and the message?"

She told him what her avatar looked like with a nostalgic smile. "The animation went inside the keyhole of the handcuff and magnified into a distorted bitmap. I saw a series of numbers that I copied down. It was a bank-account number. The animation zoomed out and the cursor appeared again, blinking, before it wrote the last line, 'You were never plain. Love, Robert.'"

A perplexed look crowded Dante's face on hearing the word 'plain'. "Ah, I remember now . . . Yes, definitely . . . you're far from plain."

"Thank you," she said. "I had my pen and paper ready. I watched the screen do a slow countdown: 10,9,8,7,6,5,4,3,2, and 1, and appearing centered on my screen was my avatar, but bigger."

"The bank account had to be outside the country, right?"

"It was actually a safe-deposit box in Lucerne, Switzerland; the box there held another copy of all the Strand dark-soil documents and an extremely respectable amount of money in bearer bonds."

Dante was quiet for a moment. "How respectable?"

"Very respectable."

He sipped again. "Bearer bonds are instant cash anywhere in the world, no questions asked. Question is, was someone after that money or is Rendition trying to call you back into the fold?"

"Good question," she said. "What do you think?"

Dante hesitated. "I'm inclined to think Rendition wants you back. I would think that they were not so pleased about losing their prized asset. You made many of their cases. Every government has secret groups. Like most elite organizations, once you're in you really can't leave."

"Not to change the subject, but what happened to Gennaro?"

"What do you mean?"

She shifted her shoulders, sipped and spoke. "I don't know. Just seems that he's from Naples, and from what I gathered there was some kind of screw job and he got boxed up and sent to Rome, like he's supposed to act docile and wait for his retirement pension. What exactly happened?"

Dante put down his mug. "It's a very long story. What do you know about the Camorra?"

"Besides reading Roberto Saviano's book and reading the newspaper coverage of the garbage strike in Naples? I had heard about them working with the Russians to counterfeit American money, but that was before my time. I imagine they function in principle like the Mafia we have in the United States."

Dante picked up his coffee mug again. "You're headed in the right direction, except the Camorra and the Sicilians run it more like the early days in your country. They're extremely violent and very old-fashioned with codes about silence, Omertà, and vendetta, revenge-killings. Personally, these thugs claim to be 'men of honor' but I find them revolting. Real *cafoni*. People like them keep the southern part of this country from progress and self-improvement."

"What does all that have to do with Gennaro?" she said.

"Gennaro was an auditor in Naples in the late eighties and early nineties, around the time Giovanni Falcone and Paolo Borsellino were cleaning all the shit out of the stables in the south. Falcone and Borsellino were doing the task of Hercules. Gennaro uncovered a trafficking scheme connecting the Camorra, the Ndrangheta in Calabria, and the Sicilians. He was on the verge of diagramming out the whole scheme, paper trail and all from Naples to Gioia Tauro and Reggio Calabria and of course, Palermo. Don't let appearances fool you: Gennaro is an extremely smart, analytical man."

She had already learned that the previous day. She noticed now that Dante had the intent, focused look that she admired when she had met him.

"If he was on the verge, what happened?"

"He was told to drop it, drag his feet, since his work threatened so many people. Gennaro was onto something huge. Absolutely huge. He was threatened, I imagine, and I think he backed off. I don't know a hundred percent for certain, but I think he met with Falcone and Borsellino. Rumor says he worked with them at first and that led to convictions; but the two magistrates kept him out of the limelight. They were like that. Then they were killed and he dropped it. Everyone in this country was shaken up by those killings. Everyone! First, Falcone was killed, and then Borsellino, months later. I remember it like yesterday."

"At that point he must have pissed off enough people to get transferred to Rome."

Dante looked drained. "No. That came later. In 2008."

"He was in Naples during the garbage crisis?" she said, and saw Dante nodding his head.

"When Gennaro dug in his heels, ready to apply himself to the investigation and knock down a few of the top assholes in that garbage cartel, his superiors got very nervous. As I said, rumor had it that

Gennaro had set in motion successful convictions from his first collaboration with Falcone and Borsellino. Gennaro backed off, mellowed out into the shadows after the two were assassinated, and I think his wife begged him to restrain himself, but when the garbage crisis hit . . . Gennaro pulled out his best work. He was well on his way to exposing the corruption from the boot and all the way up the leg. Then he gets reprimanded and he's sent to Rome. Complete kick in the balls and wind out of his sails."

"Then his wife died? Talk about hell."

Dante's face went as pale as the belly of a fish. "Gennaro's wife didn't just die. She was murdered. The Camorra."

"My God, I didn't know. How?"

Dante wouldn't look at her. "Please don't ask me that. It's too upsetting. It was payback for the earlier convictions and a warning to him if he persisted in Naples with the garbage business. Bastards waited and waited years, but that is the nature of vendetta."

"Christ, I didn't know," she said.

"So what do I call you? Alabaster or Bianca?"

"Call me Bianca," she said, "and we should review the Bevilacqua research, but let's do it out here and not inside. I'll explain why."

13

Gennaro sat at the counter of his favorite trattoria, eyes closed, chin up, mind and mouth ruminating on the flavors. Donato, his friend on the other side of the counter, had given him a new dish to try.

"What do you think?" Donato asked, head cocked and hands working the short cloth.

Gennaro held both his hands up. He chewed, moved the food from one side to another, swallowed and opened his eyes.

"I like it," he said.

Donato threw down the used cloth. "I knew it. This makes me happy."

Gennaro held up an index finger like a judge and Donato's hands went to his face in near defeat.

"While the tortellini is *perfetto* and the meat inside is delectable," Gennaro said, "the Madeira sauce could be the downfall. Tread carefully there: this sauce borders on sweet and I think you need just a touch of acid."

"I used some marsala and an ever so slight touch of truffle butter, but only ever so slight," he indicated with a pinch of his thumb and forefinger. "I should consider lemon or a touch of zest."

Gennaro raised his index finger again. "Exactly. We are in agreement. The meat? What exactly did you use? I loved it."

"Short rib."

Gennaro winked at the ingenuity. *"Bravissimo."*

Gennaro's cell phone went off. He had put it in his front pocket since he was sitting down. He hadn't wanted to put it on the counter because he was afraid that he would forget it. Again.

"Ah, damn it," he said, "my balls are vibrating. Excuse me."

Donato nodded, flung the short cloth over his shoulder and walked away to give Gennaro privacy.

It took Gennaro a second to recognize his caller. "Alessandro? For the love of God, don't you have a woman in your life? It's Sunday."

Gennaro had preset his volume setting higher than usual because his hearing was failing him.

"Boss, that's the first time you've asked me a personal question in all the time we've known each other. Eh, no. No woman, but I appreciate the—"

Losing patience and needing to swerve away from the sentimental, Gennaro switched to dialect. *"Che cazzo voi?"*

"Boss, I called to say that Dante and Bianca want to meet to discuss . . . you know, the project. You know the place a block away from the Egyptian. We're meeting there."

"I know the place. I'll leave now and meet you there."

Gennaro snapped the lid down and put the cell on the counter. Donato was wiping down the already clean counter with his cloth. He motioned to the cell phone with his chin. "Got to leave? Work?"

"Pain in my ass. On a Sunday, too—I don't understand this younger generation of workaholics. That's all they do and think about."

Donato shook his head and mumbled the imported word for workaholics, *"Stacanovista.* So, does this workaholic have a woman in his life or not?"

Gennaro stood up, put the phone in his rear pocket, shook his head, and placed a few Euro on the counter. "The last thing that Alessandro has seen or touched belonged to a chicken."

Tony the Egyptian was a local fixture who had operated a pasta cart— ironically—not far from the Pasta Museum near the Quirinale Hill. The genial man had first begun circulating his mobile culinary delight thirty years before in the out-of-the-way places in Rome, like the Baths of Caracalla or the Basilica di San Clemente, before braving the busier streets, where he found broader acceptance and more welcoming stomachs.

Romans, like most Italians—or most Europeans and quite a few Americans—had their issues with the various immigrants: Africans, Albanians, Libyans, Moroccans, Romani, and Turks. But Tony the Egyptian seemed exempt from it all. As much as Gennaro disdained take-away food—*da asporto*—he conceded that the man's cooking was tasty and the servings plentiful, even joking that if, for some reason, the man were threatened with deportation, all of Rome would converge on the Piazza Venezia to extend collectively their middle fingers in protest.

Gennaro hadn't planned on visiting two *trattorie* in one day; he thought it perverse, and it made him superstitious. When he arrived he saw a garden of torsos at tables. He started to look for their table the way a cat sticks his head up at the sound of a can opener. He knew that they were there but he didn't know where.

The proprietor, Nunzio, was standing at the front of the house. Local rumor had it that his family had owned the plot of land on which the trattoria was built since the early days of the Republic. Gennaro thought it was bullshit, but the few tourists who came to the area ate it up. Nunzio rarely broke a smile under that canonical beak nose of his. He patrolled the floor in his uniform of navy-blue pants and blinding-white dress shirt, open at the collar, thick gold chain minus the crucifix at his neck, and wisps of his black and graying chest hair protruding upward and outward against the plackets. Despite his uncommon name, Nunzio said little. In fact, the more he saw a customer frequent his place the less he said. He saw Gennaro and pointed to the table in the back, in the corner.

There was no choice of chairs at the table so Gennaro had to sit down next to Alessandro. Bianca and Dante sat opposite him. The corner was meant for romance—the only thing that seemed to be missing was the candle-wax-stained straw of a cheap Chianti bottle. Gennaro's stomach surprised him with a growl.

"Have a seat, Boss," said Alessandro.

Gennaro remembered to retrieve his cell and place it on the table near the forks next to his plate. An attractive waitress delivered a plate of toasted black bread topped with taleggio cheese and three kinds of mushrooms.

The waitress asked him, *"Acqua minerale o naturale?"* Gennaro sensed her surprise, and that of the table, when he said, "Naturale." She left and they looked at him.

"Heard a report that *acqua minerale* has higher levels of arsenic and manganese," he said.

Dante handed everyone except Bianca a summary sheet. The waitress set down a small appetizer.

With paper in hand and eyes on the single page, Dante read: "*Amici di Roma* are loosely organized and relatively autonomous, with Lorenzo Bevilacqua as president. He created this organization, playing off the name of the *Associazione Culturale Amici di Roma*, which has provided students, tourists and educated visitors to our country with outstanding guided tours for decades, since their staff is picked from our best universities. Bevilacqua, appropriating their good name, created an import-export company with some shady characters."

"Criminal backgrounds on any in the cast?" Alessandro asked.

"No," Bianca said.

Which meant she knew the material as well as Dante. Which meant that, at the very least, she had helped with the research. *Interesting.*

"Ties to known low-lifes?" Gennaro said.

Dante said, "Not here. What I mean is that, on this side of the scam, all his confederates are squeaky clean. But when you start looking at his business associates in America you start to see some questionable characters. In New York, his colleagues have had problems with the IRS; one of his shipments that had come into Port Elizabeth in New Jersey was cited for Customs irregularities. Same with another shipment in New Orleans."

"These irregularities with antiquities?" Alessandro asked. Gennaro waited for an answer. It was a good question.

Bianca answered again. "Artwork. In both cases the shipments were impressionist paintings."

Gennaro wiped his mouth after having some of the bread and enjoying the meatiness of the mushrooms. "Impressionists from Rome? Expecting Impressionist art here is like finding good food in London."

"That's exactly what tipped me off to Bevilacqua," Bianca said. "The financials get really murky when you try to trace shipments once they go to the United States."

Alessandro's eyes came up from his page. "What does he claim to be importing?"

Dante exchanged a look with Bianca, and she gave him the sign to answer the question. So she was not just involved. She was leading the investigation, Gennaro was thinking as he observed the two of them. *Very interesting.*

"An assortment of things," Dante said, "but mostly American in theme: electronics, clothes, jeans, some wine—all those things kids and the middle class with money want to say that they have. You know, status items."

Gennaro had set his paper face down when the waitress returned. The next course was a large flatbread with parcels of duck confit, small dollops of goat cheese, and dried cranberries. Everyone stopped to admire the dish, and he began to think this was a good place for a meeting.

"All well and good," Gennaro said, "but we need to count this Bevilacqua as a suspect or not. We don't have the time or the budget if we want to keep this project secret. Our professor has cast the line in the water so we have to go with the bites. Anyone approached the professor?"

Everyone turned heads to Alessandro.

"I spoke with the professor," he said, "and he tells me that he's inundated with the usual questions about where exactly the eagle was found, the condition of the artifact, and when the public can expect a glimpse. He's gotten the academics and archaeologists chasing him too, but nobody has crawled out of the forest and offered a bribe to see the eagle one-on-one. No mention of money at all, he said. He did say, however, that he has had one academic pestering him about wanting to see the artifact and offering some kind of exchange: you-let-me-see-this-and-I'll-let-you-see-that type of arrangement. The professor said that he had a feeling about this guy."

Gennaro was surprised at the contribution that the cranberries made to the dish. He had expected pine nuts instead. "I get feelings all the time, Alessandro. We can't afford to rely wholly on gut instinct. It's dangerous and misleading."

"This academic have a name?" Bianca said. "A university?"

Alessandro appeared to be enjoying his portion of flatbread. "That's the thing. Moretti couldn't get much out of the man. I wrote down the man's name, but beyond that—nothing. He's American though."

Gennaro chuckled. "We're pulling at moss. What is he, a defrocked academic who got too close to a graduate student? An amateur art historian? Maybe he's an enthusiastic collector? Maybe he's a multimillionaire wearing tweed in hot weather? We can be here all day speculating. None of it means a thing."

"The name?" Bianca said. "Did the professor say what this man offered in exchange for private time with the eagle?"

The wine cleared Alessandro's palate. "Professor Moretti said the academic was willing to arrange for him to have a private tour of unseen artifacts, starting with a bronze eagle, Roman, circa 100 AD. As for the university in America: none. The name is Alan Ancona. I don't have the business card, but like I said, I wrote down the phone number and e-mail address the man gave to the professor."

Dante looked excited. "The same Ancona I've been reading about in the papers?"

"The same."

Dante explained. "Ancona has an office given to him by the Church. He's been asked to appraise items in the Vatican Collection. He's managed to lie low."

"Lie low?" asked Bianca.

"Some sex scandal is getting all the news, but I read about him in the Arts section. Small article," said Alessandro.

Gennaro was relishing his second helping of flatbread. "So what? He has an eagle. The Aquila was made of either silver or bronze, so this intellectual has access to another one. So what?"

"How'd you know they were made of bronze or silver, Boss?" Alessandro asked.

"Alessandro, I can read."

"The information you copied down from the professor, please," Bianca said, her hand out to Alessandro. He handed her his small spiral notebook, flipped open to the appropriate page.

Bianca read out Alessandro's printing of the name. "Ancona at gtu. You wrote this the way it had appeared on the card? The 'at' in the e-mail address too?"

"Just as Professor Moretti read it off to me." Alessandro took another bite of his flatbread.

"What's the problem?" Dante said.

"The 'gtu' is odd. For a university one expects 'edu.' The only academic institution that I can think of with the acronym 'gtu' is in Berkeley, California. The phone number's area code isn't Berkeley's, but that doesn't mean anything since it's most likely a cell phone, possibly an office somewhere in Rome. From the card I wouldn't know that he's a professor. There's no PhD after his name."

"From the way Moretti talked, he kinda assumed the man was an academic."

"Going through the mosses," Gennaro added while looking down at his plate.

Bianca tapped her finger against the writing. "The local part of the e-mail address bothers me."

"The what?"

Alessandro whispered 'chiocciola,' the word for both 'snail' and the @ sign.

Before Gennaro could comment, the waitress had arrived at the table with the next dish. He forgot who was doing the ordering, but he wasn't complaining. The food kept coming. While she set the main plate down, Bianca tore a piece of loose-leaf from Alessandro's spiral notebook and copied down the Alan Ancona information. She busied herself with more writing while Gennaro parceled out servings.

The waitress announced the dish as: *"Pasta all'Amatriciana,"* and recited by rote that the dish was made with specially procured and butchered *guanciale*. Both the pasta and sauce were made on the premises. Gennaro lowered his head to smell the dish while Nunzio silently poured the wine with the watchful eyes of an ancient poisoner.

Alessandro had to ask about the wine, and the man answered, "Frascati," before placing the bottle onto the table.

Bianca ignored her serving. Dante noticed, and Gennaro noticed him noticing, but neither said a word. Alessandro mumbled between mouthfuls that the dish was heavenly and that he liked the peppers and the thick tubes of bucatini pasta.

Gennaro could not keep himself from grumbling.

Alessandro said, "You don't like the dish, Boss?"

"I like it but this chef plagiarized the recipe." He forked his pasta in a way prosecutors would describe as, 'with mean intent.' "The pasta is good. The sauce is good; the plagiarism is in the pig."

Dante was attentive. Even Bianca lifted her eyes up, the pencil remaining still in her hand.

"Cured hog cheek—the *guanciale*—was meant to impress us, but that'll change to pancetta when the tourists go away; and that's the give-away. I had this dish over at Osteria di San Cesario. Anna Dente Ferracci and her mother Maria Savina Dente made this dish for me. I was in their divine presence—lovely ladies—and when they heard me speak they knew—" His complimentary finger was in the air again. "They *knew* I was from Campagna. What an evening, I tell you! This—" he pointed to his plate, "is but a pale imitation. They imitated everything, even down to the choice of wine: 'Luna Mater.' Steal, Alessandro, but steal and make it new—add a touch of your signature."

"I think I've got it," Bianca said.

"Got what?" Gennaro asked.

Bianca excused herself from the table and walked over to a handsome young man with a laptop eating alone. They exchanged words. The table watched Bianca typing on a few keys, writing something on the same torn-out piece of paper she was using. A few more smiles were exchanged. She returned to the table waving her piece of paper.

"Why did you use his laptop when you brought your own?" Alessandro asked.

"Ah, I've been having some issues with it and I was lazy."

"I'm sure his ugly face and one eyebrow didn't make a difference, did it?" Dante said.

She ignored him.

Motioning his fork like a baton, Gennaro asked, "What did you discover?"

Bianca placed the paper onto the table and ironed it out flat. "I kept reading Ancona at gtu and the 'gtu' bothered me. So I started thinking about California and had a hunch. Then I wanted to verify my hunch so I looked for another place in California. On the laptop, of course."

Three blank faces were waiting for her, their forks vacant.

With the calculating demeanor of a coroner she said, "Here, Dante: I want you to pronounce the 'gt' as individual letters. Leave out the 'u'."

She handed the piece of paper to him but folded it in half.

Dante took the paper slowly, looked down and, feeling like a schoolboy learning his alphabet, he enunciated "gee," paused, and then went to the next letter, "te," and handed Bianca back her piece of paper.

Silence.

Bianca unfolded the lower portion of the piece of paper. Dante read out the entry. "Ancona at Getty-u."

"The Getty is a museum in California that uses four vocabulary databases, all trademarked and proprietary. The Getty is very well known for its antiquities collection, and as coincidence would have it, they have experienced a recent scandal regarding items in their collection that—shall we say—were not properly acquired."

A fork dropped. Gennaro snatched the piece of paper. "So, if we can prove a connection between this Ancona and Bevilacqua, we might have a case."

The waitress came over with a dessert tray of ugly but delicious cookies. *"Brutti ma buoni?"*

They declined dessert. As they walked out, Alessandro tapped Dante's shoulder. *"Complimenti!"* That research you summarized on that one sheet was very impressive. Good work."

Bianca looked at Dante and smiled. He lowered his head. Gennaro enjoyed the pantomime and then paid the bill, since it had been a working lunch. On a Sunday, of all days.

But Gennaro left feeling very self-satisfied. He had resisted the urge to send the waitress over to the antisocial Nunzio with cookies and have her say to him, *"Buono ma brutto."*

14

They each went their separate ways.

Dante decided that he had to visit the *barbieria* on Via della Vite. His head was overdue and he wanted to see Americo, whom he called uncle, out of respect, since the man had done his hair since he was a child and had given him his very first shave ever. Dante's father had taken him to the shop and his father's father had taken his father there, so it was a matter of family tradition. For as long as Dante could remember, Zio Americo was a short man, thin with a full head of hair, thick eyebrows, and Martin Scorsese glasses with aspheric lenses. The family whisper was that Americo's grandfather was one of Garibaldi's best friends and advisors—a *consigliere*, in the old sense of the word. To encourage speculation, he had secreted in the corner nearest his chair an Austrian Model 1849 caplock rifle, the so-called 'Garibaldi rifle.'

Zio was an ancient *maestro* of the razor and scissor in his tailored white lab coat. Though he now moved slowly with old bones about the shop's marble floors, the man's mental acuity could undo others young enough to be his great-grandchildren. Zio was a man of the professional ritual: he would have his client safely ensconced in the red-leather chair, the drape around the shoulders and, after discussing the requested cut, he would begin his continuous clicking, snipping, and lifting of scissor and disinfected comb. He eschewed the modern trend of using the electric razor for cutting hair on the head, claiming that it damaged the hair.

Once the haircut was completed, Zio, resorting to a trade secret rarely practiced elsewhere, would burn the ends of the hair, explaining to those who asked why that the flame removed the hairs that stuck out and the heat sealed the shaft of the cut hair. The smell of singed hair was part of the charm of the shop. The next ritual Zio enacted upon his charge was to render a vigorous scalp massage by hand, not with the vibrating device that the other barbers wrapped around their one hand. Zio said craftsmanship always begins and ends with a pair of hands, while machines of that sort were for incompetent men with dissatisfied women.

Their conversations varied, but in recent years Dante would ask his adopted uncle when he planned to retire and what his plans were, mostly to give Zio a chance to exercise his wit. He said that he had to work to support a Brazilian lover, or because his investment in video-tape machines had failed, or because he was constitutionally incapable of idleness, or because he had to pay the veterinary bill for Camilleri, his Cane Corso. The most recent was that he had to work because he had missed the opportunity of sudden fame, like the old man who had ridden through the crowd during a Berlusconi speech on his bike, loaf of bread in one hand, yellow rose in the other. He had once told Dante that he could reinvent himself, like an American, and become a Moyle since he had the rudimentary skills, if one were to discount the difference in anatomy, but he dismissed the thought because he had neither the time to convert to Judaism nor a flattering skull for a yarmulke.

Dante closed his eyes as the hot towels rested on his face for the shave. Zio stropped his razor with the rhythmic wrist flexibility of a cellist. This stage of the visit was when Zio would declaim a canto from *La Divina Commedia* or a passage from Manzoni, or depending on his mood, sing a muscular sonnet of Buonarroti. But if he felt particularly spiritual, as he did when the day felt heavy with clouds, he recited with the most heartbreaking sincerity the poetry of Guido Guinizelli.

Dante paid and asked only then, as he always did, after Zio's only living relative: a son, an unmarried lab tech. Everybody bent their noses crooked rather than say it aloud that the man might be gay.

Alessandro went over to the Viale America to swim in the Piscina delle Rose. *Bambini* were scattered throughout the blue water of the Olympic-size pool that had hosted the water-polo competition in the 1960 Summer Olympics. These children, like armies with their different-color suits, were playing oddly named games of 'make the wave' or 'battleships and submarines'; their slick heads and goggled eyes turned to hear the loud commands of their generals; their playful screams of dramatic destruction and triumphs dotted the blue water surrounded by the two-tier boundary of concrete and adult spotters.

He kept to the far side where he claimed a lane for swimming the mantra of meters, flip turns at each end, absorbing the underwater concussions of everything and everyone to the right of him on the way down and to his left on the return, as his arms turned over one stroke after another to climb up and down the water. The children were refreshingly polite. When they realized that he was there they granted him his space to do his tediously boring adult exercise: back and forth for what they considered forever. But once they thought the thought they forgot it upon returning to the latest maritime development: a young girl had declared herself a general, which incited protests.

Up and down Alessandro swam, goggles on, finding himself in a silent world where the water welcomed him and washed away, with each pulling stroke, all the negativity of the week. He thought of all of Gennaro's insults and let them float away. He thought of Dante's recent injuries and how he might bear some responsibility for the events that had swirled that assault into existence. He found forgiveness and humor when his manager's voice replayed in his head. He rationalized that, with respect to Dante, the universe has its own logic and chaos.

The swishing caress of the water against his ear as he turned to breathe reminded him that all of it was transitory, none of it worth getting upset about, because everything would flow. In that flash of face for air, warmth from the sun, he kept his eyes closed, opening them only when they looked to the bottom of the pool to know where in his journey the wall was approaching him so he could flip over, pivot and angle his body sideways like a thin wisp of wet thread to put himself through the invisible eye of an imaginary needle in front of him, gliding as long as he could before he had to use his arms and feet.

He felt inspired to swim an extra few thousand meters. No matter what his muscles might say later, tomorrow, or days later, he swam and swam, creating his own ebb and flow of time, defying the sun and making the moon jealous. When he rested he felt his shoulders ache in a good way, and when he opened his eyes and took in the bright world he felt more alive, much lighter, grateful to be in the here and now. A young woman walked past him, turned to look at him and smiled when she realized that he had caught her looking. It felt good to feel desire and be desired. He wanted to flirt but decided, why ruin the late afternoon.

In the locker room he spun his suit dry in a metal contraption that subjected his trunks to centrifugal forces. Leave it to the Germans to engineer it, but an Italian would've created a design that wouldn't have made this clever device look like an aluminum trash can. Then to the shower, where he lathered himself with body soap to rid his body of the chlorine and kid piss. He used an excessive amount of conditioner to rinse the chemical coarseness out of his hair. After drying himself off, he took a quick look in the mirror, went over to his locker, opened it and got dressed. He slung his small carry bag over his shoulder.

After having swum a distance he would do the mathematical calculation: five thousand meters is to five kilometers is to three miles, so he felt like a god but ached like a human.

Gennaro walked.

He walked in the heat and wished for autumn; walked to clear the rooms of his mind and lighten the load of food in his stomach; walked past the Christian and pagan monuments and the recycled places—once pagan now converted to Christianity. Gennaro ignored these public displays because he found them to be relentless reminders of mortality, just like graveyards speak to finality and churches of the inevitable. Out of the nine hundred churches in Rome, Gennaro resigned himself to sit in the pew of one of the out-of-the-way ones.

He sat in the Basilica di Sant'Agnese Fuori le Mura. He found that he needed the company of dead women to remember the one he lost long ago. Here he had Agnes, patron saint of virgins, Constantia, leprous daughter of Emperor Constantine, and Emerentiana, foster sister of Agnes. The Basilica of St. Agnes was not the Aversa Cathedral that he and his wife, Lucia, adored, but it had the catacombs, had that

Romanesque architecture, that lighting and those brown and red tones that appealed to his aesthetics and sense of intimacy. He contemplated the apse mosaic and the arches for a time, and then found a seat.

One of the canon regulars nodded to Gennaro as he walked by the pew, mistaking him for one of the religious. Hardly. Gennaro stared up and down the stony wall. There were times he disliked Rome. It was a city where archaeology and geology were as badly layered and confused as an apartment wall that had suffered several bad paint jobs. Just when you get to the bottom of something, its true surface, you realize that it is shit stacked on top of older shit on top of another layer of even older shit. Gennaro felt blasphemous having such profane thoughts in a sacred place, but when he considered that Agnes and Emerentiana had both died violent deaths at the hands of the Romans, he realized that this violent world was the real one. Only for a brief moment would he be inside these walls that kept it all at bay.

Dante didn't know it, nor did Alessandro, and he hadn't expected Bianca to know, but today was the anniversary of Lucia's death. He smirked as his inner voice told him that Lucia would have elbowed him and told him that he should have picked Santa Maria Maddalena for his self-pity session because Lucia said that her best friends were prostitutes.

He certainly had a hard time courting her after her first marriage. That asshole had abused her, screwed around on her, but she had gotten him good one day with a hot iron. The police had a heyday with their reports, which he had read. They ridiculed the bastard while he was on the floor waiting for medical attention: 'That little lady there did this to you? We find that so hard to believe—a big, strong guy like you and a tiny woman like that. What's that, Signora? It was an accident, I see, he walked into the iron. That's right. I understand.'

Lucia struggled after leaving her first husband. Her family didn't help. 'You made your bed and you sleep in it,' her mother said. 'God gives us only the tribulations we can endure,' the priest said, 'so he can teach us the ways of virtue and patience.' She wanted to scream at all of them, *"Vaffanculo!"* Lucia was a strong-willed woman; a beautiful one, too, and smart. But since she had been the one to initiate the divorce she was persona non grata and nobody would hire her. That a woman worked at all in that small town should have qualified as a miracle.

The whores came to her aid. She had known most of them from childhood, and because she was kind to them, never judging them or their vocation, they were kind to her. After the iron incident, she joked that one way or another a man had to pay for it. She had so little in those early days, but when her friends came around she would make whatever food she had or at least offer them some coffee. And when she cleaned up she would find that they had left her money under the saucers, or elsewhere in her apartment. Their kindness saved her from complete destitution.

Of all people it had been a Jew who had gotten Lucia to the independence she needed. In the next town over a shop owner in need of a seamstress hired her, offering to pay her by the piece. She got the job by batting her eyelashes and selling the man a line of eloquent bullshit, but she knew nothing of sewing. She only hoped that she could learn the trade fast. After a few slow starts and some botched efforts, an elderly woman across from her, hair pulled back tight, dressed in black, invited her over and said in a low voice, "Here, sit next to me and watch me. Keep your mouth shut and learn."

Day after day, Lucia learned the craft of stitching and eventually developed, as all the great seamstresses do, a unique style of her own. The Jewish lady, Giuseppina, would smile as she sat next to Lucia, approving her work with soft-voiced compliments. They would talk and share lunches. Lucia saved her money and moved from her stifling town to the next one over to be closer to her work. She saved more money with the idea of establishing her own shop. At the end of the workweek, she asked Giuseppina whether they could meet for coffee, that she had something important to discuss with her. They agreed to meet at Giuseppina's apartment.

Even on weekends Giuseppina wore black but allowed her hair to run somewhat truant from the barrette and pins. Lucia sat there, fingers lightly holding her saucer, waiting for her host to return from the kitchen with some homemade almond cookies that she had brought with her as a gift. Giuseppina loved almond cookies.

"Giuseppina, you've been kind to me. I've been thinking of opening my own shop and wish to invite you to work with me."

"That's so kind of you, but I'll do fine."

"But, my dear, your hands—forgive me for noticing—are getting arthritic."

The woman held up her hands. "These hands have created the world in which I live." She spread her arms wide to convey the space of the apartment and its contents. "I have always put my own money away. A woman should always have her own money and not rely on anyone. I would say the same to men, dear."

At that moment a young man whom Lucia and the other women had seen visiting Giuseppina at the shop walked in. He was a handsome man straight out of the movies, with the Mastroianni part and combed-back black hair and lively, humorous eyes. All the women would watch the man when he visited, letting their hands do the work from memory while their eyes imagined scenes and things only women could imagine. Giuseppina would sit quiet in her chair.

Alberto said hello and Lucia likewise as the man unloaded the bags and put away the food into the refrigerator and cupboards.

Lucia spoke in a lower voice. "Giuseppina, you can't have your son devote his good years to taking care of you."

A pause, and a long, seductive, whimsical smile made its way from cheek to cheek. "Who said that he was my son?"

Lucia sat back in her chair, absorbing the inference. "But he's so young . . ."

Giuseppina nibbled on a cookie. "What can I say? I like to teach." Another nibble finished off the cookie. "Look, Lucia, you open your shop. Be free and save your money. You don't need a man. If you find one, watch him, observe his character, and then decide. That doesn't mean that you have to marry him. Men are weak and they'll take anything off the street to do their cooking and cleaning."

Giuseppina's eyes bored intently into Lucia, "There are good men out there. Some women can be stupid and mistreat them, for women are no better than men. We don't like to be alone and we are cats with each other. Alberto? Alberto is a good man and I adore him. He takes care of me and I know it. You? You take care of yourself, and if you find an Alberto then so be it. But you decide that and not God."

Lucia opened her shop. She dealt with the Camorristas and paid her protection money with reluctance, but she would pay it. During Gennaro's investigation into the Camorra, years later, she asked him to back down some because she was growing fearful for his safety. He never thought that they would harm her first.

That fateful day Gennaro was at the office when the Polizia di Stato, the state police, showed up in front of his desk requesting that he accompany them. He saw the body, saw the blood, saw the fight she had given the attackers, and he understood grief. He understood the hidden truths of literature that he read: Orpheus and Eurydice, Paolo and Francesco, Hadrian and Antinous, Alexander and Hephaestion; understood the untranslatable language of anguish.

Lucia's funeral was a solemn affair. Giuseppina came in black, her hair grayer. The old lady, now in her nineties, still walked with her handsome Alberto at her side. She asked Alberto for a few moments to speak with Gennaro. Alberto leaned down and gave his condolences to Gennaro before he went off.

Giuseppina sat down, her face tense but dry. She put her hand on Gennaro's thigh and said to him, "I'm an old woman at an age that your wife should have lived to see. She was like a daughter to me. You were good to her and for that I'm grateful, but I ask that you promise me one thing, and only one thing."

Gennaro would always remember that conversation and that promise vividly.

"Promise me that you'll find those responsible for this. Promise me that, because I'll deny God and wait in Hell for them."

"I promise," he told her.

"Good, because what the Devil has planned for them is nothing compared to what I've got waiting for them."

Giuseppina left with Alberto. She died not more than two months later; and he had no doubt that the woman had kept her word. Last Gennaro had heard: Alberto never married.

Gennaro sat there lost in thought. He snapped out of his reverie only when he realized his face was wet.

Bianca continued her research on Bevilacqua. The late afternoon into the dark evening found her in another cyber café, legs tucked under, eyes scrutinizing the flickering screen, her fingertips flitting across the keyboard.

God, she loved this.

15

Gennaro was in a deep sleep, in that unknowable darkness where hours are hazy, long, and later lost; where the dreamer is cradled in the fragile web of knowing and not remembering; where, if the dreamer does wake, he remembers for a moment before his return to sleep, but if he falls back asleep, he forgets everything in the morning, only remembering vague fragments of this or that or something blurry and impossible for words. In small fits of waking he, the dreamer, turns and returns to the reconstruction of a deceptive memory or a new fiction; but in this case for Gennaro it was a semi-erotic dream involving Lucia. They hadn't yet made love, but the eroticism had come from the warmth of the summer heat, the reds and yellows he had been seeing in the dream.

In this dream they were courting, though these days it is called dating. She was cautious and he was patient. Anticipation was the aphrodisiac. She had invisible scars but he knew that without touching her. It was as if she feared suffocation but he let her breathe. They were having a pleasant picnic together on the island of Ischia.

At an unforgiveable hour, the phone rang. It was Alessandro.

"We've got a problem," he said.

Gennaro was groping for the light as the voice met his ear. "No, you've got a problem."

"Big problem, Boss. I'm serious."

Gennaro could tell that Alessandro had turned away from something by the way his voice had changed, as if he was looking for more privacy, but Gennaro did not care. He had awoken with an erection that was now quickly wilting. Also, the light and the voice had settled it. He was awake and there was no going back to sleep, even though it was—he glanced at his watch, five-thirty in the morning.

"I'm serious too," he said. "Now listen to me, Alessandro, this had better be good, because I'm in a foul fucking mood—not that you would know the difference. So what is it?"

"It's Bianca."

"What about her?" Gennaro's annoyance now wilted, replaced by a prickly sensation of panic: first it was Dante's assault and now this bit of news.

"Somebody broke into her place."

"Is she okay?" Gennaro became aware that he had unknowingly clutched the top sheet.

"Oh, she's all right, Boss. She wasn't even home at the time. Good thing, I guess, because whoever broke in really turned the place over."

"Where was she then?"

"Don't know. All I know is she must've been coming home, saw the police were already on the scene, and turned the other way. Some neighbor of hers, I guess, called saying that she'd heard a racket."

Now the inspector in Gennaro was waking up as well. Things were finally beginning to happen. "She turned around? Where the hell did she go then? That must mean the police haven't talked to her. Or worse, they'll assume that something happened to her and they'll start looking for her."

Alessandro's voice changed again. Must have been another turn, a look away for privacy. Alessandro's softer voice returned too: "I'm sure that the police aren't in a hurry to go looking for her right now, but they will eventually. Bianca is at Dante's. Dante called me and I called you."

Gennaro sighed. "That's wonderful: a children's game of telephone. I don't get it, Alessandro. You call me—thank you for waking me up—but how do you know what the police know? How did you know that her place was tossed?"

"That's why I called you, Boss." That damn change in Alessandro's voice again was starting to annoy Gennaro. "I mean I wanted you to know she's all right and at Dante's and all, but the real reason I called is that there's someone here who knows you and I thought you'd want to talk to him. He's a hundred-percent certain he wants to talk to you."

"Who?" Gennaro said.

Alessandro said it in a low register, as if it was a dirty word. "A cop.

Actually, he's a detective. I was standing with all the nosy neighbors on the sidewalk here and he sees me. I don't know this guy, Boss, but he recognized me, asked me my name and next thing I know he mentions your name and he asks whether I can get you down here, and that's how it is I called you."

"That's how it is? Alessandro, I don't know any cops. I definitely don't know detectives."

Alessandro, like a kid, taking satisfaction in his calculated victory, said, "Oh, yeah you do, Boss. You know this detective and he knows you."

"Listen to me, Alessandro. I'll spell it out to you again so even your little head understands. I DON'T KNOW cops and I DON'T KNOW detectives."

"He says his name is Isidore Farrugia."

It took a moment for the familiar name to register. "Jesus Christ, I'll be right there. Give me the address."

Alessandro rattled off the address. Gennaro didn't bother making his bed. He ran to the bathroom with his penis flopping up and down.

Isidore Farrugia had been working up the ranks when Gennaro met him years before in Naples, when the anti-Mafia task force had convened for his preliminary report on the money-laundering operation out of Sicily into Naples that had been reaching as far north as Milan. Farrugia was no more than an acquaintance at the time, but his reputation had preceded him. They became friends the day Lucia was murdered and for months afterwards. The detective had been the first one at the house; he had handled the scene procedurally, and attended to Gennaro personally.

Farrugia came from Calabria, of mixed blood, as far as his so-called colleagues in Rome were concerned. His mother was Spanish, dark, and his father an even darker Calabrese and those two in union produced a son that was beyond the Sicilian shade. Isidore Farrugia was an impressive man: wiry, long in the face with large round eyes, thin black eyebrows and at the time when Gennaro had met him, majestic curly hair and wispy black sideburns. He could pass for a twin of Alexander the Great straight out of that mosaic of the conqueror fighting the Persian Darius. In terms of his policing pedigree, the man had started out undercover in Taormina, infiltrating small-time Mafia mousetraps set for tourists, but quickly had graduated into riskier stings in Palermo and had worked more undercover operations that Borsellino had started.

After the Borsellino and Falcone assassinations, Farrugia's cover was considered compromised. After Lucia was murdered and Gennaro was shipped north, he heard through the worn-out grapevine that Farrugia had also been relocated. Gennaro was never sure whether it had been because of a genuine concern for the man's safety or racist politics. What Gennaro did know with certainty was that Farrugia had been keeping tabs on him. The man had taken Lucia's death to heart, for the brutality of her murder had disturbed him. Farrugia's mother had been collateral damage in a vendetta in his hometown of San Luca. Gennaro kept in contact until their new jobs and new cities separated them; their nascent friendship had then simmered into nonexistence.

Gennaro arrived and spotted Alessandro immediately. Farrugia he didn't see until he had seen the back of the man's head. His hair was shorter, but the body was still wiry. Not only that, but Farrugia emanated the same intensity even from across the street with his back turned. Making detective grade must have really irritated his Roman colleagues, but fuck them. If anyone deserved it, it was Isidore Farrugia—the man hadn't been counting the hairs on his boss' ass to get the promotion. Farrugia had never married. He took his job seriously and considered it an act of honor to do his duty to the letter of the law, although he did occasionally get dyslexic when it came to getting results.

Farrugia's head turned almost to profile, as if he had heard something. His head had that slight tic of someone knowing that somebody else was watching him. He turned, clean-shaven, face taut, sideburns gone, ready for confrontation. His hand was instinctively at his waist as his eyes scanned the sidewalk.

A cocked smirk broke the symmetry of his face as soon as he spotted Gennaro.

He started walking, and Gennaro saw that the man's eyes were pointing to an empty spot on the sidewalk where they could talk. Gennaro's hand told Alessandro to stay fixed and he went to speak with the detective.

The two men shook hands and embraced quickly as friends do.

"You look like your usual piece-of-shit self, except harder and older," Farrugia said.

Gennaro took it in stride, but the man was correct. It wasn't until after Lucia died that he began to use profanity and sarcasm, building that notorious reputation for repartee. "I see that you've got some gray and I imagine you're still a pebble in a few pairs of shoes."

"I do my best."

Gennaro, nodding in the direction of Alessandro, because his mother had taught him never to point, asked, "How did you know he was one of mine?"

"I have my ways. This woman in this apartment, Bianca Nerini—I take it you know her?"

"I do."

"Also one of your own?"

"You can say that," replied Gennaro with a slight shrug.

"Eh, you and her a . . ." he asked with his two index fingers parallel to each other and meeting and separating.

"No, nothing like that. She's an acquaintance."

Farrugia paused and eyed Gennaro. "Acquaintance enough that two men get out of their beds to look after her? I'm no Commissario De Luca, but I'm inclined to think she's important to someone. I'm not supposed to discuss an investigation, but for the sake of conversation and friendship I'll think out loud while you eavesdrop. You understand?"

Gennaro nodded.

"I show up on this shit assignment because the idiot squad that arrived to investigate a break-in suspects a missing person. No signs of foul play but you know they have to start thinking of kidnapping and all the other ideas they get from watching all that bad television. God knows, if I hadn't gone there they would be arguing about which way the perpetrators had left the toilet paper on the spindle, face up or down. Now, let's be honest with each other for old time's sake. You wouldn't happen to know anything, would you? I didn't think so from the way you're looking at me. Good, so let's say, for the sake of conjecture, that she's safe somewhere and for some reason that should remain a mystery for now, she needs to stay out of sight . . ."

"I would say that's a reasonable assumption," Gennaro said.

The detective smiled; his eyes and eyebrows lifted up, indicating the apartment above the street. "This woman is rather odd. I don't want to insult your friends; but, I mean, I go into her apartment and I find functionality and austerity that I haven't seen since I visited Monte Cassino. Mind you, while I'm not expecting to find a Paola Navone kitchen, I've been inside many homes, and contrary to rumors on the force I'm no monk myself. But there's nothing in that apartment but nice shoes, a small wardrobe in one armoire, enough cookware to get by with, and a ton of computer shit. There is no evidence of a lover— male or female, we can't assume these days, right? The woman has no lingerie. I didn't see pictures anywhere of any kind. Not a picture of family or friends. No pet. No pictures of a pet. I didn't even find so much as a vibrator or a television in the place for entertainment. No books, either. What the hell am I to think? Is this woman a mental case? A recluse? The oddest thing I find are a ton of SIM cards and—"

"SIM what?"

"SIM cards, those things you put into cell phones. And that's the thing, Gennaro, there were at least ten or twelve of the damn things still inside their plastic packaging. And, oh, I forgot, one disposable cell phone. This is weird, no? There's no paperwork in the entire place, no bills, bank statements, or personal letters. Nothing. She even has a paper shredder and that was empty, too. I don't know whether I'm in the house of one of those androids or in the presence of a ghost."

"How'd you get her name or know about the break-in?" Gennaro watched the police down the street. They had let the vestibule door close and lock. The next cop trying to get back into the building was bitching about the door.

Farrugia was observing the same scene. "Damn idiots; to think they get to carry guns. The name we got from the landlord who, of course, does not live on the premises and who, of course, was aggravated with a phone call this early in the morning."

"Of course. The break-in?"

"Signora on the floor beneath the apartment. Old enough to be God's mother, an insomniac, and my guess, the building snoop. Every building has one: they know who comes and leaves and with whom, who flushes the toilet and at what time, who is cheating on his wife, which wife lets the handsome young delivery man stay longer than normal; you know, the usual. This woman called in about the ruckus above her head. She had enough good sense to know that something was not right, had enough of a mind to call the police and not take it upon herself to investigate the noise and get herself killed."

"What could she hear if there was nothing in the apartment?"

"She said it was the sound of their walking all over the hardwood and marble floors that had driven her to distraction. She did hear some crashing sounds though. Kitchen drawers and contents turned over—that kind of thing. My guess is that these goons knew that they wouldn't find a thing almost as soon as they got started, so they staged a little drama to make their presence known. Had she been home, my guess is that we'd have ourselves a different scenario: the kind with chalk on the floor."

"A message, then?" Gennaro added.

"Exactly, a message. We both know who are good at leaving messages, don't we?"

"You think mafia? Seriously? C'mon, Isidò, we know each other. I'd have come to get you myself if those scumbags were involved, but this girl isn't like that. No way."

"Are you sure? I told you what my eyes are thinking and what my stomach feels. She's hiding from someone and that someone is letting her know that they know where she is. If I were you, I might suggest that she get help or keep moving, but you and I know—" he raised his finger for emphasis, "that if it's the people we both know, there really is no place to hide. And there's another thing I need to tell you."

Gennaro shrugged his question.

"You know that old spy under her apartment, the one who called it in? She said that she saw two men leaving the building. She couldn't give much of a description because they had their backs turned to her, and they parked in a spot with no street lamp. All I've got is 'two huge thugs in dark shirts,' which isn't much to go on, but you know what? The old bat that said she couldn't see anything, so she says, managed to write down the license plate number. Y'know, I can't figure these old women out. They act blind and the next you know you find out that they know the answer to a crossword clue five people down from them on the subway and it was for a puzzle they'd seen last week. But I digress: a green Fiat."

"Rented?"

"That was hard, wasn't it? The car was rented, out of Fiumicino. That's a real help, I know. Unless our old friends down south are getting creative for names, I have the name for one American who rented the little green shit box with tinted glasses. We can assume his buddy is also an American."

"Americans?"

"That's right, pardner," Farrugia replied, imitating a cowboy out of one of Gennaro's old films. "They're Americans. I'll run the names through Interpol and the usual databases later, but I've got to imagine that two Americans in that little car must've been very uncomfortable. From what the Signora said these two are tall, so they must've had their knees up around their ears. That must've made for a hell of a sight."

"I guess it isn't mafia, then."

"Let's not assume anything. Here's my card. My mobile is on the back. None of the damned morons I work with here has that number. I learned a new American word that I like to use for them; 'assclown'. English surprises me now and then. You take that card. You can count the fingers on one hand the people who have that number."

Gennaro took the card, put it in his pocket, and joked. "I'd be afraid to ask which finger."

Farrugia had started to walk away.

"Isidò . . ."

The other man stopped, turned back and came closer to hear him.

"Isidò, you know I appreciated your help back then. I know we fell out of touch, but any progress, on your end, finding, you know, Lucia's . . ."

Farrugia shook his head. "No, old friend, no progress. But that doesn't mean I've given up. You know that there are some things in life that leave sand in your heart, and that was one of them. Before I depart this life for the next I'll either have the bastards, or one gigantic pearl."

Gennaro appreciated the mixed metaphor. It didn't matter that it was wrong, it just mattered that someone else understood.

16

"Thank you for having me," Bianca said. "It's temporary, I promise."

"Sure you're all right? You don't seem the least stirred by what happened."

Bianca resisted the urge to tell Dante that he should have said 'shaken up,' but 'stirred' could also work. She pointed to the terrace.

"What?" he said.

She walked over and gently pushed him outdoors.

"I don't understand you, Bianca, what's with—"

"Your place is bugged—at least the kitchen is and I have no doubt the rest of the place is also."

"Okay," he said, "I can understand your being upset with what just happened, but let's stay calm about the matter. I'll find out what Alessandro has to say when I call him later. He went over to your place to see what happened. Why the hell am I whispering?"

Bianca shut her eyes and tapped her forehead. "Ugh, how stupid. If Alessandro is there somebody'll get his picture."

Dante held her at the shoulders. "You really need to get a grip on yourself. Listen to yourself. You sound like one of those government conspiracy cases you hear about in America."

"Dante, America is where I come from, and I've been involved in investigations like this. Some nondescript person sits in a car, or across the street somewhere, and nonchalantly snaps photos without anyone ever noticing. Then someone else will take those pictures, isolate every single person in the frame, and run them through facial recognition software for licenses, passports, you name it. And then they'll try to see if there's an association between any person they identify with me."

"Bianca, listen to yourself. Calm down."

"Fine. Come with me and keep your mouth shut."

And with that she grabbed his hand and pulled him to the kitchen and carefully disassembled the switch plate as Gennaro had done that night. She pointed to the bug. He had the grace to look more curious and astonished than defeated. They returned outside.

If Dante was furious—and she certainly would be—he was disciplined about showing it. He ran both of his hands up the sides of his head, trying to think. She stood there awaiting his response.

He extended his arm, indicating the kitchen. "What the fuck was that?"

"A bug."

"I know it's a bug." He started pacing in small steps, back and forth. "Christ, what the hell is going on!"

"Do I need to tell you to calm down now?"

"If that's there—" he pointed again to the kitchen through the closed glass sliding door, "it's like roaches, right? You find one; then there have to be others. Somebody is listening. Were they listening when you explained everything upstairs?"

She paused until he stopped pacing. "I combed through the room and most of your place. Yes, there are others, but not in your bedroom."

Dante had a stunned look. "You what? I don't believe what I'm hearing. You searched—and there are others?"

She nodded.

"There are others but none in my bedroom. Why not there?"

She shrugged but he was working into a major tantrum and wasn't really communicating any more.

"You know I'm trying to overlook the fact you rummaged through my things, don't you?"

She stood there placid and still. "You need to calm down. You think that whoever planted them didn't go through everything before I did? As for why they didn't put some in the bedroom, don't you think they watched you for a while before they seeded the place? They had to know your schedule and your habits before they came in."

He was dumfounded. "Are you listening to yourself? Worse yet—I'm beginning to believe you."

Bianca stepped closer to him. "I'm sorry this upsets you. I'm really sorry that I've involved you in my past life, but that's how they work. The bedroom is probably not bugged because they—I don't know—watched and saw that you don't bring women home, and maybe they have no intention of hearing you snore."

"I don't snore. And whether I bring someone home or not is none of anyone's business! What about your place? Is it bugged?"

Bianca didn't want to tell him that he did snore, so she settled on his other comment. "You're right, it's none of my business, and last I checked: no, it wasn't bugged."

He stood there and glared. "You know what pisses me off? After hearing your story about how all upset you were when you came home that day and found someone had gone through your place, what did you do? You got angry. But, despite it, you didn't seem to have a problem, no crisis of conscience apparently, to go on an expedition in my private place. That's right, you just go right ahead with your little electronic field trip."

She crossed her arms. "You needed to recover and you were in no condition."

Dante's hands got expressive. It looked as if he was washing them by the way he was turning them over. Finally he put them up to his lips prayer-like. "What happens now? I assume that this is your group of people, Rendition, right? Give them what they want. They want the money then give them the money. You can't go to the authorities because they are the authorities, right? Go and figure out how to make peace with them. There has to be a way to save face; some way to discuss the matter over a table."

"Are you insane? You think I can just pick up the phone and say, 'Hey, guys, my bad, leaking all that information you killed someone to cover up. Let's kiss and make up. How's one pm tomorrow for lunch?' Think, Dante. This is the government; it's no different and no better than any of those multinational corporations."

Dante faced her. "Bianca, if that's true, don't you think that if they really wanted you dead they would've found a way to put you in a landfill somewhere?"

"It's only been two years, Dante. Maybe I've finally run out of time and identities. You can't run forever, you know."

Dante was wagging his finger emphatically. "No. No. No. Listen to me. You're smart but not that smart. I live in a country, remember, with three thousand years of history where people have revenge in their bloodstream. Trust me, somebody wants you dead, they'll make sure it happens." He started counting out on his fingers. "You know about Borsellino and Falcone. That's two. There's Pinelli; there's, uh, Carlo Giuliani, Moro, and Pasolini. And let's not forget our glorious parade of murderous emperors and family psychopaths."

"Okay, I get your point, Dante. But, you know, is it possible we're looking at this all wrong?"

"What do you mean?

"You say that if my government wanted me dead I'd just disappear, like that." She snapped her fingers for effect. "Perfect. But my place wasn't bugged. Yours was."

Dante didn't say a word at first then asked, "Your point?"

She put her hands on her hips. "Maybe all this recent shit has to do with your freaking lost eagle, Moretti, and Bevilacqua. Think of that? What about your spelunking friends? You said they were 'competitive types'— your description for them, not mine. Any of them electrical engineers?"

"We are speleologists, not spelunkers. Spelunkers explore caves. No, they're competitive, I'll give you that, but they wouldn't resort to bugging my place. Plus how would they know about you to go and ransack your place?"

"One of them could've seen us go down that day you showed me the mosaic. You said they were territorial, and you pulled your fictitious eagle out of someone else's territory. Who knows? I don't care if it's caves or sewers—no difference to me. All I'm asking is, is there a chance all this could be tied to the lost eagle?"

Dante sat down. She joined him at the table. The sun brushed overhead and a cool breeze swept across the terrace.

"I don't know." He thought for a second. "What about those internet messages you were getting?"

"What about them?"

"Talk to him—her—them. Find out what the person wants. They said they wanted your help and let's face it—they warned you that 'they' knew where you were. It turns out they were right."

Bianca had a blank face. "You're kidding, right? Uh, 'Hello, what do you want? Oh, by the way, did you bug my friend's place and do something to my apartment?' Get real, Dante. Whoever that person is, they're the last person I want to speak with right now. This isn't online dating where you can block someone from contacting you or a social network where you can control who sees you and who doesn't."

Dante shrugged. "I'd rather rule them out instead of fighting a two-front war."

"They're all or nothing. Rendition doesn't go halfsies, remember?" His face indicated that he hadn't understood so she said: "They don't do things half-ass, Dante. Somebody went through my place back then, and I have no doubt that they were also behind Strand's disappearance."

Dante's shrug was beginning to seem like his trademark. "You don't know that for certain. Strand disappeared: no body, no crime, right?"

She gave him a sideways look. "You're an idiot if you believe that."

"We have to make a decision and go with it in order to figure what the hell is going on. That's all that I'm saying. It's your choice, but I would think it through about having some kind of communication with this mysterious IM person. Be reserved and you . . ." He was snapping his fingers, in search of the phrase, "you feel them out, as you say. Anyway, I've got to go to work. There's food in the fridge and you're already familiar with the place, so I'm sure you can figure out the rest, if you haven't already."

Bianca wasn't about to apologize again. She let Dante get up from the chair, waited, and then said to him before he opened the glass sliding door, "I want to review my latest research on Bevilacqua with you, Alessandro, and Gennaro. Again, I'm sorry about everything. I didn't mean to call you an idiot. We just need to be careful about what we discuss when we're inside."

"Understood. I'll let them know. I need to get going."

Gennaro saw Alessandro on the phone when he came into the office and asked, "Dante?"

Alessandro nodded after he had hung up. "He's fine. He said that we should all meet to discuss some research."

"How's Bianca?"

"Dante said that she said that she was fine."

Gennaro heard the answer, stood there, and looked at Alessandro.

"What is it, Boss?" Alessandro said.

"Oh, nothing. Just, when a woman says 'I'm fine,' you know that you, the situation, or both of you, are fucked."

17

Alessandro peered cautiously around the edge of Gennaro's doorframe. The two pairs of eyes met and observed each other without saying a word.

"I haven't got all day, Alessandro!" said Gennaro. He was in a reasonable mood, which was unusual since he had been sleeping so little, with the green Fiat, the Farrugia information, and the two Americans on his mind. But the day was young.

"Since we're having a working lunch or early dinner we thought you should pick the place." Alessandro had his small spiral notebook out and flipped through a few pages. "Bir & Fud in Trastevere has excellent pizza with a board for tasting beers. Trattoria Monti on Via San Vito has, I hear, a tortolloni with runny egg yolk, and one of the secretaries who went with her boyfriend, an American, said it was delicious—that it was 'to die for,' which is apparently a good thing in American. But if you feel adventurous and want to go over to the Testaccio neighborhood, we can try Perilli: they're strong on roasts and have quite a few nice pasta dishes, but I'm a little queasy about *pagliata*." His pencil made its trip down the page. "Wine is good at Perilli and since you like fish, Boss, you might like the fillet of ricciolo at Settembrini. Urbana 47 is also good, but if your heart is set on seafood I say we do La Gensola."

Gennaro, feeling his stomach both conflicted and persuaded, sat behind the desk looking sad at Alessandro. A part of him wanted to strangle him for his Anglicisms: 'to die for' and 'your heart is set on,' as if the man spent his leisure time watching sitcoms for American teenagers and undeveloped adults.

"Alessandro," he said, "I have two questions for you."

"Sure, Boss, what do want to know?" Alessandro said, flipping closed his spiral notebook like a gunfighter returning his pistol to his side.

Gennaro sat back in his chair of uncomfortable leather. "First: where did you learn your English? Second: why do I get to choose where we eat?"

"Like Dante, I learned it in school, but only well enough to have mixed success when the tourist season came and I could practice on the American girls." Alessandro's eyes betrayed a recollection of the hornier days of his hormones that he now cataloged as nostalgia. Gennaro knew the look. "Both Dante and I read a lot of English, but he reads more than me. I watch TV and try to imitate American English. He listens to the radio more than TV, because he likes the English pronunciation on BBC Worldwide and he doesn't like American sitcoms. Me? I tried the radio, but mostly I just try not to put vowels on the end of my English words that end with a consonant, or hold my double consonants for three beats. And I still don't, after all these years, understand what the Americans or British mean when they say that they have a 'schwa sound' and we don't."

Gennaro admired the struggle. "I doubt Americans know what the hell a 'schwa sound' is, but both you and Dante speak well. I learned my English from years of making mistakes, but I had some in school and then I took lessons with a tutor in the San Gregorio Armeno area. I can tell you stories of Christmas-time in that area: the fish stalls in Porta Nolana and the holiday fireworks. Did I ever tell you that I met my wife during the holiday fireworks? I found out that she went to the same tutor because she wanted to learn English for customers who came into her shop for a small mend and repair."

"I didn't know that. That's quite romantic, Boss. Uh, you decide where we're going?"

"Thinking of Naples makes me think of *capitone*, so I think I'm in the mood for seafood. Let's go with La Gensola. I heard they have a nice *collatura* from Campania."

"Collatura?"

Gennaro could only stare. How could someone who acted as his own private Zagat not know this? "Collatura . . . *la collatura di alici* . . . strong anchovy sauce." He wondered whether he should explain to Alessandro the many ways Neapolitans make yellow eel, their *capitone*.

"Right, Boss." Alessandro started out the door, but said before leaving, "Oh, your second question as to why we're asking you to pick the place?"

Gennaro had started to read a memo when he looked up. He had forgotten the second question.

"Because you're paying, Boss," said Alessandro.

Gennaro was too amused to be angry. "Of course. I always pay one way or the other."

Osteria de Gensola was an out of the way place in the Trastevere neighborhood. It was unassuming, letting the food do the talking; a place to dine in ambience that doesn't intrude itself. The main room was rich with calming wood and tan tablecloths, with one table dedicated solely to desserts.

Bianca arrived with Dante just moments after Alessandro and Gennaro had taken a table. Dante pulled out her chair for her. Gennaro confessed that he was excited about the food since the blackboard out front and the slim, printed menu inside detailed specials from Campania and Sicily that he hadn't seen in most restaurants in Rome. He was thinking of changing his mind about seafood for his meal.

Gennaro insisted that he be entrusted with ordering for the group and joked that he should have the privilege since he was footing the bill—expensing the meal, of course, to Accounting, who he said were little birds with no balls, which meant they couldn't fly very high or far but compensated for it by making loud noises whenever they saw the opportunity. He clucked his arms and chirped 'cheap, cheap, cheap.'

For the appetizer he ordered three stuffed zucchini blossoms, baked figs, sliced and stuffed with Gorgonzola cheese, drizzled over with a special anniversary issue of Giusti family balsamic vinegar, and a dish of fried stuffed olives. For the *secondi piatti*, he requested two impressive dishes: the beef with *eggplant stracciato*, which was an indescribable blend of beef cut in strips with shredded eggplant, and a childhood favorite of his, *Coniglio alla Ischitana* or Rabbit, Island Style: the island being Ischia, not Capri.

The waiter, when he had heard Gennaro speak the dialect, was eager for all of them to sample a small taste of the house *vermicelli con le vongole* or vermicelli with clams, indicating that the clams had just been delivered. They all agreed to eat more slowly than usual as they discussed the research and reserve places in their stomach for slices of a chocolate Caprese cake.

Between dishes the expected questions were asked. 'Bianca, are you all right?' 'Do you need to replace anything?' 'If you need anything, please don't be afraid to ask.' 'How do you like Dante's place?' And the expected advice was given. 'It's just temporary' and 'Things happen, but it's not the end of the world.'

Before dessert arrived, there were the rounds of after-dinner drinks on the table. Bianca placed her laptop next to her small glass of Fern-et-Branca, each nearly camouflaging the other with blackness. While Dante started on his drink, an Averna, Alessandro held his order in his hand, rotating a snifter of Grand Marnier while Gennaro sat there patiently with his yellow herb-infused Strega, which, like all things Sicilian, was an acquired taste.

"Shall we start?" she said.

Alessandro shifted in his seat. "You're giving the presentation?"

Bianca's head turned to the side to look at Dante, who sat up like a called-upon pupil. "Need to make a confession. While I did the presentation last time, it was Bianca's work. I presented it at the time so not to involve her, but in light of what has happened recently, I think it's safe to say she's involved. How they found out about her I don't know, but Bianca helped us last time and she's helping us again. As you've already surmised: she is an outstanding analyst."

Alessandro accepted the explanation. Gennaro watched and sipped. Dante sat back and said nothing more.

Opening up the clamshell screen and pivoting the laptop so Gennaro and Alessandro could see it also compelled her and Dante to modify their seating slightly so everyone at the table could examine the documents that she wished to review.

"I need to preface the analysis on Lorenzo Bevilacqua with a quick exposition on the import-export business model," Bianca said, "because how Lorenzo exploits it is crucial. As you know from your own work there are two variants of the import-export model. Variant one: businessperson wants to do business abroad but lacks the overhead so he enters into a contract with a management-services company to ship products abroad. Let us assume, for now, that this businessperson has marketing and relationships abroad. The management-services company is there strictly to minimize overhead—combine small shipments from several companies, get bulk rates, streamline the customs process, whatever. Variant two? Type two is a company with money, but no customers abroad. This company hires out a trading company to find buyers for their products. And as you would expect, there are finder's fees for the trading company. That's two types of import-export models in a nutshell. Type one, someone takes care of Customs and ships to customers. Type two finds customers."

"But we know that there's a third way, which is intentionally complicated because it involves established importers and exporters who hire out independent contractors, who are themselves exporters, to find them more trading partners. The independent contractors can, themselves, hire out more independent contractors, so you can see that in this last variation on a theme we have a web of backroom deals and complicated paper trails for keeping track of what went where and to whom."

"We've seen those kind of operations in our work," Alessandro said, "any one of these independent contractors, when the fog clears, could turn out to be a shell company, a fictitious, here-today, gone-tomorrow company. Endless paperwork."

"Or it could be traced to an individual, who is legally untouchable because the blame is somewhere downstream," added Dante.

Gennaro sipped, enjoying the sight of his employees actually being smart. It made for a pleasant change. Dante continued holding his hand to his chin, imitating Rodin.

"With that quick review in mind," she said, "we need to refresh our memory about the ways smuggling is covered up. We first need to look at the basics of the legalities in place to prevent smuggling. I want to use an example. Let's talk about diamonds. Once upon a time, the G8 countries were asked to figure out ways of preventing terrorists from using diamonds to finance their operations. I won't review how those organizations were using diamonds because that has been done to death. What is important is to understand the proposed solution the G8 countries created."

She clicked on a file to show them a formal-looking certificate. "This is a Kimberly certificate: an internationally recognized and agreed-upon certificate which says a diamond is conflict-free. In popular parlance, the diamond is not a 'blood diamond.' Theoretically speaking, all diamonds on the world market should have a KP certificate to prove they're clean. We know that is not the reality. Same goes for artwork and antiquities. There is no established standard for provenance. Think of families trying to collect artwork the Nazis stole."

Bianca closed out the certificate and kept talking as she moved the mouse around the screen.

"Rhetorical question, gentlemen: What does all this have to do with Lorenzo Bevilacqua, his companies—note the plural—his dubious connections to other American companies and contractors, and his potential interest in Roman antiquities?"

Nobody said a word as Bianca looked around. The waiter served the chocolate Caprese cake.

"Museums have to compete with each other," Bianca said. "We can think of them as small businesses or large companies with certain tax privileges. Type two: import-export model. Instead of executives we have academics, curators, and diplomats trying to launch exhibitions and capture public monies and government grants and loans. Politicians hover around to make what they can out of exhibits as PR events. Museums are also customers looking for new inventory to make money. Inverse of type one. It's a very competitive business when your inventory is one-of-a-kind. I know that I haven't gotten there yet with looting. It's true that many museums have tried to stem the tide of archaeological looting, but let us look at the evidence.

"I mentioned the KP certificate. Museums have tried something similar. In 1970, in Paris, various museum-sponsored delegates drafted the UNESCO Convention on the Means of Prohibiting and Preventing the Illicit Import, Export, and Transfer of Ownership of Cultural Property. Isn't that a nice long title for a conference paper? I won't bother to explicate what that entailed, but suffice it to say that the idea was to establish, for the very first time, a means of protecting cultural artifacts and sanctioning offenders. The problem? The Convention meant nothing until a country ratified its proposals as legislation. Case in point, the United States, always quick on its feet, implemented legislation in 1983. Thirteen years late is better than never, I guess.

"In those subsequent thirteen years Guatemala was stripped nearly clean, as was Peru, as was southern Italy—almost, until southern Italy created the Sicilian Art Police, the *Commando Carabinieri Tutela Patrimonio Culturale*, who use satellite imagery and surveillance. It is my understanding that museums simply conceded the artifacts in question if the Art Police showed up on their doorstep—they instill that much fear. The Sicilians apparently learned how to deal with museums and looters, particularly after the 1980 scandal over Sicilian silver from Morgantina.

"Today, the counter-argument from the museum is to say to the deprived country that they are better equipped to maintain the looted artifact. It's a nice way of saying possession is nine-tenths of the law. Case in point is the Elgin Marbles, but I can also tell you that that argument is still being used. Another example?" She clicked open a news article. "The Nigerian government tried unsuccessfully to reclaim a sixteenth-century West African bronze plaque taken by the British military in 1933, so you can see that whether it's 1812, 1933, or today, relics are a viable commodity on the world market with a very gray cloud over how museums can safely and legitimately acquire them and how governments can safeguard their own treasures.

"One of the suggested solutions to looting these days is to return to the old practice of partage, where objects from archaeological digs are divided between the country of origin's national museum and the archaeologist's home institution. I don't need to mention that Italy has always been one of the richest countries for archaeology, but now that the Roman underground is facing slow, but unorganized excavation, with no standard or oversight in documentation, who is not to say that we have the perfect stage for opening Pandora's Box?"

"Be fair," Dante said. "The Beni Culturali is actively involved in monitoring discoveries, and I can tell you that the Roma Underground has been nothing but honorable. Not to mention we have Perceval, the cooperative of archaeology graduate students. I know many people in these organizations and they are all decent and dedicated individuals."

"But who is policing them?" Gennaro asked.

"Let's not point fingers," Alessandro said. "Gennaro is right though—all it takes is one crooked person in the Culturali, one in Roma Underground, or even a graduate student with mounting student debt, to make a looting scheme work. I'm sure there are regulations in place we don't know about, and let's assume there is honor. But let's not lose sight of the fact that we have a suspect, Lorenzo Bevilacqua, and either we prove or disprove his involvement, or move on."

Gennaro raised his glass to Alessandro's cool head, which he felt he kept sharp like his pencils.

"Here is how I think Bevilacqua is doing it." Bianca pulled up scans of financial documents. Many of them were unintelligible, with blue, bruising stamps on the pages, illegible initials and graphite smudges, but official looking nonetheless. These documents were in the background. In the foreground she clicked open very clean, formal and pristine documents.

"Wow, that's a world of difference," Dante observed.

"Let's start at the top level," she said. "As you can see, these documents are immaculate. Why? These are the tax documents filed with the IRS and every one of these files—" she moved the mouse around the screen, "represents individuals, or small businesses, or larger companies associated with Bevilacqua. They could be trading partners, independent contractors . . . you get the idea. They all know Bevilacqua. All these files are claims for tax deductions for artifacts donated to a museum."

"Hold on," Dante said. "You're telling me that all these people know Bevilacqua and they are getting tax benefits for donating antiquities to museums? I presume all the museums are in the United States? Then why don't the authorities just audit these individuals and companies? And how does Bevilacqua make money from this?"

Bianca enlarged one of the tax files so they could see the larger dollar amount an individual put down for a deduction.

"It's not so cut-and-dry. US tax law does not require the filer, whether an individual or a company, to state how they obtained the artifact. The museum, which bears the responsibility of assessing the value of the artifact, provides the receipt that the filer will use as the basis of the claim for a deduction. As long as the filer has that receipt from the museum, he or she is in the clear. Until we have hard laws in place to force taxpayer-funded museums to reveal the provenance of their acquisitions there is no recourse; and even then, looters will move to the private market of non-funded museums."

"So," Gennaro said, "Bevilacqua and his web of associates and companies procure artifacts for the museum and they in turn give him a kickback on the tax benefit?"

"That's my thinking, but there's more," she said.

"I can see money being made from creating paperwork to accompany an artifact, especially if you have friends in Customs," said Alessandro.

"And if you have a cultural organization like the *Amici* with Bevilacqua out front and the Church and Ancona in back," said Dante.

"Which brings me to Ancona," she said, eyes on her keyboard.

Bianca double-clicked an image and enlarged it. It showed an amphora, about 30cm high, with much of the decorative paint intact.

"This is an amphora, of course, and that—" the arrow pointed to a dark stain at the top, "is resin, which makes the amphora extremely valuable, because it is rare to find jars with it intact; and these initials here," she showed with the mouse arrow, "tie the amphora to a famous potter who lived in Augustus' reign. This amphora, once discovered, was duly registered, put into a plastic bag, into a box, and sent off to a warehouse, owned by this company," she enlarged one of the many documents and highlighted a company name. "This company turns out to be a trading partner with Bevilacqua. Now, we have this other photo here on the right. The photo is from an exhibit on Imperial Roman pottery in a museum in the United States. Notice anything?"

There, in the middle, was the identical amphora, right down to the resin.

"The amphora on the right is identical to the one on the left."

"You don't know that for certain," said Dante. "I'll admit that these two jars look very similar and the resin makes them striking but none of us here are experts."

"I concede your point, but I want to point out another coincidence," she said.

"The paperwork that accompanied the amphora to the United States was filled out by an appraiser. His interest is in Etruscan and Roman antiquities. I have several photographs of the appraiser sitting with Bevilacqua at several charity fund-raisers for numerous art galleries and several museums."

Gennaro lifted his hand. "Bianca, I've given testimony in numerous anti-Mafia trials where the court stupidly had me sitting two seats down from known Mafiosi. Just because I appeared next to them in a picture or on television doesn't mean I consort with them."

"Good point, Gennaro. But the business that donated the amphora to a US museum has been very busy in Rome and all over Italy in the last five years. I did some more digging and discovered that the business owner is an independent contractor to at least five of Bevilacqua's companies and associates."

"So what?" Alessandro said. "It might just mean that the man is good at what he does."

Bianca had a smile waiting for him. "Ah, but the tax receipt for the amphora shows who did the appraisal. Want to guess?"

Alessandro, seeming eager, said, "Let me guess: another associate of Bevilacqua?"

"More than that. It turns out that the man is Alan Ancona."

Now Gennaro was getting truly interested. "The one with the museum e-mail address?"

Bianca was wearing a huge grin. "With the museum that was cited for improprieties with its Greek and Roman art collection. The Italian courts took that museum to task over an artifact from Morgantina."

"Silver?" said Genanro.

Bianca said, "No, a statue of Aphrodite. The earlier Morgantina scandal, over the silver, was in 1980. The museum, as a result of this scandal, agreed that they would not accept either donations or acquisitions without paperwork if the artifact had a pedigree prior to 1995."

"Then," Alessandro said, "if this amphora is slated for an exhibit, it must have documentation. Correct?"

"That's the problem. The museum should have had to show documentation, but that brings up a peculiar coincidence. The amphora on the right is in the US, but the amphora on the left should be, according to Culturali paperwork, here in Rome."

"In a Bevilacqua warehouse. That should be easy enough to prove," Alessandro said.

Dante shook his head. "By the time we put the request to pull it from the warehouse, the damn thing could show up back on the shelf, like it never disappeared, if it is ever returned. The museums have the artifact in their possession."

"It matters and doesn't matter," Gennaro said. "I think Bianca has shown us that we have our middleman on the hook. We need to talk to Moretti. Alessandro, please get the car and drive Bianca back to Dante's place. Thank you, Bianca. Dante, I want you to take a trip with me."

"Me?" Dante said, surprised.

The waiter handed the bill to Gennaro.

"Of course," Gennaro said, hand in pocket. Again.

18

Alessandro dropped her off at Dante's place and offered to walk her to the door. But she jingled her copy of the keys for the place as her answer before she closed the car door. Alessandro, she realized, was just being his sweet self and his chivalry was sincere, but she was tired from talking so much.

Giving her presentations had tired her but she felt good about the analysis she had given Alessandro, Dante and Gennaro. She was a firm subscriber to Occam's scribble when it came to analysis: *'entia non sunt multiplicanda praeter necessitate,'* or, 'entities must not be multiplied beyond necessity,' or better, as Aquinas himself said, more or less succinctly, in the vernacular, 'keep it simple, stupid.' But this business with Bevilacqua, even simplified as far as necessity would allow, was a convoluted mess.

She peeled off the laptop strap and poured herself a glass of water. She plugged the battery into the adapter for a fast recharge then debated whether she wanted to do some work out on the terrace or not. Interesting that she thought of it as work. It'd been a long time since she had done anything of an analytical nature and this "Bevilacqua Affair," as she called the assignment on the internal memo in her mind, was exercising those skills again. She found it amusing how old, abandoned habits could resurface with such enthusiasm.

In her early days with Rendition she had her General Accounting job by day and her covert assignments from Rendition at night. The money was fantastic and the assignment, unless otherwise specified, had no due date. She felt like a free-lance assassin where she hunted down facts. But rather than have the attitude of 'I've got to nail the bastard,' she felt that she had that dispassionate, almost lawyer-like or clinical zeal that doctors possess, of letting data speak for itself and letting the mind impute the conclusion.

Bianca had a twinge of self-doubt though: there was a small, faint whisper of 'Let's burn the bastard Bevilacqua at the stake.' But she resolved herself to accept that the sensation was really a form of jealousy. She admitted that she admired his resourceful nature. As far as she knew, his profits were from the worlds of art—a victimless crime, at least at the semantic level. True, the Italian cultural patrimony was being shipped overseas, but how many people knew a thing about Etruscan art, or had heard about processional crosses and King Lalibel, who had built the eleven rock churches in the Lasta Mountains, or knew of the influence the Venetian artist Nicolò Brancaleone had on Ethiopian artists.

The water was refreshing. She decided that she would engage this project. Let the facts say what they would and let others decide Bevilacqua's fate.

Outside, she pulled the table and chair in closer so she would have her back to the wall and nobody could read the screen. Her battery light was blinking green. She set up her workspace and, after plugging in all the USB ports, she unhinged the screen and booted the machine up. She thought of the day when Windows would turn on instantly instead of doing mysterious internal gyrations like an antique television set. She checked her Wi-Fi and found a signal amongst Dante's neighbors to hitch on for Internet access.

Pondering Dante's earlier suggestion to string along the mysterious IM chatterer, she enabled the IM, which she had disabled along with her networking capability earlier, to avert interruptions at the meeting.

Older pleas for assistance popped up with their dates and times. If anything, this chatterer was persistent. Bianca could see that the person was online. She resurrected her own avatar and stared at the mystery chatterer's avatar.

Bianca smiled with admiration. The faceless female head for an avatar had changed. At first sight she thought that the chatterer's avatar was a rip-off from mythology, or that she was dealing with one of those tedious Dungeons & Dragons dolts she despised, who hadn't moved on to either the Renaissance Faire crowd or to the SciFi conventions, or become one of those self-declared New Age religion devotees that made up contradictory belief systems while humming and drumming. Bianca despised those forms of identification, but this person intrigued her; the avatar intrigued her.

The avatar, with its nice color contrast, looked as if it said 'Loki.' But if you looked carefully the avatar really said 10ki. The puns lay in the distinction. Loki, in Norse mythology, was the god of multiplicity and duplicity, a sovereign of air or fire, taking animal forms since he was a shape shifter; and he was a master prankster. 10k, on the other hand, is a federal reporting form for a public company's performance, not to be confused with annual reports mutual-fund members receive in the mail and throw out after failed attempts at reading the execrable prose. The small case *i* that this virtual friend added to 10k, Bianca thought, must be her way of declaiming 'I am 10k,' which her former self, Alabaster Black, would recognize. It meant that, if this person worked for Rendition, she specialized in suspect public companies.

She stared at the empty dialog box and felt all of Hamlet's indecisiveness, all of Prufrock's cowardice. Should she or shouldn't she?

If she did, how would she play this game of Question and Answer? It didn't help that the closing lines of an Eliot poem were in her head, because a teacher had made her memorize it—it wasn't until she had come to Italy that she realized that Eliot had cribbed from the *Inferno*. The question is whether the flame would stay still or not.

Bianca decided that it was time for Alabaster Black to return, using Dante as her guide: observe, play along, and then decide.

She typed into the empty white space. "Why do you think I can help?"

After a pause, the windowpane below the dialog space informed her that the other person in the chat was typing out her reply. 10ki must have hit the return key because the response said, "B cuz u r AB."

Bianca—now Alabaster—stared at the chat shorthand and typed, "U seem 2 think so. Y?"

10ki typed back, "Not 100%. Need 2 know 4 certain . . . up 4 me giving u a test?"

Alabaster thought that had taken balls: ask me for help, tell me I'm in danger, but ask me to prove myself to you.

She typed quickly: "?" It was a nice spiteful ambiguity.

More typing ensued. "U r in danger, as am I."

"W/ whom?"

"R"

Alabaster looked at the single letter. She didn't like the ambiguity coming back at her, though she felt confident that this was simple cat-n-mouse talk and that they both knew the meaning.

She felt adolescent about it, but she typed back to 10ki: "R or are?"

10ki replied again, but this time with a larger R in bold red font, which brought the conversation momentarily to a halt.

Alabaster made the first move and typed, "U said u want 2 test. Curious."

The windowpane told her that typing was happening on the other side of the divide, wherever that was in the world. It must have been a long message even for textspeak. Then the reply appeared in the box.

"1st need 2 say y be4 I start. Reason 4 test is I must know u r not R."

She took that long to type that? But then Alabaster realized that 10ki had every right to worry about whom she was chatting with, although Alabaster deduced that 10ki had found her first, knew whom she was, before waiting for confirmation that she was who she said she was.

10ki typed, "There?"

Alabaster hit the keystroke to tell 10ki: "Si."

She saw that 10ki was typing so she waited for the reply.

"I'll throw clues only AB would figure out. Red R wld know sum but AB wld figure out rest. Game?"

"Si"

"Clue 1: HMG-CoA. Red R wld know."

"Keep throwing & tell me when dun."

"Clue 2: MP. Red R ditto."

"Throw."

"Clue 3: CoQ10. RR again."

"Throw."

"Clue 4: 1987-2001. In MP IPO init w/ CS = king. RR"

That certainly was the longest clue given. 10ki was typing again, according to the windowpane.

"Clue 5: last one."

"Throw."

"SM & EHR w/ PEP nightmare. Wasp next. AB territory now."

There was a pause and Alabaster concluded that this was it: five clues, likely clues embedded within the clues, with four of them in the working knowledge of Rendition. But the last clue was the one that would prove to 10ki that Alabaster was who she said she was and not part of some Rendition entrapment scheme.

Alabaster was starting to feel peeved about having to prove herself, while at the same time understanding the mutual mistrust, feeling that she had no answers of her own—like how 10ki claimed that 'they' knew where she was since *that* had come to pass with the apartment break-in. There was no healthy reason to conjecture what would have happened to her if she had been home.

Annoyed, irritated, and impatient at seeing the window showing no activity, Alabaster tried to find something to say in response to these clues. 10ki hadn't suggested a timeline or real-time answers. She wondered what she should say: 'I accept?' or 'When do we talk next?'

The message that popped up from 10ki sent the clichéd chill up her spine. It would have been appropriate to write: "R u there?"

Instead, 10ki wrote in Italian textspeak: "C6?" for *'ci sei?'*

Without thinking, Alabaster typed more textspeak into the untouched field: "Dm c sent," which in Italian is *'Domani ci sentiamo.'* 'We'll talk tomorrow.'

Alabaster had her clues; it was time to be Bianca again.

19

As they walked, Dante asked Gennaro, "You said you wanted to take a trip. Where to?"

"You'll see."

"Will it take long?"

"Are you in a hurry to get home?"

"No. I just thought I'd ask," Dante replied, opening the door on the passenger side of Gennaro's twenty-year-old Panda. He clicked his seat belt into place, while Gennaro put the key into the ignition, turned the engine over and put the AC on for the two of them. Then, rather than put the car into gear, Gennaro started squirming his butt back and forth into the seat as if his back needed scratching. Dante tried not to stare.

"You all right?" said Dante at last.

"I'm fine," Gennaro answered, then started pulling his shirttails up and out of his pants, loosening the top two buttons of his shirt and crumpling his collar. He took his light blazer off, squirming with some intrusion into Dante's personal space to get out of one of the sleeves.

"Here, put this jacket on the back seat for now and grab me my hat on the back seat."

"Okay. You sure you're all right?"

"I said I was fine." Gennaro took the retrieved hat, a Fedora, ruffling up his hair before donning it. "We ready now?"

"I have no idea."

Gennaro put it into gear and nosed the car into traffic.

"What's with the look?" asked Dante, noticing the drab olive fedora with the narrow brim and burgundy band. Gennaro wasn't quite the Columbo of reruns and would never pass for Alain Delon, but the hat certainly gave him character.

"I'll explain later, and besides, I like the old-time look. I'd look like an idiot like these kids today, copying the American look with jeans

Gabriel Valjan **157**

hanging off their ass. Jeans were a status symbol in my day but so was ordering piss-water American beer. By the way, straighten up your tie. I need you to look neat."

Dante pulled down the visor to have a look into the small rectangular mirror that didn't give much of a view, but enough for him to see his neck, fingers, and tie. "I don't get you."

"You don't? Let me ask you something and I'll try and keep this professional," said Gennaro, eyes on traffic, hands on wheel, but looking occasionally Dante's way. "You've known Bianca, how long now?"

"Uh, don't know, I'd say about three months."

"And you've never asked her about her personal life? Three months is sufficient time, I think, to ask some reasonable questions about friends, family, work. Right?"

Dante rested his arm on the car door. "Yeah, I guess. But come to think of it, that just never came up in conversation. I'd meet her every day at *Due Fratelli* and one thing led to another. I showed her some of the underground because that's my hobby and I might've made her a meal. What's your point?"

Gennaro skillfully cut someone off to get into the right lane for the roundabout, ignoring the car horn and expletives behind him.

"Bianca proposes this hoax—brilliant idea, I must admit. Then we just heard this detailed analysis—also brilliant—over late lunch. Doesn't any of that provoke questions? I mean, c'mon Dante, you and I know that someone doesn't just access IRS documents like that." He snapped his fingers. "Christ, I'm still waiting for an expense report to clear at the office from two months ago, and it took me an entire fiscal quarter to prove to the regional bureaucrats that my mother was dead."

The car came to a stop and another round of car horns blared at Gennaro as he negotiated, rather badly, a reverse, to angle his relic of a car to parallel-park into a tight spot. Once he had the car asphyxiated between two other vehicles, he put it into park and looked at Dante.

"Where are we?" asked Dante.

"We're where Bianca lives." He pointed to the building and the floor of her apartment.

"Oh."

"Some boyfriend you are that you don't even know where she lives. Well that definitely answers another question, if you've never been to her place. Now, start thinking." Gennaro tapped the side of his head. "Remember what daVinci told us. 'All our knowledge has its origins in perception.'"

"So what are we going to do here?"

"Up there in that building is an old lady who lives underneath Bianca. We are paying her a visit. I'll talk, you don't. Let's go."

"You have no authority. You're an inspector but not that kind of inspector," said Dante, coming around the car and into the street to cross it with Gennaro.

"Fine, I'm no inspector. Let me explain something to you from the wisdom of my years. Most people are asleep when they are walking around. They walk the same way to work every day; they order the same meal every time they go to a restaurant, order it the same way, even when time and experience have proven to them that they can trust the chef to be creative. Now, if you were to wake up and act with confidence, approach life with a different attitude, then there is a good chance you could accomplish what you want before the others drift off to their next dream or realize that you've been faking it. Of course, you could reduce all I've said to 'fake it until you make it, just don't get caught,' but that is what makes me an inspector before someone finds out I'm not an inspector. Now, let me see whether your tie is straight and that you look neat. I need you to look absolutely uptight. How do I look?"

Dante wanted to restrain his honesty. "Like you just fell out of bed."

"Excellent, just what I was aiming for. Ah, would you look at that, Dante." Gennaro pointed to a black strip next to a snub of a button for an intercom on the building's directory. "What does it say?"

"It says 'B. Nerini,'" Dante said, realizing that he finally had Bianca's last name three months later. Perhaps Gennaro had a point, and he didn't know her as well as he thought.

Gennaro examined the apartment numbering. "That means we want this apartment. It says that apartment belongs to a Camilla Cetoni. Remember, I talk and you listen."

The button produced a high-pitched warble that probably cleared dust out on the other end of the speaker floors above. A surprised but cautious voice passed over 'hullo' to the more direct "What do you want?"

Gennaro, though six floors down, doffed his hat in the presence of a lady's voice. "Signora Cetoni. I'm the uncle of your neighbor Bianca Nerini and I'm here with my nephew. We wonder whether we might have a word in private with you. I spoke with a police detective but we—the family, I mean—are very confused about this upsetting turn of events. We hope to understand the situation better if we talk to a neighbor. May we come up?"

The buzzer that let them in made the glass vibrate until the door closed and locked behind them. The ascent in the elevator started off with an abrasive steel groan that did not instill confidence, but it quickly faded away and the carriage moved with no interruptions until it arrived at the sixth floor. A small delicate chime preceded the opening of the door to a dimly lit vestibule of cold gray marble. Between the sound of the elevator bell and the funereal floor and horror-film lighting Dante felt he had gone back in time to his parochial school days and that unnatural fear of anticipating Sister Superior. Gennaro was the one to knock on the Cetoni door.

His eyes first saw the flicker of black, before his mind realized that it was Signora Cetoni hiding behind the open door. A little old lady in black—was there any other kind? The tinny voice came from behind the door and, once they were inside, it closed with the conclusive finality of the lobby door. She stepped out from behind it to present herself in all her diminutive glory of one and a half meters.

"You say you're family to my upstairs neighbor? She's a strange creature. Mostly a nocturnal one, I imagine, since I hear nothing during the day. And what I do hear is only her walking across the floor. You said you're her uncle, did you? Would you two like something to drink?"

"No thank you, Signora," said Gennaro, hat in hand, looking his rumpled best. "As you can tell, I've been beside myself. I'm her uncle and this—" He pointed to Dante, "is my nephew, her cousin by my sister. He's been so upset that he can't speak, and when he does he stammers a storm."

Dante obeyed and stood there puckered, fighting a smile. This was a side of his boss he wouldn't have guessed was there.

The elfin creature began to move to the sofa. "Imagine that. The poor boy must be close to his cousin to be struck dumb. I thought from the looks of him he was one of those detectives. They always wear crisp shirts and perfectly tied ties. Eh, what can I say? You're not police?"

"No, Signora. Look at me; do I look like the kind of liability a police force would take on? Signora Cetoni, our information is limited to a confusing report from one detective. First we get the disturbing phone call that there was a break-in but no robbery. Then instead of getting information, we felt like the police were talking to us like we were one of the accused, because this man asked me questions I couldn't understand. *She have a boyfriend? She have any enemies?* And he scandalized my poor wife when he asked if she had a girlfriend, and he was not asking about women who happened to be friends. Let me be frank with you, Signora Cetoni, we ended this conversation with the police with more questions than answers. So I ask you, for my family, if you can help us in any way. All we know is that Bianca is missing. We know she's a little strange but she's a good girl, though as her uncle I should realize that she is no longer the little girl I once knew. She's a woman in this big city now."

"Where did you say you were from?" she said as she sank into her sofa.

"Tufo. It's a quaint little place for rocks and caves in the province of Avellino," said Gennaro, using his fedora the way an actor uses a prop to dismiss the lie. "Do you know it?"

"Know it? Of course I know it. The late Dante Troisi came from that area."

Dante felt a start, hearing his first name.

"My family has some Jewish blood in it, and I come from Pitigliano," the ancient said. "That's the province of Grosseto. My family and I hid in the caves from the damn Nazis. Now, to this business of your niece, I will tell you what I told the detective who I think was the one who called you. I don't know whom you spoke with on the phone but I had the senior detective all to myself. He had one of those southern names, and a very dark man. I mean his skin was dark, not his character; but just the same, I'm babbling now."

"Anything you can remember would be most helpful," said Gennaro.

"Well, like I told him, she had odd habits with her hours. She must have money because she has the top floor rented out, yet I never see her leave to go to a job in the morning. I never saw her entertain men or have any other guests for that matter. Shame to be introverted like that at a young age. Youth is for living and all the affordable stupidities while you can pay the price. I would see her sometimes leave the building, wearing rather odd clothes. She'd be wearing one of those sweatshirts with a cover for the head."

"A hood?" Gennaro asked.

"That's what I said. A hood. I don't keep up on fashion. It wasn't a flattering look, you know, because your niece is an attractive woman. Tall, but attractive. Those heels make her an Amazon though. It seemed like she wanted to hide her beauty and avoid observation. You know we are only beautiful once and then we fade. I told the detective she walked across the floor a lot. Maybe she was a nervous type and paced. She was polite to me, though, when I saw her in the elevator, but otherwise she was very quiet, like a ghost. You'd never know she existed."

Dante was starting to think that the old lady was either senile because she repeated herself and lived in the past, or that she was deliberate in withholding information. These women in black, however, were notorious for their calculating minds. They berated and nagged husbands to the point that their husbands jumped into their graves as an escape; and then these wailing widows in black silk or taffeta would mourn the departed the remainder of their lives with such drama that they would make others think that their husbands should be canonized.

"Signora, my nephew and I thank you for your time. We're very grateful. I will try and contact this detective again to see what more he can discover for us. His name began with an 'F,' I believe . . . Farrugia, that's the name."

"Yes, that was the one."

Dante had to concentrate to cover his expression.

"Thank you again, Signora Cetoni. We best go since we plan to start driving back to Tufo this evening. We flew up to Rome and we have a car rental, you see, so it gets costly. My nephew and I will show ourselves out."

"Wait," she said in a low voice intended to draw attention. "I did forget to mention one thing."

"To us or to the detective, Signora?"

"Both. I told him that I found it odd that for the last few evenings I had noticed a Fiat parked across the street. It might not mean anything but I informed this Farrugia and even gave him the license plate number, since I saw the car so often. It was a green car with two very big men in it. They always dressed the same with white shirts, black ties, and very neat looking, but definitely very tall. Did I tell you that they were neatly dressed? This Farrugia mention any of that to you?"

"No, Signora. But, like you said, it probably has nothing to do with my niece's break-in or, God forbid, her disappearance. Detective Farrugia said something to the effect that a person is not considered missing until seventy-two hours have passed or there is suspicion of foul play; but the apartment, he said, showed no signs of foul play. So, I guess the Fiat, those men, and my niece are not connected."

Signora Cetoni wouldn't hear any of it from the way she moved quickly to the window. "I don't believe that because two men don't sit in a car day in and day out, hour after hour."

"You noticed them sitting there that long, Signora?"

"I'm an old lady. What do I do but watch old films, think about the old days, and talk to myself and to those who are long gone? What can I tell you, I get philosophical when I stare out the window. I go out once a day for a walk if my bones let me. That Farrugia—who the hell would understand him anyway, with the way he switches his 'u' and 'o' when he speaks the language. There was one thing I didn't tell him, though."

"Really?" Gennaro was rotating his hat in his fingers. He walked one complete revolution of the brim, like a secular rosary, waiting for her to answer.

"These two would get out of the Fiat now and then to stretch out their legs, I guess. As I came out one day for my walk, I caught them in the lobby. I think they wanted to get into the building but I always make sure that I close that lobby door behind me when I leave. These two were making pretend with the directory, but they didn't press any of the buttons. I thought that was suspicious. One of them smiled at me, and I, of course, returned the politeness with a smile. As I opened the front door I heard the one man say to the other the word "Alabaster".

"Alabastro?" repeated Gennaro.

"No, no. He said 'alabaster' as in *inglese*. He said it in *inglisi*."

"Thank you, Signora Cetoni," Gennaro said. "You've been very kind and gracious. My nephew and I have enjoyed your hospitality. We should go."

The Signora walked them to the door. "I'm sorry that I didn't catch your names," she said.

Gennaro, without skipping a beat, said, "Mine is Brunetto and his is Benedetto."

As the elevator descended, Dante said, "Good going, Brunetto. How did I become Benedetto the Silent?"

"I had to think quick, so I thought of your namesake. The poet Dante was a Guelph, and his nemesis was Pope Boniface the Eighth, who was born Benedetto Caetani. For me, I chose another Guelph, Brunetto Latini."

"I'm impressed you remembered your history and literature. What did you make of the old crone?"

"I'll explain as we walk, but keep in mind that she is probably watching us, which is why I told her I rented out a car in Rome. Thankfully, she won't have the resources to run the plates, but I'd rather not take chances. She's a hawk under that head of sheep's hair."

Two taxi drivers, parallel to where Gennaro had parked, were in an argument. Dante got in on his side and Gennaro sat there waiting for him and waiting for the two drivers to settle matters.

When the car engine had turned over, Gennaro said to Dante, "The Signora confirmed that the two men are Americans. They also dressed the same, like twins."

"Bianca's an American and these men are American and it seems that the two men were staked out watching her."

"Exactly, and you hit the nail on the head with your choice of words: 'staked out' because they were dressed like government types. You know the look from American movies. Now when are these idiots going to move their damn cars so we can get out of here?"

Gennaro rolled down his window, which let the oppressive heat into the car but let him and Dante listen to the two taxi drivers insulting each other. The insults were relatively pedestrian, at least for Roman taxi drivers.

The animated discussion must have wound down as both drivers were going to their doors. One let off a parting salvo. *"No te sputo perchè si te sputo te desinfetto."* "I don't spit on you, because if I did, I would disinfect you."

The other driver snapped back with *"Mortacci,"* which is the short form for *"A li mortacci tua,"* which translates roughly as "may something bad happen to the bad souls of your dead ones."

And with that, the two cabbies drove off, satisfied with their work.

20

It was a day of bad omens.

Alessandro sensed that the day was off to a bad start when the tip of his pencil had broken twice: first with a Sudoku puzzle and then when trying to copy down a phone number from a voice-mail message. Dante understood the weight of the day upon waking up that morning, aching from the oppressive heat that had been smothering the city.

Gennaro felt it as he waited in line at the new Spanish place, a newspaper in his hand. He knew that Alessandro and Dante must have seen the news.

The cadence of the city remained unchanged: car horns did their thing; the buses gasped, pigeons strutted, fluttered and flew, leaving the usual mess. Early morning shoppers had already infested the open market in Piazza Vittorio. Poseidon, over at the Piazza Navona, seemingly ignorant of the sea nymphs around him, looked pissed off and ready to stab the nearest tourist with his trident.

Gennaro could relate—not that he was at the Piazza Navona, but they had one of those turnstile racks with the typical stock postcards near where he was waiting, and there was old man Poseidon, ready with his fork. As he waited in line for his food, he unfolded the newspaper and read the headline again and muttered to himself and closed his eyes, thinking about the conversation he would have to have with Alessandro and Dante about the news.

The new Spanish place was the talk of the office. It was a small start-up affair owned by a single family who ran the entire operation from counter to grill to the waitressing of the small number of tables. They had no liquor license but that didn't stop the growing number of fans from bringing their own bottle of wine for the long lunch hour.

Gennaro saw two overweight Mafiosi, deep in conversation, sitting at one small table in the corner with their eyes on the door. He knew that they were Mafiosi because they ran all the permutations on the word 'fuck'—primarily as a verb and adjective, but occasionally as a noun, gerund, and adverb. Regardless of the expensive tailoring, the car they drove, or the other refinements they might spend their money on, Mafiosi were always identified by the way they used language.

The line crept forward and Gennaro found himself one step closer to another armpit, but one step closer to food. He was seeing the counter at last. A young religious woman—of the evangelical kind who thinks they can compete against the Vatican—was working the room, handing out invitation cards to her church. She was thin, the nervous kind, full of the convert's zeal but essentially harmless. It was looking to Gennaro like one of the Mafiosi had said something rude to her, because she scurried away from the table, that sensitive face of hers about to crack into a sob. Gennaro looked at the fat face of the creep at the table. Asshole.

At last he had his sandwich and moved sideways to the register to pay for it. As luck would have it today, the register was near the Mafiosi, who got jumpy and twitchy every few seconds when the register bell chimed. Gennaro paid, said a few encouraging words about the business in Spanish, which the young lady behind the register seemed to appreciate. The Mafiosi, perhaps having had enough of the bell, rose to go. As Gennaro tried to exit he saw that a slip of paper had fallen from their table when one of them had gotten up to leave, so he picked it up and informed the man that he had dropped the paper. Not looking down at what the paper was, Gennaro simply handed it to the hoodlum.

The man looked down at the paper and said, "Fuck you."

A fine day and excellent manners. Then Gennaro looked down to find he was handing out one of the religious invitations.

Following the two behemoths towards the door, Gennaro made his way outside to find himself stuck behind a family of tourists who decided to stop right in the middle of the pavement of all places to consult their street map. *Pater familias*, looking as if he wanted to save his pride and not admit that he was lost, was telling *mater* that he knew where they were and that they were not far off from their destination, while the two teens in tow were thumbing away at text messages, simply enduring another family memory. Gennaro, trying to get around the bulk of these tourists and circumnavigate their heft and cameras, noticed that the two Mafiosi were chatting up two long-legged model types. The women didn't interest him because in Rome, like Paris, you can find the tall waifs yearning for the catwalk who spend their youth living off of carrots or celery and cigarettes. It was the Mafiosi car that interested Gennaro. It was an orange, curb-hugging Lamborghini. He memorized the license-plate number and noted the time on his watch.

Then the time he'd just looked at registered on him. "Oh, shit," he mumbled. Even by Mediterranean standards he knew that he was late for the meeting with Alessandro and Dante.

The elevator to the office didn't help since it moved more slowly than the good in the world. The warmth of the panini held to his chest made him warmer, hungrier, and sweatier inside the stuffy elevator. Gennaro hoped to God that he retired before the damn contraption collapsed.

The doors opened. Hot as it was for July turning into August, the office felt cooler once those doors had opened. Every pore on his body breathed relief. As Gennaro started to pick up his walking pace towards his office, he could see from the corner of his eye that he was headed on a collision course with the office secretary, Silvio, who had pieces of paper in his hands. Those had to be messages.

"Not now," said Gennaro walking, his arm out to deflect Silvio like an American football halfback. The two of them collided, and Gennaro made the panini's safety the priority.

"But Boss, these are impotent messages. There's even a message from the United Stater Michael Farese. You've been trying to contact him for eons."

Poor bastard. The ESL classes were of no help to him. Silvio, hearing that English was fast becoming the language of business in the EU, decided that he would master the language. A work in progress, everyone said, when they were being kind. "These are all my messages?" said Gennaro, with the wad of papers held tight to his chest.

"You betcha. And Boss, your boss wants to talk to you. He walked down but you weren't here so I think he's gonna call you at the office."

Gennaro crumpled the wad of his papers and tried to give Silvio an understanding look. Into his office he went, where Alessandro and Dante were waiting. He apologized to them, then said, "My boss might call so don't mind me if I have to answer."

Alessandro and Dante looked at each other.

"Not now," Gennaro warned them, setting his panini down gently with respect. He threw the ball of messages into the trash.

"But Chief, c'mon, it's a tradition," Alessandro said. "You've got to allow us one joke; and don't forget to ask your boss about my expense report; it's been three months."

"And Boss, don't forget I still haven't been reimbursed for that computer course he insisted I take in February," added Dante.

"I know, I know. Don't forget I have an expense report in for 1,500 Euro. He's had that in the diamond mine for three months, too."

"Allow us one joke, please," Alessandro said.

"Fine. Alessandro, you're on. Dante'll be on next time."

Maximo Cassagio came from a military family, and it showed in his dress and how he expected the office to function. The man was both a Spartan and a Puritan. There were office memos about acceptable wear for both sexes and every year Maximo tried (unsuccessfully) to tell the men of the office what color tie to wear daily throughout the year. Nobody understood how the man could have become the senior manager, least of all Gennaro, but he accepted his position under Maximo as part of the payback from pointing out the pipeline of corruption from the south to the north.

Maximo expected timeliness in work, timeliness in analysis, timeliness in returning from the lunch hour, timely bathroom breaks; and he had no compassion for the interruptions that happen in everyday life in Rome: the phone repairman is due today after putting in a request weeks ago; the satellite-television installation is today, sometime between nine am and five pm; the kid is sick with strep, and so on. Unfortunately, the expectation of timeliness did not flow backwards from his desk down to his subordinates. The expense reports were only one example.

The man had served in the military to maintain family tradition. His family retired to Palmanova, a fortress of a town about twenty kilometers from Udine and not much more from the Slovenian border. The star-like fortifications of the city, like the Pentagon, he would tell others with pride, were visible by satellite and that the town was the last bastion against the Huns. Gennaro thought it was bullshit, but his boss would have everyone believe that Palmanova had saved western civilization.

Nobody dared question Maximo; but it didn't stop others from cracking jokes about the man. The women made comments that the man's hair was mowed so perfectly on top that an aircraft could land on his head. The men, seeing that Maximo lifted weights, said that the man must have had his suits custom-made to accommodate his sheer size. The bodybuilding physique, cartoonish large head, and freakishly vascular arms and neck spurred rumors about the use of anabolic steroids. The men in the office had nicknamed him *pinolo* or pine nuts for one notorious side effect of prolonged steroid use.

Alessandro and Dante lived for these jokes.

"You know how dim *Pinolo* is?" Alessandro said. "I could tell him that he was descended from painters and then convince the big bum that Cassagio is related to a famous painter named 'Cazzeggio,' and the poor boob will think that he's a descendant of Caravaggio."

Of course, the person hearing the joke would have to know that as a child and then as an officer, Maximo Cassagio was so coddled and isolated from the real world that he wouldn't know that *'cazzeggio'* meant 'fucking around.' Which, of course, Caravaggio was not exactly innocent of.

Dante was in tears laughing when the phone rang.

Gennaro picked up the phone. Gennaro hated himself for the implicit military response: he had stood up when he had realized that it was Pinolo's voice over the line. Pinolo, like any officer, was bypassing polite formalities. Dante and Alessandro could hear the man's voice screaming out of the receiver, but neither of them could stop laughing.

"Did you get my message, Gennaro?"

"Yes, I got the message. I was at lunch. I'm sorry I missed your call."

"Do I hear someone laughing? You have a hyena in your office? The lunch hour is for eating. I don't expect frivolity on company time. You get a paid lunch hour, you know."

"I understand. I'm sorry," said Gennaro, waving for Dante to stop laughing. He threw a pad of Post-its at Alessandro. *Damn younger generation.*

The voice on the phone was not mollified. "Look, I called about this expense report that you submitted—"

"I can explain that, sir," said Gennaro, wanting to bite his tongue for calling someone much younger than he was 'sir.'

"Don't interrupt me, Gennaro. I read what you submitted and the facts on the page should suffice without explanation, without context. You should know that as an auditor. There should be no explanations. We're talking about taxpayer-money here, you understand, and I'm accountable for this office. Now, you have here a line item for a consultant . . . let me see . . . ah, yes, here it is . . . 'B. Nerini' . . . for a pricey little lunch that also included you, Alessandro Monotti, and Dante Allegretti and—"

"Yes. I can explain."

"Don't interrupt," said Pinolo, letting a pause follow his second warning. Gennaro bit his lower lip. "Consultants are, as you know, subject to my approval. Ever since the regional office set the hourly rate for all consulting services last year it has become very expensive. The public frowns upon unnecessary expenditures. Need I remind you that consultants should be a last-resort option and only after we've exhausted our internal resources?"

Gennaro wanted to say something about Pinolo exhausting 'internal resources.'

"Why do you need this consultant? Can't your ladies' man Monotti handle it? What about Allegretti? If he has enough nerve to go exploring under the city, he should have the aptitude to do whatever this consultant does for you."

"The consultant is a computer genius. The consultation was pre-liminary for a feasibility specification on a project," said Gennaro. That sounded like convincing bullshit.

"What project?"

"I'd rather not say at the moment. It could all come to nothing, but I promise to contain costs."

"Do that."

"Oh, my staff would like an update on past expense reports, includ-ing one of my—"

"I'm very busy, but send me an e-mail and I'll look into it . . . and do yourself a favor and refresh your memory on office policy about the lunch hour."

"I will. Thank you."

He hung up the phone. "Asshole."

Both Alessandro and Dante sat on the edges of their seats. The sta-tus on their expense reports was on their faces.

"Fucked again."

As Gennaro was chastising himself for using the f-word like the two Mafiosi earlier, Alessandro threw his dull pencil and Dante sighed and leaned back into his chair.

Silvio appeared in the doorframe. "So sorry, Boss, but my brain is unemployed. There is a personal call online for you. I have him holding himself on line two."

"Thank you," said Gennaro.

He pressed the blinking cube under the number pad. "Yes?"

"Good to hear your voice. It's Farrugia. Remember me, the detec-tive?"

"Of course, I remember . . ."

"Good. I wanted to remind you that I'm a detective in case you forgot."

"Jesus, Farrugia. Why would I forget? This isn't a good time for sar-casm. My boss is trying to use my testicles for cymbals, I'm short 1,500 Euros, I'm being docked pay for taking a longer lunch than I should have and I haven't even had the pleasure of enjoying my lunch yet."

"Sarcasm? I'll remind you that I'm the detective with just one word: Cetoni."

There was a silence worse than Pinolo's pause. Farrugia had him.

"What were you thinking? I go like a donkey to do a follow-up and Cetoni hands me a license-plate number that turns out to be yours. I'd love to hear your explanation."

True sarcasm. The woman did have the eyes of an eagle.

"I can explain, Isidore."

"Please do, because you're killing me here. You want to put me six feet under? I give you information that I shouldn't have, and the next thing I hear is that you and an accomplice are playing house detectives."

"No need to be dramatic, and besides, he isn't an accomplice. His name is Dante. A work colleague."

"Me being dramatic? Gennaro, do you realize that you and your friend are interfering in a police investigation? You realize that you were impersonating this missing girl's family! What if they show up?"

"I doubt that'll happen."

"How do you know?"

"I know. Dante and I visited the old lady to see whether she'd seen something and maybe forgot to tell you. You know sometimes people feel funny talking to cops. Okay, so Dante and I fudged the facts telling her we were family members. I did all the talking and Dante played dumb and mute."

Another pause. "Did she tell you anything new?"

"Yes, I'll fill you in, but it'll have to wait."

"It'll have to wait? You're killing me. You know that, don't you? We've known each other a long time, Gennaro. Don't fuck me. I'm not exactly welcome in Rome, and there're plenty of people here that'd love to see me get transferred. All they need is an excuse. You understand?"

"I understand. I wouldn't fuck you. We've known each other too long for you to start thinking that way."

"Good. We'll meet to discuss what the old lady told you?"

"We will, Isidore. We will. Have a piece of paper?"

"Why?"

"I want to make it up to you. Got the piece of paper?"

"Yeah, I have a piece. What is it?"

"Take down this license-plate number. It's an orange Lamborghini. If you move on it you might find two gentlemen of interest driving it."

"All right. I'll see you soon, Gennaro."

"I'm buying dinner to make it up to you: just remember we're both civil servants when you pick the restaurant. Bye."

He hung up the phone and leaned back in his chair and put his hands to his eyes, as if that would allow him to recuperate.

"You see the newspaper, Boss?" Alessandro asked.

"Yeah, I saw it. This is getting out of hand. I wanted to talk about that but I forgot what I was going to say."

The newspaper that morning had run an article about an idiot who had managed to get himself down into the catacombs and extract a section of a third or fourth-century mosaic, which he had intended to sell on an online auction site. His plan for sudden riches unraveled on him when the art-robber savant got himself disoriented and walked himself into a flooded area of the tunnel underground and panicked. Hours later and freaked out by all the rats, he managed to get a signal and call for help on his cell phone. He confessed to the police as they were pulling him up and out of the hole.

"I thought you might want to know that I got a hold of Professor Moretti," Alessandro said, "and I'm meeting with him. I'm getting the impression the old boy is getting really spooked, between the media and this Ancona guy hounding him. He's looking for a sit-down to discuss strategy."

"Good," said Gennaro. "Arrange the time for an out-of-the-way place. Ancona is definitely having Moretti tailed if he wants the eagle that badly. Dante? I think we need to include your girlfriend in this meeting."

There was a pause.

"She's not my girlfriend," Dante said.

"Fine, but she's a consultant and on our payroll now. Ask her to document the time she spends researching for us. I want her to invoice Pinolo for services rendered. By law, consultants on state projects have to be paid within thirty to sixty days. At least somebody will see some compensation in all this."

Silvio showed up again. Gennaro brushed him off. "Come back when your brain is working. I'm about to eat my lunch."

Gennaro unwrapped the panini with respect. He smiled because by some miracle it was still warm, thereby avoiding the sacrilege of the microwave.

The panini wore the dark stripes of its press well: the split baguette was brushed with olive oil and dressed with fig jam; inside, it was blurred with beautiful Spanish serrano ham and manchengo cheese.

Gennaro closed his eyes in devotion, as it was the only good thing about that day.

21

Café Paradiso. Bianca waited for her cappuccino and croissant. She had arrived well before eleven, when an order for cappuccino was reasonable. Any moment after eleven in Rome, or any time in the afternoon, the order would have been met with a strange stare that said, "But why?"

As she set up her laptop, she observed, for a moment, the late morning crowd off to work: mostly handsome people walking like robots in perfect suits, briefcases in their right hand and their left engaged either with the cell phone or with a Bluetooth device in the ear, talking rapidly but not communicating. Bianca thought back to the image of Lt. Uhura from her television youth, earpiece in place, exchanging information and translating for others the unseen voices from deep space. Fiction has become reality, although, unlike in the television series, no universal translator exists. Yet.

Paradiso was the ideal for her. It was a nondescript café up off the street and recessed into a curve of masonry down an obscure alley. Its only telltale sign of existence was a green neon sign for a name. The establishment was new, which meant that it was building up its clientele. Bianca could work in peace.

The handsome waiter set down her order. His girlfriend was sitting not far away, keeping an eye on her. The young girl had seen how her boyfriend had once eyed Bianca so she decided always to take her rather prolonged break there, should Bianca stay to take a seat. The last time, the threatened girl had sat down. She had pretended that time to be reading one of the popular books from America, eyes peering up and over the ledge of her propped-up hardback. This time the young girl was reading a European author.

Bianca was not one to keep track of bestseller lists, but she knew whether someone, like this insecure girl, was reading American or European authors. If the American author had his or her picture on the back of the book, it was usually a *GQ* or *Vogue* model-quality picture, whereas the European author was often photographed almost casually, as if captured in a spontaneous moment, like in a chair smoking a cigarette. Even if the author picture was on the inside jacket, Bianca could usually tell whether a book was American or European. American cover art of the author was always serious, often oddly good-looking, very accomplished and beyond-reproach, as if to say to the international audience, 'Even in America we writers who hide from humanity, who behave badly in our private lives, are glamorous, too.' European publishers, on the other hand, had remarkable aesthetics that Bianca admired: choice of binding, font selection, and paper weight, they almost seem complicit with the author in saying: 'Read the work first and then look at what I look like later.'

After thanking the waiter and smiling at the seated girl across the way, she pulled out an unlined legal-sized pad for brainstorming. The five clues from her screen said:

> Clue 1: HMG-CoA. Red R wld know
> Clue 2: MP. Red R ditto
> Clue 3: CoQ10. RR again.
> Clue 4: 1987-2001. In MP IPO init w/ CS = King. RR
> Clue 5: SM & EHR w/ PEP nightmare. Wasp next. AB territory now

She took a sip of the cappuccino, flicked her tongue over her top lip to sweep in the foam, and uncapped her pen. Using a page for a blank canvas, she clustered the clues around an invisible center, where she hoped to write in the solution.

The top end of the pen tapped against her lower lip. Pen to paper she crossed out 'Red R' first because that was Rendition's symbol. She recalled that 10ki had said that Rendition would know what was being alluded to in clues one through four. It was up to her, Alabaster Black, to solve clue five to prove to 10ki that their exchange was not a Rendition trap.

Bianca was starting to feel like her old self again. She picked up the croissant and tore it in half; the flakiness of the breakfast pastry was delightful. She looked over at the girl, wondering whether she had done any of the baking. The girl's eyes had turned downward suddenly. Bianca smiled the way only Alabaster would.

So: 'HMG-CoA', 'MP', 'CoQ10', '1987-2001', 'MP' again and 'init w/ CS = king' and the entire line, 'SM & EHR w/ PEP nightmare. Wasp next.' Pulling up her search engine, she found that HMG-CoA referred to the enzyme involved in cholesterol production and that statins, a widely prescribed medication worldwide, targeted this enzyme to lower cholesterol. The benefits of statins seemed obvious: reduce cholesterol and prevent heart attacks, strokes. She pulled up and read current articles that suggested that statins, while accomplishing these objectives, also seemed to provide other preventative benefits: reducing the onset of dementia, systemic inflammation, diabetes, and some autoimmune disorders.

So Rendition was investigating a person or a company somehow involved with statins. She had no idea what 'MP' was about so she'd skip that for the moment and see what the search engine said about CoQ10, since nothing she'd read about HMG-CoA mentioned CoQ10.

She read and read: a co-enzyme, a quinone, mitochondria, energy . . . Ah. 'CoQ10 is found mostly in the heart, liver and kidney.' There was the connection. She slurped more caffeine. The heart and cholesterol, they go together she told herself. She knew that prolonged accumulation of cholesterol in the arteries caused them to harden; the heart had to work harder to pump blood in narrowing highways until the pump just gave out. Back to statins preventing heart attacks. But how was CoQ10 involved? She made a question mark next to CoQ10 on the page.

She had finished the croissant; the last of the cappuccino had left mottled rings of tan and white along the rim and at the bottom of the large cup. Next clue.

The-2001-minus-1987-equals-14 arithmetic she wrote outside the incomplete circle. 'Init' meant 'start' in computer-programmer lingo and 'IPO' was no doubt the financial term for venture-capital fundraising—the Initial Public Offering. All this was drawing a context consistent with a typical Rendition investigation. Therefore, 'MP' or 'CS' would be either the CEO of the company under investigation or the company itself.

Alabaster thought that it was time to revisit the connection between HMG-CoA and CoQ10, so she conjoined the two search strings and found the returns extremely technical: articles written by pharmacists and other scientists who wrote in English nobody can understand. Too technical, and too little time, she thought. Remember Occam. She scrolled down the page quickly to see whether she would recognize any odd phrases or repeat patterns. She saw a slew of articles from the statin skeptics about the dangers of the drugs; and then for the hell of it, she clicked on one article by a Danish researcher living in Sweden. The man seemed credible, with an MD and PhD and a number of awards to his credit. He seemed to question the role of cholesterol in diet and the 'mirage of war' that the pharmaceutical industry had created around cholesterol. Fine. But then she saw a line of text where he claimed that while statins work at inhibiting HMG-CoA to lower cholesterol, statins also deplete the body of vital CoQ10. He claimed 'long-term low levels of a vital coenzyme CoQ10 that is crucial to energy production in the mitochondrion is dangerous.'

CoQ10 was present in the heart. She then created a two-headed arrow with HMG-CoA on one side and CoQ10 on the other; then she drew a schoolgirl's heart around the relationship. Statins lower cholesterol to prevent heart attacks; but lowering cholesterol will eventually create a deficit in CoQ10. Alabaster hadn't found any articles explaining what kind of damage low levels of CoQ10 would cause.

What did any of this have to do with an IPO for a pharmaceutical company?

She did a search again on the medication plus pharmaceutical companies. She saw too many companies in her search returns. She filtered the result down to US companies; still the list was slightly unmanageable. She did another filtering with 'IPO.'

"Bingo!" she said. The girl at the table raised an eyebrow, flustered:

the boyfriend had heard and he walked over to the table.

"Is there something I can help you with?" said the young waiter in Italian, surprised. The girlfriend's eyes lifted.

Alabaster handed him the saucer. "Yes, thank you, may I have an espresso." After he had walked away, she had her hands together as if she was going to clap them. The young girl across the way gave her another withering look.

A web result shone white against her face and illuminated her cheeks. She saw the initials she had been hunting for. 'MP' was not a CEO or a company. It was a place: Millennium Park in Massachusetts.

The IPO was for a breakaway pharmaceutical company, Nasonia Pharmaceuticals. The CEO was some reputed brash genius type named Cyril Sargent. The IPO was for the usual obscene amount, even by Wall Street standards, and underwritten by one of the usual conglomerates; and no doubt this IPO would make 'CS' a 'king.' A gutsy thing, doing an IPO in a down market, but Wall Street will find virtue in difficult times if they can convince investors that they have the last virgin in the whorehouse on sale.

The espresso was set down on the table. Alabaster thanked the waiter without looking up. The black ink and blistering crema awaited her.

This Sargent had apparently been one of the reigning creep cases from the decadent eighties, giving bravado interviews, cleaning his wingtips with hundred dollar bills at board meetings, but judiciously mellowing out some in the nineties because most of his associates had gone to Club Fed to serve long prison sentences. CS spent the next decade lurking behind the financial scenes in the millennial noughts, trying to establish credibility with philanthropies and socially conscientious investment funds. Without looking at the financials, which she would do at Dante's, CS seemed to have done well for himself. But she also knew Rendition had to have been trailing him, unable to pin a conviction or place a string of numbers under his chin so he could have boyfriends in a federal penitentiary.

It seemed Mr. Sargent had done well indeed, she read while mindlessly stirring the baby spoon in her espresso. Not only had Sargent brought the biggest bank to the pharmaceutical company, but he also had achieved a major marketing coup. He did a mea culpa with his own company's flagship statin, on the market since 1987 but whose patent had expired in 2001. The company's statin sales were in the basement. Newspapers, television and then the web had rained down fire on all statins. Sargent then unveiled his company's new medication that had the traditional cholesterol-lowering efficacy, even kept the trusted name and recognizable pill shape and color, but added a new component built into it: CoQ10.

When his new statin had hit the market, the other pharmaceutical companies, losing sales to generic equivalents as their patents expired, tried to mount a campaign to discredit him about CoQ10. They played right into his hands, because all the work had been done for him. He pointed to the growing literature about CoQ10 and the statin skeptics. Consumers ate up Sargent's mea culpa. They interpreted the company's return to the market with a safer medication, same name but 'new and improved for you because we care about your heart,' as a work of integrity. Newsweek named him Saint Sargent; Time christened him the Pharma Revolutionary; and the IPO showed that he was making a major fortune and would as long as the patent on the new drug held.

Alabaster placed checkmarks against all the clues, except 'SM & EHR w/ PEP nightmare. Wasp next.' In the center of her circle she wrote Cyril Sargent, underlining 'C' and 'S'; Millennium Park, repeated underlining 'M' and 'P'; and she didn't bother writing in the name of the recycled statin, because she figured that Rendition was investigating the spin-off company, Nasonia Pharmaceuticals, Incorporated.

She had had enough research for one morning.

She tapped the pen against 'SM & EHR w/ PEP nightmare. Wasp next' because therein lay the last clue as to why Rendition wanted Sargent and why 10ki was afraid.

Alabaster got up and looked to the back of the café to see whether the waiter was around. She thought that she should bring the demitasse back or at least let him know that she was done. He wasn't there but she did hear a book slam shut.

22

Alessandro arrived at the office pissed-off and stained.

In his walk from the Metro an idiot was texting and walked into him (or conversely, Alessandro had walked into the texting idiot), take-away coffee in hand. As Alessandro, further aggravated by the impossible elevator, stormed to his office with the big brown stain drying and reeking, Silvio was chasing him.

"Not now, Silvio. I have to change," said Alessandro through clenched teeth.

"But Alessandro, I have this nude message for you."

Alessandro stopped and turned to Silvio, "What? Never mind. What is it?" He was willing to stop because he rarely received messages: nude, new, or otherwise.

Snapping the white paper rudely from Silvio's hand, he saw the name Moretti, spelled correctly, and a number, probably the professor's cell phone. Alessandro was grateful that Silvio's Italian names and phone numbers were safe.

"Thanks, Silvio. Keep working hard on that English. I think you're doing great." He left Silvio beaming.

In the office, after he had closed the door and drawn the blinds, he motioned a hello to Dante, who was on the phone. Alessandro pulled a desk drawer open and took out a laundered and pressed shirt from Enzo's Laundromat. He took off the stained shirt and to Dante's sarcastic whistle he held it up for Dante to see. Dante gave him the thumbs-up sign.

Dante snapped forward from his leaned-back chair position when he realized that he was no longer on hold.

"Pronto," said Marco.

"Marco, this is Dante."

"Where the hell have you been? I've been calling you."

"I know that you're mad, Marco."

"Mad? Why would I be mad?" said Marco.

Everybody was a wiseass today.

"Me mad?" Marco said. "You see the news program? Why the hell am I the last one to know anything? Don't mind me; I'm just one of the founders of the Roma Underground. I've got all the groups all over me with questions. 'Marco, why didn't you tell us about the eagle?' 'Marco, when was it discovered? What does it look like?' and that's from inside the Roma Underground. You should hear what I'm getting from the Beni Culturali."

"I can imagine. I'm sorry to hear all this."

"Each group had its territory. The accountants and financial types have theirs, the engineers and medical professionals have theirs, and the agreement is that when some significant item is found, we let each other know, right? I thought that was a very simple understanding. What the hell happened? I'm looking like a real *minchione*."

Marco certainly had a way with words. He did look like a big idiot. "You're right, Marco, but we shouldn't be accusing each other."

"So who do we accuse? You think some kid from Perceval found the eagle?"

"I don't think so. Those kids are dependent on scholarships and grants either from the government or their home country, so if they got caught stealing then it'd be career suicide. You know they have to sign an agreement on ethics, don't you?"

"You're right, Dante, but that makes me think all the more that it's someone within the Roma Underground."

"Look, Marco, I have to go. My boss and his boss don't have a sense of humor about personal calls. We'll talk, I promise. Stay calm and try not to have tempers fly over this, because we could all lose our privileges to explore the underground."

"I'll try. Thanks for listening, but we need to talk more. Ciao."

"We will. Ciao," said Dante. He hung up the phone, utterly exhausted.

Alessandro swiveled his chair Dante's way. "What was that all about?"

"Marco is one of the principals of Roma Underground. He's bullshitting about the Moretti interview and about the eagle on RAI. He wants to know how the hell the eagle slipped by without any of the groups knowing about it. He's trying to calm down tempers because people are starting to point fingers at each other: the engineers are blaming my group, the Finz, and the surgeons are pointing the finger at the students in Perceval. It's a real nightmare, Sandro."

"The Finz?" asked Alessandro, picking up one of his sharpened pencils.

"As in Financial."

"And what was that bit about geeks and nerds?" asked Alessandro.

"Oh, that. Don't worry about that. Marco was getting hot-headed and name-calling."

"No. I want to know."

Dante grimaced. "Marco heard a rumor that somebody in our office knew Moretti; so since *I* work here he thinks I know something. I told him that I didn't know a thing; and besides, even if someone in our office knew Moretti that would just be a coincidence, right?"

"Right. And now the nerd has to call the geek." Alessandro held up Silvio's handwriting. Dante squinted at the white piece of paper, then sat back in his chair.

Alessandro put the paper in the center of his desk. "I've been meaning to call him since Gennaro wants to preside over another one of those status meetings. This is the first time the professor's called me at the office. I know you're going to the meeting. Did you invite your girlfriend? What's her name?"

"Bianca. And she'll be there."

"Right," he heard Alessandro reply while Alessandro keyed in the professor's phone number. After a few seconds Alessandro moved in his chair, surprised that the professor picked up the phone.

"Professor, this is Sandro. I'm fine, thank you."

Dante could hear the politeness wither.

"I'm sorry about that. I'm also sorry that this has to be a quick conversation." Alessandro picked up his pencil. "I understood it. I didn't want to leave a message. . . . How about seven? . . . I know where you are. We shouldn't talk much more on the phone. Talk soon, bye."

Alessandro hung up.

"Did he sound worked up?" Dante asked.

"The whole world seems worked up this morning. Oh, shit. Gennaro incoming."

Gennaro knocked and opened the door cautiously. "Why the door? What's with the blinds?"

"Alessandro needs a raise, Boss," Dante said. "He inflicted a striptease on me this morning."

Alessandro gave Dante a dirty look.

"Huh?" said Gennaro. "Inflicted? I feel like I'm talking to Silvio."

Alessandro used his pencil for affect. "All on account of that delayed expense report. Desperate times and desperate measures, you know."

"Spare me. The reason I'm here is to tell you we're meeting for dinner to discuss matters. You two, and Dante, bring your girlfriend. And you, Alessandro, get Professor Moretti. I want him to join us."

"Right, Boss. I just spoke with him and he'll be happy to hear it. When and where?"

"Say, about seven pm. I found a nice, pricey place on Via Licinia. Pinolo'll love the expense report after we're done. Think that time will work for your girlfriend?"

"Yes, and she's not my girlfriend," said Dante.

"Boss?" Alessandro said, "I don't know any food on Via Licinia. That area is almost all embassies."

"I found an unknown restaurant; Cuban, called Pargo," said Gennaro as Silvio appeared at his side, a piece of white paper under his eager face.

"What is it, Silvio?" asked Gennaro.

"Another nude message. It's that United Stater again."

"Michael Farese?" asked Gennaro.

"Yes. He's wandering why you haven't returned his last massage. He seems like a nice man. He says my English is rising to heights he's never heard of. I don't think he's well, Boss, so maybe call him ASAP?"

"ASAP? Why don't you think he's well?" asked Gennaro.

"Because when we were speaking he says as an impotent prostituting turnkey he needs to open cases with solid evidence or the judge will give him clap."

Thank God he doesn't know anything about the eagle, thought Alessandro.

23

They arrived at Pargo on Via Licinia.

Gennaro had picked that restaurant because he had heard that it was intimate and had fantastic *pescados y mariscos*, and he had always wanted to try Cuban food. He asked for a private table for a party of five.

The restaurant décor was unlike anything anywhere in Rome. There were tables, and there were booths for either couples or families. Both tables and chairs were dark mahogany; the booths had a backdrop of sunset-gold lighting while the chairs had leather backs. In the middle of the restaurant a delicately lit assembly of crystal panels rose from floor to ceiling as a tower, inside of which the wine was kindled like sacred wood. The waiter retrieved the desired vintage by sitting himself into a harness of leather straps that hoisted him to its location.

Gennaro asked for a booth. As they were walking to the back of the restaurant, they passed a special cut-glass door through which they saw bottles of brandies and after-dinner drinks. Off the main room, there was a designated cigar room, with humidors for those who wanted to enjoy a Cuban Cohiba or any of the other rising upstarts from the tobacco fields of the Americas: a Dominican-grown Corojo Oscuro; a sun-drenched Ecuadorian Avo; a Nicaraguan or Mexican long-leaf Stradivarius; or, if inclined to go north, a Miami-made Don Pepin Garcia Serie JJ. The owners had brought the Caribbean to Rome before anyone ever saw the menu.

Professor Moretti was the last to arrive. He found the group in the back, in the booth. If television supposedly adds five kilos, the professor looked as if he had lost twice as much and aged about ten years. The man sat next to his former student, Alessandro, who introduced him to Bianca, Dante, and Gennaro.

Like most academic types, the man had his eccentricities. He was wearing a fraying tweed coat that was rather odd for the late-July heat wave. His tie hung low, pulled down from one upturned collar of his tired-from-too-many-washings white shirt. The professor seemed amiable enough and endeared himself to the crowd by translating and explaining some of the dishes on the menu. It turned out, even Alessandro had not known, that the old man's father, also an archaeologist, had taken the professor as a youngster to an excavation of the El Chorro de Maita in Cuba, a settlement of indigenous people on the eastern side of the island, where he had first sampled *congris*, or red beans and rice. Gennaro started to feel a fondness for Moretti as his growling stomach decided on Cuban-style *pargo*—red snapper, the house special.

They decided to skip a first course since Gennaro had informed them that he had heard that the portions were substantial. However, the waiter brought out fried green macho plantains with a garlic dipping sauce for them to enjoy while they read the menu over.

Dante retained his carnivorous loyalty and decided on the lime-marinated sirloin steak, *Bistec Empanizado Campestre*. Alessandro selected a seafood dish of jumbo shrimp with wine and mixed spices, *Gambas al Ajillo*. Bianca had chosen *Lobster Havanaise,* which the menu described as an overweight lobster cooked with rich cream, spices, and that, somehow escaping Moretti's translation, involved Bacardi rum. Moretti said that he wanted the same dish as Gennaro, *Pargo a la Cubana*. Hearing this, the waiter said that he would bring the largest fish for them to share. Most of the dishes were accompanied with sides of some version of rice or with a mysterious boiled root called *yuca*.

"Professor," Dante said after the waiter had left, "we hear that you've been distressed since your involvement with the project. Please tell us."

"As you can imagine, I've been hounded by the paparazzi, which was no small thing at my age to deal with. But since there is no sex scandal and the politicians simmered down after the usual territorial squabbles, they disappeared. I'm down to two creatures with no lives of their own following me."

"Two?" asked Gennaro.

"Two tall creatures. They keep at a distance, but they're shady types, with no cameras. The other night, for example, I look outside my window and I don't see a soul, but then I look at the corner across the street and I can see the shadow of one of them. I'm fairly certain I shook them off coming here. I hopped off a Metro train as they hopped on and left them taking the ride while I took a taxi. They looked rather steamed behind the glass. Anyway as I—"

"Pardon me for interrupting you, Professor," Gennaro said. "You say you saw two men across the street. Ever see them in a car?"

The food arrived and everyone took to their forks and inhaled the aromas before digging in. Everybody had agreed to set samples of their dish on smaller plates for the others. The red snapper looked as if it were trying to swim off the bed of onions on the platter.

"No. They're always on foot," Moretti said. "Why do you ask?"

"Oh, nothing. I just thought that if these two've been doing 24-hour surveillance on you they've had to rest, right?" Gennaro separated flesh from the snapper's spine for the two of them. "I guess these two must've taken their vitamins."

"Professor Moretti, my name is Bianca. We were introduced earlier and I—"

"Oh, yes. I remember. You're Dante's friend." The professor turned to Gennaro. "A beautiful one Dante has picked, a living Beatrice."

Gennaro shook his head and served the professor some fish.

"Yes, I'm Dante's friend. As I was saying . . . you dealt with an Alan Ancona. Could you tell us what's happened between you two since the RAI broadcast?"

Moretti had begun eating but explained politely to Bianca and to the others between small bites of almond-crusted snapper. "This Ancona character is odd. First, he approaches me all curious like the other academics, asking me questions about the condition of the artifact, where it was found, how it was found. But the next time he shows up he starts making overtures."

"What did you tell him?" asked Bianca.

"For the earlier questions I kept my answers vague, like I did with the news people and scholars, I mean: I said the eagle'd been found under the Via Cavour, which is poorly lit and unexplored. I painted a really romantic picture to color in the dramatic discovery, you know? I told them that a humble speleologist who preferred to remain anonymous had been doing his usual thing when his shoulder got caught on something. Then he checks it out." Moretti used his knife and fork as props to indicate a prying-apart motion. "And next thing you know he has the eagle."

"That explains why I had Marco yelling in my ear," Dante said. "An anonymous speleologist . . . there you go. That'll set the entire Roma Underground off."

"What was I to say? I had to say something about the discovery. Nobody would believe that an old broken-down man like me is jimmying himself up and down cables with a headlamp under the city of Rome. I had to make up something credible. This isn't the Maltese Falcon, you know."

"I'm sorry, professor," Dante said. "Please continue."

"But you thought that he was an academic, right?" asked Bianca.

"I did, but then I began to get suspicious. Ancona always skirted the issue when I asked him where his post was, or what he had published. All I had was his business card. Try as I might, the man is a fox. That should've tipped me off, but then it was his overtures. Out of the blue he starts making these incredible offers: an outrageous sum to look at the eagle—which, okay, I must admit, even RAI offered to do that. But Ancona starts talking about knowing people who could help me with my situation in Salerno. I say 'What situation?' He says 'A reliable source said funding was cut off to your department and you have a smaller office,' and then, wouldn't you know it, he mentions my pension and tells me, 'It could be straightened out.' I ask myself, 'Who is this American bearing gifts?'"

"And then what? He kept calling you?" asked Gennaro, hands folded over his plate.

"Well, at first he was persistent, but then the phone calls stopped. Then the two giants start following me." Moretti's hand came up. "I almost forgot. The other thing that made me wise to Ancona was the time he mentioned his interests."

"What do you mean, Professor?" asked Alessandro.

"I think one day I must've been pestering him too much about his academic life, if he ever had one. He told me that he gave up teaching and did consulting for a private individual. Some big shot, I guess, because he never named names. Naturally, I tried to go through the back door, so I asked him his area of interest. My father's interest as an archaeologist was in the Taíno; myself, I specialized in ancient Greek, then Carthaginian, trading sites, so when I heard him mention Morgantina my ears pricked up. See, a few decades back Morgantina was in the news because—"

"We know, Professor: looting of silver and a statue," Gennaro filled in, and seeing the man's stunned face, explained, "Bianca told us. She is our consultant, an analyst. Hard to explain how she knows what she knows, but she told us all about it."

"Well, I'm impressed. This Ancona, I think, is behind these two men following me. My thoughts are; he hopes that I will go pay my respects to the eagle, and they'll get to see where it is and then they can verify it themselves."

"Or simply steal it," said Bianca.

The waiter intruded politely with the dessert menu.

"Is he offering to pay for it?" asked Alessandro.

"I would think he would, but now that the eagle is out in the news it can't just disappear without a public outcry, can it? I think all the news coverage would preclude outright theft."

Bianca said, "Ancona's been waiting this long without proof. Stealing the eagle after it's been so widely publicized would definitely be audacious, even for him, wouldn't it? I think it's possible he has a different strategy. I think he'll force our hand and somehow ask for proof that it exists, and that it be examined. There's no cost or exposure in doing that. He may not do it directly, but I could see him doing that."

Dessert arrived. The table went silent as two waiters set the plates down in front of each diner.

Moretti insisted that someone share the *Flan de Leche Clásico*, the egg-caramel flan that he used to love as a boy. Gennaro, since he had shared the pargo with the professor, decided to take him up on the offer. Dante went with the *Pudin Diplomático con Brandy*, a bread pudding doused with VSOP. Alessandro opted for a rum concoction this time, *Panetela Borracha de Ron y Piña*. The *Natilla Azúcar*, a custard dessert topped with scorched sugar, fell to Bianca.

"A bribery sting is out of the question then?" asked Dante.

The bribery question went unanswered, but the call for dessert was easily answered.

24

For Bianca and Dante, the ride back on the Vespa was surprisingly uneventful. Possibly the dog days of summer had worn down the Romans. She held onto him less tightly than usual and noticed that his heartbeat was regular, rhythmic, and serene. Curious about his earlier comment about the Roma Underground, she squeezed him around the ribs when they arrived at a red light. His head turned.

"You seemed upset with Moretti mentioning some 'anonymous speleologist,'" she said into his helmeted ear. "You said a Marco was upset with you."

Since the traffic was nil, Dante felt no need to shout. "Marco is not upset with me, but he's trying to put together a rational explanation for not knowing about the eagle. Accusations are flying around. Remember when I told you that the Underground is made up of groups who explore underground on their own time?"

"Yeah."

"I belong to the financial group. Each group has a superintendent. I'm the one for the *Finanziari*—the accountants, analysts, and auditors. Marco is a software engineer, *tecnico dei computer*, so his group is called Tecnico. He's a superintendent also but he's been a peacekeeper between the groups. As I mentioned to you that day, we have other groups; doctors and lawyers . . ."

"So Via Cavour belongs to which group?"

The light changed and Dante drove slowly enough to be heard.

"*Medico*. Those are the doctors, nurses, and other health-care professionals. So you can imagine that the first thought was that someone in that group had found the eagle and never told anybody. For really important finds we let each other know through the computer."

Another red light, which was a surprise, but neither of them seemed to be in a hurry to get home, especially since they knew the place was bugged, and conversations on the terrace were getting tiresome.

The only other place to talk in private was in Dante's bedroom, which would be . . . complicated.

"With the eagle there, you could be certain that a message would have gone through the Underground like mad. For other things, the small things, we leave them to Perceval."

"Any chance of ever discovering something and not knowing its significance?" asked Bianca.

"Not really, because with time and experience you get a good sense when you've found something extraordinary. We'll contact Perceval and the Beni Culturali, but not before we photograph the find and catalogue it."

"You don't trust them, do you?"

"Perceval or the Culturali?"

"Take your pick."

"Not that we don't trust them. We like to think of it as due diligence on our part when we photograph and document the important finds. There're so many items found these days that the Culturali can't possibly have the staff to process the finds. Like what happened to that amphora with the resin that you mentioned at our first meeting. The Culturali put a number to it and filed it away for the experts and scholars." Dante gunned the Vespa through the intersection. "Now it's on display in America."

They arrived at the curbside; he took off his helmet but Bianca still had her arms wrapped around his midsection.

"Let me ask you. Does this agreement that exists among the groups also exist with the graduate and post-docs?"

"Perceval?"

She let him go, took off her own helmet and dismounted from the Vespa. As she stood there she handed him her helmet. "They're a group of kids, most of them are starting their careers, and they have their hands in the dirt, so to speak, every day, right?"

"Those 'kids,' as you call them, are highly educated professionals: archaeologists, archivists, classical scholars and medievalists, you name it. Would they have a motive? Sure, but they're their own group. Everyone in the Underground has a lot of respect for Perceval. We also can't afford to piss people off. Like anything, there's politics involved. But no, they're not part of the agreement."

Bianca touched his shoulder. "I didn't mean to dismiss what they do. My point is they can roam the entire city, right? They're not bound to any territorial obligation?"

"Well yeah, that's true, but whenever there's a find, it's usually by one of our groups, so when Perceval comes in, one of our people is always present. It's like a procedure, see . . . we'll find something, tell each other so we can document it; we document it, then we call Perceval if they're not on site, and they, in turn, call the Culturali. It's like a chain-of-command thing."

"You said if they're not on site. Does that mean it's possible that they can be on site?"

"Sure, why not? Like you said, they roam the city. We never know when we'll find something. Things don't always go according to plan. We still photograph and document our finds, though, but I can assure you that the Culturali don't show up in five minutes. This is Rome after all, mother of all bureaucracy."

"So Marco is thinking it's an inside job. Either someone in the Medico found the eagle and ran with it, or someone from the Perceval is trying to make a name for themselves. But he's not pointing the finger at the Culturali?"

"I can't assume what Marco thinks, but I know one picks their fights carefully with any agency. He's upset that the procedure fell apart and he doesn't want enthusiasm to unravel the group. Does he suspect corruption in the Culturali or Perceval? Who knows! It's not unheard of for bureaucracy to be corrupt, Bianca, but Marco is angry because nobody got to document the eagle. And if something scandalous were to happen to that eagle he's worried that the Underground will get blamed and we'll lose the right to explore the city. He knows that he can't control either Perceval or the Culturali, but he'll be damned to see the Underground take the blame."

As they walked up to the apartment door Bianca had to ask one final question, "That amphora with the resin . . . we know that the Culturali assigned a number to it for the warehouse, but did the Underground photograph and document it?"

Dante placed the key into his door and paused. "Of course, we photographed it and assigned it a reference number. It's in our digital library. Marco's group discovered it."

He expected Farrugia in a few minutes. The table on the balcony was set. The menu was intentionally Calabrian.

For the starter Gennaro had planned *sardella*, a paste of anchovies and sardines set on fire with red pepper, soothed with salt, packed tight and meant to be spread on bread. Gennaro, wanting Farrugia to taste home, thought he would serve toasted crostini with sardella, topped with minced onions and tomatoes. He then had made homemade fusilli for his *ricci di donna*, using, appropriately enough, one of Lucia's knitting needles to wind the eggless pasta down the steel into spaghetti-like spirals. It was just a small portion of pasta meant to calm Farrugia as he explained his visit to Signora Cetoni.

The main course was grilled swordfish steaks with wedges of lemon, drizzled with *salmoriglio*, another simple but tangy sauce made with olive oil, garlic, lemon, and oregano. Farrugia should be swimming down the coast after this meal. The only traitor to all this food was the wine from Tuscany, a Vernaccia di San Gimignano, because Gennaro had no choice but forgive Calabria its lack of good white wine.

Farrugia, like Dante, was that odd Mediterranean creature who obeyed the clock; but unlike Dante, the hands of the clock never held absolute control over how the man might show up. This time Farrugia was civil and knocked on the door.

Gennaro's apartment was a modest one in the Trastevere neighborhood. The smallness of the place wasn't stifling since he asked for so little out of life. He figured that the less he owned, the less he accumulated, the more he felt free and unburdened. His needs were basic: a safe place within walking distance of a decent meal, if he was too tired to cook for himself. Though his place was in a secret corner of the ancient neighborhood, his neighbors were certainly not geriatric or dull, what with all the bars, restaurants, and music clubs around them.

"I brought some pastries," said his guest.

Gennaro could tell that Farrugia's eyes had, out of habit, sized up the apartment for the number of possible entryways, exits, and blind spots. He was welcome to do so, since Gennaro neither had anything to hide nor steal. He had clothes, probably out of date. He wore no jewelry. His television was nothing like the plasma monstrosities that deserved their own room. His furniture was respectable enough. All he cared for was, should the robbers decide to deprive him of his humble belongings, they would at least leave him the picture of Lucia that he had on the table accompanied by a small round glass of water and a solitary rose. Which was exactly the first thing Farrugia moved towards when he saw it. He looked at Gennaro for permission to pick up the frame to look at her.

"Go ahead." Gennaro moved around the kitchen with the plates. "The picture is of us on holiday in Sardinia. We had just summited Monte Corrasi in that picture."

"It's painful sometimes to look at a beautiful woman." The detective returned the frame to the small table next to the couch.

"Let's go out to the balcony and eat," said Gennaro.

"Sardella?"

"Think I'd serve you snails? I hope you enjoy this sardella on crostini. I had wished for a bottle of Ciro but the wine merchant had none in stock. We'll have some wine later. I have a surprise for you."

Farrugia stood there silent and motioned to the chair opposite him, suggesting that Gennaro sit down. "Don't worry about the Ciro wine. The foot can live without the toe," said Farrugia, alluding to the anatomical locations of Ciro and Calabria.

The crostini crinkled and broke with each bite to release the savory earthiness of the sardines against the fierce sun-baked *pepperoncini piccanti*. Both men relished that first taste of the meal. The pitcher of cold water sat on the table sweating.

"You know we need to talk, Gennaro," Farrugia said when the food no longer demanded their attention. "That visit of yours to the old snoop? I had bent the rules about an investigation when I talked to you, then you go with some mute to playact Sherlock Holmes and Watson behind my back. You do realize if this case becomes a missing persons or worse, I could find myself behind a desk processing drunks and whores for the remainder of my career?"

"It won't be a missing person's case; of that I can assure you. The mute, by the way, is Dante. We work together. You like the sardella?"

"It's very good, thank you. This Dante was the Benedetto character and you, Brunetto? And I am to assume without asking that in your way of ways you know that this Bianca Nerini is safe and sound."

"I was Brunetto, yes. Nerini is safe and sound."

"She a witness to something serious?"

"Not sure. We both deduced that someone is after her and they were content to leave her a message. The old lady, Signora Cetoni, confirmed for me that the two voyeurs in the green Fiat were Americans because they spoke some English."

"She talked to them?"

"Not exactly. She told me that she was going out for her constitutional and saw them at the intercom board, like they knew where they were going. And don't take it personal that she didn't mention it to you. As I said, people don't always like talking to the police."

Farrugia crunched crostini a moment. "She had enough sense to copy down the license-plate numbers and enough trust to give them to me. That puts her ahead of the norm. So what did our two visitors say to Signora?"

"Only one of them spoke and not to her, but to his partner. The one said to the other, 'alabastro.' No, no . . . 'alabaster.'"

"Marble?"

"Exactly what I had thought at first, but I don't think so. I got to thinking, if I were looking for someone and I discovered something that I had to communicate to my partner—what would I say?"

"I think I follow. So we're partners, you and I, and we've been staked out for days waiting and . . ." Farrugia swallowed the last of his sardella crostini.

"Looking and hoping for a break and I find it first."

"We find the place somehow, possibly from other sources, but we can't confirm it unless we get in. Easy enough to get into any building: follow behind someone returning home, ring a bell and make some inquiry or pretend to make a delivery, but then how do we know we have the exact apartment?"

Gennaro brushed some crumbs off his lips.

"They were at the intercom board not to ring someone for the purpose of getting into the building. They were looking for someone. We can infer that they intuited the correct floor and apartment from the intercom board because they recognized a name. They didn't steal anything in the apartment, though . . ."

"There was nothing to steal, Isidò. The place was bare. All they did was trash what was there."

"I understand that and I agree with you that it was a message of some kind. I have no doubt that, had she been in the apartment, we might have an assault, a rape, or a homicide. Let's forgo those possibilities at the moment. Until you spoke to Signora Cetoni you had no idea that B. Nerini was a woman, correct? Yet they knew that they had the right person, right? So back to our noun: we have our seekers, we have a place, but we have no thing sought."

"Unless our person, B. Nerini, is the thing."

"Exactly. Now, as partners about to commit a crime, we both have to know with some certainty that we have the right person, so I'm with you in that vestibule, leaning down to look at the intercom board. What do I do to confirm this to you?"

"You read the name: B. Nerini."

"Yes, but that is not what I say to you."

"You said 'alabastro.'"

"'Alabaster.' The old lady said the one man spoke to the other in English. I read in Italian an alias, but tell you in English the name."

"So. Our Bianca Nerini was once named Alabaster."

"There's more food, isn't there?" asked Farrugia.

Ferrugia leaned back with a rare beatific look on his ascetic face. "The *Pesce Spada al Salmoriglio* was excellent. I might've thought you'd pulled the fish right out of the Strait of Messina yourself. The wine was also perfect: dry, green, and with just the right amount of acidity."

"We can wait a few on the pastries," Gennaro said. "I'll put the coffee on too. Until then, it's my turn to talk. I need to ask you a favor—actually, three favors."

"Sounds like you really need help. If I can do it, I will. What is it?"

Gennaro motioned to the closed doors of his balcony. "For now, please don't ask why I'm asking these favors. First, I'd like for you to get one of your electronics specialists, someone you trust in the department who's very good at surveillance work. I need him to comb through my place and check to see whether I'm being bugged."

Farrugia squinted a little and it was not from the sun. He nodded.

Gennaro pulled a folder from under the table that he had hidden on the seat of one of the empty chairs and handed it to Farrugia. "Items number two and three. Inside that folder are two pieces of paper. One is an inventory slip done up by the Beni Culturali for an Augustan amphora with intact resin. The artifact was found underground several months ago. I won't say more about it until I hear from you what you've found out about it. I need a status, please. The slip should allow you to trace the artifact to a storage warehouse."

"Okay." Farrugia peeled the copy off of the second page inside the folder. "And number three here is an address for one Professor Moretti. What do I do with Professor Moretti?" Farrugia asked.

"Nothing with Moretti himself. He claims that he's being followed by two men."

"Really? Any chance it's our two Americans?"

"It's possible." Gennaro pushed back his chair. "But please be discreet."

As Gennaro stood there, about to make his way back into the kitchen for coffee and pastries this time, Farrugia replied, "When have I not been the invisible man?"

25

Bianca had always believed that 'feminine intuition' was the kind of nonsense thinking that protected men and women in the world from rational thought; but she admitted that she felt uneasy with Dante's insistence that they go underground.

She warned Dante that it might not be safe to venture underground that day despite his call to Marco and the latter's assurance that there would be no harm. Marco had portrayed tempers as calmed after having passed over boiling.

Despite Bianca's protest, Dante subscribed (apparently) to the specious logic that the eagle was still very much on everyone's mind. Tensions ran high above and below the surface, and though nobody could blame him personally, others in other groups saw the Finz not as fellow speleologists but as sell-outs of the greatest archeological find since Bedouin shepherds had uncovered the Dead Sea Scrolls. Fresh on everyone's mind, he reminded Bianca, were other recent and equally stunning discoveries in Rome: the painted images of Peter, Paul, John, and Andrew in the Santa Tecla catacomb; or the alleged grotto, the Lupercale, of Romulus and Remus under the palace of Emperor Augustus.

He called going underground "social". She called it "political". "Political" was much more dangerous.

"What're your plans today?" he asked her.

"I don't know. I thought I'd do some research."

"I'm off to the Forum of Nerva into the Cloaca Maxima."

Bianca consulted the geographical and territorial maps she had in her head. "Are you crazy, Dante? That's Medico territory. You want the surgeons to take you apart alive without anesthesia?"

"Marco said it was fine. I've done this in the past. Members from different teams do cross over and explore other sections from time to time. The rule is that you let the presiding team direct the exploration.

Marco knows I'm coming and I think this is a good way to help keep the peace between the Finz and Medico."

"Gennaro told me you were idealistic, but now I don't know whether you or Marco are idealists or just simply idiots."

"Fine, insult me then." Dante grabbed his gear bag.

"You're really going?" asked Bianca.

"I'm *really* going. What does this look like, a picnic basket?" he said, bowling the bag towards her but not releasing its handles.

"Then I'll join you."

"You can't, Bianca."

"Why not?"

"First, I've already got my hands full diplomatically going there on my own. I'm sure some words will be exchanged, and I can't be doing that and keeping an eye on you at the same time. Second of all, you're not properly trained. The last time I escorted you, I took responsibility for your safety. Third, and most important, you're not one of us, and your presence underground will definitely spark more questions, if not resentment. They might think you're an embedded journalist or something like that."

"I'm going. Just tell them what everyone else thinks."

"What's that?"

"Tell them I'm your girlfriend."

"My English is pretty good," said Dante, blocking her as she tried to get her jacket. "I think I am saying 'no' correctly."

Bianca stared at him. Her first thought was to knee him in the balls, but she knew that she was a guest in his house—apartment, technically, but a guest no less. Leaving Dante on the ground writhing and calling on the saints as he held his nuts would simply be . . . rude.

"Okay, let me try reasoning with you, Dante. Right or wrong, I'm the one who set this all in motion by giving you the idea of setting up a hoax. The professor is in Ancona's crosshairs, shadowed by two spooks, because Alessandro—not you—involved him in this scheme. The only thing you've done was to sell my idea so that your boss and your friend could put their careers on the line. Maybe you saw yourself climbing up the ladder if all went well? Which brings me to my point . . ."

"Which is?" said Dante, eyes boring into her despite his calm voice.

"Like I said . . . I should go because I'm responsible. Mind you, I'm not responsible for how the turf was divided up. I'm not responsible for picking where the eagle was found or—"

"How generous of you, Bianca, to concede that you have limits. Fine, then you come along. Fend for yourself. Just remember to keep your helmet on, straps tight, and headlamp on, and keep your eyes focused ahead. Don't you worry about me being a weight on my line at all."

"Why do you say that?" asked Bianca.

"Oh, I don't know . . . maybe I'm just too busy climbing up out of the sewer," Dante said after she walked out of the door in front of him and he slammed the door behind them.

She thought that, rather than having her arms around his body for the ride on the Vespa, she'd like to put her fingers around his throat. It'd just take one decisive squeeze.

Then it came to her that this was a very Italian thing to feel. Perhaps she was making a home here more than she'd realized.

Alessandro was indecisive about his plans that evening.

He wanted to get out—the only question was where to go. He thought of going over to Piazza Navona and visiting the café-bar Antico, or maybe venturing over to the wine bars in the Campo de' Fiori.

Then he remembered that Bar del Fico down the street had just reopened after a two-year hiatus, adding a pizzeria and restaurant. Some of his friends complained that the renovations made the place more French, like the wine-bar Etablì around the corner. But they had agreed that the improvements had been much needed. They joked that they would quit going there if the elderly chess players under the fig tree started wearing berets and striped naval shirts.

He thought of the clubs for after dinner, but he had no idea what his mood was. At Club Gilda he had seen too much of the paparazzi.

The place called Ex Magazzini had live music but he hadn't a chance to check who would be performing that night. He was lazy. He recalled that the last time he had gone out clubbing with friends was when they had packed off as a group to Brancaleone on Via Levanna.

He decided to find dinner somewhere on the piazza and then see whether he would have enough room in his stomach for a splurge on a *granita di caffè con panna* at Tre Scalini, where he could sit outside and watch the sights.

After a pleasant meal at a small restaurant, he allowed Tre Scalini to extort their twelve Euro from him for the privilege of using a chair at one of their famous red-decked tables. Sitting in Navona was a very touristy thing to do, indeed, but Alessandro enjoyed Bernini's *Fontana dei Quattro Fiumi* and how the baroque master had assembled his representations of the Danube, Ganges, Nile, and Plata rivers. He liked the history around the piazza: stadium grounds from the time of Domitian, fallen into disrepair; the name *Navona* flowing into Italian via a bastardization of the Greek word *agon*; and Bernini's Nile, a Borromini design, with the veil either shielding her eyes from the Christian supremacy of *Chiesa di Sant'Agnese in Agone* or reflecting, in allegorical language, pagan ignorance of the river's origins.

Alessandro was watching the crowds in the glow of the golden lights against the cobblestones, when he heard a voice.

"Quite a beautiful evening, isn't it?" she said with a touch of a Hungarian accent that did not, as most people would think, make her sound like Dracula.

Alessandro couldn't help but look at her. His thinking fell into something that felt like a bad translation of an American noir writer, the only American books he really enjoyed reading. He couldn't resist going along with the terrible voice-over narrating the scene to him. The espresso in the *granita* had already jumped his nerves and sent the distress signal to his hormones.

'Her Italian was fine but the legs were better. She stood there, three-quarter legs and one-quarter torso in a dress, looking like the girl next door but acting all street-smarts, all sin, ripe for a night on the town.

Nice shoulders, a little knobby on the ends; the bare skin flawless, without blemishes on the arms, the face, the legs; and all the rest of her was a secret that she let out at night but hid from the lampposts.'

She was talking, making small chitchat, but Alessandro knew how to make an automatic polite face from sitting in too many meetings with Pinolo. His mind wandered elsewhere on her geography. 'This Magyar beauty had some Germanic features: hair somewhere between blonde and brown, the eyes caramel brown, tall but not Scandinavian-tall, with a touch of the Rom, the gypsy blood in her, that imbued the skin with an exotic complexion.'

Alessandro realized that he had agreed to one drink with her. She smiled, he smiled, they talked and all the visual cues indicated that he had some workable charm, some success with this woman because she touched him now and then, laughed at his jokes, tried to get him to talk about his job, about what he liked to do in his spare time, about his hobbies. Alessandro refrained, wanting to preserve some mystery to him and avoid the endless drone of macho accomplishments like the guy next to them at the bar. He did have to thank the chatterbox, though, because she suggested a quieter place for them to resume their conversation.

They ended up at his place. He ignored the Marlowe voice saying, 'Bad move, kid. This actress has read you like a bad script and'll brush you off like lint in the morning. Snap out of it kid, 'cause you know nothing good'll come of it.'

She had pushed him back, unbuttoning his shirt, peeling the sleeves off his shoulders. The kisses came hot, insistent, without much thought where they landed, though every single one of them was strategic. Alessandro found that he was trying to participate but she persisted in dominating him. He could taste the drink that he had with her, taste her lipstick, and his head spun while she rode him up and down, up and down, as his head went round and round faster. The images went around in front of his open eyes: he saw her eyes staring into his, felt her panting in his face; her nails digging into his shoulders either to secure her own pleasure or to pin him down; and then with his eyes closed, behind them he saw Marlowe in his trench coat, hand over his face.

Alessandro came to in the middle of night. His bedroom had been turned inside out, but it had been done with the neatness of a maid who had just turned over a room. Everything was almost in its place, but he knew his place well enough to know when things had been rearranged. He checked his wallet: all the credit cards were there. The money was there, as were his identification and license. He got up from the bed, nearly falling over until he realized that he had forgotten to pull up his pants. Pulling the zipper up felt gratuitous.

What had she wanted, he asked the Marlowe in his head, but the detective had abandoned him. He searched and searched until he realized finally that only one thing was missing, one thing stolen: his small spiral flipbook with his notes from Bianca's presentation.

He wished that he had one of his sharpened pencils so he could stab himself for his stupidity.

The last time Bianca had heard the word 'cloaca' had been in biology class, the day they had dissected frogs. In Latin it meant 'drain' or 'sewer.' The Forum of Nerva is but one of many possible points of access into the Cloaca Maxima. The great sewer.

Even the sewers of Rome have history. Tarquinus Priscus had begun it, Tarquinus Superbus had finished it, and Marcus Vipsanius Agrippa, the naval genius behind Augustus Caesar's victory over Marc Anthony at Actium, had done the rest to modernize the waterway into the world's largest sewer system. Modernity had come to the sewer in 33 BC, she added, as she put on the thick jumpsuit that Dante had tossed her way. She wanted to ask Dante why this suit seemed thicker than the one she had worn at the Oppian Hill where they had seen the "Vendemmia" mosaic together, but he was still angry with her for being there at all.

Dante saw her struggling with her straps. He came over and roughly straightened, buckled, and cinched them all into place with pulls, tugs, and slaps. Without saying a word, he taped the bottom of her legs with duct tape, jammed her sleeves down into the gloves, taping them also, and without looking at her, he pulled her hood up from behind her head, tied it, secured the headlamp in place and left her there for a moment hermetically sealed off and trussed up. All she had to do was pull up the respirator mask that hung somewhat loosely around her neck to cover her mouth and pinch it into place on her nose. Dante seemed to be looking for some other odds and ends in his endless supply bag.

"This is a whistle," he said, and without looking at her clipped it onto an empty belay hook near her shoulder. "This is a buck knife in case you have to cut a tangled line. Think twice before you use it." He clipped the knife with a small hole at its base into another empty clip at her waist. He showed her a waterproof flare, explained nothing since he had rolled it in front of her for her to read the instructions.

In short, he was being juvenile. Typical male.

The Medico group had gone ahead of them. Dante could see that their bags were orderly, as was to be expected of surgeons and medical professionals. Marco had let them know that Dante was coming. He had also told Dante on the phone that the Medico team today was a party of four. Dante recognized the names in the team and recalled that he had never had problems with any of them, although Adriano could be a testy son of a bitch. Adriano was one of Rome's primadonna surgeons, and while well respected professionally, he had a hideous temper. Everyone had heard about the time Adriano was trying to clip an aneurysm and started throwing spent surgical equipment at a nurse who was trying to help the anesthesiologist with troublesome tubing. The patient lived but the surgeon and nurse got into a fistfight afterwards.

All Dante could think of when he had heard that story was the third commandment, 'Thou shalt have no other gods before Me,' with DeMille music thundering in the background and Heston's beard and hair waving in the wind.

Dante plunged into the darkness with Bianca following behind. Agrippa's idea of modernizing the waterway was to provide masonry to enclose the open latrine. There was darkness and the sounds of watery movement.

But the smell that wafted invisibly through this realm of light deprivation was what made the Cloaca Maxima what it was. As the human body descends, it is enveloped by the putrification of millennia. Some speleologists became immune to the swirling odor of fermenting ammonia, petrol, and death. Dante was not one of them. The mask was an absolute necessity.

God only knew what Bianca was thinking at this point. But, she was the one who had insisted on coming.

The irony was that the patron goddess of the sewers, the Etruscan goddess Cloacina, who even appeared on a Republic denarius, was also protector of sexual intercourse in marriage. If she were truly an aspect of the goddess of Venus then Botticelli had painted in the wrong kind of spume for his *Birth of Venus*.

Down they went. Below, he could see the glow of the lighting that the Medico team had set up. The water was a moving exhibition of human indiscretions and disrespect since time immemorial: rude waste of all kinds. The only modern items in the passing parade of flotsam were spent condoms, floating along like a diaphanous but sickly jellyfish. Whatever could float above coasted by in waters colored to a shade somewhere between the battered brown and the oxidized green of an old, neglected penny. The underground had its own inhabitants, like the ocean's depths, things that hadn't seen the light or met the air above. There were the occasional rodents, but this river was likely their conduit to the afterlife. Here and there were mud, bones, and sherds of amphora and other pottery scattered about, as matter-of-fact as diamonds all over the ground in South Africa today.

Voices ahead became audible.

The four men of the Medico team ahead of them were examining a turn in the pathway that led to unmapped territory. From their talk it was clear this path had been blocked from mapping because there had been a question about secure footing. The waters had apparently subsided enough in the heat of August to make a sound estimation. As

Dante approached, they saw him and their conversation also subsided. When they saw Bianca it ended abruptly.

Dante did his best to overcome the frosty reception. He introduced Bianca as his girlfriend and fellow financial expert. They said nothing. Dante, for the most part doing a soliloquy, explained that his group was working with the engineers in Marco's group on funding to purchase a remote-controlled robot. With some good cheer he announced that an enthusiastic supporter of the Roma Underground had set up a contest with a handsome cash prize with a scholarship at several technical colleges for students who designed the best subterranean robot.

For the next hour or two the actual atmosphere was fetid while the human one remained tense, about to crackle. One of the Medico team members was busy writing notes while another colleague discussed logistics and plans for a SCUBA dive underneath the Coliseum and the hopes for setting up an underwater lighting rig. Dante interjected that he had hoped to drum up some money from supporters for the rig. No one responded. It was as if Dante was a schoolboy receiving the permanent cold-shoulder treatment.

It came time to surface. One of the Medicos, Dante couldn't see who it was behind the masks, mumbled something about 'Ladies First.' Dante was second in line on her line and parallel to her was a twin line for the Medico ascent. Adriano was already working up it. Bianca must have been getting the hang of the ascenders because she maneuvered her ascent in the harness quickly.

Dante was beneath Bianca on the line. Adriano was to the side of him. Looking up he could see Bianca's progress. He was proud of how quickly she had learned to belay the ropes. Occasionally he would feel Adriano tapping into him as the two of them worked their way up into daylight. The first tap was imperceptible. The second one felt like a mistake. He had looked to his side and Adriano grinned. The third time the tap was just a bit too hard to be an accident. Adriano's face had that wiseass look from the schoolyard that said, 'go ahead, say something.' Dante ignored him.

A few feet more and nothing. Maybe it was all in his head.

The ropes were getting taut and strained from all the weight grouping together as the bodies on the two lines inched closer to the bright hole above. Bianca was ahead a short distance, certain to be the first one out.

"Your girlfriend has a nice ass," said Adriano.

Dante ignored the comment.

"It makes sense to me now that you couldn't know who found the eagle. Marco was right. You wouldn't know."

"Huh? What are you talking about?"

"I mean, I don't blame you. A nice ass like that and I wouldn't be paying much attention to my work or to the underground." That cruel grin again.

"You'll want to shut up, now," said Dante.

"C'mon, you're a man and she's a woman. I'm giving you a compliment here. She's your girlfriend and we all know in the beginning of a relationship that all you do is—"

Dante stopped on the line. "Shut up and don't talk that way."

A few more inches up the line and Adriano started again. "Sensitive, aren't we?"

"Forget it," said Dante.

"If you say so. I meant to pay you a compliment. A girl like that, I'd show her a good time. If I really wanted to impress her, I bring her down here and show her around, like you're doing today, but I have to say your girlfriend really knows how to belay. Good strong legs. Nice."

"Adriano . . . why don't you just shut the—"

"If I really wanted to impress her I'd show her the Vendemmia. Play that right and I know just where that'd get me," he said.

Like Cain with Abel, or Jacob with Esau, he could resist the temptation no more. He grabbed hold of Adriano, seizing up all movement with tight tension on both lines.

Bianca above had looked down periodically at the top of Adriano and Dante's heads and saw their headlamps jerking beams across opposite walls. She heard them talking with Adriano's voice escalating in pitch. She stopped her ascent to listen. The two men were arguing. Dante was offering excuses about something thrown in with invectives, while Adriano was spitting accusations and insults. Bianca could feel the humid August air above her and she climbed up more.

Adriano and Dante had not moved. Men below Adriano were yelling but Bianca didn't know whether they were shouting encouragement to Adriano or telling both men to shut up and carry on. More exchanges and the lines started jumping: Adriano and Dante were fighting in mid-air.

You've got to be kidding me.

She peered down and saw Adriano cock back his fist and slam Dante in the face; her line swayed and she felt the torque of the impact at her waist.

That's it. She unclipped and unhinged the knife and cut Adriano's line. There was the sound of a receding scream and of men below yelling to get out of the way. The sound ended with a pleasant splash.

Dante looked up in shock to see Bianca clipping the knife back to her belt. He began to climb up. By the time he reached the top, she was already outside and stripping off her suit, using the knife to free herself of the duct tape. She didn't say a word.

Dante undressed. They both heard and ignored the yells that percolated up and out of the open hole. After Dante had packed his supply bag, he secured another line for the Medico and tossed it down to them. Then he faced Bianca.

She hinged the knife closed and tossed it back to him. "Didn't have to think twice before using it."

26

The shower was neither hot enough nor long enough for Bianca to feel clean. She lathered; she scrubbed; she rinsed and she repeated. All she thought was that she was now a carrier of microbial flora or alien spores, a giant petri dish with legs.

As she swept back her hair under the showerhead, she looked down at the rivulets of water swimming around her feet, converging into one stream towards the drain, and all she could think was, where does all that water go after her eyes forget the sight of it?

Tying off the sash on one of Dante's robes, she walked down the stairs to find him sitting on the sofa, head cocked back, arms out like Christ crucified, an ice bag over one eye. The ice cubes and bag slid forward as he heard her approaching.

"You were right," he said. "I shouldn't have gone."

"Of course I was right," she said, then realized he was more humble that most men she'd known, something she should encourage. "Sorry, that was a bitchy thing to say. How's the eye?"

"I'll survive." He shifted his still-solid ice cubes around in the bag. "This is such a mess: the underground situation, not the eye."

"Plan to call Marco and tell him?"

"No, he'll hear about it. Everyone knows Adriano is a hothead, so any word out of his mouth that I started it would be seen immediately as bullshit."

"Outside chance that Marco had set you up to take an unexpected lesson?"

"That Marco wanted me to have an altercation with Adriano or . . ."

"Or that he counted on Adriano attacking you? C'mon, Dante, the Roma Underground is Marco's life project, and while he doesn't know all the details about the eagle, he needs an outlet. You're the superintendent of the Finz, and what better scapegoat?"

Dante tapped his ear and then twirled his finger in the air as a reminder that his place was bugged.

Bianca shrugged. "I don't give a shit at the moment. You relax and recover from your boo-boo. I'll be outside to enjoy the nice polluted air."

'SM & EHR w/ PEP nightmare. Wasp next' sat there immobile on the screen. The cursor blinked like her eyes.

What the hell did that mean?

The air out on the terrace felt quite liberating even if she had to remind herself that it was August heat.

For sheer simplicity and desperation, she typed in 'SM' into a search engine and had to laugh at the expected search return: Sadomasochism. Lots of it.

Odd, she thought, because she had always assumed that the fetish would be properly spelled out 'S' ampersand 'M'. She toyed with the search results from 'SM' and 'S&M' and noticed that with 'S&M' the returns were far more sexual, whereas mere 'SM' provided some diversity, though nothing worthwhile. Fearing the blank wall of a dead end, she looked down the first-page search results for any key words, thinking that 10ki might be one of those intelligence types who believed in embedding clues in repeat patterns. Code specialists communicated with crossword clues, so, why not?

Page one said nothing obvious, just the usual definitions about the kink, so she clicked the link for page two, and she felt her ass sink deeper into the chair with a Eureka realization.

At the top of page two was a hyperlink to 'ROI Measurement for Social Media Marketing.'

Damn it, of course: sm was social media.

She ignored 'ROI' because that was Return on Investment, economic camouflage for profit margin. She pulled out her legal pad and reviewed her concentric circle and the clues she had written into the center of the heart. She had a name, Cyril Sargent; a place, Millennium Park, and a company, Nasonia Pharmaceuticals, Incorporated.

Time to brainstorm. The theme was pharmaceutical, broad and

wide, but specifically, a statin. Bianca thought of the 'Five Ws' and wrote down in a column:

Who⇨ Cyril Sargent
What⇨ ~~statin copyright loss?~~ IPO of Nasonia Pharma
When⇨ ?
Where⇨ Millennium Park, MA
Why⇨ $

She put down her pencil. The 'When' had to be in the near past since Rendition was still investigating him, so she crossed 'When' off her 'Five Ws.' The 'Why' is self-evident: to make money, duh. Crossed off. 10ki had to be the principle Rendition person reviewing Nasonia's Form 10-K.

Bianca stared at the legal pad. If she were 10ki and was trying to prove that Sargent had done something suspect, how would she do it? Nasonia was his new pet project and she verified online that his coup with the statin and CoQ10 patent had stayed with the parent pharmaceutical company. Conclusion: Nasonia was indeed the next venture, and 10ki was anticipating the dog would bark again.

If she were . . .

She tapped and tapped the pencil into the legal pad until the sharpened graphite point broke. The answer was obvious as Rome: the present is built on the past.

The gut instinct she had—although not provable—was that Sargent would repeat his past coup by providing a new twist on an existing product or idea, then lock it in with a patent. That was exactly what he had done with the statin. He took a class of medications with a long history, a bunch of HMG-CoA reductase inhibitors with a losing market to generics and a growing body of innuendo about possible side-effects, and turned the whole damn thing on its head. His parent company had a blockbuster drug about to go belly up with an expiring patent and what does he do? He patents a new product and inverts the bad press with a clever marketing program and slogan: 'We care about keeping your heart safe,' or something like that.

Bianca rewrote her 'Five Ws,' modifying and adapting them.

> Who⇨Cyril Sargent
> What⇨IPO of Nasonia Pharma
> Where⇨Millennium Park, MA
> How⇨Social Media

Bianca was feeling Alabaster Black's adrenaline again. She was one step short of finding the modus operandi. Each malefactor has a signature, and the clever ones vary the way they sign their crimes; but the experienced eye finds similarities in the way the unclean hand commits the act. 10ki could genuinely be stumped or she could merely be inexperienced.

The rest of the clue said, "EHR w/ PEP nightmare." Bianca looked at 'EHR' and said "thing," and with 'PEP nightmare,' said, "phenomenon," and then said, "These two have to be connected either to the past—something involving his statin triumph—or to the present, his new IPO."

Dante slid open the glass door. "Everything okay out there?"

"Fine," she said and returned her eyes to her legal pad.

EHR. What was it? It was unlikely that a search engine was going to tell her on the first return what 'EHR' was, but she typed and tapped the Enter key.

"I'll be damned. That makes sense. Absolute sense."

The 'How' question just deepened with the answer on her screen: Electronic Health Record.

The 'PEP nightmare' confounded her so she wrote down on her legal pad:

> (*Past*) statin ⇔ Social Media & Electronic Health Records?
> ⇔ Nasonia (*Future*)

Bianca massaged her temples, because a headache from too much thinking was coming on. Wasp next?

She could smell Dante cooking something delicious despite the closed glass door. Tucking her laptop under her arm, she decided to concede that she was closer than before yet so far from a satisfactory, logical answer; and the clock was ticking to a countdown when she had to prove herself to 10ki.

"While you were outside, Gennaro called," Dante said.

"Really? What did he have to say?"

"He wanted to know if you can come in to work tomorrow with me."

"What did you tell him?"

"I told him that I'd ask you. I didn't want to assume," he said as he found the plates and put them on the counter.

She smiled. Right answer. Again.

27

Rome in August is a most peculiar time of year.

The city transforms into something eerie, the oldest ghost town in western civilization. Clothing shops will shutter their windows for the month, then a movie theatre blacks out its marquee, then the exodus will really take an ominous turn, with bordellos, pharmacies, and restaurants closing. Soon enough it is just the tourists with their maps, the monuments, and the taxicabs cruising up and down the layout of the city in search of fares. The heat remains.

Bianca did go to work with Dante. The ride up the elevator seemed longer and hotter.

Once inside his office with its two sets of fans circulating the air, Alessandro, Bianca, and Dante sat down around the table as Gennaro called the meeting to order.

"What the hell happened to you?" he said. "Need I get an insurance policy on you?"

Dante's black eye had bloomed into a plum. The pupil darted sideways along a respectable slit.

"No," said Dante, and then explained how he had acquired the eggplant eye.

"We might start thinking about one for Moretti though," said Alessandro, "if we don't come up with something soon. We can't hold off the public forever. They're going to want to see the eagle."

"The public is on vacation," Bianca said. "I'm more worried about Ancona and his associates. I doubt they'll accept any more delays. And with feeding the media so little and it being a holiday month, I'm sure they'll start asking about the eagle after getting tired of hearing which American celebrity forgot to wear underwear in public."

"Still, I'm worried about Moretti," Alessandro said. "You heard what he said last time. He said that he had two people following him. That can't be good. Ancona will want answers soon."

"Where is Moretti, by the way?" Gennaro said. "Somebody invited him, right?"

"I thought *you* did," said Dante, pointing at Alessandro.

"Why are you looking at me? I've just been telling you I can't get ahold of him on my cell."

"I'm looking at you because he's your friend," said Dante.

Alessandro stood up. "What, am I some kind of fucking idiot? Since I brought him into this I'm supposed to invite him, too?"

"Now you're blaming me for your bringing your professor into this?"

"This whole thing was your idea in the first place. No, wait, your girlfriend does your thinking and she fights your fights apparently—"

Dante went for Alessandro but Gennaro stood up, grabbed him by the arm, and whistled once and loudly. Alessandro and Dante settled down.

"Now, children," Gennaro said, "this is simple enough to resolve. Alessandro, keep trying to get the professor on the phone. Thank you."

The door opened and a frightened Silvio appeared in the doorframe with a dark figure behind him.

"Oh, great," Gennaro said, "just what I need. It's Berlusconi. What is it, Silvio?"

"So sorry to interrupt, Chief, but this man behind me insisted he see . . . he says his name is—"

"I know who he is, Silvio. Let the man in," Gennaro said, waving the guest in, and pointed to the empty chair next to him. The man sat down, making a weak smile to those opposite him at the table.

Silvio began his exit when Pinolo appeared with a fresh haircut, bristles sharp enough on top to provide traction.

Gennaro couldn't help but imitate George C. Scott, picking up papers and twirling around, "O, Mother of God, what have I done to you?"

Pinolo barked out to Silvio, "Wait for me outside," and to the entrapped office crowd he held up another expense report. "Cuban food this time? I'm looking at these figures and I've got to wonder, Gennaro, if you eat with all the tourists."

"No, sir. I don't. I can explain. May I sit down?"

"You may. Oh, you'll explain it to me. It seems like you're inviting more people to your lavish feasts. Let's see . . . this time dining in the Caribbean we have a new member, P. Moretti. Another one of your consultants?"

"Actually, the principal consultant," said Gennaro.

"But what happened to consultant B. Nerini? Oh, never mind. I see he was also in attendance." Then Pinolo noticed the distinguished dark man in a suit sitting calmly next to Gennaro. "Who is he? Another consultant?"

"A guest. We were planning on lunch later. You're not paying, I can assure you," said Gennaro.

"And who is she?" Pinolo snapped, using the paper as a pointer.

Gennaro remained seated. "Allow me to introduce you to Bianca Nerini, consultant."

Bianca stood up and extended her hand. Pinolo shook it, reflexively, then pulled the expense report to his chest and motioned again with it. "Need I remind you, Gennaro, that you ought to read the memo that all visitors should be issued a pass and have their names visible at all times while on the premises."

"Yes sir, I must reacquaint myself with that memo."

"Since you have a guest and I've embarrassed myself on your account, I'll excuse myself now."

He closed the door with some drama and was seen outside the window having words with Silvio.

"For once I feel sorry for Silvio," said Dante.

Gennaro stood up and with his left hand motioned for Bianca to rise, and with his right motioned likewise to his guest. "Bianca, may I introduce to you an old and dear friend of mine, Detective Isidore Farrugia . . . and Isidò, may I introduce to you Bianca Nerini."

"Pleasure," each said to the other over handshakes. Farrugia sat down, interest etched into his face now, as he unbuttoned his suit jacket.

Turning to Farrugia, Gennaro said, "And my boss whom you just met is Maximo Cassagio. He's from Palmanova and the boys've nicknamed him Pinolo, but not to his face."

Farrugia nodded in understanding.

Alessandro introduced himself and shook hands with Farrugia. "Sorry about Pinolo. He's a real asshole."

"I can see," responded Farrugia with his handshake.

Dante smiled and introduced himself. "What he said about Pinolo is true, unfortunately. Big head, little balls, and a real pain in the ass."

"My condolences."

Dante slapped Alessandro on the shoulder as a way to apologize to him about earlier.

"Excuse me, I need to find myself some coffee," said Bianca.

"Things not stimulating enough for you," said Dante, as Bianca started to walk out of the room. She didn't reply.

Before she closed the door, she heard Gennaro whisper to Farrugia, "They're boyfriend and girlfriend."

She found an abused but hardy espresso machine in a side room.

Silvio was standing there at the sink looking down at a book. He was looking particularly depressed as he was reading his text. Bianca thought she saw tears brimming in his eyes. Although they had been introduced, they had never spoken to each other, though she had witnessed his attempts at English.

"Are you upset, Silvio?"

"Just frustrated with reading, Ms. Bianca," he said. His clear English surprised her. She loosened the arm of the espresso machine and something fell loose and something fell off.

She was about to say, "Shit," because that is what most people say when they experience the unexpected, but she refrained. No need to set a bad example.

"Tell you what, Silvio," she said. "Help me make the espresso and I'll try and help you with your book."

He handed her the book with his finger in it so she could take it and know the place where he was having difficulty. He started working the machine parts into place as she looked down at the open page. It was an excerpt from *Huckleberry Finn*.

"Your teacher has you reading this?" she said.

He opened the cabinet and pulled out a demitasse and saucer. "Ms. Bianca, I'll never learn my English at this rate. People around the office make fun of me, but I want to improve myself. I don't want to be an anybody the rest of my life."

He twisted the arm in place after tamping the coffee. The strong smell of Illy espresso cut the air. The espresso started to trickle into the small square cup.

"I understand," she said, "but I want to tell you that this is a very difficult text, even for Americans. There is slang; there is incorrect grammar for speech and—"

"But my teacher says children in your country can read this, and he said that this *Huckleberry Finn* is like us Italians with our regional dialects. Maestro calls it 'regional vernacular' or sometimes he says 'patois.'" Silvio pulled the demitasse out from under the running spout and placed it on a saucer for her. "He means to show us that English is without standards."

After taking the saucer in one hand, the book in the other, she said, "Let's sit down over here."

He pulled out a chair for her and pushed it in for her as she sat down before taking a chair of his own.

"I think what your teacher meant is that *Huckleberry Finn* is an example of non-standard English. This excerpt you're reading is Mark Twain, the author, imagining how a boy and a slave might've talked in those days, which was decades before he wrote the story. That's the nineteenth century. Not everyone talks this way in my country now. Sure, there are regional differences, like accents or dialects. I think that's what your teacher was trying to show you."

"Like us with our regional Italian."

"Sort of, but I don't want you to be discouraged. You're studying a very complex passage, complicated for its social criticism of prejudice and slavery. Because your instructor tells you a child can read this doesn't mean a child understands the implications of the text. A child might understand the sounds if someone reads it to them; but the ideas behind the language are far more difficult and adult. Did you know that this novel is studied in universities and was even banned at one time?"

"Really? I never went to university, Ms. Bianca. I didn't know that I was reading a higher-level book. You make me feel not so stupid."

"Nobody makes you feel stupid, unless you let them, Silvio. Remember that."

"This *Finn* is still very confusing to me. Maestro wants us to write a short composition in English, of course, and I don't know how to describe Huck. He's a white southern American and there's his friend, the slave Jim, who people in the text call 'boy' and 'nigger.' I looked up that word in my dictionary and it's a very bad word, very racist, for a black person, but then when I look online and in newspapers at the library I see that nobody calls a black person a black American, but an African-American. I know I shouldn't call Jim that other word. Do I call Huck a southern white-American and Jim a black southern African-American? See, here in Italy we know that not all Africans are black, so all this black and white and hyphens confuses me. I don't understand these hyphens, Ms. Bianca. In Italian we use adjectives if we want to describe color."

"If I were you and wanted to avoid the whole issue I'd use the word slave. It'll be understood that he was black. That way you avoid the hyphen altogether."

"Ah, you are very smart. I see what you say." He closed the book. "Hyphens make no sense. We'd never say a Calabrian-Italian, you know."

She knocked back her espresso, which was just what she needed. "By the way, Silvio, I saw Pinolo was yelling at you after he closed the door. Was it because the visitors weren't wearing passes?"

"No, Ms. Bianca. It was over something else."

"Oh, I see. I'm sorry to hear about that."

"It was over Shakespeare."

"Pinolo knows Shakespeare? That's surprising. Must be *Merchant of Venice*." Even in the little time she'd been with Dante, she'd learned that a day didn't go by without Pinolo's reminding someone in the office how his hometown Palmanova, not far from Venice, had saved Italy from the Huns and then the Turks.

"No, Ms. Bianca. He asked me who invited the Moor."

Ah, Farrugia, the Sicilian-Italian. She finished her espresso, but before going to the sink, she said, "You're doing just fine, Silvio. Even people who've gone to college couldn't do what you're doing."

"You think so?"

"I know so," she replied with a smile and an encouraging hand to his shoulder.

Bianca returned to the office and took a seat.

"As I was saying we can't stall longer," Dante said. "Moretti is being followed. I got socked in the face and we've got Pinolo on us."

"I'd love to have seen Adriano's face when Bianca cut the line on him . . ." Alessandro said. "'Waaah,' and then splash into liquid shit."

Dante made an exasperated face, as Bianca and Farrugia eyed each other.

"Oh, please, allow me my moment, Dante," Alessandro said with a laugh. "Any chance we can get Pinolo in one of those harnesses?"

"Are we done yet?" said Gennaro. "No word from Moretti?"

Alessandro nodded. "One."

Farrugia leaned forward and directed his speech at Bianca. "As I understand your operation, Alessandro has a point about Ancona wanting the eagle. It's inevitable, though, something is to be said with most of Rome on vacation that we have time on our side with respect to the media but not to Professor Moretti."

"What do you mean?" asked Gennaro.

"The two men who've been following Moretti," Farrugia said. "I've looked into them."

"Americans tied to Ancona, right?"

"Possibly tied to Ancona, but not Americans," responded Farrugia, looking directly at Bianca. "No. The two are SIMI, former SIMI operators who now work free-lance."

Bianca looked confused. "What is SIMI?"

Gennaro put his hand on hers and said, "*Servizio per le Informazioni e la Sicurezza Militare*, the Italian version of military intelligence."

Alessandro's pencil stopped moving.

"These two are former operators," Farrugia said, "out of work since the 'yellowcake forgery,' but they've shown up peripheral to some suspicious spying allegations."

"'Yellowcake forgery' as in uranium for Hussein from Niger and that load of bullshit about weapons of mass destruction?" she said.

"One and the same. That was when they left SIMI officially. They've been suspected in shadowing international business leaders, politicians and Italian magistrates."

"Real cloak-and-dagger stuff, eh?" Dante said. "What's the likelihood of them freelancing, as you said, for Ancona or Bevilacqua?"

"I don't know. For all I know they also could be investigating Ancona and Bevilacqua."

Gennaro spoke up. "We can't really do anything until we get a hold of Moretti. If you've gotten this information on his two shadow men, then you must know where he is."

"I know where I've seen him last. At his apartment."

"I've called him a hundred times already," Alessandro said. "No answer."

"Well, I guess that's it for now," Gennaro said and stood up.

Farrugia said to Gennaro, "Your place is clean. No bugs. I need to talk to Bianca. Alone."

"Go on, all of you back to work," said Gennaro.

Farrugia sat back down. The rest headed to the door.

"Wait, Dante," said Gennaro. "Would you please go downstairs to the pharmacist and get me some anti-acid pills?"

"Why me, Chief? Why don't you ask Silvio?"

"Because Silvio will return with cream for hemorrhoids."

"You really not feeling well, Chief?"

"I'm not feeling well. Pinolo. Moretti. Blame it on August. Here's the money, now go."

"Bianca, I'll be back," Dante said.

When he was gone, Gennaro said, "Bianca, please sit down."

"But Dante will be right back," she said.

Patting the chair, Gennaro said, "Please have a seat, dear. Close the door. That elevator will come with the Second Coming; and besides, it's August. I doubt Dante will find a pharmacy. They're all closed. He's young and healthy; so he wouldn't know."

"Please close the door and have a seat," said Farrugia with noticeable authority.

She closed the door, took the seat, and got comfortable. Silvio walked by and smiled at her, looking as if his day had improved.

"Now," Farrugia said, "we should talk . . . Alabaster."

28

"Can you believe he did that to me?" Dante said. "He sends me out to get heartburn pills from a pharmacy when he knows damn well that practically all of Rome is closed!"

Bianca kept walking, saying nothing. She didn't trust herself to open her mouth at the moment.

"Hey, aren't you even listening to me?" He grabbed her elbow and spun her around to face him.

Bianca grabbed him at the wrist. "Don't touch me. You're the one who lives here. You should know that no pharmacy would be open."

They kept walking. The Vespa was within sight.

"Please stop," he said.

They stood in the middle of the sidewalk, repeating the Italian drama she'd seen a hundred times on sidewalks, in cafés, in apartments: the alpha female and wary, repentant male.

"I'm sorry, okay," he said. "I was just angry that Gennaro pulled that stunt on me. Everyone is getting on edge. You're right. I should've known finding an open pharmacy would be like expecting condoms on sale in front of the Vatican."

"Stop whining." She turned her back on him and looked for the Vespa.

"What the hell's gotten into you?"

She whirled around. "Go ahead and say it. I'm acting like a bitch!"

"I would never say that, or call you that."

"It's what you're thinking, isn't it?"

"Hold on," he said, sounding maddeningly reasonable. "I'm not the one who walks around so secretive all the time. You do. I'm not the one who's hiding from the world. You are. Now, what the hell is going on, Bianca? Did Gennaro say something or his detective friend Farr . . . ?"

"Farrugia. His name is Farrugia and he knows. They both know."

"Know what? I don't get . . . you mean *they know*? Gennaro? Farrugia knows? How's that possible?"

Her anger at him had drained away. It should have been directed at herself in the first place. "I must've left a trail or a loose end. How stupid could I be?"

He took her hands. "Bianca, you're far from stupid, but even you have to realize that you can't run forever. You hold yourself to this impossible standard."

"Let's sit down over there on the bench," she said. Both walked over and sat, silent for a moment, looking at the empty streets and taking in the existential silence of an abandoned Rome.

"Farrugia knows Gennaro from when the two of them worked on the big anti-Mafia case that led to Gennaro's wife, Lucia, being murdered," she said. "It seems that Farrugia was sent to Rome, and pretty much treated like a has-been on the police force. His superiors give him the shit work: a few homicides, some overdoses, illegal immigrants—you can tell that it's a big step down from his days on the Organized Crime Bureau or whatever they call it down there. He explained it all to me; it's all politics. Farrugia drew the detail assignment on a breaking and entry, possible burglary that morphed into a missing-person case. That turned out to be me. It is my luck to draw a wildly overqualified inspector. Like a good bloodhound, he tracked me down."

"I have a confession to make," said Dante, and he explained the charade he and Gennaro had pulled on her neighbor, Signora Cetoni.

Bianca stared into his face silently. She was still trying to take it all in.

"You're not mad?" Dante said.

"At this point, I don't care. I'm sure Gennaro meant well and had no idea what he would find. Farrugia took the detail and ran with it, and here we are sitting on a bench in hotter-than-Hell weather."

"So is Farrugia closing the missing-person case? He found you. I mean he found Bianca Nerini. He doesn't have to say he found Alabaster."

"No. He's leaving it open. He wants to exclude the possibility that someone on the police force is watching the case. I don't know what he wants in exchange. He's afraid that if he puts in a report, whoever broke into my place will show up. I'm thinking that Farrugia will want to piece together my background."

"What the hell for? I can see him delaying the report so you can help us with Moretti and the eagle, but I doubt he's trying to figure out your past."

"Detectives are obsessive types, Dante. Not much different than completists who want everything in their collections. The smallest missing piece drives them nuts. And let's not forget that, like most detectives, if they can leverage a criminal to get bigger game, they'll do so."

"But you're not a criminal. You were doing a job and, well, life got complicated on you."

"Yeah, it certainly did. That doesn't stop Farrugia from wanting to crack Bevilacqua and Ancona, and if that means sacrificing me he might just do that."

"You really don't trust anyone, do you?"

"It's an occupational hazard."

"Well, you have to trust at some point. If anybody shouldn't trust a soul it should be Gennaro. Look at what happened with his wife. You know that somebody he was working with was on the take. The mafiosi went after his wife to send him a message. My point is if Gennaro trusts Farrugia, you should too. I know Gennaro and he wouldn't jeopardize your safety."

"Why should I trust Gennaro? He gave me up to Farrugia, didn't he?"

"That was unintentional. Maybe you don't have a choice now. Don't you trust me?"

Silence. She wanted to tell him she trusted him, she really did. But she couldn't lie. And she knew too well that Rendition was patient enough and clever enough to plant someone close to her. So she spent her energy resenting him for asking her to trust him. It might not have been fair, but it was where she was.

Dante raised his eyebrows twice. "You're really insulting me, Bianca, you know that? I let you into my home, put myself at risk, take care of you, cook, and respect your privacy with whatever you do with your laptop there. I can't tell you how many times I see you on that terrace with your pad of paper reminding me of Alessandro with that fucking pencil of his. It's like watching a bird peck for seed. TAP . . . TAP. Do I ever say anything? No. I come home one day and get attacked with two goons asking for 'Alabaster.' Did I blame you for that? No. Did I say anything to Gennaro or Alessandro? No. And this last time with Adriano, did I blame you?"

"I think you do. You didn't want me to go with you into the sewer. I still think Marco might've been behind that. I wouldn't expect anything less from your cavemen club."

"Not cavemen. We are urban speleologists."

"Whatever." She adjusted her laptop strap across her chest and stood up. "Take me home."

"Fine. I need to stop by the butcher's shop to figure out our lunch." Dante got up from the bench, fishing for his keys in his pocket.

"Eat by yourself. I want you to take me to my home."

He drove the Vespa in silence. The empty streets, the stoic monuments added to the slow crawl of time that it had taken to drop her off at the usual spot near the Hotel Diocleziano.

Her last words to him were meant to sting. "Don't call me."

Gennaro and Farrugia sat alone in the office.

"You're quiet, old friend," Gennaro said. "Mad at me that I didn't take you for Cuban food?"

Farrugia, standing, went over to the window and looked down at the cityscape. The August sun did not descend with the punishing intensity of his Calabrian youth. To him Rome was central Italy, and he tried hard not to subscribe to the divisive prejudices of looking at his compatriots as either northern *polentoni* or southern *terroni*. But he knew the likes of Pinolo the minute he had laid eyes on the man.

"Not mad. But my stomach is thinking," said Farrugia, letting his finger release the blind.

"What does your stomach say about Moretti?"

"That I need to find him quickly." He returned to his seat. "If these SIMI thugs get a hold of him and squeeze him and this sting operation is found out as a hoax, they'll harm the old man out of spite."

"And Bianca?"

"You mean Alabaster? She's agile and resourceful. I think for the moment she's spooked. Perfectly normal . . . she'll need to calm down and collect her thoughts. Then she has to make a decision: stay or run."

"If she runs, then what? Would you pursue her?"

Farrugia shrugged. "I have no reason to believe she's committed a crime. If she stays, it'll be out of a sense of camaraderie, or sheer intellectual challenge. She has a keen mind, no doubt there, Gennaro, but the question is whether she's as ruthless as she is for the sake of survival."

"Is this your stomach talking or are you reading her character, based on something else?"

"Remember our talk on the sidewalk that day? I asked, 'Is this woman a mental case? A recluse?' She's clearly not agoraphobic, but the degree to which she has no personal effects in that apartment told me that she has few or no attachments, emotional or otherwise."

"I remember you saying that you thought you were handling a ghost. But I have to say if she's skittish she seems to be adjusting well since she's been living with Dante."

"A ghost needs to haunt someone."

"She didn't take the news well when you presented her your findings about the two Americans in the green Fiat. I guess you weren't expecting her to be suddenly forthcoming."

Farrugia drummed his fingers along the top of the desk. A breeze high up in the building rattled the blinds, intruding on their conversation.

"Why would I expect her to reveal a thing? She has no reason to. Those two Americans in that car are a legacy from a past dispute." He drummed some more. "But now she has the hardest task that faces the intellectual type."

Gennaro threw up his hands.

"What's that?" he asked.

"When the internal logic collapses, the hardest thing for the intellectual is . . . to trust and ask for help," said Farrugia, tapping his temple with his finger. "I rather hope she finds the courage."

On the way to a cyber café Bianca found her answer.

Mounted above a multi-story hotel was a billboard baking in the Roman sun that advertised the latest drug in a bold red and white color scheme that reminded her of a sugary soda beverage her friends used to drink after school, a drink which she disliked intensely because of the burning carbonation.

She knew that she must have looked like a pathetic tourist, staring as she was at that billboard, a tourist left alone to contemplate something like the Coliseum, which Romans walked past daily, a place that had been a patchwork of overgrown grass and weeds at the time of the visit of the great German poet and writer Goethe.

She saw the '-pril' ending to the drug name and thought immediately of the soothing rains of Chaucer's opening line. "Whan that Aprill, with his shoures soote, The droghte of March hath perced to the roote."

Then, under the drug name, she noticed the announcement, in Italian, of course, "Proven effective in clinical trials."

Damn.

'-prils' were ACE inhibitor drugs used to treat heart failure, hypertension, or high blood pressure, and prevent strokes. It made her think of Sargent's new statin that claimed, although not fully corroborated, to stall strokes, Alzheimer's disease, and a miscellany of other disorders with the addition of CoQ10.

The "Proven effective in clinical trials" blinded her like the opening of a curtain on a lazy day in bed. It was clear: Sargent had used social media in some way during clinical trials. Had he inappropriately used electronic health records? Nonetheless, there was a connection.

'SM & EHR w/ PEP nightmare. Wasp next.'

While an ACE inhibitor is not Sargent's statin, his use of social media somehow involved health records and created some kind of nightmare and 10ki was suggesting that Sargent was about to repeat it again.

Her need to plug into cyberspace was making her fingertips twitch. She found her cyber café, purchased a time card and went to a docking station to connect her laptop.

A few keystrokes later she found that there was no coverage or even insinuation of any scandal or suggestion of impropriety about Sargent's use of social media. What references she found on his use of social media were so vague that they left the reader to wonder how Sargent used social media at all. More keystrokes but nothing on Sargent.

The keyboard clicked and clacked as her fingers worked the keys. The 'aha moment' came when she discovered that the Federal Drug Administration had no official statement or policy on the use of social media and clinical drug trials.

"Bingo!" she said, but disturbed no one since the café was bereft of nerds or geeks. Even *they* were away in Rimini for some time in the sun.

Somehow Sargent had capitalized on social media and used it to grease the pipeline for his new statin. The question she knew that remained for her was: what was 'PEP' and what exactly were the details to the 'nightmare'?

She typed in PEP and the results exhausted her patience: 'Post-Exposure Prophylaxis'; 'Pulmonary Embolism Prevention'; 'Penile Extension Project.'

She brainstormed: a clinical trial is a project, so that made her think of project management, and after scurrying down some false leads she read that the crucial limiter on all projects was time. She said to herself, "Like, duh," and ignored the kiosk keeper's curious stare.

Then the link appeared: a PDF of a Powerpoint presentation by an industrious Indian doctor with multiple degrees, including a doctorate and a string of alien acronyms at a British hospital in which he spelled out a mathematical formula to calculate the rate of enrollment for a successful clinical trial.

It was so much better than the 'aha moment' or a 'Eureka' that she pumped both hands up in triumph, so amped with adrenaline that she couldn't yell out her exultation. The kiosk keeper was tsking his head side to side, as if he had seen the exact replay a thousand times a day.

She pinged 10ki.

29

An hour later after a tossed-back thimble of caffeine, 10ki answered.

10ki typed, "A to Q?" which was the taskmaster's shorthand for 'answers to questions.'

She keyed in her answer for the first clue, "Statin."

"Correct."

"MP . . . Millennium Park, Massachusetts."

"Correct."

Bianca, feeling confident and assured, proceeded with, "CoQ10 + statin."

"Right again."

Bianca, trying to minimize the details, typed for the fourth clue. "Patent expiration. Statin reborn; king = Cyril Sargent; & spin-off venture = Nasonia Pharma."

"Right again. Now for the hard part."

"Social media to open electronic health records, which coaxed or tweaked enrollment timeline 4 clinical trial. Thought is repeat with Nasonia," and almost signing her name, she typed, "AB = Alabaster Black territory," and added, with pride, "QED."

The cursor stood alone in a sea of blue screen, blinking, and the more it blinked the more it seemed a distress signal.

Finally, 10ki typed, "SM, correct; EHR, correct; Wasp, incorrect. Close enough, Alabaster."

It may have made her look petulant, but the need for perfection provoked her response. "Incorrect? Nasonia = IPO."

"Yes, IPO. Always possible repeat performance but u need to be literal about name."

By now, Alabaster was angry and confused so she typed, "?"

"Nasonia = 3 species of a type of wasp. Genome: global pesticides & potential drugs for diseases from sequencing."

Bianca sat back in her chair, feeling wrung out. Cyril Sargent was starting a company that had a plan, probably establishing a multiple-patent monopoly, to sequence an insect's genetic map. She had no idea what the significance was about that particular wasp, but it apparently piqued Sargent to name a company after a winged pest.

"Have to go but need ur expertise 2 save time: 10ki files: Lorenzo Bevilacqua &/or Amici di Roma &/or Alan Ancona."

Blink the cursor did again in a calmer ocean.

"Sure. Give me 2 days. Thx."

The kiosk keeper watched her leave, as did the two pairs of eyes in a green Fiat across the street.

There was a knock. It was old-fashioned, even rustic, but as effective as the electronic buzzer.

Simple and unpretentious was the rap of the knuckles against the door—the door opened. Dante was on one side, Bianca on the other side, as if nothing had ever happened.

She smiled. "May I come in?"

He smiled, said nothing, and widened the opening for her to return home.

30

Detective Farrugia parked his *civetta* in an alley in the San Lorenzo neighborhood.

As he jerked the emergency brake up he couldn't help but think that the sound was like wringing a chicken's neck, a sound that brought back his childhood. Farrugia saw as he looked around that some of the buildings in San Lorenzo still retained scars from the massive Allied bombing but that street art managed to cover up the ugly past with respectable scenes in vibrant colors.

The home office had given him an unmarked car. It was like any public-service employee with a personality: it gave him grief in the morning when he wanted air-conditioning, reacted with stultifying slowness mid-day when he tried to use the windshield wipers to clear the grime and pigeon shit, and seemed to want to race home at the end of the day to do nothing.

Alfa Romeos and Fiats were the staples of the Italian police fleet, and everyone on the street could identify them. There was the unique color stripe on the side, the unique roof color; the unique plates and banal white block letters on the car door to declare the specific branch of law enforcement. Even without their livery, they carried the feel of police cars, and a trained eye could still spot them. So when Farrugia needed an undercover car, he specifically requested the vehicle he had now—a ten-year-old Volkswagon Golf.

Of course, that Farrugia was behind the wheel did nothing for anonymity.

Moretti rented an apartment in San Lorenzo because it was near the public university, La Sapienza. The professor, like most priests of the mind, had never married nor had children.

Farrugia enabled the car alarm—another less than discreet noise, followed by a flash of lights. It made sense for Moretti to be near other professors, to be near students. The environment here was quiet by day with the students in class, while the nightlife could certainly keep an old man young, with its curbside cafés filled with lively debates on art, literature, and politics. Except that, in August, the neighborhood was even more of a ghost town than the rest of Rome as the students fled to their homes, which must give Moretti plenty of quiet time and alone time.

It was the "time alone" that worried Farrugia. Silvio had been phoning the man day and night: no answer. There was no need to bother with e-mail since the man didn't own a computer and disliked electronic communication. And if anything had happened to him, there was no one left in the neighborhood to notice.

And so Farrugia was here.

The apartment was accessible from the rear by a wrought-iron stairwell. A heavy industrial steel door, acting as the fire exit from his floor, was open, seesawing and creaking with a metallic swagger. Farrugia climbed up the grating with caution, putting on the set of crime-scene gloves he always kept in his pocket. Best to use this entrance since Moretti's "visitors," if he had any, wouldn't use the front desk.

Stale air emanated from the hallway as Farrugia widened the door and heard the protracted groan. A twittering light from the ceiling in the hallway was giving off the spasmodic bursts of a distress signal. The light bulb had been loosened. Following the numbers on the doors, he found Moretti's apartment. No light or shadows could be seen under the door and a slight nudge confirmed that it was locked.

He looked both ways like they do in the movies before he took out a slim leather case and unzipped it. A colleague from the FBI whom he had met at an international conference and had helped on an organized-crime case had made him a set of lock picks as a thank-you gift. American lock-picking sets were supposedly registered in DC, his colleague had told him over coffee that day, but not this one. Marc Weber Tobias, the greatest lock-breaker ever, had designed this kit, the Special Agent had told him.

It seemed to work. Two seconds later the lock turned. With a flip, he swung the pick back into the carrying case and drew his weapon as he pushed the door slowly. The far window let the August air exhale a breath through the drawn red curtain. Even in the gloom, he could see the place was in shambles. The scene reminded Farrugia of one of those northern paintings, perhaps Gerrit Dou, with its inexplicable light source and forbidding chiaroscuro.

When the curtain lifted up again from a big belly of air, the light stimulated an urgent sound from the taped mouth and bulging eyes of a bound man on the floor.

Farrugia was kneeling beside him in an instant. The professor had taken a good beating, eyes swollen and duct tape slapped across his lips. To add to the disrespectful thrashing the old man had endured, his "guests" had rolled him up in a shower curtain with red and white petals. Farrugia started unrolling the professor from out of the curtain, but stopped to look and verify the floral pattern, which he then ignored when he had realized that the professor had noticed that his rescuer seemed more concerned with the shower curtain than with freeing him.

"This'll hurt when I pull it off," said Farrugia.

The professor nodded.

Farrugia took a good hold of a corner of the duct tape and yanked it decisively.

Moretti closed his eyes, the pain so great he couldn't scream, but the tears welled up and ran down the sides of his face. Farrugia freed the man's hands from another wad of duct tape, and looked to the sink for a glass to give the man some water.

"Very sorry about that. Here," said Farrugia, giving Moretti the water and watching the man gulp without dignity. "How long do you think you were tied up?"

Moretti held up two fingers and kept drinking, the water running down the sides of his mouth. He was quite parched.

"Two days?" Farugia said.

"Two men," Moretti said, his voice still raspy. "I told you two men."

Farrugia wondered where the hell the detail he had assigned to watch those two men had gone. Moretti had been beaten and then rolled up like a used carpet and had remained that way for . . . yes, it had been two days. The last status he had received from the two undercover agents had indicated that everything was fine, until he tried to contact the professor himself. Then the day he had gone to meet Gennaro and heard that Silvio had been having no luck reaching the professor had made Farrugia realize that the math was just not adding up.

"They wanted to know about the eagle," said Moretti.

"Of course they did. Can you tell me anything distinctive about them? Dress? Speech?" He didn't want to suggest an American accent, but he was expecting it.

"They spoke Italian, but when they were rummaging around, they slipped into some dialect; sounded almost Slavic."

Friulian or Resian, but not American. Farrugia worked the makeshift bindings off the man's limbs, checking at the same time to see whether any bones were broken.

"Think maybe they spoke Slovenian?" he asked.

"Not quite, but it had that touch," the professor said, rubbing his hands to restore the circulation.

"Probably mercenaries. No bones seem to be broken, Professor, but I'd like to take you to the hospital to make sure your cuts and bruises are looked after. They take anything?"

"My notebook, but I had nothing that'd implicate any of us."

"Cell phone?"

"Heh. They took that but it won't do them any good."

"Why do you say that?"

The older man moved his haunches from side to side to access his back pocket, from which he extracted the SIM card.

Farrugia took the small wafer between two fingers. "What made you take the SIM card out?"

"That night at the restaurant the young lady, Bianca, told me it was a good practice. If they'd gotten hold of this card then they would've been privy to all my contacts and that would've jeopardized everything."

Smart old dog.

"I'm glad you're still with us," said Farrugia, lifting the old man to his feet and assisting him in steadying himself.

"So am I."

"What did you tell them?"

"I said the eagle was at a lab for verification and that even I didn't know which lab. I said it was all for secrecy's sake. These two hoodlums weren't happy with hearing that, but I guess they must've heard some students or the cleaning lady with her cart in the hallway because they ran off. I was in and out of consciousness at that point."

Yes, they must have been run off. Farrugia knew that the rolled-up shower curtain had been meant as the last stretch in a one-way ride.

Bianca's return had surprised Dante.

They ate dinner together, hardly saying a word let alone revisiting the argument. Afterwards, Dante did the dishes and tidied up. Nothing had been resolved between them, nothing had been said, but was her arrival here a form of apology? Did it mean she'd decided to trust him? He sat down on his couch, picked up his book and was about to start reading it when he realized that she was on the stairway looking down at him.

"Is it comfortable, that sofa?" she asked.

"For sleep? Not really, but it'll do." He opened up his book to look for his last paragraph.

"Oh," she said, almost self-conscious, as if she were at a loss for words.

He had never seen her at a loss for words. And she was still standing there. "Something on your mind?" he asked her.

"Does it bother you that people always seem to refer to us as boyfriend and girlfriend?"

"Not really. Does it bother *you*?" he asked, not looking up, though he stole a peek and saw that she was standing there, indecisive.

Before she turned to walk up the rest of the stairs she said, "I don't know if you need a reminder or not, but you're allowed to sleep in your own bed, you know."

"I didn't know."

"Now you do." She walked up the last few steps to the landing and went to bed.

31

Dante lay there in his bed reliving the three mysteries of man.

The first mystery had begun years ago when he, like most boys, would stare at the blank sea of a bedroom ceiling imagining his first woman. The second mystery came years later when he, after some experience, and she, who had finally arrived also with some experience, would lie on the bed, afraid of what to say, uncertain whether to stay, or all too certain of what to say and do. Then they both stared at that ceiling, waiting for the appropriate time. The third mystery, yet to come, was of gratitude that someone would endure with him against the darkness under the white stare of the ceiling.

Maybe . . .

He freed one hand to tilt the digital face of the alarm clock to verify the time.

The digital clock said 11:34.

He stared at the clock. It was a small black box that had red numbers for a face and a pulsating colon for a heart. He adjusted his pillow. It was one of those nights that felt older than it should, much later than it was, but the red digital numbers said the same time upside down: HELL.

Her hand moved across his midsection and he felt the stupid urge to flex his abdomen to prove he had a firm stomach. His insecurity about whether he was worthy prevailed on the edge of sleep. He and Alessandro had argued that mere mortals have a four-pack abdomen and the diet-crazed have six whereas those with a spider heritage have eight.

All the mysteries coalesced into one luminous blur as sleep overtook him. He had fantasized about Bianca. She was now incarnate next to him. He did worry about the morning because he was feeling so at ease with their experience that he had nothing to say, but thought that if he continued to say nothing, she would be offended. And then, of course, he worried what she might say, since she was the hyper-rational one, almost without a need for emotion.

He escaped into sleep, thankful for whatever it was to be in the moment. The morning seemed so far away.

The cell phone rang. His. He could tell his from hers because hers never rang when he was with her. He also knew it was his because she kept hers next to her laptop, snuggled into the little pouch on the strap.

Thankfully, the whirring sound did not awaken her.

"Pronto," he said, eyes still closed.

"It's Gennaro," the voice said in a very caffeinated tone for an early hour.

"What's up, Chief?"

"Moretti is at San Pietro Fatebenefratelli."

Dante sat bolt upright.

She murmured at the disturbance.

"You all right? That didn't sound good," said Gennaro.

"I'm fine. Moretti is in the hospital? What happened?"

"Cuts and bruises and a little dehydration but nothing serious. He's fine. A little shaken up. Just getting looked at to rule out anything dangerous. I'll explain when you get here. I'm here with Farrugia; Alessandro is on his way. I'd like for you and Bianca to come down here as soon as you can."

"Sure, Boss. We'll get there soon." He ended the call.

The hand across his chest and the warmth of her breath as she nuzzled his neck distracted him; he closed his eyes for a moment.

That ended when he heard a sound downstairs.

Had it begun with a few rat-tat-tats on the door and escalated into a fist-pounding tantrum, he could see his neighbors calling the police. Unless it *were* the police making the noise, then his playing the angry resident answering the door would play into their script and then justify the ensuing festivities. Then he could be humble.

But neither angry intruders nor the *Raggruppamento Operativo Speciale* tried to pick the locks.

Dante woke Bianca up and placed a finger on her lips. "Ssshhhh. Lock yourself in the bathroom and call Farrugia from my cell. Explain to him somebody is at my door. He can find us by tracing the cell phone."

She nodded almost without hesitation, took his cell and slipped out of bed.

He eased his way down to the living room. The inexpert metallic prodding at his front door that he'd heard from upstairs continued. Then he saw the door handle turn unsuccessfully.

Then Bianca stood next to him, wearing quickly thrown-on clothes, just as Dante was. She held up the cell, which was still on. He thought she'd agreed far too easily.

They watched and then heard a jiggling noise and another inept turn of the door handle. Bianca pointed to the bottom runner of the door, where Dante saw two flickering shadows.

The terrace was too high up and too dangerous to climb down from. Dante felt no choice but to confront his unwelcome guest or guests. Since he had no peephole to the door, he had to assume that at least one person on the other side of the door was bent over to jiggle the doorknob. He motioned to Bianca to stand aside.

She backed away, returned a moment later with a kitchen knife. He would have to get used to her courage.

As the doorknob turned again, Dante grabbed it, turned it and pulled the door open, then grabbed the shirt attached to the arm and slammed the man into the doorframe. As had been expected, there was a second man, who countered Dante's move with a gun pointed at the side of his head.

Then he found himself trumped when he felt the sharp point of a chef's knife at his neck.

"Let's be reasonable here," said the man jammed into the doorframe. In American English.

"I'm willing to use this," said the man with the gun behind Dante.

"Use it and you'll be breathing out of the side of your neck," said Bianca behind him.

"Seems like everybody here speaks English," said the man in Dante's grip. "He'll put the gun down if you let me go, and I'll show you identification. Or better yet you can reach into my breast pocket and pull out my identification yourself."

"Or even better yet," Bianca said, "your friend either hands me the gun or drops the rounds on the floor, including the one in the chamber."

"Not happening," said the man with the gun.

Bianca edged the point of the knife forward for him to feel her disappointment. He closed his eyes, feeling the pain and the reality of being outmaneuvered.

"Fine," Dante said, "then the two of you introduce yourselves and tell me why you're breaking and entering my apartment."

The man in Dante's grip said, "Special Agent Murphy, FBI, and the one with the gun, Special Agent McGarrity, also FBI."

"Are all cops Irish like in American movies?" asked Dante.

"No, just the black ones," said McGarrity. "Are all Italians mafia?"

"Aren't you two out of your jurisdiction?" Bianca said. "This is Rome, Italy, not Rome, New York."

The man in Dante's hands squirmed. "Hey, if you want the CIA instead we can accommodate you with just one phone call. In fact, they're an upgrade. You won't even hear the doorknob next time."

"Lose the sarcasm," Bianca said. "Why are you here?"

"We're here for you, Alabaster," McGarrity said, "and not the gentleman who has my partner in the death grip. How about we all take this inside and have a civil conversation."

"Am I wanted for a crime?" asked Bianca.

"No," said Murphy and McGarrity simultaneously.

"Watch." McGarrity slowly eased the gun away from the back of Dante's head and holstered it, and held both of his hands up. "Now call off your boyfriend. And maybe somebody here has some coffee?"

Dante relaxed his grip. Murphy stood up. Dante tried to straighten out the man's lapels as a no-hard-feelings gesture. As McGarrity stepped in, Bianca closed the door.

"Thank you," said McGarrity.

"I'll put on some coffee," said Dante.

"Okay," Bianca said, "what's this about?"

Murphy was the one to take charge. "Let's lay everything out on the table. We're FBI and you're Alabaster Black. You disappeared about two years ago. You went to Lucerne, then a few other places, had a few name changes, and now you're here."

Bianca put the knife down. "What of it? Should I stop you there and let myself be amazed at your display of brilliant deduction, or should I allow you to continue?"

"Everybody's a wiseass these days." McGarrity pointed to the chair and Dante nodded that he could sit down. "Charlie, have a seat and stop playing the hard ass. You're not very good at it."

Dante poured the coffee and all four of them sat, enjoying the first sip of Lavazza together.

"I'll be straight, Ms. Black or Ms. Nerini—whichever name you want us to call you. We're a couple of field agents with a shitty boss back home. He gets a jacket across his desk one day on a Robert Strand. The file came up because some distant relative who knew somebody who knew somebody was wondering if there was an estate—pure fishing expedition. We caught it because said crappy boss has to show that somebody did something with it, so this other person raising the stink can go away all peaceful and quiet. The problem was, the more I looked at the Strand file the more the hair on the back of my neck started to stand up. I worked Homicide then Organized Crime before I went to the Bureau, and there are some instincts that don't die."

"And you think Strand was murdered?" asked Bianca.

"I'd bet on it. There was never a body, but foul play isn't unreasonable. I start digging through the dossier, and that led me to other papers, and before you know it I'm in a forest. Now Special Agent Murphy here has an eye for patterns—he's one of those people who does cryptograms in his head. Anyway, Charlie here pointed out one day while we were wading our way through the cardboard-box forest that he saw in the headers of some financial reports the letters 'AB'.

And Charlie said, 'You know, Mike, this AB has to be the team leader or something like that, because AB shows up everywhere the names Robert Strand and preta appear. Right up until Strand disappears.' At the time, I didn't know what preta was, but thanks to Charlie connecting the dots, we soon found reasons why his death made sense. Then our question became 'where's AB?' After all, Robert Strand apparently disappears and AB disappears? It's curious. Especially since a hundred million US in bearer bonds disappeared from Strand's estate at the same time. That relative who schmoozed a Senator must've known about that hundred million."

Dante nearly choked on his coffee. He knew Bianca hadn't seemed to worry about money, but a hundred million?

"You sound ambivalent about Strand's disappearance," said Bianca. "You have doubts?"

Murphy decided to contribute to the conversation. "No, we assume that he's dead. Anyway, we combed the government databases for anyone with the initials 'AB' and—"

"And you filtered by gender and narrowed it down further by financial-related occupation. Hardly rocket science."

"No, it's not rocket science," said McGarrity, "but the funny thing is when you start going into the field and start talking to people, it's amazing the things you'll discover."

After a small sip she said, "Like what?"

"You start formulating a profile of a person based on trends and phenomena. Then, as Charlie will tell you, patterns start to emerge," said McGarrity with his demitasse below his lips. "The patterns led us to Rome."

"Your boss allowed the two of you to do this all on taxpayer money?" Dante said, thinking of Pinolo refusing to pay for business meals. "No wonder people want to go to America. Money must grow on trees."

"You have no idea how much taxpayer money is wasted, Mr. Allegretti, especially when your boss wants to look busy. But the real reason is our high-ranking pain in the ass."

"Just cut to the chase," said Bianca.

Murphy was the one who put his demitasse down. "For years there have been rumors that there is a covert government entity called Rendition. The same rumor said that this organization used a red 'R' as its logo. We looked at those reports, and while the IRS is good at putting the screws to people, the reports we saw—your reports—operated on an entirely different level. It was like intelligence work you can respect."

"That would sound like something your CIA would do," said Dante.

"Quite true," said Special Agent McGarrity. "But if it involves the murder of a US citizen, like we believe it did with Strand, then it's our territory. The CIA can handle the players abroad if we can prove the murder was international."

"Who's to say it wasn't a home-team effort?"

McGarrity shrugged, "Who's to say. Stranger things have happened in our nation's past, but with any agency a president has to issue some kind of mandate. Title 28 empowered the Bureau to cover domestic matters and govern internal intelligence. The 1947 National Security Act legitimized the CIA. And given the lack of boundaries in today's world, we would have to wonder where Rendition fits into things. See what the disappearance of one American will do?"

Bianca took her last sip. "You mean one wealthy American who supposedly had technological innovations that could upset economic markets and power ties. You have all this in motion because some relative wants an inheritance."

Special Agent Murphy leaned forward. "It is a sad fact that some Americans are worth more than others. We know you were a government accounting clerk who somehow found a way to live abroad. We aren't asking you how. I'm sure we can always find a way to interrupt your ability to finance your stay or suddenly make you unwelcome in other countries no matter how much money or how many identities you may have. We only care about what you might know about Rendition."

Bianca was quiet. "I had always heard Rendition was a rumor. You both know that the CIA has what is called the OGA."

McGarrity smiled and said, "You mean Other Government Agencies. Yes, we know it's a wide umbrella term that can cover the moon's shadow."

Dante interrupted, once again thinking of Pinolo. "From where I sit the two of you still have a boss to report to, and it seems very probable that his personality hasn't improved in your absence."

They looked at him and reflected on the truth of his words. There was always a boss.

"So we need to decide what to do," Dante said.

"No," Bianca said, "first we need to go to the hospital."

Dante nodded. "More coffee anyone?"

32

On the ride to the hospital, Dante's cell phone rang. It wasn't Farrugia.

"What the hell is wrong with you, Dante?" Marco said. "I let you into Nerva and you bring your girlfriend and she goes psycho on Adriano."

Dante cupped the receiver to tell Bianca, "It's Marco."

"Of course it's Marco. Remember me? I'm trying to hold the Underground together and now I have practically all of the medical staff in Rome against me. You better hope I don't need medical care, and the same goes for you and your girlfriend. What was she thinking?"

"That Adriano is an asshole," said Dante.

Murphy and McGarrity turned their heads since they couldn't pretend that they were not listening.

"Tell me what I don't know, but to cut his line? You could've just left him to air out."

"He punched me in the face," said Dante.

"Well, if you got seriously hurt, there was a doctor right there."

"Besides busting my balls, what do you want, Marco?"

"Calm down. Look, do you know anything about this eagle or what? If you know something you would tell me, wouldn't you?"

"Bye, Marco." Dante clicked his cell shut and threw it on the smoldering dashboard. "How the hell do you two manage in this small car?"

"It's the only one the boss allowed us to lease," said Special Agent McGarrity, hands lifting off the steering wheel apologetically.

Gennaro was standing outside the examining room with Alessandro and Farrugia when he saw the crowd of four approaching them.

Dante made the introductions, and it seemed the two mysterious Americans were FBI agents. Who were apparently now on their side? After the round of handshakes Professor Moretti emerged from the room, overwhelmed by the crowd outside his door.

The departing doctor was all smiles and cordial until he saw Dante and Bianca.

"How are you, Professor?" asked Dante.

"I'm fine," Moretti said. "I explained everything to Farrugia. Who are these gentlemen?"

Alessandro introduced the professor to the two Special Agents, and Gennaro was relieved to find that the professor didn't recognize them.

Gennaro was the first to say it. "We should talk, so let's find a place to eat."

As the crowd moved down across the glaring white hospital floor, counted amongst the happy, healthy group of people who leave a hospital of their own accord, unaided by wheelchairs or orderlies, Gennaro pulled on Bianca's arm.

"You trust these two?" he asked.

"Not yet," she said, "or not entirely. But we have no choice."

Alessandro came through for breakfast. Even with most of Rome gone, he knew of a chef at a fantastic bed and breakfast on the Corso Vittorio Emanuele II who couldn't afford to go anywhere for the holiday month.

"Where we going?" asked Gennaro.

"A small quiet place near Largo Argentina and the Pantheon," said Alessandro. "The food is good, but we've got to make sure when we leave that we leave a good amount of money. My friend Fiore is doing all the cooking, all the serving, and he's stuck in Rome because he's paying his mother's medical bills back home in Ragusa. We can eat well and help a friend at the same time."

They all grumbled except the Special Agents, who struggled to understand Alessandro when he slipped into dialect about his friend's special situation.

Fiore met them at the door and showed Agent Murphy a place to park the Fiat in the back, where the car would be safe and unseen. Farrugia's Golf, they abandoned on the street. Fiore showed them around the desolate bed and breakfast before seating them in a master suite with an improvised table set for eight.

The room was spacious, immaculate and decorated with white-on-white décor, giving it a cool, calm, placid atmosphere. A respectable-sized plasma television was mounted on the wall with an immortal ficus tree under it. A simple blue curtain hung from a rod to keep the sunlight out. Against the wall was an unframed black-and-white photograph close-up of one of the gods from the nearby fountains in the Piazza Navona.

Understanding that he would have two American guests, Fiore made sure that eggs figured in his dishes for them. He presented them with egg-and-ham bruschetta, a frittata with mozzarella and zesty herbs; and he made one especially Italian treat for them: anise rings, along with copious amounts of strong coffee, orange juice and fresh fruit.

For the rest of the group, Fiore knew that they were partial and receptive to a breakfast south of Naples, so he gave them a choice of either *mandorla* or coffee granita or *cremolate* with chunky pieces of peach to enjoy with their brioche. While Murphy and McGarrity ate as if they had just become famous, lost that fame, and regained it on a fortuitous reprieve, the rest of them dipped and bit their brioche again and again.

The moment came when the plates were gone and the table was cleared.

McGarrity folded his napkin and placed it neatly in front of him, then wagged his finger at Farrugia. "Detective Isidore Farrugia . . . I never thought I'd have the privilege to share a meal with you. I followed your work for the Maxi-Trials and the subsequent convictions. You have no idea how much the guys in OCB admired you. How were you able to turn Mafiosi?"

Farrugia tried not to look surprised. "A fox can learn to jump a barbed-wire fence. While I appreciate your attempt at flattery, Agent McGarrity, the credit, as you know, should go to those no longer with us."

"No flattery, Detective. I meant it sincerely. The Maxi-Trials changed the United States Organized Crime Bureau. The only unfortunate outcome for us across the Atlantic is that federal prosecutors had to create a domino factory in order to get convictions. I don't think a man who has committed multiple murders warrants special rights in order to get his testimony. If we had everyone confessing to get better deals and lighter sentences, heaven would get overcrowded."

Farrugia's face reflected no emotion, not even a twitch, which took a little doing. "We have our penitents here also, but it isn't up to me to do the negotiating for a parking spot in Hell."

"I assume you were also a political casualty?"

"You tell me, since you've followed my career. I don't presume to have anything in common with you aside from the occupation. But you could say something along the lines that I was passed over. I'm not exactly known for being a politician."

McGarrity slammed the table hard enough to make everyone's eyes jump, except Farrugia's. "I knew it. I thought I saw the pattern. You're a modest man, Detective. I like that."

"While I have your high esteem, please explain to me why you were sitting outside Ms. Nerini's apartment and why you turned her apartment over?"

McGarrity paused and looked at Bianca, which was interesting. Then he proceeded to explain: Robert Strand, his plans for *preta* plants, his apparent demise, the organization called Rendition, the missing bearer bonds, Lucerne, and the cases and conclusions of reports of one Alabaster Black. The redecoration of the apartment was just for show since they knew they wouldn't find a thing. It was meant as a psychological tactic. It had failed. But, Farrugia had to acknowledge, it was their only failure so far. Except, perhaps, underestimating the nosiness of Italian neighbors.

While the group listened, Farrugia took small sips of his ice water. When McGarrity had finished, Farrugia asked, "Did you find anything in Ms. Nerini's apartment that proves she is Alabaster Black?"

"No."

"Can you prove whether she was then or is now a member of Rendition?"

"No." The Special Agent held his hand up. "Please hear me out. If an organization like Rendition exists, it has no oversight, and there's always the possibility of corruption when there is no oversight. Is a committee an answer? While I deplore bureaucracy, Detective, I do believe in checks and balances. If nobody checks Rendition, then who's to say that they are any better than the mafia? I'm sure one can look back in time and find sound reasons for the mafia. Well, that time has passed. We've had laws on the books to safeguard investors since the S&L scandals and we have entire divisions of law enforcement dedicated to white-collar crime. Although far from perfect, laws now define 'victim' more accurately, and such laws should've ended Rendition's existence."

As McGarrity spoke, Farrugia glanced over at Bianca, who had her eyes staring ahead, brazen as one of the Medici women.

Farrugia cleared his throat. He put his hands on the table and showed his palms to McGarrity and Murphy.

"I can't help you with Rendition, but we here around this table are interested in a particular fox, and I think you'd be very interested in making sure he doesn't jump the fence."

"How do you propose to do that, Detective?"

"You've met Bianca Nerini. I defer to her and her colleagues. I only ask that you two be honorable, which means all communication will stay within this present party, which means any surveillance, like electronic bugs, should stop. If we can't act with honor amongst ourselves, then we are no better than the people we claim to detest, and our existence insults those who were murdered for profit. As for how we prevent a certain wolf from jumping the fence, I would like to teach you a Sicilian proverb: 'Ogni vulpi porta amuri a la sò tana'; and my old friend Gennaro can translate it for you. Excuse me."

Farrugia walked out for a breath of air and to compliment Fiore. But before he did, he heard Gennaro clear his throat. "Every fox brings love to its own den."

33

Alessandro seemed like a kid with a new toy, his eyes wide open and wet smile broadening, surfing the channels on the plasma television. The only thing missing was the drool.

Dante stepped up to Sandro's right side. "Anything good?"

"Amazing depth and . . ." He stopped inexplicably in mid-sentence when he realized Bianca was on his left.

"Go on, don't mind me," she said. "I can see from the screen you're not talking about the porn channels. It's a common male affliction."

Dante glanced at her. "Porn?"`

"No, sports and television."

"Hold on, wait." Sandro spiked the volume up on the Free Channel. The coiffed mannequin head was announcing, "Breaking news development. Latest in from the field says that Professor Rinaldo Moretti has been seen and treated at a local hospital. To our correspondent Giancarlo Ragonese . . ."

"Those assholes can't even get my name right," Moretti said. "It's Renato not Rinaldo."

The two Americans, Farrugia, and Gennaro went to join the party.

"Sssh, Professore," said Farrugia, eyes on the screen.

On the smooth plasma was a perfectly assembled talking torso, also with helmet hair, with his finger in his ear to signify the high-tech flow of real-time conversation from field to office.

"Yes, it's true. An unnamed source has confirmed that Professor Renato Morelli was treated today here at San Pietro Fatebenefratelli for what appeared to be cuts and bruises from a possible altercation." The newsman pointed up to some floor of the hospital as if he were indicating the precise treatment room.

"Moretti!" yelled the professor.

Sandro increased the volume two bars.

"Was he hurt, Giancarlo?" asked the Free Channel newsman, giving a painfully concerned look that could have been equally misconstrued for constipation.

"All I was told from our source was that the professor had some lacerations, one of which required stitches, and then he was discharged, safe and sound."

Everyone looked at Moretti. No stitches.

"Tell us, Giancarlo, did the esteemed professor say that he had been attacked?"

"Negative. These injuries remain mysterious but suggest physical violence. As you know, the professor has been reclusive and has been under intense scrutiny since his appearance on our channel about the spectacular find in the Roman underground. There is a shroud of secrecy around the eagle, as you know."

"Shroud of Turin!" heckled Moretti.

"Yes, we know Giancarlo. Is there any indication that the professor seemed distressed?"

"Our source said the professor was charming, interacting with his attending physician, and that he even flirted with his nurse. We just don't know the cause of these injuries. Although the professor has had to endure extraordinary media attention, which I'm sure has caused him some unwanted stress. It is unconscionable to believe that anyone would want to hurt him, especially when the public at large awaits his verdict on the eagle. Back to you in the studio."

"Thank you, Giancarlo, for this provocative breaking news. Questions remain: who hurt the professor, and what is the latest on the eagle? Now to other news. Fishermen in the Strait of Messina have captured on video a giant squid being eaten by a sperm whale. Fascinating dramatic footage when we return."

"Great," Moretti said, "I'm reduced to a sex-crazed geriatric on the verge of a nervous breakdown and imminent tragedy. They've reduced me to several clichés. Take your pick."

"It's all just color," said Farrugia. "I've been called worse."

"Now you know why I don't watch television for the weather," said Gennaro.

"How the hell did they find out the professor was at the hospital?" asked Bianca, taking the remote and hitting the mute button.

As usual, she had cut to the meat of the matter. "That damn doctor," said Dante.

Farrugia sat behind the wheel of his unmarked car, Gennaro next to him, and McGarrity and Murphy in the back seat.

"This is a really nice car, Detective," said McGarrity.

"Thank you." He turned over the engine. The air-conditioning kicked on. He thanked the Virgin Mother silently. His luck was improving.

"Think it's safe to keep our Fiat parked here?" Murphy asked.

"It'll be fine. Sandro's friend doesn't mind. Fiore has the keys and I'm sure you wouldn't mind if he takes it out for a spin now and then, since he isn't going anywhere on vacation. Sandro says Fiore is very responsible."

"Not a problem," said McGarrity.

"So how are we going to do this?" Murphy asked.

Three heads turned and looked at Murphy and then looked at each other.

"We draw out Ancona, right?" asked McGarrity.

Gennaro looked at Farrugia, who gave the matter some thought, now that he had these new resources to use.

"The question is who?" he said. "Who will draw Ancona out?"

"I don't understand this answering questions with a question, Isidò," said Gennaro.

Farrugia turned askew in his seat to face Gennaro and also to include McGarrity and Murphy in his thoughts.

"Ancona sent those men after Moretti. Dante thinks that the doctor leaked the story to the news because there's some feud within his archaeological group. All fine and well, but Ancona has to figure Moretti isn't going to go to the police."

Farrugia saw that McGarrity wanted to say something and stopped.

"That news coverage might as well be as good as a police report, right?" McGarrity said. "Bianca explained that Ancona and Moretti had met in the past. This man wants to see the eagle for his client Bevilacqua, so it wouldn't be in his interest to push Moretti too hard. Rough him up, yes, let him know he's serious. But we've got to figure Ancona is going to check up on Moretti, since the professor is his only link to the eagle."

"Exactly," Farrugia said. "We need to make Ancona more anxious about the eagle. We don't know for certain if Bevilacqua is involved yet, but Bianca is certain that Ancona is dealing relics on the market for museums and private collectors, so we focus on the first lock in the canal."

Gennaro interrupted with, "How do you suggest we do that? Bevilacqua or no Bevilacqua, Ancona or a chain of collectors . . . there are three cops in this car so none of you can just walk up to Ancona and start a conversation, wearing a wire, like in the American movies, without him knowing it. Don't look at me because I'm not that good an actor to go undercover."

"Signora Cetoni might disagree."

"Signora Cetoni is not a suspicious underworld figure. That we know of. Bear in mind, like Bianca said, this Ancona has been in this business for a while, so he'll insist on credibility, want proof either with cash backing the conversation or an artifact ready to change hands."

"I think you just gave me the idea, Gennaro," said Farrugia.

"What did I say?"

"Yeah, what did he say?" asked Murphy.

"We might need an actor, but we'll definitely need an actress."

McGarrity gave Farrugia directions to the cheap hotel on the seedy side of Rome where they were staying.

Pulling the car up to the curb and then putting it into park, Farrugia and Gennaro looked at the neighborhood and surveyed both sides of the street, from curb to rooftop. He knew that there were some bleak and squalor-filled places in Rome, but he didn't think things got this bad.

Murphy was the first to open his door and exit. McGarrity was next, but seeing that Farrugia was still thinking, asked, "What is it?"

"Your boss must really hate you."

"You don't know the half of it," McGarrity said, and closed the passenger door.

34

Bianca had closed her laptop before Dante had come to bed that evening. At least one of them had slept well that night.

Not hearing from 10ki concerned her.

What concerned Dante the next morning was the weather: the way the light cast itself down from the sun across the sky; the way the air, like a sheet, hung unmoving and unforgiving. He told her that, where the ancient augurs had entrails to read, he used the August weather to divine his daily dose of destiny. But only in August, as it was the month that had always bothered him most.

They went through their usual morning routines as if they had been married; and for quite some time. After his and then her shower, his shave, her make-up, coffee and a fast bite together, they discussed Farrugia's plan. Both of them put on something fashionable that suggested they had money but enough discretion not to flaunt it. They found the office from the professor's directions.

The office was not far from Tremini Station, with a nondescript entrance at street level, pockmarked marble, dirty from years of diesel fumes, one heavy door, a polished call box with one nameplate and a mounted camera that left no room for pigeons above the doorframe.

Bianca pressed the buzzer. They both looked up at the camera. Bianca could swear that it had blinked for a close-up of their faces.

"May I help you?" a woman's voice said in office Italian.

"Mr. and Mrs. Rossi to see Mr. Ancona," said Bianca in slightly broad English.

Pause. Another paired look up at the observant eye.

"What's this in regards to?" returned the voice in a pissy tone.

"Between us and Mr. Ancona," she said. "Feel free to mention the name Professor Renato Moretti." She used an annoyed voice only another woman would understand. Dante stood there like a dutiful husband, an accessory.

A buzzer unleashed the door. It took both of them to wedge the slab of steel and glass open so they could enter the building. Frigid air-conditioning sucked them in. Coming towards them they heard the clicking of heels across a sheet of marble buffed down to its veins.

"This way, please," the secretary said without introducing herself. No handshakes, either. She walked as if she was the uncontested queen of office bitches. With the blasé unconcern of an airline stewardess demonstrating the life vest, she pointed to a set of double doors. "Mr. Ancona is inside." Then she disappeared to wherever it was that she had her throne.

Before them they saw two chairs, the backs facing them, as if placed there especially for them to meet Ancona, who sat behind an enormous desk. One look at him and Bianca immediately thought 'mortician' or 'don' from the Mario Puzo novel, for Ancona was a well-dressed man from the waist up. He was fiftyish, with his hair combed over and slicked back like a Hollywood star from a bygone era. His shirt was starched, the tie knotted nicely, and his eyes said 'fear me.'

Bianca had an entirely different interpretation of the man from her research. Blue-collar upbringing, single child of sacrificing parents who had sent him to parochial schools, saved from destitution by academic scholarships to one of the Ivys, where he knocked out stellar grades in a predictable double-major in economics and business administration. Upon graduating, he somehow found a way to finance an MBA before the degree had cachet. Like Robert Strand, if he had taken a few severe turns climbing up the evolutionary tree.

The desk was made to look busy with numerous papers scattered about. Ancona sat there poised with a pen, looking up with a smile. He didn't get up, but rather pointed to the two chairs with his pen. He returned to signing his papers to remind them that he was not only busy but under no obligation to politely accept their interruption, since they had no appointment.

Bianca was most surprised at the sight of the crucifix behind Ancona, high up on the wall. Christ in his passion looked down at them across the millennia with an exasperated, tormented expression, as if saying that his suffering was done and hers was about to begin. Thematically appropriate, below the Lord were two frames of Ancona, one with several smiling crimson-garbed men who were, she verified upon squinting, cardinals, while in the other photograph Ancona, age unknown, knelt in front of the Pontiff.

"How may I assist you, Mr. and Mrs. Rossi?" said the man, still signing documents.

Bianca spoke. "You were referred to us. My husband and I are redecorating our villa and we were interested in consulting your services, since we've heard you've done extraordinarily well for your clients."

"Mrs. Rossi, please forgive me for being so curt, but I'm not an interior decorator." He looked up for a moment as he finished his sentence, then returned to his signing.

Pause.

Dante said nothing. Bianca waited.

Ancona rose to the occasion. "My assistant informed me that you mentioned Professor Renato Moretti. I'm curious as to what Professor Moretti may have had to say about me. The professor and I spoke briefly over the matter of the imperial eagle. I had asked if I could have a look, but that conversation came to nothing. Your connection to Professor Moretti?"

Dante took a turn. "My wife and I attended one of his lectures in Salerno. To be quite accurate, we took a cruise around Sicily and up a short part of the coast, and the professor provided a daily commentary on the important Arab, Greek, and Norman strongholds. The professor seemed to suggest that you were . . . persistent about the eagle when we last spoke to him before his visit to the hospital."

"Merely enthusiastic, Mr. Rossi. I heard about his visit to the hospital. That reminds me—I should call him to wish him a speedy recovery. As for the eagle, since the professor wouldn't show it to me for official reasons, I figured I'd wait until it was cataloged like everyone else to see which museum will receive the honor. You mentioned that I was referred to you, Mrs. Rossi. I presume it was Professor Moretti?"

"Oh, no, not Moretti," she said. "You came recommended to us through a business friend of ours."

"Really?" he said with the fake business smile like that of a supervisor enduring an interview, knowing all the while that he'd never give the job to the applicant.

Bianca looked right at Ancona. *"Amici di Roma."*

Ancona dropped the pen.

But it took him only a moment to recover. "I belong to several cultural organizations, Mrs. Rossi. If perhaps you gave me a specific name I would feel more comfortable discussing business with a stranger."

Dante started his play. "My wife and I try to limit name-dropping to a minimum. It's a gauche practice, and frankly the people we know in *Amici* prefer their names be kept out of public scrutiny. It's a form of modesty that I'm sure you've come to appreciate, Mr. Ancona."

A smile, a look over to Bianca, who smiled, and then they both faced Ancona and smiled as if the tea service was just perfect. They were ready to take this act on the road.

"I was merely suggesting that it is only proper to check references, for business reasons," he said.

"That won't be necessary," said Bianca, "unless of course you prefer we take our business elsewhere."

Ancona stood up. "I think that might be best, Mr. and Mrs. Rossi, since I conduct business only with those I have the utmost confidence in, either through years of association or upon the highest recommendation."

Bianca and Dante also stood up.

"That's really a shame to hear," he said. "But it's good to confirm that you have business principles and discretion. Either way, my wife will get what she wants without you. You would've made it easier, but she's a resourceful woman."

"In the art world, I doubt anyone has had more success than I in procuring items for either the museum or the private collector. What exactly is it that you are looking for?"

"The eagle, of course," Bianca said.

Ancona either started laughing or choking. After he had cleared his throat, he said, "Mrs. Rossi, I admire your determination, but even I couldn't get near it. You also know the rest of the country is waiting, as are archaeologists, historians, and museum curators . . . you can see my point that for the eagle to simply go into private collection would provoke an international outrage. Now if there were some other antiquities you and your husband might like for decorative purpose, I can help you."

"We should go," said Bianca. "Thank you for your time, Mr. Ancona. My husband thought since you knew Moretti that you'd be one step closer to the eagle. As for other antiquities, I wouldn't need your help since I have unlimited access to antiquities."

"Unlimited access?" Ancona said. "I'm sure that's a bit of an overstatement."

"Hardly, Mr. Ancona. Let's not be naive. I use the same methods that you use. I have reliable sources in the underground and I get word now and then when something has been discovered. I am contacted before the item is cataloged—sometimes even after it is cataloged—and then I make the necessary arrangements."

Ancona sat down and looked Bianca over slowly. "Please sit down. I'm enjoying this conversation. You realize that you'd be accusing me of several crimes from what you described, and implicating yourself at the same time."

"And yet you're not denying it," she said, staring down at him and then smiling. "You can go right outside that door and run down to any official you want. Tell them what I just said and I'm sure that someone in the police, the Beni Culturali, even the Swiss Guard, will pat you on the shoulder and tell you they'll get to it when they get to it."

"I think we might've started off with a misunderstanding, Mr. and Mrs. Rossi." Ancona rolled his pen between his fingers. "I can help you with some things, but the eagle is too much in the spotlight at the moment. As I said, to have it go into private collection is simply too provocative and risky. Furthermore, I don't even know where it is at the moment. Professor Moretti is very secretive."

Dante cleared his throat. "Professor Moretti made no secret of it that the artifact is in a lab. Given that, it was not hard to discover which one."

Ancona seemed to experience a tic, since his right hand scratched behind his ear several times.

"What if I were to suggest," Dante said, "that as collectors we were to obtain the eagle but then decided for philanthropic reasons to donate it to a museum."

"And why would you do that? You go through all the trouble of obtaining the eagle and then give it away?"

"C'mon, Mr. Ancona. Think of the publicity. We give the eagle to say, the *Amici di Roma* in the United States with the suggestion of, say, donating it in our name to a museum in California. It would be excellent public relations and good for business, and it would put the eagle in our country. The Italian government's argument that the eagle needs proper care and should be accessible to scholars is answered if the precious bird is in a museum."

"And you don't think the Italian government wouldn't have a much stronger legal argument than that?"

"Of course they would. But should another scandal emerge, I believe that the Italian government and the public would be sufficiently distracted."

"A scandal? What scandal?" Ancona asked.

"I don't know. Maybe something to do with politicians, maybe something to do with rogue elements in the underground . . . anything is possible, you know, Mr. Ancona, if you have the imagination."

"Imagination aside," Ancona said, "there is the matter of finance, and I'm not clear what my role in all this is."

Bianca went inside the breast pocket of her jacket and extracted a folded piece of paper that turned out to be quite large when unfolded. Ancona was watching her with curiosity, looking at her eyes as she reviewed the paper. He tried to be patient but he licked his lower lip and lightly tapped his pen.

"I've always detested carrying a pocketbook," she said, "so I carry what I need in my jacket pocket. We are simply asking you to use your influence in getting the eagle into the United States."

She folded the paper back up and handed it to Ancona.

As Ancona unfolded the paper with care she said, "That should be all you need in the way of references, Mr. Ancona." It should indeed. It was a bearer bond for one million, American, from her collection. That much money was instant credibility. "There is more where that came from should 'financing' require it. Need I remind you that the charming thing about that piece of paper is that it is untraceable and instant cash anywhere in the world?"

"Is this for me?" asked Ancona.

"As a retainer, of course," said Bianca.

"Of course," replied Ancona.

35

Farrugia was sitting at the table at the trattoria, waiting for them.

He folded the newspaper over and ironed the seam straight, the editorial section facing him. The editors had printed two cartoon panels as a Question and Answer to provoke public response. Each panel was the iconic image of Italy as a long-legged boot with Sicily as the football and Sardinia as the football in flight.

The cartoonist of the left panel had shaded Sicily and the southern part of the country, from Campania downward, as green; mid-section up to the Marches and over to the northwest corner of Piedmont, as white; and Lombardy on eastward, as red.

The wit of the right panel had turned the national colors of the flag on their side. He asserted fiscal authority with a green wedge from Lombardy down to Tuscany, a swath of white purity from Trentino down to Lazio, leaving the back of the leg, the boot and Sicily in Communist red. Inexplicably, Sardinia was a satellite of green, fiscal turf.

Farrugia rumpled the paper in annoyance and set it aside when he saw the group approaching the table. "How'd it go?"

"Ask Bianca. She did all the driving," said Dante as he sat down. Alessandro, Gennaro and Moretti also sat down without speaking, deferring to her.

He turned to her.

"I think he went for it. He pretended he wasn't interested, but when I told him we knew the lab where the eagle was, I think he was secretly annoyed that Renato would tell us and not his henchmen."

"And when you told him that all you needed him for was getting the eagle back into your country?"

"I think he saw it as the easiest job in the world. No work for him as long as he has the Amici front and Bevilacqua controlling the docks in the States." She paused to place an order for a rustic cacciatore.

"How did he respond to your comment that you had 'unlimited

access to antiquities'?"

"I think he was suspicious, but the sight of the bearer bond was enough that he could barely keep his tongue from falling out."

"Think he might think it's too good to be true?" Gennaro said. "We come in opening the barn door wide open."

"He *should* be suspicious," Farrugia said, "which means he'll act cautious and ask for some kind of good-faith gesture."

"That's where Dante comes in," said Bianca.

"I do? How?"

Both Bianca and Farrugia looked at him, though her eyes were playful. His were not. The rest of the table were merely watching the chess match.

"You need," she said, "to talk to someone you trust in the Underground and ask him for something that is really valuable, but—here's the important part—something that hasn't been documented by anyone. And I mean no one—not Perceval and certainly not the Beni Culturali. Ancona has to think we're just as good as he is."

"Dante, please describe the Ancona office from the street to the den," Farrugia said.

Dante's description was admirably methodical, from the outside camera, the bitchy receptionist, the marble floors, to the twin picture frames of the ecclesiastics. He repeated most of the conversation verbatim, not minding that he was a supporting actor in the drama, and emphasizing Ancona's fetish for signing papers.

"What the hell could he be signing?" Farrugia said. "The last thing someone in his position would want is a paper trail."

"Perhaps they were just for show," Bianca said, "something to make him seem busy?"

"If he were a lower-level bureaucrat, perhaps," Farrugia said. "But a man in his position rarely has the need to appear busy to strangers."

The waiter set down the main courses, since nobody had arrived hungry enough for an antipasto. Farrugia and Gennaro crossed themselves because they had ordered a vegetarian dish in observation that it was Friday evening. They shared the vegetarian lasagna made with the usual noodles and cheese, which included cremini, porcini, and portobello mushrooms.

"Excuse me," Alessandro said, "but can one of you describe the receptionist?"

Looking up from a morsel of chicken Bianca said, "Tall on legs, mouse-brown hair, small tits . . . why are you looking at me like that, Dante? A woman can't say 'tits'? It's not like any of you are still altar boys. Anyway, she wasn't around us much; in and out like that. I think she might've been Hungarian."

"Definitely Hungarian but . . ." Dante made a so-so motion with his hand. "She had a touch of the exotic."

Bianca looked at him, upon which he said, "And she's right. Small tits."

Alessandro turned pale. "I think I might've fucked us."

He explained the meeting in Piazza Navona, excluded the biological details, and explained the morning discovery that his notebook was gone.

Eating proceeded solemnly after the revelation.

36

Agents McGarrity and Murphy sat at a table with Farrugia, waiting for Bianca.

She had called the meeting; she had picked the café, her favorite in the Piazza della Rotonda across from the Pantheon. Bianca figured that they could wait, knowing that the Detective wouldn't mind her exercising her interpretation of Mediterranean time. Let the Agents stew.

So she walked around the inside of the Pantheon, admiring as she had done numerous times the pagan walls and the columns from Egypt working together to shift sixty tons of weight that was dedicated to Marcus Agrippa but that Hadrian had built. This was Bianca's favorite place in Rome for a reason.

She admired the oculus, the hole in the dome, because whether it let in a small amount of rain, a dash of snow, or left a yawn of sunlight or moonlight on the geometric floor below—the open eye in that roof was to her the most potent of all of Rome's metaphors of power. The opening allowed and controlled the only source of light within that space, and whatever was left on the marble below was all that Rome herself would reveal each day to whoever walked there, as it had always been throughout the millennia.

She left a rose on the tomb of Raphael.

Farrugia, naturally, was the first to see her walking toward them. He said nothing as McGarrity checked his watch. Murphy squinted in the glare and scanned the piazza impatiently. Farrugia signaled to the waiter, who also did not see or know Bianca was coming, to bring an espresso for the lady and place it at the empty setting.

As she approached, Farrugia stood up to acknowledge her presence while the other two men wondered why he was standing, when suddenly they saw that she was there. Bianca and Farrugia exchanged greetings in Italian as the waiter appeared with a smile and placed her demitasse on the table, saying in soft Italian, "Caffè for the lady." She thanked him.

She took her seat. "Have the bugs been removed from my apartment?"

Farrugia leaned back to get comfortable in his chair; his look to McGarrity reminded him that he also expected and would appreciate an answer.

"Yes, they have," said McGarrity.

"And you know about Sandro's encounter?"

McGarrity and Murphy nodded in unison like students.

Farrugia asked, "You're certain that this woman Sandro met was the same one you encountered at Ancona's office?"

Before Bianca could say a word, Murphy said, "I understand being cautious, but isn't that a bit paranoid?"

She finished her espresso, and then turned to Murphy. "We have no choice but to be overly cautious. And am I paranoid? Let me ask the two of you one question—and one of you answer me honestly—did you bug Dante's apartment?"

Both men shook their heads.

"I thought so, because the bugs are still in his place. I asked you to get rid of all the bugs and you did. My place is clean, thank you. The bugs in Dante's place are either from Ancona or someone else we don't know yet."

"We didn't bug Dante's place. Why would Ancona?" asked McGarrity.

"Dante is a member of the Roma Underground. Or it's possible that Ancona discovered Moretti's only lifeline in Rome: Sandro."

"Excuse me." Farrugia held up a hand gently. "If that be the case, then bug Sandro."

Bianca smiled at him. "I would agree. Here's my thinking: you're Ancona and you do a background check on Moretti. You discover Sandro, do a check on him and find out that he shares an office with an auditor who happens to explore the underground in his spare time. Who would suddenly become very attractive to you then? Dante. Besides, do we know that Sandro's place wasn't bugged?"

"We can check his place," McGarrity said, "and we'd be happy to check Dante's apartment if you like?"

"Please do, but don't remove them. Ancona knows we're playing a game."

"What do you suggest then?" asked Farrugia.

"Proceed as planned, but we have to make sure that whatever Dante digs up whets Ancona's appetite for more. The race is between whether we get enough evidence on his operation first or he cuts his losses."

"You do realize that if and when he cuts his losses it could mean your life and Dante's?" asked Murphy.

"And Moretti's . . . and Sandro's," Farrugia said. "Ancona will make sure he leaves no dust when he leaves the table."

"I know," said Bianca.

McGarrity rapped the table with his knuckle, a nervous habit. Apparently, no one had ever told him how annoying it was.

"You think all this because of Sandro and his romantic romp?" he said.

Bianca tilted her sunglasses midway down her nose. "Agent, suppose you're an auditor working sixty hours a week. Your boss is some asshole who ties up your reimbursements for months to just bust your balls. You go one night, have a nice dinner, solo, go for a dessert, and you meet a woman who rides your bones all night, disappears by morning. Think you'd forget what she looked like?"

Farrugia folded his hands and kept quiet.

McGarrity gulped some air. "All right, good point."

Murphy got up. "We should go. We'll check Dante's and then Sandro's place and let you know what we think. If we find bugs we'll leave them as is."

"Thank you," she said.

Farrugia waited for the two agents to get halfway across the piazza, then asked, "You trust those two?"

"Not because I have a choice. May I ask you a personal question, Detective?"

Farrugia let her know that she could.

"You don't work with a partner, do you?"

"No."

"May I ask why?" She kept her sunglasses lowered so he could see in her eyes the genuine interest in his answer.

"I work alone," he said simply. "I'll call for help if I need it but I don't expect it. My partner was killed years ago with his entire family, including the family dog, as a reprisal. Ever since then I prefer to work alone. Here in Rome, my superiors seem to prefer it that way."

"I'm very sorry," she said.

"That was your personal question?"

"No, but after hearing just now about what happened to your last partner I thought it would be insensitive to ask what I wanted to ask you."

"Ask," said Farrugia.

"When it comes down to a partner, which quality matters most to you—love or trust?"

"Trust," said Farrugia without hesitation.

The answer lingered between them across the table before Farrugia offered clarification.

"Love is good, but with trust you have everything."

37

Dante couldn't sleep, so he walked around the second floor some. He took the stairs and paced the first floor, slid open the terrace door and went outside. The heat disturbed everything, yet there was something peaceful, serene, about standing there nude under the moon and hoping for a breeze that his mind told him would never come. He looked out at the city: it was alive and seemed to acknowledge his living there, showing him a car, only one, its lights on as it meandered down the course of the street in silent speed, its destination of no matter, meaningless.

Insomnia had given him that hour of solitude. He decided to return to bed. He went back up the stairs now, treading them softly as he approached his bedroom. Once inside, he stopped for a moment.

Bianca was on her side, facing him. She was, as Dante, nude, the sheets thrown down the bed in protest, her body motionless as a photograph left wet and exposed, appearing ethereal. No sooner had he thought this, while gazing down at her, then her eyes opened.

He felt suddenly embarrassed.

Then her hand reached up and pulled him towards her and as he came onto the bed she eased herself under him to let him in.

Farrugia folded over the envelope and tucked it into his light jacket. He opened the door and made his way to the infamous elevator when, out of the corner of his eye, he saw a figure and heard the increasing volume of a voice approaching him from his left. The man intending to collide with him was new to the lobby.

Farrugia did the instinctive scan as he continued walking—polished black shoes, grayish blue slacks, thick belt and hand on holster, white shirt, black tie, some nameplate with an identification badge on a retractable string, and, above the poorly tied knot, a weak face trying to look authoritative with a few missed spots from his shave that morning. A rent-a-cop.

"You . . . STOP . . . you need to sign in at the desk. New rules."

Farrugia held up his hands since the security man, his hand still on his holster, seemed keen on playing cowboy. He followed the man back to the desk.

The man handed him a ledger book. "Write the name and the business you're visiting on the line there. I'll give you a visitor's pass and only then can you take the elevator."

Farrugia looked down and saw B. Nerini written on the first line. "With so many visitors you must be a busy man," he said, scribbling down his information.

"What's your name?" the man asked, trying to decipher the detective's distinctive scrawl.

"Are you asking me so you can write it down for my visitor's badge?"

"No. You can do that."

"Isidore Farrugia."

"What kind of first name is that?" the rental cop asked, following his question with an uncomfortable chuckle.

Farrugia looked at the man and let the moment of silence speak his contempt.

"San Isidro is the patron saint of Madrid. Isidre is the Catalan version. San Isidre is an area in Valencia," said Farrugia, waiting for the blank visitor's pass that the man now standing behind his desk did not seem in a hurry to create for him.

The guard handed him a blank pass.

"So you're Spanish? I thought I detected a difference in your Italian," said the man, now looking for something on his desk for Farrugia to write with.

"No. I'm Italian." He clicked open his own pen, taken from inside his breast pocket, saying nothing more so as to let the other man stew in his confusion. He noticed that the man had inadvertently handed him two blank passes. The cardstock stuck together.

"Might I see some identification . . . a driver's license or something official?"

"Would work identification be acceptable?"

"Long as it has a picture," said the man behind the desk.

Farrugia handed him the billfold and watched the man flip open the brown leather and see the badge and then the small flap with the rest of the details.

The man looked up. Farrugia said nothing, staring back at the man as he handed his identification back to him. The guard handed him a plastic sleeve and a pincer clasp.

"Thank you," said Farrugia, damning Pinolo in his mind for the entire inconvenience.

"I see you've experienced the Visitor's Desk in the lobby," said Gennaro.

Alessandro stood up and read from a piece of paper. "Effective immediate, all visitors must report to the Visitor's Desk in the building lobby and present a valid form of identification in order to obtain a pass and visit offices on the premises." Alessandro held up one finger and continued. "A visitor should inform the guard of the office that they intend to visit and the correct floor should the office exist on multiple floors." A second finger went up. "The visitor should wear the pass visible at all times." Last but not least, he raised a third finger—his middle finger. "Upon leaving, the visitor should relinquish the pass and write the exit time in the Visitor's Log."

Silvio, passing outside the office's closed door, stopped, saw Alessandro, and looked around to see the intended recipient.

Gennaro recognized the exasperated look as Farrugia found himself a chair. When the detective looked up, he smiled when he saw Moretti and Bianca presenting their badges.

"Pinolo's got balls," said Farrugia.

"That's speculation," said Dante.

"Speculation is the theme of my visit," said the detective, fishing out the envelope he had curled up and stuffed into his jacket pocket. He undid the clasp and pulled out some surveillance photographs.

"Professor and Dante . . . please look at these photographs and tell me if you've ever seen these men."

Moretti took the photographs; Dante joined him, looking at them over Moretti's shoulder as the older man filed one behind the other.

"These are the men who were following me," said the professor.

"And you, Dante? Are these the men who attacked you?"

"I'm not quite sure since it happened so quickly. I'd know the voice if I heard it again." Dante took the pictures and looked at them slowly.

"And what about you, Professor—think these two are the same ones who attacked you?"

"I'm certain they are, but I can identify only one of these men from the attack. I can't say with confidence about the other one." He pointed to the man in the photograph in Dante's hands.

"But both of them were watching you from across the street?"

"Most definitely. These two are the ones I said were following me."

"That's good enough for me for now," said Farrugia.

Gennaro held up his hands wide, waiting for Farrugia to explain the two mystery men.

"The photos are from two colleagues whom I had asked to look into the Professor's first complaint. I'm not clear how they slipped my colleagues to attack the Professor, but these two thugs have a long record. Unfortunately, we couldn't do anything with them while they were watching the Professor—until they decided to attack the Professor. If we find them and the Professor identifies them, we can arrest them."

"So they've disappeared?"

"It appears so."

"Criminal records?" asked Alessandro. "For what?"

"Extortion, intimidation, suspicion of homicide, but no convictions since none of the victims or their families would file a complaint. Up until now all their criminal activities had been confined to the area between Naples and Palermo. This is their first trip to Rome, from what I can tell."

Gennaro looked perplexed. "Any connection to Ancona?"

"None that I can tell. Now that we know where Ancona's office is, we can try and follow him discreetly, of course, or see whether these two show up. We tapped his phones, but from the looks of his phone records and banking statements, he's doing all his work the old-fash-ioned way. He has to be using a courier system."

"Maybe his Hungarian beauty is doing some legwork for him," Alessandro said.

"Too early to tell. Her record is clean, her papers in order. Either she's avoided being caught or she's new to his operations. I didn't see any record of her traveling to the United States, so I assume she's part of his local enterprise."

"What do you propose?" asked Dante.

"I'm still trying to track down the manifest for an amphora found underground. Gennaro gave me the invoice for it a while ago. It's like looking for the missing link. I've never seen such a mess of paper-work. Since Civitavecchia is the main port, I have to believe—want to believe—Ancona is using it somehow to smuggle artifacts out of the country. I meant to ask whether you've called your friend in the Roma Underground?"

"I left him a message to call me," said Dante.

"If you have the amphora invoice," Bianca said, "I could see what I can do with it."

Farrugia stood up, pulled the amphora document from his billfold and handed it to Bianca and then asked Dante, "Is Pinolo's office on this floor?"

"No, it's up one floor, to the right when you come out of the eleva-tor, down the hall. But you do know that your Visitor Pass restricts you to the floor you're visiting. I believe the world ends if you deviate from that."

"Of course it does. Pinolo's a manager. He has his own bathroom up there?"

"Uh, yeah, but it's locked," Dante said. "Managerial privilege."

"And it's intriguing that you know that. Is the bathroom door vis-ible from his office for him or his assistant to see?"

"No. He has no assistant, has the office to himself, and his door has grayed-out glass."

"Good. I should go. Gennaro, I'm coming over for dinner tonight."

"You're inviting yourself to dinner these days?" said Gennaro. "Bring wine then."

Farrugia took the elevator up one floor, and in a matter of moments picked the lock to the bathroom door. That the executive outhouse was palatial was an understatement. Air-conditioned. A full-length-mirrored wall with the marble countertop sink, glistening fixtures and a stack of hand towels were waiting for him when he entered. The urinal was marked off between two dividers to the right of the counter; barricaded behind an oynx door was the toilet, nice and self-contained like a millionaire's private island. The remaining excessive obscenity was a leather couch with perfectly stacked magazines and a single copy of the Financial Times, standing out in all its flamingo glory on a coffee table.

Farrugia took out the extra cardstock visitor's pass from the guard downstairs and undid his own Visitor's Pass from its plastic sheath. With his pen he drew a caricature of Pinolo as a mouse with a small penis, smaller testicles, and long tail and entitled it *Topo Pinolo* in the space for the name, then fastened the artwork by the pincer clasp to the coat hook behind the toilet-stall door.

38

The other end of the line picked up and he heard the expected, *"Pronto."*

"Dante here. You haven't returned my call. You get my message?"

"Yeah, I got your message. What is it with you, calling me only when you need something? And besides, you left me a message only yesterday. Why such a hurry? It's August, remember."

Dante smiled. Marco was still somewhat indignant, but if he were using his not-sure-whether-he-was-joking-or-simply-sarcastic voice, he could be managed. "I know and I'm sorry to appear so impatient, but this is important."

"Important for you, maybe, but why should I assume it's important for me?"

Marco sounded as if he was talking on his cell phone while walking outside, just as Dante was around the terrace while Bianca fiddled with her laptop wearing a wide-brimmed hat to protect her from the sun.

"I'm sorry that I can't get specific," he said, "but what I'm asking for is important, not just to me but to the Underground."

"Well your message didn't say what it was that you needed, so tell me."

"I need bait. Something really attractive, but an item that hasn't been seen by anyone in the Underground, Culturali, or Perceval, for that matter." He got it all out in one large gush then rubbed his temple, waiting for Marco's explosion.

"Is that all?" Marco said. "Why didn't you say so? I think that I have Nero's fiddle in a drawer here somewhere. Or would you rather have the sandals of Christ? What do you think I am, Dante? First, you bring your girlfriend down here and let her loose—"

"Adriano is an asshole, you know that, so let's not revisit that conversation. Do you have something or not?"

"Adriano is a jerkoff, agreed. But I'm the one who's trying to keep the Underground afloat. As to what you want, please light a match for me so maybe I can see what you're seeing. Does your request have something to do with the eagle?"

Dante hesitated.

"Well?"

"It's like this, Marco. I need an artifact for bait because I'm involved in an investigation into smuggling. The reason I need something compelling and undocumented is in case someone in the Underground, Beni Culturali, or Perceval is on the take." Dante paused to let it all sink in.

"Shit, you're not kidding, are you?" said Marco.

"This is why it's important to the Underground. The way I reason all this is that someone on the outside is using someone, maybe several someones, on the inside. I have an eye on one person, and I need to see whether he'll take the bait. If he does then I can figure out how he does it and bust him."

"*You* bust him? You might have all the evidence, but you're not that kind of cop, Dante. Unless you're not telling me that the cops are involved."

"A cop *is* involved. Do you have anything that I can use for bait, or not?"

"A cop? One cop? Jesus, that really makes me sleep comfortably. If what you say is true, Dante, the corruption involved has to be an order of magnitude beyond what you and I can imagine. What evidence do you even have for any of this?"

Dante heard him breathing. Marco was probably pacing his small balcony in a fit of hand-to-head like one of those mechanical bell-ringers in a cartoon. "I can't go into too much detail but there was an amphora we discovered a while back."

"Yeah, I remember that. It had an intact resin seal. Quite a find, but we crated it and sent it off to the warehouse."

"And according to the paperwork, it's still in the warehouse waiting to be cataloged, examined, and restored. But the artifact is, in reality, sitting in a museum in California."

"California?" Marco practically screamed. "That can't be and even if it were, there have to be papers to attest to the find, the pedigree."

"Forged. I don't know exactly how it was done, but it's gone, so I'm back to asking you what I asked at the beginning—do you have something for me?"

In an almost whisper-like tired voice Marco said, "Yeah. I have something. Not Nero's fiddle but good enough. I'll bring it to you at work in the morning."

"Thank you. Morning is fine. Make sure you get a Visitor's Pass." Dante hung up before Marco could respond.

Bianca had closed the top to her laptop.

"What's wrong?" he asked.

"Nothing. I had hoped to hear from someone and I didn't," she said. "But I think I might've figured out how Ancona is doing it."

The evening delivered the affliction of humidity to further oppress what the sun had scorched all day. Farrugia's wristwatch said it was almost seven pm, but the second hand was racing to make it official. He had a bottle in hand, the end result of the eternal debate within himself: bring white wine or red wine to Gennaro's place. He had no idea what his old friend had planned for a meal, and since he had already invited himself he wasn't about to call Gennaro and insult him by asking. Red wine it was.

Farrugia knocked on the door, presented the wine first, then himself.

"The heat is too much so I'm making something simple, if you don't mind," Gennaro said. "Open the wine. Glasses are there and talk to me while I make the meal." Gennaro walked back into his kitchen pointing out where in the cupboard his guest could find the wine glasses.

"It's about the surveillance photographs from this morning," said Farrugia, extracting two wine glasses and exploring a drawer for a corkscrew.

Gennaro was making a substantial bruschetta. He had the bread cut and placed on a large serving board. In a bowl he had added some milk to the goat cheese and was whisking the mix. "What about the photographs? Moretti said that they were the two who were following him. Dante wasn't so sure, but it stands to reason that these two might've been one and the same."

"True, but I'd left out one small detail."

Gennaro bashed a head of garlic, peeled off the skin, and rubbed the garlic onto his large slices of bread. On the stove was a small skillet, and next to it he had sliced some pancetta, set aside a crop of arugula and a bowl of sliced plum tomatoes. Farrugia was trying to understand the presence of a lemon on the counter.

"You remember the 'small detail' of your little cartoon of Pinolo," said Gennaro with a big grin.

"How did he like that?"

"He ranted and raved like an idiot and we laughed until it hurt. He could have simply tossed it in the trash, and no one would have been the wiser. Of course the entire office received an e-mail memorandum on 'humor in the workplace and the sanctity of the washroom.'"

Farrugia smiled. "But, of course, Pinolo is doing what he does best."

The pancetta sizzled and sent up an aroma of sweet and savory pork. Gennaro pulled out the flash-sautéed meat and set it aside and anointed the bread with the cheese spread. He parceled out the pancetta on top of the tomatoes he had deployed, topped all of it with arugula and pulled out a zester for his lemon and distributed the citrus across the heap on top of the bread. The final touch was the sprinkling of white balsamic vinegar.

"Pour the wine, please," said Gennaro, lifting an island of bread onto a plate for his guest.

"The two are connected."

"Connected? You mean mafia? Eh, Isidò . . . what is it you are trying to tell me? Everyone in the office assumed mafia when you told us that it was these scumbags' first trip to Rome. What are you struggling with?"

"Yes, mafia, but I skipped over to which family these two belong."

Gennaro sipped his wine. "Does it matter?"

"It does, I'm afraid," said Farrugia and he mentioned the family name. Totaro.

The blood drained from Gennaro's face. "You're thinking they were involved in Lucia's death."

"They would've been too young at the time, but I'm certain that they were working up their reputations in the family business at about that time to know who had taken the contract."

"I thought that the family was put down during the Maxi-Trials," said Gennaro in a low voice, his appetite appearing diminished.

"For the most part . . . yes, but you know the mafia is like a hydra—cut one head off and another grows somewhere else. These men are probably soldiers, and they either merged with whoever had taken over leadership or they simply jumped to whoever was left standing."

"But you said you're not sure that they're connected to Ancona."

"There has to be a connection, even though I haven't found it yet. If the connection isn't with Ancona, then it has to be with Bevilacqua. We connect them to Bevilacqua and him to Ancona, we complete the circle."

"That's only the beginning, Isidò. Connect all that and you still have a shark swimming somewhere around Sicily, Naples, and who knows where else."

"I know. I know."

They ate in silence.

Gennaro took his wine glass and planned to sit down in his living room. He touched his friend's shoulder before leaving the kitchen, telling him to not worry about the dishes. Gennaro felt heaviness in his heart, as if he had just seen a child's gravestone in the cemetery.

39

Bianca looked at her wristwatch. Two am.

She lay back, unable to sleep, the heat unrelenting as a cliché, and no word from 10ki. Finally, she got up, put on a long thin shirt and went downstairs.

Out on the terrace she sat down and powered up her laptop. She had nothing better to do but try, even though her communication attempts were beginning to feel like she was using her laptop as a Ouija board. After opening up the chat console and selecting her old avatar, she wondered what she'd say on the screen.

"R u there?" she typed finally.

She compared the dark screen with the Roman sky. She was there with her small square beacon of light under a canopy of stars, distant but razor sharp as glass shards scattered across a dark carpet. As a child she had thought, upon seeing the twinkling of the stars, that life outside our planet was communicating to us in code. She wondered how many before her and after her would look up at those same stars and perceive the same beauty and feel the same terror at our utter insignificance.

An electronic chime disturbed her pessimism.

"I'm here & :-(2 b MIA."

Bianca disliked emoticons but she set it aside, happy to have finally received confirmation that 10ki was still around. She knew that she had passed the test so she paused, thinking how to proceed with the next step in this virtual relationship. She remembered that, originally, 10ki had asked for her help.

"Y," she typed.

"Work on wasp. Pushing 4 results & resolution."

"Resolution in sight?" Bianca typed, remembering as Alabaster how Rendition could get insistent about analysis. Their rush seemed to feed an enthusiasm for what they wanted to see, and after the Strand case she concluded that Rendition was dedicated, above all, to the objectives and pursuits of the intelligence community.

"Hardly. Case = complicated & Red R threatening."

That was a first: 'threatening.' Had Rendition crossed over to threatening an analyst, overtly, for not delivering? That was not, or had not been, Rendition's style. As long as she said that she had taken a case as far as she could and had given it her best effort, Rendition had no problem. That had always been the agreement: on your own, but do the best that you can. Times must have changed.

But then again, Alabaster Black never had a case that she couldn't complete. 10ki was his or her own person.

Bianca decided to be forward and ask, since 10ki had opened the door with 'threatening.' "U said while back U & I in danger. Explain."

She was curious how fast and forthcoming her correspondent would be with this personal question. Bianca half-expected a delay so she looked up at the sky again. The stars had not moved though the earth had. Their twinkling had not stopped though it was the refraction of light and not aliens sending signals. That was a shame. Man should be humbled, again.

Ping.

"Fibbies sent after u. Red R threatened u might tell all."

Fibbies was a nickname for the FBI. That explained McGarrity and Murphy, but she wouldn't tell 10ki that even if the FBI knew all there was to know about Rendition, proving it was another matter. Rendition was completely decentralized and nobody knew anyone else within it. The question was whether Rendition felt sufficiently threatened to become proactive and neutralize her.

She groaned, having eased unnoticing from cliché to euphemism.

"How r u threatened?"

"Don't think R wants me 2 make case. 2 much $ involved 2 big a loss 4 pharma, lobbyists, etc."

10ki was right about the cascading et cetera. Drugs developed from the wasp genome, while having a multinational-research aspect to them, have no patent restrictions, unlike the Human Genome. So nothing could prevent someone like Sargent or his Nasonia company from owning an entire line of important future drugs. Benchtop scientists from around the world who were unlocking the secrets of the parasitical wasp were thus deprived of any monetary gain as well as any scientific recognition: they sign away their intellectual-property rights the day they accept to work for him. And one man wound up controlling a host of lifesaving drugs.

Bianca thought of other clichés: politicians on purse strings; lobbyists in bed with big business; big-bad-wolf Pharma. Annoying with a ring of truth. Another damn cliché.

She wanted to tell 10ki that if she should present the findings and Rendition chose not to act upon the information, then the work was done. The analyst had held up his or her part of the agreement. But Bianca also knew the price of knowledge and discovery. She had to rationalize the consequences when she heard about the deaths surrounding her cases: Edward Wilburs of Alliance and his aneurysm; Horowitz of Manor Enterprises and his cerebral hemorrhage; Randall Wilcox of Fox Engineering, car flipped over between two silent highway lanes. All that rationalization had worked, that is until Robert Strand had shown up.

10ki had to have a different set of circumstances on hand. Sargent hadn't given 10ki another side to the investigation.

Bianca typed: "Ur in an ethical bind. Damned if u do. Damned if u don't."

"I know. Like 2 get files 2 u in case something happens 2 me."

Bianca wasn't sure that what 10ki had would prove the existence of Rendition, lock away Sargent, or at least terminate his plans. Sargent had already left his mark in using social media for patient recruitment. The FDA had to establish rules there.

They signed off.

Bianca closed the lid on the laptop. The stars still twinkled and would continue to twinkle no matter whether humanity improved or destroyed itself.

40

As Bianca took pride in conquering Dante's espresso machine, she thumbed through a doorstopper of a book she had pulled from his bookshelf.

Five-hundred short stories convinced her that this writer must have been one of those timid, agoraphobic souls who lived in a room of typewriter-ribbon tins. As she sipped her caffeine she was taken with the author's portrayal of women, his compassion for the maltreated and victimized. Some of the language, especially that used in the court scenes, consisted of antiquated formal legal terms, but the man's output was nonetheless impressive. It was also a lethal missile if thrown or bone-breaking if dropped.

Dante, who had gone to meet Marco that morning, came in with a metallic announcement of keys and a parcel under his arm.

"Is that it?"

He nodded and placed the brown-paper-wrapped box on the counter next to the thick book. She looked at it and had wondered why all secretive things are wrapped in brown paper—the classic PBW that always alerted the postman that porn was being delivered.

"What'cha reading?" he asked, clearing the machine for a *doppio*.

"Scerbanenco. Think Ancona will like it?" Her eyes indicated the parcel.

"Fool if he didn't." He touched the top of the parcel for emphasis. "If this doesn't establish our credibility, then the man doesn't know his antiquities."

"Untraceable?" she asked.

"Untraceable. No documentation whatsoever." He slurped his espresso. "Nobody even knows it exists yet."

"Excellent. Let's stay in and read. I've been enjoying these short stories. I'll call him tomorrow and make an appointment."

God rested on the seventh day. Gennaro did not. Grief and the need for revenge never sleep.

He tried to reason with Farrugia's discovery, but he couldn't. Reason had retired. The idea that these two thugs might have knowledge of his wife's killers made Gennaro want to strangle that bullshit term psychologists call "closure." There was never closure with violent death or sudden interruption, the shock of loss.

At first Gennaro rationalized that the murderers were probably dead themselves—the internecine feuds that had ignited sometime during or after the Maxi-Trials had left a trail of bodies. What was there to gain in knowing the names and faces of his wife's killers? It didn't bring her back. It didn't soften the wound. It would do nothing to alter the image he continued to carry in his head of the blood on the floor and the walls, the scene that had greeted him when he had come home that evening.

Farrugia would say that knowing they were dead would bring 'justice.' What justice?

Gennaro put on the television in search of a classic movie as distraction. Nothing interested him. He searched the radio, found a Mozart aria playing.

But instead of the Mozart, he heard in his heart the thundering trombones, strings and timpani of Wagner. The Ride of the Valkyries.

Bianca picked up her cell phone. It was Ancona.

"Mrs. Rossi, it's Alan Ancona. I apologize for disturbing you on a Sunday, but I was wondering if you and your husband could meet with me? It seems that an engagement has suddenly come up. The matter, unfortunately, forces us to decide sooner rather than later about us working together. My engagement requires that I leave Rome before Ferragosto."

"Before August fifteenth? I see." She cupped a hand over the receiver and signaled to Dante to bring pen and paper to her. She scribbled that it was Ancona calling for an earlier meeting.

"I agree that this is all rather unforeseen," Ancona said, "but as we discussed together, it would only take some small token to establish our mutual collaboration. If you have something, we can meet; otherwise, it'll have to wait until I return to Rome, which I don't see any sooner than late autumn."

She wrote down for Dante. *Obscure meeting place!*

"I understand, Mr. Ancona," she said. "Business is what it is. My husband and I were just talking this morning about a lovely piece that we thought would be perfect for you. We're confident that you'd be quite pleased with it. I daresay that when you see it, I think you'll be happy to take on our request to help us move the item we wish for into our collection. And a few others that we've marked."

"Others? There are other items that you wish to be sent abroad . . . ?"

"A few small items that I'm sure you can handle, in addition to the one we discussed."

"Really? I would love to know the details but I think it best we review them in person."

"Agreed. Since your engagement accelerates our timeline, we would need to move in person. My deposit should be sufficient for the key item in my collection, but I'll let you decide once you see the other items if another transaction is necessary. How about we meet Tuesday? That should give us sufficient time to arrange for us to have all our items in one place, making it easier for you to do what you must from a single location."

"Tuesday is fine. Where do I meet you and Mr. Rossi?"

Dante handed her the paper, and she read. "The catacombs of Domitilla? We can meet above ground at Via delle Sette Chiese."

She could hear either hesitation or surprise in his breathing over the phone.

"Mrs. Rossi, I'm curious as to how you propose we enter the catacombs. It's my understanding that the basilica's entry into the underground is unsafe, and the Vatican has assigned an order of priests and brothers to oversee the catacombs. The Holy Father has also granted exclusive access to a team of German archaeologists."

"Please don't worry, Mr. Ancona. These catacombs are the largest in Rome: fifteen kilometers of a necropolis. I'm sure there's room for everyone. We shall see you in the evening . . . say nine pm?"

"Nine pm it is," he said.

Marco disliked sitting alone at the pastry shop. He was anxious, caf-feinated, and feeling the fool for meeting with Dante that morning. Now, Dante told him to meet the cop who was fielding the sting.

As the prinicipal of Roma Underground, Marco oversaw all the training with ropes, harnesses, and aquatic gear. He enforced safety clothing, hygienic precautions, and established a consistent system for documenting discoveries underground. He coordinated, best as he could, diplomatic relations between Roma Underground and the Beni Culturali and the student group Perceval. It was Marco who had discovered the "Vendemmia" mosaic that Dante had shown Bianca.

The name 'Roma Underground' wasn't some clever gimmick that he had come up with off the top of his close-cropped head. He knew his history and named the community of urban speleologists from the various professions across Rome after a work by the archeologist, 'the Columbus of the Catacombs,' Antonio Bosio, author of the 1632 edi-tion of *Roma Underground*. Marco had originally planned to call the group 'Bosio' but settled on the book title instead. Of everyone in-volved in this entire scheme, he had the most to lose. And now he was meeting with the one cop on which all this depended.

Only one other man, a dark man, with a distinctive confusion of Spanish and Calabrian features had walked into the shop. He was wear-ing a white linen shirt, tan slacks, and polished shoes, and motioned his 'ciao' to Marco as if he had known him for decades. Marco smiled reflexively.

"Detective Farrugia?"

"Marco? Dante's friend, correct?"

"Yes. Please sit down, Detective." Marco beckoned a waiter to the table. "Dante spoke to me this morning about our needing to meet."

Marco ordered an Agrumi soda, lemon, and Farrugia asked for a plate of cookies, chocolate with hazelnut, Baci d'Alassio.

"You gave Dante what he needed?" Farrugia asked after the person had left with the order.

"I did. And you're the one supervising this operation?"

"I am. I understand that you have concerns. Dante and I know that you took considerable risks to help us, but I want to assure you that the risk is worth it. I appreciate your discretion."

Marco paused to let the waiter deliver their order. "He said that this might take down a smuggler."

"It will, if all goes well. I'm sure Dante explained to you why he needed an artifact that had no documentation.

"His exact word for it was 'bait'."

"It's hard to know whom we can trust. We aren't even sure of the full extent of the parties involved. But I can tell you that this individual we've targeted is the one we believe is the link between Italy and the United States."

"Really? How are the cookies?"

"Quite good. Try one, please," said Farrugia with a slight push of his plate to Marco.

Marco ignored the lemon tartness to enjoy the chocolate and hazelnut combination. Farrugia pulled out his cell phone and read a text message.

"Any news?" asked Marco, mumbling his question through his chewed-up cookie.

"Dante. The meeting has been set for him to take the items."

"Items?" said Marco with expected surprise. "I gave him only one item. Where's this meeting?"

"The Catacombs of Domitilla."

"Are you all crazy? That site is impenetrable, plus it's under Vatican protection."

"They have Swiss guards walking around?"

"No, that's not what I meant. The Vatican has German scholars and the Divine Word Missionaries overseeing the site."

Farrugia chewed on a cookie, watched Marco, swallowed and said, "With the latest bank scandal, I think that the Vatican has other worries at the moment. And besides, you can't tell me that portion of the underground is not accessible by other means. I'm not suggesting walking into the church and climbing down the cellar steps. A man of your expertise must know of more than one route."

"Why do I feel you and Dante want more from me?"

"That brings us to our special request. But I promise it'll be worth it to you."

The detective explained; the speleologist listened, shaking his head.

41

Farrugia agreed to meet with them. Fair enough. McGarrity had given him the name of some out-of-the-way café between Tremini and the Vatican.

Hell could not have provided a better day. Outside felt like a broiler. Everyone who had no place to go for the holiday smoldered. The two special agents watched Bus 64 let off passengers, including two pick-pockets doing their best to walk nonchalantly from their undetected crimes. As soon as the doors had closed, the agents saw a commotion amongst the passengers, but they laughed it off because it was out of their jurisdiction.

"'Morning, Detective," said McGarrity, who had stood up and offered the ritualistic handshake while his partner remained seated.

"'Morning." Farrugia ordered himself a cappuccino, right from where he was standing, saving the waiter a trip to the table.

"Mind filling us in?" asked Murphy.

"Bianca and Dante are meeting with Ancona tonight. Nine pm. They'll meet near the Catacomb of St. Domitilla. Dante's arranged for Ancona to have a taste to lure him in. The idea is to have him agree to moving a shipment for Bianca to the United States."

"How much does Ancona know? I mean, we know Dante's place is bugged, right? He could've overheard everything."

"He heard what we wanted him to hear. Bianca and Dante played it up that the preview item is a major rarity. Should make it worthwhile for Ancona."

"And this Catacomb . . . St. Domitilla . . . what does Ancona know about it?" asked Murphy.

"Enough to know it's a challenge. For now, he knows that he'll meet Bianca and Dante there, but it's reasonable for Ancona to figure out that the rest of Bianca's shipment will be in the vicinity. I'll expect him to ask Bianca and Dante to show him the goods, since they're more work for him to ship out to the States."

McGarrity was looking curious. "Ancona will want to see the eagle. Everyone's been salivating over it, so you can bet that . . ." Something in Farrugia's face made McGarrity stop talking.

"The bait that Dante has *better* work, because there is no eagle," said Farrugia.

The clink heard was Murphy dropping his small demitasse spoon. McGarrity sat there blank-faced.

"Now that takes some real balls," Murphy said. "How do you suppose Dante and Bianca will get past his questions? They can't stall him."

"That's why the trap has to be seductive," said Farrugia.

"Seductive enough for him to overlook not seeing the eagle and assume it's in the stash?"

Farrugia nodded his head and slurped some cappuccino. "Nothing will stop him from looking through the crates Bianca has for him after he closes the deal. Ancona is a businessman, so I suspect he'll start talking about exposure and risk. Ask for more money."

"You said Dante made all the arrangements, right? Can we be sure that Ancona isn't one step ahead of all of us after overhearing Dante's conversation? Casing the Catacombs before the meeting? Having Dante followed?" Murphy realized he was pushing, but he wanted to let Farrugia know that he had experience as well.

"No doubt that Ancona had Dante followed. I approached Dante's friend to get the bait since Ancona knew that Bianca and Dante would be in the apartment. All Ancona knows is that Dante asked for something without a paper trail. That conversation gives Ancona Dante's contact in the Roma Underground, but Ancona has to sit and wait. He might go so far as to have Dante's friend followed, but I'll put my money on Ancona just sitting and waiting. His friends—be they in the Roma Underground, Beni Culturali, or Perceval—can give him a report on Dante's friend. No harm there. It gives Ancona another name in the Underground and another avenue to get better goods for his clients, if he thinks he can bribe Dante's friend."

Murphy watched Farrugia take a sip of his cappuccino. Murphy had pushed away his small dish, which had nothing but crumbs left over from breakfast.

"There's always the chance that Ancona could double-cross Bianca and Dante tonight. If he knows where the antiquities are stashed in the catacombs from following Dante's friend, and he thinks that the eagle is also there, then there's nothing stopping him from taking everything. He doesn't even have to wait for them to show up tonight."

But Farrugia had anticipated this thinking. "He'll want the money since he's moving more merchandise. He'll want to see Bianca and Dante. Ancona doesn't have enough time to evaluate the situation and do away with three people."

"And what if Bianca brings him the bait, he steals it, and tries to do away with them both then and there?" McGarrity said. "No loose ends, including Dante's friend. All Ancona has to do after that is ship the loot to his contact abroad."

Farrugia nodded. "It is a possibility. Nothing was without risks." He took a final sip of his cappuccino. "It's one-part collector's greed and two-parts easy money. I'm counting on Ancona looking at easy money. You're right, and that's why I hope Bianca's trick will work."

"What trick is that?" the two men on the opposite side seemed to ask simultaneously.

"You'll see. Let's hope it all works out."

The Catacomb of St. Domatilla is the oldest in Rome to contain human remains. In addition to the haunted-house atmosphere of the numerous caves, spread out over nine miles, the necropolis is also the only one to contain a fresco of the Last Supper from the second-century. To the layperson it reeks of stale air, squalid lighting, and echoes of romantic movies like *Quo Vadis*, with pious Christians meeting underground to hide their faith from the oppressing Romans. In fact the Romans usually couldn't be bothered with persecution. One day they ignored the Christians and another day they found ingenious ways of martyring them. The tourist can enter the city of the dead through the sunken basilica but Dante and Marco knew of another entrance.

Dante had picked the catacomb for that reason and for another: an experienced guide is necessary to navigate the caves, with their uneven floors and low ceilings. Whoever could hide the archaeological treasures in the catacomb also had to be skilled enough to make his way out of the treacherous caves. Dante had calculated that if Ancona were to steal the loot that Marco had secreted into one of the caves, he would do so only with the help of his contact inside the Roma Underground.

Above ground, nearing nine pm, Bianca and Dante waited for Ancona on Via delle Sette Chiese. It was neither bright nor dark out but adequately dim. She held a small wooden box. He felt nervous but his nerves went numb when he saw the car pull up and park. Its lights went off, and Ancona emerged. Then a few seconds later, two other figures erupted from the two rear doors. Bianca stared straight ahead.

"'Evening," said Ancona, without bothering to introduce his two companions.

He held his hand out. "You have something for me, Mrs. Rossi?"

"I think you'll find it appealing."

"I had hoped it would be the eagle, but I understand that this small token of yours is a good-faith effort to gain my confidence and trust. Intriguing box."

Bianca touched the side of the box. "The box is necessary. The wood gives the appearance that we're shipping wine. Everything down below is crated as if it were wine shipments. Some items are packed in straw, others in pre-formed containers carefully concealed. The Rossi vineyard in Napa is one that my husband and I have expressed an interest in making profitable. I'm sure you can see that in the near future we might need your services for shipping us grape varietals, equipment, wine blends from Italian vineyards, amongst other things."

"Yes, other things. And all of this has to be shipped to you in the States and you'll need the right . . . the right expertise, the right touch of paperwork when the situation demands it, since we're only talking about wine and nothing else."

"Exactly," she said.

Ancona handed the loosened lid to a cohort behind him. He looked at Bianca and Dante first before looking down into the box and shifting around the special wrapping.

"A first-century millefiori glass dish," Dante said, not bothering to disguise his love for the artifact. Marco had certainly come through. "You can still see the craftsmanship of each individual petal. A similar find was discovered in London years ago, but this dish is, as you can see, intact without any wear or damage."

"Exquisite," said Ancona. One of the two men from behind him leaned forward to look at the dish but retracted his head along with his curiosity when Ancona had turned to him.

"Are you still interested in moving our goods?" she asked.

"And these 'goods' are in the catacomb?"

"They are. About ten boxes are down below. All of them are crated, varying in size, of course. They have the Rossi vineyard insignia. All they need is to be moved and expedited, using whatever methods you think best."

Ancona put the lid on the prized dish and handed the box to one of his men.

"You understand that physical labor is involved, and a large cargo like that would require influencing the appropriate bureaucracy here and abroad. It will require more financing, although I certainly appreciate your gesture with the millefiori. You have excellent taste, Mrs. Rossi."

"Shall I pay the same amount as the last time?" she asked and smiled.

He returned the smile, knowing that they were just being polite with each other since naming the amount of money would be vulgar. They agreed. She gave him another bearer bond.

"Mr. Rossi will tell you where the artifacts are. You have your associates move them. When should I expect to see them in the States?"

"In about three weeks. If you should give any thought to donating any of your collection to a museum I do hope that you'll contact me."

"I plan to keep what is mine," she said, "but I appreciate the offer."

Dante drew a schematic map and handed it to Ancona.

42

Despite what you see in the movies, a stakeout and takedown are about as dramatic as watching Samuel Beckett's *Waiting for Godot.*

A numbing banality comes in the endless hours in a cramped car that seems to get smaller and more confining with time. Conversations with a partner start with complete sentences and degenerate into grunts and half-syllables. Endless cups of coffee. The squawks from the dispatch radio or into a cell-phone sound, at first precise and savvy, but after a few hours, one or the other parties on either side of the line begins to sound like a parrot with gastrointestinal distress. Everyone waits for the adrenaline rush from the word, "Go!"

Farrugia had only half of these problems, because he had not counted on bureaucratic bullshit. His superior would allow him only two men: the same two Farrugia had assigned to follow the men who were following Moretti, and who didn't notice when they roughed Moretti up. He had three men, including him, to cover both the Catacomb of St. Domatilla and Ancona. Three men above ground were not enough fish or loaves to work a miracle.

Half an hour into the waiting game at Via delle Sette Chiese with his colleagues in another car—yet another *civetta*—he received a blessing of blessings in the form of a call from Marco.

"*Beda Madre,*" he said, hands clasped together and looking up at the roof of his parked car.

"Dante is with me and I have three cameras," said Marco.

"Where did you get cameras?"

"No time to explain, detective. One camera is directed at the loot."

"The others?"

"There's another in one of the recesses along the exit, so each member can be positively identified. The last camera is with me. Hand-held."

"Beautiful." The resultant films would be like one of those surveillance videos on American real-crime shows. The prosecutor would have multiple angles on tape. He then realized that Marco was still talking.

Marco found the time to explain that he was always thinking of technological improvements in working underground. He was nattering on about wanting to install an underwater lighting system so his speleologists could swim under the Coliseum safely. Farrugia was audience for Marco's enthusiastic essay on how it could be done, how much it would cost, and the consequences for archaeological surveying, because he had been pleased at his sudden good fortune.

"Marco?"

"Yes."

"Sorry to interrupt you. It's all interesting but how many crates do you have down there?"

"Uh, about nine or ten."

"Enough to need two men?"

"One of the crates is a two-man job, but most of these boxes one guy can carry. You'd need several trips, of course. I didn't want to make them too big and interfere with the exit camera's angle in seeing their faces."

"How many trips would you say if it was more than one man?" asked Farrugia, checking his watch.

"I'd say three trips, including the big one that needs two men. Why?"

"I think our visitors are arriving. Sit tight a minute."

A small truck pulled up and three men emerged. Two of them were unmistakably button men from some mafiosi clan. Farrugia knew the type immediately by the way they walked and gestured to each other. A hundred years ago they might have carried the signature sawed-off shotgun of the Sicilian hills, the lupara, but today they carried the inevitable Kalashnikov. That made Farrugia nervous for Dante and Marco. The third man was the odd man. Unarmed. He seemed normal enough. Farrugia was ambivalent now that he knew the boxes were enough for one man to carry. It left the other hand free for the Kalashnikov.

"Marco?"

"Yes."

"You've got two men, armed, and a third man, unarmed. Stop talking now and start filming in a few minutes."

"Done."

Dante and Marco were crouched down in the darkness when they heard the footsteps. The schematic directed the men through long stretches of hewn tufa stone a block away from the church to a square open area where the wooden crates were stacked. Unmapped territory. Impressive work Marco did, considering the catacombs are nearly a hundred acres of land with a million tombs. He made sure that the spot was away from any tourist group, yet not so far into a corner that it couldn't be found. Dante and Marco had spent quite some time traversing the underground, the 'Callixtian Complex,' since they had to avoid German scholars and Divine Word missionaries on the premises.

Filming started. Marco flipped open the small square screen viewer. Dante looked to his side and saw ancient graffiti scratched into the wall registering the day of death. The ledge for the dead was there but the bones were gone. Or most of them, at least. He read the graffiti again: 'Cuius dies inluxit,' said the scrawl. 'The day in which he shone.' He wondered whether the bereaved had intended 'in luxit' rather than 'inluxit.' 'The day in which he entered light.'

Voices. The third man was behind the two men, but he turned to survey the payload of antiquities. He leaned down and mumbled that all the wood was nailed up. No time for satisfying his curiosity. He set aside one box. He was instructing the two of them, but neither Dante nor Marco could hear him well. The two goons were armed. They saw that. They each slung the straps to their Kalashnikovs over one shoulder and each picked up boxes. Marco's hand trembled a little.

Though it was cold below, Dante could feel a drop of sweat form and wait before it decided to roll down. The two big men had turned around and headed for the exit with their boxes. Three good-sized boxes in each man's hands to make six. Dante knew that Marco had placed real antiquities in them. All documented items. The third man was prepping the next trip. He set two medium-sized boxes aside, one for each man, leaving the biggest box for the two-man carry and the last small one for him.

Marco's hand calmed down some since the armed men had left. He kept a steady hand filming the third man. Tedium is what Dante felt. His mind wandered to Giovanni Battista de Rossi, founder of Christian archaeology. Would the scholar agree with him on 'in luxit'? The conflation of the preposition 'in' into a portmanteau with 'luxio' could be a medieval mistake. Not unusual.

Footsteps returned. Marco's hand wobbled. The third man ordered each man to take one of the medium-sized boxes. He said, "Save the big one for last." More tedious waiting. Dante imagined that he could hear the deceased scholar, de Rossi, from his grave in the Agro Verano reminding him that the medieval scholar thought knowledge was a free gift of God. That explained why teachers would never make much money. Dante smiled. The dead man would also tell him that the Scholastics were dwarves on the shoulders of giants. The giants were dead pagans, of course, and not buried in these claustrophobic chambers under Rome.

Plodding footfalls and that dragging sound of dirt again. The two musclemen gave an understanding look to their foreman and each grabbed a side to the box and began the long lug.

Marco and Dante's eyes met and thought the same thing: confusion. The third man was lingering. The last parcel was easy enough for him to take and follow his accomplices. Why didn't he leave with them?

He picked up the wooden parcel at last, but he didn't head to the expected exit. It seemed that the man had another idea. Marco continued filming. His hand was calm since the guns were gone. Staring ahead, they were waiting and watching when they heard a squeaking sound. They hesitated because they suspected the sound. Marco looked at Dante and Dante looked at Marco. They each had the same look of understanding.

A mouse with twittering whiskers ran down Marco's arm. Marco jumped. The camera flew.

Dante caught it in mid-air.

The mouse fled the scene. Tomorrow Marco would transmogrify Pepino the Mouse into an Orwellian rat. But it was too late. The third man saw them, too, and ran away.

Dante took off after him down the ambulacra, away from the planned exit.

Where was he going? Dante reached into his pocket to find his flashlight. The fleeing man must have thought the same thing because he illuminated the path in front of him with his own flashlight.

That was odd. The man had a flashlight. He had planned to come to the unlighted corridors. Dante could see the man's back and the passageways a few feet ahead of him.

There was the very distant sound of water. An aqueduct? The Acqua Vergine? This area *really* must be unmapped. This was not the tunnel from Castel Sant'Angelo to the Vatican for Pope Alexander VI to visit his mistress and children. The catacombs that were growing further behind them had been discovered in the Renaissance and then renovated in the late nineteenth century; but this passageway was *sub terra ignota*. Damn. The Latinists would correct him: *subterra ignota*. He should push together where he spliced words.

Dante did not like this at all.

It was getting colder. He was a speleologist, not a qualified cataphile—that is, not an explorer of catacombs like those he had read about in *National Geographic* who would disappear below Paris for days at a time, a week at a time at the most, sometimes mapping out passageways, other times attending secret raves or painting murals beneath the city. Dante was not prepared to become Jean Valjean, nor did he have the string to guide him out like Tom Sawyer or Theseus.

The dirt smell was metallic, the darkness darker, and the two beams from the flashlight his only guide.

The man ahead had slowed down. Was he also lost? That would not be good for either of them. Dante thought like a tourist for a moment.

To the left and right of him he could see wall niches, small ones, about two to three feet in length, some even smaller. A dead-children section: infant mortality on display. Further on he saw more niches with bones and some frescoes for the wealthier children. Bereaved parents must have thought that burying their children near martyrs would ensure resurrection and salvation.

Where was he?

The sound of feet: his and the other man's. The other man switched off his flashlight.

Dante could hear himself panting. He could hear the other man breathing hard as well. Dante knew that he had to be close. He turned off his flashlight also, placing it into his pocket. He let his hand touch the wall to guide him. All he had now was the growing darkness and the odor of ancient dirt. It was a waiting game for human sound.

His eyes went steadily into the darkness, hoping to see something move, but the darkness was impenetrable. He had to be near. Dante could still hear the other man breathing, could hear his own breathing. It was he, Dante Allegretti, against his unknown guide in this necropolis, the man with the small wooden box.

Each man was taking small scrapes of tufa for steps.

Dante's hand continued to grope along carved-out volcanic earth, entering recesses and grazing over dry bones that he would not think about now. He stopped again. Dante didn't hear any footsteps now. He waited, his hand crawling inside a cubiculum. He grabbed a bone. A femur. Child's or not it was all that he had for a weapon. He crept slowly, trying to keep his feet silent.

That squeaking noise again? Mice? No. They tend to whistle. He heard it again—a soft scratchy pattering sound.

Rats . . . damned rats. He gripped the femur and planted his foot forward and outward.

He stepped on something solid.

An awful high screech came up from below and the air around his head gave way to an unexpected breeze. The sound of something solid hitting the wall near Dante's head. A whiff of dust went into his hair and up his nose. Dante swung with the femur and connected with real, living bone.

"*Porca vacca!*" the other man yelled.

The man could damn cows and the national football team for all he cared because Dante had hold of the man's good arm and was not about to let go. He used the femur to tenderize flesh and bone until the other man went down.

Dante fell down on top of him, gasping, flailing him with the bone. The other man was gasping too, trying to defend himself, scratching and kicking, trying to escape from Dante. He hit Dante with the wooden box. There was a solid sound of wood against skull.

Dante rolled over in momentary agony, but combat adrenaline kept him moving. If he didn't, the other man would get away.

He caught the man's heel with his hand and pulled it hard into his chest. Two leg bones now. Dante thought for a second to bite the leg. Dust kicked up. Dante had begun to wonder whom the rats were cheering on. Fists, some yelling, more creative curses, and more femur drumming flesh and bone. The man was down again and Dante rolled onto him.

And suddenly, this fight felt familiar. Dante had the man straddled as he pulled out his flashlight and turned it on.

"Adriano?" said Dante.

"You bastard!"

"Me? A bastard? You're the one trying to steal the eagle."

"Steal it? You idiot, I'm trying to save it. Do you really want it shipped to America?"

Dante rolled over and collapsed onto the hard volcanic tufa.

"What about Ancona? What about the other things he stole? You're his inside man."

Adriano was still gasping. "I admit . . . I helped Ancona. That was the past, but I'd never let him have the eagle. It's . . . it's too significant."

"And those two men?"

"Ancona's. They're taking the crates to Civitavecchia. Ship goes out tonight. Ancona leaves by plane."

"Then we better move," said Dante, catching his breath at last. He got up and extended his hand to help Adriano up.

"What about the eagle?"

Dante took the box and threw it into the darkness.

"What the hell is wrong with you?"

"Adriano, there is no eagle. It was a trap to get Ancona and Bevilacqua."

"What? Who's Bevilacqua?"

"I'll explain," said Dante as the two men started walking back in the direction of Marco.

"Am I in trouble?" Adriano asked, certain of Dante's answer.

"I'm afraid so."

"Think I need a lawyer?"

"Probably, yes."

"Think I can help get Ancona?"

"Yes."

"Still think I'm an asshole?"

Dante smiled. "Oh, yes."

"Good. I'm glad to know some things haven't changed."

43

As Farrugia could see for himself when he burst into the office, Alessandro's Hungarian love was every bit as exotic as he had described her to be.

"How did you get in?" she asked in a very loud, offended voice as she stood up on her spindle legs.

"Easily enough. I'm the police, and your security company gave me the code to enter the premises. Your landlord also knows. Now where is Mr. Ancona?"

"Don't you need a warrant or subpoena for any of this?"

But she was just trying to buy time. Farrugia ignored her, walking past her to the doors behind her.

A disheveled Ancona, tie undone, was behind his desk, trying to feed his paper shredder more than its mouth could handle at one time.

Christ on the wall on his cross, the smiling cardinals, and one infallible Pope were not enough to save Ancona from the scourge of steel handcuffs.

Silvio wheeled the television from the conference room into the office after Marco had called Dante. Everyone fell silent as the Free Channel came on. Moretti still held the grudge that the station had mangled his name the last time. Gennaro was chewing on a loose piece of skin on his thumb. Dante and Bianca were sitting on the couch. McGarrity and Murphy took up the last amount of free space in the crowded office. Alessandro was twirling a number-two pencil, a Ticonderoga. Sharp.

Prune-faced Giancarlo Ragonese's head took up the screen, finger embedded beyond the reasonable expectation of wax from his ear, looking earnest. A small ribbon ran under the man's chin: "Latest breaking development: art scandal."

"This is Giancarlo Ragonese reporting to you from St. Peter's Square with an astounding revelation that will surely reverberate through the halls of government and international politics."

Moretti wanted to heckle the screen when he saw Ragonese, but the room shushed him in unison.

"Sources say that an ongoing investigation into the thefts of antiquities from the Roman underground has yielded a ringleader and co-conspirators, domestic and foreign. Details are not entirely clear at the moment but it seems that many rare and valuable items, before being cataloged and processed for warehousing here in Rome, were mysteriously going missing until authorities caught a recent break. The exact mechanism for these disappearances remains uncertain."

Moretti groaned at the cliché. 'Recent break.'

The constipated mannequin continued with his report.

"The big break came when a ticket for an amphora was traced to a warehouse; but when authorities consulted the warehouse and sought proof of the amphora—considered quite valuable because the relic was sealed with resin—they found the drawer empty. Detective Farrugia who heads this investigation alleges that this amphora is in the United States, at a prestigious museum in southern California. We are showing you now two photographs: one picture from when the item was unearthed and the second photograph from the American museum. As you can see, one doesn't need to be an expert to recognize the distinctive resin plug. The American museum has declined to comment at this time."

The home-office reporter, listening to Ragonese, was nodding his head as if he were following the unfolding mystery.

"Detective Farrugia, a veteran of organized-crime investigations, holds firm in his belief that a syndicate is behind the amphora's disappearance. Inspired by the amphora and by the recent scandal over inappropriate Vatican banking uncovered by the Guardia di Finanza, the detective staged a hoax to draw in this syndicate. I guess we can call this a case of the detective following his hunch."

This time, the others joined Moretti in a groan.

"Farrugia was so successful that he had all of Rome and the art world abuzz, quite fooled, because the fantastic discovery of the last eagle is nothing more than a fraud, aided and abetted by the testimony of the academic curmudgeon Professor Rinaldo Morelli."

Moretti received some sad looks as consolation, which he waved off. The studio reporter asked, "How was the syndicate exposed?"

Inserting his finger into his ear as if he were straining to hear the question through his earpiece, Ragonese said, "It seems that Farrugia had contacted Roma Underground and asked them to crate up discoveries as part of a scam. He used these crates in a ploy to see who would arrive to export the valuables abroad. Sources here say that the crates were placed in the Catacomb of St. Domatilla. Leadership in the Roma Underground, using surveillance cameras, filmed men removing the crates and transporting them to Civitavecchia where they were to be placed into shipping containers headed for the United States at night. That was when the heroic detective and his team descended."

"So these precious artifacts have not left Italy?" said the man in the studio.

"No, they have not. The men caught on film have dubious pasts, although I regret to inform you that at least one member of the Roma Underground appears to be implicated in all this: one Dr. Adriano Lingetti. The doctor is cooperating with authorities and naming names. As with cases like this, one comes to expect a penitent. We all are acquainted with the adage that repentance does the soul good. As I speak, Detective Farrugia, members of the Financial Police, along with the Organized Crime Bureau, have arrested one Alan Ancona, who is an art collector and importer/exporter, with ties to several well-known museums around the world. Rumor has it that Ancona had in his possession another valuable artifact and forged documents of transit. These documents supposedly use the names of local and provincial politicians both here in Rome and in Milan. You can expect more on that news when I have it. We can be certain, however, that all of Mr. Ancona's recent activities with museums are being vigorously reviewed. I must mention that two of the men on film arrested with Mr. Ancona have ties to mafia activities in Naples, Palermo, and Calabria. I await confirmation but these men are alleged members of the Totaro crime family who, as many will recall, were responsible for numerous assassinations during the Maxi-Trials. The two men also seem to fit the description given by the esteemed Professor Morelli."

Moretti held up his hand but it did no good.

The newsman kept talking but Alessandro turned down the volume when Farrugia and a colleague appeared in the doorframe.

And inevitably, Pinolo stomped in and was about to say something about the large congregation in one office, about guests not wearing identification badges, when Farrugia's colleague handed him an oversized envelope.

"What's this?" said Pinolo.

"For you," the man said. "Enclosed are invoices for the consulting services of Bianca Nerini and Professor Renato Moretti."

Pinolo thumbed through the invoices and gasped at the total amount on the last page.

"Who are you? On whose authority?"

"Oh, I'm sorry. I'm Inspector Paolo Ferraro with the Finance Police and liaison officer with the FBI's Organized Crime Task Force and the American version of forensic accounting. Seated over there are Special Agents McGarrity and Murphy, who have assisted your office throughout the investigation."

"I wasn't aware of their involvement," said Pinolo.

Gennaro stood up and turned his computer monitor towards his superior.

McGarrity stood up. "My partner and I are grateful for the help we've received from your office. Thanks to these people the FBI has been able to gather the proceeds of this investigation and forward them to US Attorney Michael Farese for a case against Bevilacqua for RICO violations, amongst other crimes."

Pinolo looked at Gennaro, papers in hand from Ferraro with eyes registering confusion from what McGarrity had just said.

"But I've sent you memos daily," Gennaro said. "Don't you read your e-mail?"

"If this is an international investigation then I shouldn't have to pay any of this," screamed Pinolo.

"In the long run, that is true," Ferraro said. "But for now you do have to pay. Don't worry—the Italian government will make sure that your department is reimbursed. Just fill out the correct paperwork and in due time . . ." the man stopped talking since Pinolo had turned and started to walk away.

"I'll wait for you downstairs," said Ferraro to Farrugia, but not before handing his business card to Bianca.

Once everything had settled down in the office Farrugia found himself a seat. Gennaro went against his own principle and offered to call for take-out, but everyone said that they should go out for a celebratory dinner later.

Dante asked, "The case looks good against Ancona, but what happens with Bevilaqua? Think Ancona will give him up?"

Farrugia looked at Bianca then Dante before he answered the question. Gennaro thought his old friend looked uncharacteristically smug.

"I think Bianca's trick can almost guarantee that they'll be a race to see who tells the most compelling story to the American authorities— Ancona or Bevilaqua."

"Not sure I understand. What trick?" asked Dante.

"All I will say is that both Ancona and, from what I'm told by Ferraro, Bevilaqua, turned pale when someone explained to them the significance of the symbol on the side of the crates."

Dante said, "I don't follow."

"Bianca had a nice graphic logo designed and placed on the sides of the crates. A simple, but prominent red 'R,'" said Farrugia with a smile of enjoyment.

Dante and Gennaro looked at her, stunned. McGarrity and Murphy—like partners who have known each other for too long and could complete each other's sentences—had their eyebrows raised.

"Why are you looking at me like that?" she said. "I told Ancona that we represented a vineyard. 'Rossi Vineyards.' Simple. I didn't imply anything beyond that. Now, if you'll excuse me, I've got a gift for Silvio."

Bianca asked Silvio to make her an espresso in the break room. He proceeded to go through the routine mechanically while she plugged her laptop in for a connection.

"I have something for you, Silvio." She hoisted a bound document from her carry bag. "Think of it as a small gift."

He placed the demitasse down in front of her and saw the document.

"You didn't have to do that, Ms. Bianca."

"It's nothing, really. It's a novel that's on the Internet. I downloaded it and had it bound so you can read it as you continue to work on your English."

"Thank you. What is it?"

"Last time we talked you said that your teacher had you reading snippets of *Huckleberry Finn*. You asked some important questions about prejudice and racism, so I thought I'd give you another important novel that addresses the same themes, but from a different perspective."

"What is the novel called?"

"See for yourself."

Silvio carefully pronounced the title. *"Blake; or, The Huts of America."*

"The novel was written by a man named Martin Delany; it was his answer to Harriet Beecher Stowe's *Uncle Tom's Cabin.*"

His eyes quickly read over a phrase in the opening paragraph: 'a contest for the presidency of the United States' and he looked up and thanked her again, promising to work hard at improving his English.

Early the next morning Bianca arose and dialed up a doppio espresso for herself on Dante's DeLonghi while he continued sleeping. She rummaged through various English-language webs on her laptop, like any normal half-awake Roman, in search of the latest of the late-breaking news that was usually nothing more than half-tease and half-fact, before she found a half-dozen articles that would seem like nothing more than fractals of unrelated news, but she connected them together.

She read about smuggling, about a prominent cultural organization, and about local police and international experts in organized crime questioning members of the Totaro family.

After she had downed her espresso she checked her Instant Messenger. She felt amused to see 10ki's icon. She sent a message.

"Haven't heard from you much."

"Been busy but I heard about the work in Rome," 10ki typed.

"What did you hear?"

"Screws being put to Ancona 2 talk & pressure on Bevilaqua." 10ki added, "Nice."

Bianca had too many questions going through her head. News was fast. Even the Italian news had a disordered sequence of events. She looked at the icons on the screen and saw a line of pulsating periods at the bottom of the windowpane, indicating a message was being typed and incoming.

Distracted, she decided to let 10ki run the conversation, so she waited.

"AB best R had."

"Thx."

Again, the periods pulsated.

She looked back at the screen and saw a blank square announce itself in the space between her and 10ki's icon.

The square filled in with white. Bianca waited for more.

Then, in front of her eyes, a bright red line, guided by an invisible hand, started to form the cursive letter 'R.'

Either the surprise or the delayed effect of the caffeine throbbed in her head.

Next to the crimson R, in a simple font, appeared the typed statement: "We need your help. Again. Will you come to Boston?"

Bianca almost closed the laptop lid shut as if it would keep either the message or question hidden. Her lips went dry. She gave it some thought. She pried the lid up and with clicks of the mouse, terminated the windows.

She was about to power down the laptop when another console

window popped up and white periods marched out slowly across the darkness. She waited, curious.

Letters appeared on the screen, forming a sentence. She read it and wanted both to believe and dismiss what she saw: *You were never plain.*

Wasp's Nest

By Gabriel Valjan

The Second Installment of the Roma Series

Coming November 2012

1

It was cold. Damn cold. New England cold.

Alabaster Black had inserted herself into Boston in February where days of sand, salt, and snow were chased into shorter nights by stinging frost and sub-zero temperatures. She had given up Rome for this?

She trudged her way through a public alley she thought would be a short cut. She had meant to leave in August, but that also meant leaving Dante and their fresh love affair. She finally left Rome in January. It also meant leaving a small circle of friends, the first real circle of friends she'd had since college: Alessandro, Gennaro, and Farrugia. Even now, she missed Silvio and his honest but mangled English.

Why, she asked herself. *Why?*

She reminded herself she had to come to Boston for the Sargent case, renewing her work with Rendition on, she hoped, her terms. The few details on Sargent, his questionable business practices, his pharmaceutical company—all so very enticing, all so challenging. Or was that rationalization? She crunched through the graying snow. Of course, she might have also left Rome to flee Dante, flee and sabotage their intimacy.

Trust her employer, Rendition, again?

There was an issue. There was the matter of history. Rendition had done enough in the past to warrant paranoia. There had been enough of that in Rome, and before Rome, but here she was in Boston.

Damn snow.

Alabaster looked ahead, down the narrow path in front of her. A trailer-truck much too wide, it would seem, to fit into the alley, but it tried nonetheless, emitted an awful mantra of bleeping noises. There was something absurdly perverse and insistent about Boston drivers. She struggled to find her footing, cautious and uncertain.

A lumbering truck fired heavy sounds behind her and barreled down the alley. Rendition and its simple red 'R' for a logo flashed through her mind as she saw the white headlights and the square jaw of the grille coming towards her. She couldn't confirm anything about the drivers—whether they were oblivious as most Bostonians, arguing perhaps about their damn Red Sox or the Patriots—because the white glare had grown brighter and closer.

Her hand against the alley wall felt a handle. She didn't think. She pulled.

And found sanctuary.

Her heart pounded as she felt the sweat tingle against her skin. The truck passed by outside the door. She felt it in her feet and up into her bones. There was that obscene lumbering sound of freight bouncing side-to-side, honking a few seconds later when the one truck met the other at the end of the alley. One species of driver greeting another. Not Rendition, then. Rendition would have exited more gracefully.

Never attribute to malice that which can be adequately explained by stupidity.

She walked into a kitchen—a restaurant kitchen, to be precise. One head turned, saw her, but said nothing. She was a wet cold mess and knew it.

In front of her she saw a man with his back turned to her and a young man in his late teens; the one who had seen her. It looked to be the chef and his sous-chef. This must have been a small, nascent restaurant because there was no line, no corps of manic workers hustling to plate dishes and move the appetizers and entrées. There was no ethnic illegal doing dishes or any uniformed men and women flowing in and out in a frenzy through split doors. This was a restaurant either in the throes of birth or approaching death.

"Here is the mootz-a-thell, Chef," the kid said, placing a bowl near the chef who was busy prepping something while working on yet another dish. She admired their synchronicity. This hard work was for what? One couple in the dining room? Was this hustling kid sous-chef and headwaiter, too?

"The water was on. Cannellini to be al dente in fourteen minutes, Chef," the kid barked out.

The man in white was stooped over in intensity with establishing his mise en place. She found a clean spot on the wall to lean against to watch creation taking place. "The sheet out of the oven, yet?" he asked in a booming voice. His head never looking up.

"Caramelized overnight, Chef. The prosciutt' is ready, Chef."

"Need my pasta," was the next loud request.

The kid was sweating, and she saw a cloud of steam rising up and heard the wet sound of weight shifting from a pot into a colander.

"Pasta al dente, Chef." The kid came around the counter, pasta in bowls for his boss. "Orecchiett' is on."

"What is wrong with you?" the chef screamed, and she watched the hardworking young man turn into a young boy. "It is mozzarella not 'mootz-a-thell'. Prosciutto not 'prosciutt.' Everything in Italian is pronounced. Every syllable is enunciated, you understand me, Michele? You say it the way you spell it. Orecchiette not 'orecchiett.'"

The kid looked crushed.

She had seen what happens next a thousand times on the streets of Rome, behind glass in cars or in trattorie: the chef starts to use his hands. Italians express the range of their emotions the way a conductor uses a baton.

"Pay attention to me, Michele. You wouldn't say 'espress,' would you? You'd say 'espresso.' You say 'cappuccino' not 'cappuccin.' You wouldn't say 'tirami', you say 'tiramisu', don't you?" With that exposition of sample vocabulary, he tapped the kid on the chest and gave him a quick hug and apology for his outburst.

"Chef, there's a lady standing there," Michele said, now that the food was complete. She admired his sense of priorities.

The chef turned sideways to see Alabaster.

She shook off the last of the dampness, looked at the counter, and said, "Pasta e Fagioli," emphasizing her pronunciation of 'beans,' saying it properly and not, 'fazool,' like Italian-Americans are often heard saying.

The chef's surprised face broke into a smile.

While the kid served the house, Alabaster reviewed the line of bowls. When she said, with perfect vowels and consonants, 'belle orecchiette,' the chef looked as if he were ready to cry.

"Sit," he said, pointing to a small table against the back wall. "There is plenty left over from what will go out to the customers. And the weather . . ."

She slid her laptop case under the table and took a seat. "Thank you, that's very kind."

"You speak Italian heavenly."

"*Ti ringrazio.*"

"Lived there? What part?"

"Roma." She quickly named restaurants. The man hung his head in nostalgia, with the understanding one has when he has sat at those very same tables, eaten there, and conversed with the people. He sighed "Roma" the way a man remembers his first love.

He poured her a glass of white, a 2009 Sigalas Santorini, to enjoy with her 'pasta e fagioli.' The pairing of the wine's bright minerality and acidity was vindicated by the saltiness of the caramelized prosciutto.

"I made it like a proper pasta dish instead of a soup," he said. "I want my customers to experience a different aspect of this rustic dish."

"You have many customers yet."

"I'm working on it. The economy is tough. I'd like to add staff, expand on supplies and my menu, but things are tough. Deliveries are even worse."

"How do you mean 'worse'?"

"I ordered a beautiful prosciutto di San Daniele. Nothing yet." The man threw down his small cloth he used for wiping off excess sauce during plating. "I don't know. In my mind I get paranoid and think my competitors bribed the deliveryman. You know, everyone knows everyone in this town and there's no telling what competition in hard times will do. I shouldn't burden you with my troubles. You're eating."

"The kid?" she asked.

"Good kid. Hard worker. Screwed-up family, but he wants to better himself. I call him Michele but his name is Michael. He ran away from home. Like me, he's from Brooklyn, and fell in love with Italian food and culture. What can I say?"

"Italian?"

"Me? No. I'm a Jew from Brooklyn, God's honest truth. But I love Italian cuisine, the way of life. I trained here and then abroad. What I'd give to go back, but I have to make this work first. Sometimes I worry about what I got myself into. This is my life savings." Again the emotions of hands, back and forth, up and down in the air. "The overhead here is insane, the city, and Bostonians. I'd tell you what I think of Bostonians, but you probably know that already. Tough crowd, but loyal if you've earned it."

"This was a wonderful meal. Please let me give you something for it. Least I can do. Not every day I have a chef cook for me in his own kitchen."

"No. Absolutely not, I insist. Hearing you speak *la bella lingua* is payment enough. Want to do something for me? Please tell your friends about my restaurant. Tell them to order my 'pasta e fagioli.'" He sat down a tall fluted glass and poured her a drink. "Try this. It's a little different and you might think 'non-traditional for an Italian meal,' but tell me what you think." She witnessed a nice amount of the bubbly, gold liquid riding up to midway on the glass. "Have a sip, please."

She nosed it. Apple. Tart. Nice astringency with a touch of acidity. She tasted it. Clean, some wood, and dry.

"Reminds me of prosecco. Palate-cleansing," she said.

"Exactly. And here's the beauty. It's from New Hampshire. Farnum Hills Extra Dry Cider."

"My name is Bianca Nerini," she told him, instinctively pulling up the alias she used in Rome. What did it matter, since he is a Jew from New York who is now an Italian chef, probably fluent in the language? She had sampled his food, heard his Italian pronunciation. Impeccable. His sous-chef is Michele not Michael.

Alabaster noted his name, the name of the restaurant, and its correct address and entrance.

She was impressed. Michele returned with the verdict. The customers loved the dish. There was an order for dessert and with that she wished them well as Bianca, thanking them again, and went on her way to her new home.

Nearly run over but she had found good food. There was work to do.

2

He could have passed for a banker. Passed for the mailman. Passed as the man down the hall who walks by a thousand times, says 'hullo,' day in and day out, but his name dances on the tip of the tongue, stays buried in the brain, unavailable for recall. His is the face seen at the bar when the fight breaks out, but nobody can describe him when the police arrive. Complete milquetoast.

He was also in Boston. Returning home on the Red Line after secreting himself into the back of the room at an open lecture at Harvard because he enjoys obscure Latin authors. He had just listened to a discussion on the fragmentary *Cynegetica*, three-hundred twenty-five hexameters on hunting by the third-century Marcus Nemesianus. The impassioned professor had announced at the end of the lecture that next week's discussion would cover eleven eclogues erroneously attributed to Titus Calpurnius. He would argue that they belong to Nemesianus.

Waiting on the platform for the inbound train to downtown Boston that should arrive soon—theoretically, at least—he stood there inside a throng of students, shoppers, and tourists. He showed no signs of impatience, content to turn his mind to the question of the authorship of the eclogues. He knew that the train was coming when he heard the long shrill metallic groan of the train taking the curve into Harvard Square T-station. He would ignore the latecomers in the distance who would try to run down the ramp to make the train, jamming themselves into the first car. He habitually took the car towards the rear so he would not be one of the first faces exiting.

He found his seat, it is a crowded car. A man of indeterminate age marked off the seat next to his by throwing down a hefty shoulder bag, nearly crushing his feet, and then casting down another bag, a backpack, which he swung around, barely missing him.

He said nothing. His face expressed nothing.

Once seated, his neighbor wrested off his winter coat, intruding in his personal space without a smile or an 'Excuse me.' The rude man, divested of his baggage, then proceeded to check all his mobile devices. The non-descript man could see that the cell phone had no messages. The man next to him thumbed a quick text or a Tweet, not knowing that it was all rather useless because there was no reception or possibility for a signal between Harvard Square and the next stop, Central Square. Clueless.

The two men seemed settled in for the ride. Bodies stood and held sway with the train's movements either by balancing like urban surfers or by hanging on from overhead straps like military airborne on a plane from which they hoped that they could jump soon. Finding at last that his phone was incommunicado, the rude man thumbed further buttons, and it began to emanate something that must have passed for music. Treble flattened to a rhythmic buzz, bass all but gone, only the bare skeleton of the melody line and harmonic tempo remained.

The man let his mind drift to Nemesianus. It had been many years since he read Haupt's *De Carminibus*, which identified Nemesianus as the author of the last four Eclogues. Haupt had offered some argument for keeping the remaining seven with Calpurnius.

The tinny music became more insistent. A simple, three-chord development, classic AABA melodic structure. The train entered the darkness and there were the flickering images of advertisement speeding past like a movie made from the thumbed edge of a matchbook as the train neared Central Square.

Then came the sniffling.

The unencumbered man blew his nose into a piece of tissue that had outlived usability, but its owner nonetheless thought he could parcel out one more meager area for his stuffed-up nose. Nobody looked when the man inhaled and made that gurgling winter-cold sound.

Haupt. Calpurnius. What was it that the professor had seen in those other seven to lead him to ignore the differences Haupt had seen?

The music changed again, to another three-chord ballad-like ditty, the progression through tonic, dominant, and subdominant, drawing the man's attention against his will. Music always had that effect. He could listen with rapture; he could listen with disgust, as he did then.

But he couldn't not listen.

His neighbor used the snot rag to wipe his watery eyes after he had frayed the last of the tissue with a trumpet blast.

Again annoyed, he turned his mind to hexameter.

The music modulated into the dominant minor. The inconsiderate miserable next to him coughed without covering his mouth. Disgusting.

Charles Street into Park Street station is another opportunity for an anonymous dark tunnel and more metallic screeching. It was less than two minutes between stops. He stood up before the darkness came and squared himself off in front of the man with the bags to take the door when it opened. He knew that there would be sound, a bend in the rails that would jolt the unseasoned traveler forward.

It went dark. The train took the curve. Those who ride the train daily take the mechanical rounding of the rail with unknowing habit, reflexive muscle memory. He lunged forward and whispered an indecipherable 'Excuse me' in the dark.

He got off early at Park Street and went for the concourse. He knew that in the next stop or two the seated man would loll back and forth and others might think that he was asleep. It would likely be the third stop—Broadway Station—that the train might reveal the other man's true state.

The body would fall forward to the floor. Dead.

The MBTA police would come and investigate the disturbance, then the Boston Police Department (BPD). It would take little time for the inevitable conclusion: ice pick through the larynx. There would be the cataloguing of all those bags and their contents, a review of surveillance films at every station since the victim had boarded the MBTA train; but there would be nothing.

Just crowds of people; and if anyone had noticed a man getting up near the victim before the lethal darkness swallowed them up, they would still have nothing. A hat hid the hair. Sunglasses obscured the face. Gloved hands would preempt fingerprints. Nothing left for them except snot rags to bag.

He had already walked the concourse to get above ground. Gone. He was a man of no qualities but of certain skills. On assignment in Boston.

Acknowledgments

Without the encouragement and praise of friends and colleagues at Dana-Farber Cancer Institute, my short story "Alabaster" would have remained simply short fiction in the drawer and not the novel, *Roma, Underground* today. Therefore, first and foremost, I must thank Margaret Taggart and my fellow nurses and caffeine addicts, Maura Pevear, and Mary McKenna for their insistence that I let Alabaster have a life.

I owe a debt to Dean Hunt, dear friend and editor of my grammar and syntax, who has endured three reiterations of the novel, all my short stories and novels, and my numerous and unforgiveable violations of the English language. He should know by now how much I value his friendship.

Dave King, who line-edited the manuscript before it went to Winter Goose Publishers, has become a collaborator in my writing, and a friend. From Fellini to piranhas to Salvo Montalbano we have laughed.

I have also had Deb Well read and comment on *Roma*, and I'm grateful to her for all the constructive criticism for what worked and what didn't and for sending me to the desk to revise and rewrite with food and wine. Patricia Lovett is another reader who has provided me with feedback. I am also grateful that she read *Roma* by flashlight during Hurricane Irene.

I am thankful to Winter Goose for believing in me; Jordan Adams accepted me, James Logan edited the manuscript, and Jessica Kristie counseled me on marketing. Thank you.

Last but not least . . . the debt that I am unable to repay. I wrote this novel while undergoing treatment for cancer. The humor afforded to me by the Italian author Andrea Camilleri through his creations of Catarella, Mimì Augello, and Salvo Montalbano nourished me. The RAI production of the Montalbano series with Luca Zingaretti entertained me. And entertaining me with his stories of Boston's lost West End and with his stories back in the day as a designer at Filenes was the late Warren Larivee. He regaled and sustained me when time stood still and I faced Mortality. He took me to every single treatment and was a friend in ways that defy definition. At my most vulnerable time in my life, he was there. I would write what became *Roma* every day and then go to my 'treatments' with Warren at my side. Although Warren is now gone I still hear his laughter and his voice in my head. Gratitude, Humility and Love do truly seem like insufficient words—mere abstractions of human thought. It is to Warren and through his example I understand Love, Loss and Gratitude.

About the Author

Ronan Bennett short-listed Gabriel Valjan for the 2010 Fish Short Story Prize for his Boston noir, "Back in the Day." Gabriel's short stories and some of his poetry continue to appear in literary journals and online magazines. He recently won first prize in ZOUCH Magazine's inaugural Lit Bit Contest. He lives in New England but has traveled extensively, receiving his undergraduate education in California and completing graduate school in England. *Roma, Underground* is his first novel.

Photo By Patrick Lentz

Follow Gabriel
Website: http://gabrielswharf.wordpress.com/
Facebook: http://www.facebook.com/pages/Gabriel-Valjan/291400997547203

Look for **Wasp's Nest** November 2012

CPSIA information can be obtained
at www.ICGtesting.com
Printed in the USA
FFOW01n1853230514
5517FF